Praise for Philip Kerr's *The One from the Other*

"Philip Kerr is the contemporary master of the morally complex thriller. . . . [*A German Requiem*], set mainly in postwar Vienna, has an affinity with Graham Greene's *The Third Man* but—dare I say it?—equals or surpasses Greene (and the Carol Reed film featuring Orson Welles), because it doesn't shy away from the Nazi-saturated substratum of the Viennese milieu. And then I discovered—and devoured—Mr. Kerr's new noir, *The One from the Other*. It crystallized my dissatisfaction with recent le Carré novels (clumsily didactic) and made me rethink my addiction to Alan Furst's oeuvre (brilliant but a bit too thickly varnished with romantic glamour). . . . The achievement of Philip Kerr's novels is that he takes his Chandler/Hammett-style detective, that lone figure in the (largely ahistorical) mean streets of the urban jungle, into the midst of a far more highly charged historical backdrop, a different, more profoundly mean—indeed, evil—sort of mean-street neighborhood, the crossroads of history and tragedy. Mr. Kerr has set his detective on an *Inferno*–like trajectory that takes us deep into the heart of darkness."

—Ron Rosenbaum, *New York Observer*

"Several elements account for the excellence of the Gunther books. First, Kerr is a fine novelist; in terms of narrative, plot, pace, and characterizations, he's in a league with John le Carré and Alan Furst. Moreover, he has done prodigious research into an era that ended well before he was born. The political, historical, military, and cultural details feel absolutely authentic. If you want a sense of what Nazi Germany was like, day to day, not many novels equal these. Finally, Kerr was truly inspired to place a detective-turned-private-eye at work in Nazi Germany. Private eyes investigate crimes, and where in human history can we find more cosmic crimes than those of the Hitler era? The question was whether Kerr would be equal to the challenge he set for himself. He has been. . . . One of the bright spots in this always readable, often troubling novel is the suggestion, near the end, that Kerr's good German will return again."

—Patrick Anderson, *The Washington Post*

"Because he never had any illusions to begin with, Gunther is the ideal narrator for Kerr's bleak tale of the dirty deals made by victors and vanquished alike. Having learned that there's no way to distinguish 'the one from the other,' the cynical P.I. has the moral clarity to see through the deceit and hypocrisy of both friend and foe. He's the right kind of hero for his time—and ours."

—Marilyn Stasio, *The New York Times Book Review*

"It is to be sincerely hoped that a very large number of readers buy this book so that Mr. Kerr won't be tempted to abandon Bernie Gunther again, and that his adventures will continue for many years. Even if the author wants to torture his hero, he shouldn't do it to his readers."

—Otto Penzler, *The New York Sun*

"No novelist 'gets' Germany and Europe before, during, and after World War II as well as Mr. Kerr, not even Alan Furst. . . . There seems to be little of which Mr. Kerr is not in command—noirish turns of phrase ('His teeth were big and yellow, as if he usually ate grass for dinner'), pacing, atmosphere, story, and historical facts and events."

—Roger K. Miller, *The Washington Times*

"Kerr's book is his spectacular follow-up to his extraordinarily brilliant Berlin Noir trilogy. Kerr is the only bona fide heir to Raymond Chandler that I have ever come across; his German private detective Bernie Gunther would have been respected by Philip Marlowe and the two of them would have enjoyed sitting down at a bar and talking. One of the things that is so amazing about Kerr's four Bernie Gunther novels, to me, is that while the books are ostensibly hard-boiled mysteries, they gave me a glimpse into the incomprehensible horrors of the Second World War and the Holocaust in much the same way D. M. Thomas' *The White Hotel* and Spiegelman's *Maus* once did. For me they are all works of art that for a moment enabled me to grasp the unimaginable, before my mind clouded over and returned to the safety of the quotidian."

—Jonathan Ames, Salon.com Book Awards

"Kerr's stylish noir writing makes every page a joy to read."

—*Publishers Weekly* (starred review)

"Grim and gripping, with the author's customary sure-handedness in evidence."

—*Kirkus Reviews* (starred review)

"Once more, Kerr demonstrates his mastery of a time well-mined in fiction but still rife for exploration."

—Sarah Weinman, *The Baltimore Sun*

"Kerr's expertly plotted tale glistens with period detail and punchily cynical asides. A–."

—*Entertainment Weekly*

"A welcome return [of Bernie Gunther] . . . A somber, melancholy, compelling work, *The One from the Other* stretches the notion of entertaining fiction to [the] breaking point. . . . Philip Kerr impressively sustains the novel's parched, opportunistic, bottomlessly compromised world. Where next for Bernie Gunther?"

—*The Times Literary Supplement* (London)

"It is a highly entertaining book, imaginatively conceived and smartly executed. Although it stands as a remarkable work of historical fiction, fans of hard-boiled detective stories will not be disappointed."

—*Historical Novels Review*

## ABOUT THE AUTHOR

Philip Kerr is the author of seventeen previous novels, but perhaps most importantly, the four featuring Bernie Gunther—*The One from the Other* and the *Berlin Noir* trilogy (*March Violets*, *The Pale Criminal*, and *A German Requiem*). He also wrote the cult classic *A Philosophical Investigation* and five bestselling children's books (as P. B. Kerr). Kerr was chosen early in his career as one of *Granta* magazine's Best Young British Novelists and was hailed by Salman Rushdie as "a brilliantly innovative thriller-writer." Born in Edinburgh, he now lives in London and Cornwall with his family.

# THE ONE FROM THE OTHER

A BERNIE GUNTHER NOVEL

Philip Kerr

PENGUIN BOOKS

PENGUIN BOOKS
Published by the Penguin Group
Penguin Group (USA) Inc., 375 Hudson Street, New York, New York 10014, U.S.A.
Penguin Group (Canada), 90 Eglinton Avenue East, Suite 700, Toronto,
Ontario, Canada M4P 2Y3 (a division of Pearson Penguin Canada Inc.)
Penguin Books Ltd, 80 Strand, London WC2R 0RL, England
Penguin Ireland, 25 St Stephen's Green, Dublin 2, Ireland (a division of Penguin Books Ltd)
Penguin Group (Australia), 250 Camberwell Road, Camberwell,
Victoria 3124, Australia (a division of Pearson Australia Group Pty Ltd)
Penguin Books India Pvt Ltd, 11 Community Centre, Panchsheel Park, New Delhi – 110 017, India
Penguin Group (NZ), 67 Apollo Drive, Rosedale, North Shore 0632,
New Zealand (a division of Pearson New Zealand Ltd)
Penguin Books (South Africa) (Pty) Ltd, 24 Sturdee Avenue,
Rosebank, Johannesburg 2196, South Africa

Penguin Books Ltd, Registered Offices:
80 Strand, London WC2R 0RL, England

First published in the United States of America by G. P. Putnam's Sons,
a member of Penguin Group (USA) Inc. 2006
Published in Penguin Books 2009

1 3 5 7 9 10 8 6 4 2



PUBLISHER'S NOTE

This is a work of fiction. Names, characters, places, and incidents are either the product of the author's imagination or are used fictitiously, and any resemblance to actual persons, living or dead, business establishments, events, or locales is entirely coincidental.

THE LIBRARY OF CONGRESS HAS CATALOGED THE HARDCOVER EDITION AS FOLLOWS:
Kerr, Philip.
The one from the other : a Bernie Gunther novel / Philip Kerr.
p. cm.
"A Marian Wood book."
ISBN 0-399-15299-7 (hc.)
ISBN 978-0-14-311229-7 (pbk.)
1. International relations—Fiction. 2. Munich (Germany)—Fiction.
3. Vienna (Austria)—Fiction. I. Title.
PR6061.E784O54 2006 2006044817
823'.914—dc22

Printed in the United States of America
Designed by Paula Russell Szafranski

FOR JANE

*God, give us grace to accept with serenity the things that cannot be changed, courage to change the things which should be changed, and the wisdom to distinguish the one from the other.*

—REINHOLD NIEBUHR

# THE ONE FROM THE OTHER

## PROLOGUE

# *Berlin, September 1937*

*I remember how good the weather was that September. Hitler weather, they used to call it. As if the elements themselves were disposed to be kind to Adolf Hitler, of all people. I remember him making a ranting speech demanding foreign colonies for Germany. It was, perhaps, the first time any of us had heard him use the phrase "living space." No one thought for a moment that our living space could only be created if someone else died first.*

*I was living and working in the space we called Berlin. There was plenty of business there for a private detective. It was all missing persons, of course. And most of them were Jewish. Most of them murdered in back alleys, or sent off to a KZ, a concentration camp, without the authorities bothering to notify their families. The Nazis thought it was quite funny, the way they did that. The Jews were, of course, officially encouraged to emigrate, but because they were forbidden to take their property with them, few did so. Still, some people devised several neat tricks to get their money out of Germany.*

*One such trick was for a Jew to deposit a large sealed parcel containing various valuables, and labeled the "last will and testament" of so and so, with a German court of law before going abroad for "a holiday." The Jew would then "die" in a foreign country and have the local French or English court request the German court to forward the parcel containing his "last will and testament." German courts being run by German lawyers were usually only too happy to comply with the requests of other lawyers, even French and English ones. And in this way quite a few lucky Jews managed to be reunited with enough cash or valuables to start a new life in a new country.*

*It might seem hard to believe, but another neat scheme was actually devised by the Jewish Department of the Security Police—the SD. This scheme was seen as a good way of helping Jews leave Germany and, in the process, of enriching certain officers of the SD into the bargain. It was what we called the* tocher, *or Jewish peddler, scheme, and I first had experience of it as a result of the strangest pair of clients that ever came my way.*

*Paul Begelmann was a rich German Jewish businessman who owned several garages and car dealerships throughout Germany. And SS Sturmbannführer Dr. Franz Six was the head of the SD's Jewish Department. I was summoned to meet them both in the department's modest, three-room suite of offices at the Hohenzollern Palais, on Wilhelmstrasse. Behind Six's desk was a picture of the Führer, as well as a host of legal degrees from the universities of Heidelberg, Königsberg, and Leipzig. Six might have been a Nazi crook, but he was an extremely well-qualified Nazi crook. He was hardly Himmler's ideal-looking Aryan. Aged about thirty, he was dark-haired, a little self-satisfied around the mouth, and no more Jewish-looking than Paul Begelmann. He smelled faintly of cologne and hypocrisy. On his desk was a little bust of Wilhelm von Humboldt, who had founded the University of Berlin and who, famously, had defined the limits beyond which the activities of the State should not go. I guessed it was unlikely that Sturmbannführer Six would have agreed with him there.*

*Begelmann was older and taller, with dark, curly hair and lips that were as thick and pink as two slices of luncheon meat. He was smiling but his eyes told a very different story. The pupils were narrow, like a cat's, as if he was anxious to be out of the SD's spotlight. In that building, and surrounded by all those black uniforms, he looked like a choirboy trying to make friends with a pack of hyenas. He didn't say much. It was Six who did all the talking. I'd heard Six was from Mannheim. Mannheim has a famous Jesuit church. In his smart black uniform, that was the way Franz Six struck me. Not your typical SD thug. More like a Jesuit.*

*"Herr Begelmann has expressed a wish to emigrate from Germany to Palestine," he said smoothly. "Naturally he is concerned about his business in Germany and the impact that its sale might have on the local economy. So, in order to help Herr Begelmann, this department has proposed a solution to his problem. A solution you might be able to help us with, Herr Gunther. We have proposed that he should not emigrate 'pro forma,' but rather that he should continue to be a German citizen working abroad. In effect, that he should work in Palestine as the sales representative of his own company. In this manner he will be able to earn a salary and to share in the profits of the company while at the same time fulfilling this department's policy of encouraging Jewish emigration."*

*I didn't doubt that poor Begelmann had agreed to share his company's profits not with the Reich but with Franz Six. I lit a cigarette and fixed the SD man with a cynical smile. "Gentlemen, it sounds to me like you'll both be very happy together. But I fail to see what you need me for. I don't do marriages. I investigate them."*

*Six colored a little and glanced awkwardly at Begelmann. He had power, but it wasn't the kind of power that could threaten someone like me. He was used to bullying students and Jews, and the task of bullying an adult Aryan male looked like it was beyond him.*

*"We require someone . . . someone Herr Begelmann can trust . . . to deliver a letter from the Wassermann Bank, here in Berlin, to the Anglo-Palestine Bank in Jaffa. We require that person to open lines*

*of credit with that bank and to take a lease on a property in Jaffa that can be the premises for a new car showroom. The lease will help to validate Herr Begelmann's important new business venture. We also require our agent to transport certain items of property to the Anglo-Palestine Bank in Jaffa. Naturally, Herr Begelmann is prepared to pay a substantial fee for these services. The sum of one thousand English pounds, payable in Jaffa. Naturally, the SD will arrange all the necessary documentation and paperwork. You would be going there as the official representative of Begelmann's Automotive. Unofficially, you will be acting as the SD's confidential agent."*

*"A thousand pounds. That's a lot of money," I said. "But what happens if the Gestapo ask me questions about all this. They might not like some of the answers. Have you thought of that?"*

*"Of course," said Six. "Do you take me for an idiot?"*

*"No, but they might."*

*"It so happens that I'm sending two other agents to Palestine on a fact-finding mission that has been authorized at the highest level," he said. "As part of its ongoing remit, this department has been asked to investigate the feasibility of forced emigration to Palestine. As far as SIPO is concerned, you would be part of that mission. If the Gestapo were to ask you questions about your mission you would be entirely within your rights to answer, as these two others will answer: that it is an intelligence matter. That you are carrying out the orders of General Heydrich. And that for reasons of operational security, you cannot discuss the matter." He paused and lit a small, pungent cigar. "You have done some work for the general before, have you not?"*

*"I'm still trying to forget it." I shook my head. "With all due respect, Herr Sturmbannführer. If two of your own men are already going to Palestine, then what do you need me for?"*

*Begelmann cleared his throat. "If I might say something, please,*

*Herr Sturmbannführer?" he said, cautiously, and in a strong Hamburg accent. Six shrugged and shook his head, indifferently. Begelmann looked at me with quiet desperation. There was sweat on his forehead and I didn't think it was only as a result of the unusually warm September weather. "Because, Herr Gunther, your reputation for honesty goes before you."*

*"Not to mention your dedication to making an easy mark," said Six.*

*I looked at Six and nodded. I was through being polite to this legal crook. "What you're saying, Herr Begelmann, is that you don't trust this department or the people who work for it."*

*Poor Begelmann looked pained. "No, no, no, no, no," he said. "That's not it at all."*

*But I was enjoying myself too much to let go of this bone. "And I can't say as I blame you. It's one thing to get robbed. It's quite another when the robber asks you to help carry the loot to the getaway car."*

*Six bit his lip. I could see he was wishing it was the vein on the side of my neck. The only reason he wasn't saying anything was because I hadn't yet said no. Probably he guessed that I wasn't going to. A thousand pounds is a thousand pounds.*

*"Please, Herr Gunther."*

*Six looked quite happy to leave the begging to Begelmann.*

*"My whole family would be extremely grateful for your help."*

*"A thousand pounds," I said. "I already heard that part."*

*"Is there something wrong with the remuneration?" Begelmann was looking at Six for guidance. He wasn't getting any. Six was a lawyer, not a horse dealer.*

*"Hell no, Herr Begelmann," I said. "It's generous. No, it's me, I guess. I start to itch when a certain kind of dog cozies up to me."*

*But Six was refusing to be insulted. So far in this, he was just a typical lawyer. Prepared to put aside all human feelings for the* greater good of making money. "I hope you're not being rude to an official of the German government, Herr Gunther," he said, chiding me. "Anyone would think you were against National Socialism, the way you talk. Hardly a very healthy attitude these days."

I shook my head. "You mistake me," I said. "I had a client last year. His name was Hermann Six. The industrialist? He was less than honest with me. You're no relation to him, I trust."

"Sadly not," he said. "I come from a very poor family in Mannheim."

I looked at Begelmann. I felt sorry for him. I should have said no. Instead I said yes. "All right, I'll do it. But you people had better be on the level about all this. I'm not the type who forgives and forgets. And I've never turned the other cheek."

It wasn't long before I regretted becoming involved in Six and Begelmann's Jewish peddler scheme. I was alone in my office the next day. It was raining outside. My partner, Bruno Stahlecker, was out on a case, so he said, which probably meant he was propping up a bar in Wedding. There was a knock at the door and a man came in. He was wearing a leather coat and a wide-brimmed hat. Call it a keen sense of smell, but I knew he was Gestapo even before he showed me the little warrant disk in the palm of his hand. He was in his mid-twenties, balding, with a small, lopsided mouth and a sharp, delicate-looking jaw that made me suspect he was more used to hitting than being hit. Without saying a word he tossed his wet hat onto my desk blotter, unbuttoned his coat to reveal a neat, navy-blue suit, sat in the chair on the other side of my desk, took out his cigarettes, and lit one—all the while staring at me like an eagle watching a fish.

"Nice little hat," I said, after a moment. "Where'd you steal it?" I *picked it off my blotter and tossed it onto his lap. "Or did you just want me and my roses to know that it's raining outside?"*

*"They told me you were a tough guy at the Alex," he said, and flicked his ash on my carpet.*

*"I was a tough guy when I was at the Alex," I said. The Alex was police headquarters, on Berlin's Alexanderplatz. "They gave me one of those little disks. Anyone can pretend he's tough when he's got KRIPO's beer token in his pocket." I shrugged. "But if that's what they say, then it must be true. Real cops, like the cops at the Alex, don't lie."*

*The little mouth tightened into a smile that was all lips and no teeth, like a newly stitched scar. He put the cigarette back in his mouth as if sucking a length of thread to poke in the eye of a needle. Or even my eye. I don't think he would have cared which. "So you're the bull who caught Gormann, the strangler."*

*"That was a very long time ago," I said. "Murderers were a lot easier to catch before Hitler came to power."*

*"Oh? How's that?"*

*"For one thing, they weren't nearly as thick on the ground as they are now. And for another, it seemed to matter more. I used to take a real satisfaction in protecting society. Nowadays I wouldn't know where to start."*

*"Sounds suspiciously like you disapprove of what the Party's done for Germany," he said.*

*"Not at all," I said, careful with my insolence now. "I don't disapprove of anything that's done for Germany." I lit one of my own and let him fill in the double meaning and entertained myself with a mental picture of my fist connecting with the kid's pointy jaw. "Have you got a name, or is that just for your friends? You remember those, don't you? All the people who used to send you a birthday card? Always supposing you can remember when that is."*

*"Maybe you can be my friend," he said, smiling. I hated that smile. It was a smile that said he knew he had something on me. There was a sort of twinkle in his iris that came off his eyeball like the point of a sword. "Maybe we can help each other. That's what friends are for, eh? Maybe I'll do you a favor, Gunther, and you'll be so damned grateful you'll send me one of those birthday cards you were talking about." He nodded. "I'd like that. That would be nice. With a little message inside."*

*I sighed some smoke his way. I was growing weary of his hard act. "I doubt you'd like my sense of humor," I said. "But I'm willing to be proved wrong. It might make a nice change to be proved wrong by the Gestapo."*

*"I am Inspector Gerhard Flesch," he said.*

*"Pleased to meet you, Gerhard."*

*"I head up the Jewish Department in SIPO," he added.*

*"You know something? I've been thinking of opening one of those in here," I said. "Suddenly everyone seems to have a Jewish Department. Must be good for business. The SD, the Foreign Office, and now the Gestapo."*

*"The operational spheres of the SD and the Gestapo are demarcated by a functions order signed by the Reichsführer-SS," said Flesch. "Operationally, the SD is to subject the Jews to intense surveillance and then report to us. But in practice the Gestapo is locked in a power struggle with the SD, and in no area is this conflict more hotly contested than in the area of Jewish affairs."*

*"That all sounds very interesting, Gerhard. But I don't see how I can help. Hell, I'm not even Jewish."*

*"No?" Flesch smiled. "Then let me explain. We have heard a rumor that Franz Six and his men are in the pay of the Jews. Taking bribes in return for facilitating Jewish emigration. What we don't yet have is proof. That's where you come in, Gunther. You're going to get it."*

*"You overestimate my resourcefulness, Gerhard. I'm not that good at shoveling shit."*

*"This SD fact-finding mission to Palestine. Exactly why are you going?"*

*"I need a holiday, Gerhard. I need to get away and eat some oranges. Apparently sunlight and oranges are very good for the skin." I shrugged. "Then again, I'm thinking of converting. I'm told they give a pretty good circumcision in Jaffa, if you get them before lunchtime." I shook my head. "Come on, Gerhard. It's an intelligence matter. You know I can't talk about it with anyone outside of the department. If you don't like that, then take it up with Heydrich. He makes the rules, not me."*

*"The two men you're traveling with," he said, hardly batting an eye. "We would like you to keep an eye on them. To see that they don't abuse the position of trust in which they find themselves. I'm even authorized to offer you some expenses. A thousand marks."*

*Everyone was throwing money at me. A thousand pounds here. A thousand marks there. I felt like an official in the Reich Ministry of Justice.*

*"That's very handsome of you, Gerhard," I said. "A thousand marks is quite a slice of sugarloaf. Of course, you wouldn't be the Gestapo if you didn't also have a taste of the whip you're offering me in the event I don't have the sweet tooth you were counting on."*

*Flesch smiled his toothless smile. "It would be unfortunate if your racial origins were made the subject of an inquiry," he said, stubbing out his cigarette in my ashtray. As he leaned forward and then back again in the chair, his leather coat creaked loudly, like the sound of heavy raindrops, as if he had just bought it from the Gestapo gift shop.*

*"Both my parents were churchgoing folk," I said. "I don't see that you've got anything like that to throw at me."*

*"Your maternal great-grandmother," he said. "There's a possibility she might have been Jewish."*

*"Read your Bible, Gerhard," I said. "We're all Jewish if you want to go back far enough. But as it happens, you're wrong. She was a Roman Catholic. Quite a devout one, I believe."*

*"And yet her name was Adler, was it not? Anna Adler?"*

*"It was Adler, yes, I believe that's correct. What of it?"*

*"Adler is a Jewish name. If she were alive today she would probably have to add Sarah to her name, so that we could recognize her for what she was. A Jewess."*

*"Even if it was true, Gerhard. That Adler is a Jewish name? And, to be honest, I have no idea if it is or not. That would only make me one-eighth Jewish. And under section two, article five of the Nuremberg Laws, I am not, therefore, a Jew." I grinned. "Your whip lacks a proper sting, Gerhard."*

*"An investigation often proves to be an expensive inconvenience," said Flesch. "Even for a truly German business. And mistakes are sometimes made. It might be months before things returned to normal."*

*I nodded, recognizing the truth in what he had said. No one turned the Gestapo down. Not without some serious consequences. My only choice was between the disastrous and the unpalatable. A very German choice. We both knew I had little alternative but to agree to what they wanted. At the same time, it left me in an awkward position, to put it mildly. After all, I already had a very strong suspicion that Franz Six was lining his pockets with Paul Begelmann's shekels. But I had no wish to be caught up in the middle of a power struggle between the SD and the Gestapo. On the other hand, there was nothing to say that the two SD men I was accompanying to Palestine were dishonest. As a matter of course, they would surely suspect that I was a spy, and, accordingly, treat me with caution. The chances were strong that I would discover absolutely nothing. But would nothing satisfy the Gestapo? There was only one way to find out.*

*"All right," I said. "But I won't be a mouth for you people and say a lot of stuff that isn't true. I can't. I won't even try. If they're bent then I'll tell you they're bent and I'll tell myself that that's just what detectives do. Maybe I'll lose some sleep about it and maybe I won't. But if they are straight, that's an end of it, see? I won't frame someone just to give you and the other hammerheads at Prinz-Albrecht-Strasse an edge. I won't do it, not even if you and your best brass knuckles tell me I have to. You can keep your sugarloaf, too. I wouldn't like to get a taste for it. I'll do your dirty little job, Gerhard. But we let the cards fall where they fall. No stacked decks. Clear?"*

*"Clear." Flesch stood up, buttoned his coat, and put on his hat. "Enjoy your trip, Gunther. I've never been to Palestine. But I'm told it's very beautiful."*

*"Maybe you should go yourself," I said brightly. "I bet you'd love it down there. Fit right in, in no time. Everyone in Palestine has a Jewish Department."*

*I left Berlin sometime during the last week of September and traveled by train through Poland to the port of Constanța, in Romania. It was there, boarding the steamer* Romania, *that I finally met the two SD men who were also traveling to Palestine. Both were noncommissioned officers—sergeants in the SD—and both were posing as journalists working for the* Berliner Tageblatt, *a newspaper that had been Jewish-owned until 1933, when the Nazis had confiscated it.*

*The sergeant in charge was Herbert Hagen. The other man was called Adolf Eichmann. Hagen was in his early twenties and a fresh-faced intellectual, a university graduate from an upper-class background. Eichmann was several years older and aspired to be something more than the Austrian petroleum salesman he had been before joining the Party and the SS. Both men were curious anti-Semites, being strangely fascinated with Judaism. Eichmann had the greater experience in the Jewish Department, spoke Yiddish, and spent most of the voyage reading Theodor Herzl's book about the Jewish State, which was called* The Jewish State. *The trip had been Eichmann's own idea and he seemed both surprised and excited that his superiors had agreed to it, having never been out of Germany and Austria before. Hagen was a more ideological Nazi who was an enthusiastic Zionist, believing, as he did, that there was "no greater enemy for the Party than the Jew"—or some such nonsense—and that "the solution of the Jewish question" could lie only in the "total de-Jewing" of Germany. I hated listening to him talk. It all sounded mad to me. Like something found in the pages of some malignant Alice in Wonderland.*

*Both men regarded me with suspicion, as I had imagined they would, and not just because I had come from outside the SD and their peculiar department, but also because I was older than them—by almost twenty years in the case of Hagen. And jokingly they were soon referring to me as "Papi," which I bore with good grace—at least with a better grace than Hagen, who in retaliation, and much to Eichmann's amusement, I quickly dubbed Hiram Schwartz, after the juvenile diarist of the same name. Consequently, by the time we reached Jaffa on or about October 2, Eichmann had a greater liking for me than his younger, less experienced colleague.*

*Eichmann was not, however, an impressive man, and at the time, I thought he was probably the type who looked better in uniform. Indeed, I soon came to suspect that wearing a uniform had been the principal reason he had joined the SA and then the SS, for I rather doubted he would have been fit enough to have joined the regular army, if army there had been at that time. Of less than medium* height, he was bow-legged and extremely thin. In his upper jaw he had two gold bridges, as well as many fillings in his long, widow's teeth. His head was like a skull, almost exactly like the death's head on an SS man's cap-badge, being extremely bony with particularly hollow temples. One thing that struck me was how Jewish he looked. And it occurred to me that his antipathy for the Jews might have had something to do with this.

From the moment the Romania docked at Jaffa, things did not go well for the two SD men. The British must have suspected that Hagen and Eichmann were from German intelligence and, after a great deal of argument, gave them leave to come ashore for just twenty-four hours. I myself encountered no such problems, and I was quickly issued a visa allowing me to remain in Palestine for thirty days. This was ironic as I had only intended staying for four or five days at most, and caused much chagrin to Eichmann, whose plans were now in complete disarray. He railed on about this change of plan in the horse-drawn carriage that carried the three of us and our luggage from the port to the Jerusalem Hotel, on the edge of the city's famous "German colony."

"Now what are we going to do?" he complained loudly. "All of our most important meetings are the day after tomorrow. By which time we'll be back on the boat."

I smiled to myself, enjoying his consternation. Any setback for the SD was fine by me. I was pleased if only because it relieved me of the burden of inventing some story for the Gestapo. I could hardly spy on men who had been refused visas. I even thought the Gestapo might find that amusing enough to forgive the lack of any more concrete information.

"Perhaps Papi could meet them," said Hagen.

"Me?" I said. "Forget it, Hiram."

"I still don't understand how you got a visa and we didn't," said Eichmann.

*"Because he's helping that yid for Dr. Six, of course," said Hagen. "The Jew probably fixed it for him."*

*"Could be," I said. "Or it could be that you boys just aren't very good at this line of work. If you were good at it then perhaps you wouldn't have chosen a cover story that involves you both working for a Nazi newspaper. Moreover, a Nazi newspaper that was stolen from its Jewish owners. You might have picked something a little less high profile than that, I think." I smiled at Eichmann. "Like being a petroleum salesman, perhaps."*

*Hagen got it. But Eichmann was still too upset to realize he was being teased.*

*"Franz Reichert," he said. "From the German News Agency. I can telephone him in Jerusalem. I expect he will know how to get hold of Fievel Polkes. But I haven't a clue how we're going to get in touch with Haj Amin." He sighed. "What are we going to do?"*

*I shrugged. "What would you have done now?" I asked. "Today. If you'd got your thirty-day visa after all."*

*Eichmann shrugged. "I suppose we would have visited the German Freemason colony at Sarona. Gone up Mount Carmel. Looked at some Jewish farming settlements in the Jezreel Valley."*

*"Then my advice is to go ahead and do exactly that," I said. "Call Reichert. Explain the situation and then get back on the boat, tomorrow. It sails for Egypt tomorrow, right? Well, when you get there, go to the British embassy in Cairo and apply for another visa."*

*"He's right," said Hagen. "That's exactly what we should do."*

*"We can apply again," cried Eichmann. "Of course. We can get a visa in Cairo and then travel back here overland."*

*"Just like the children of Israel," I added.*

*The carriage left the narrow, dirty streets of the old town and picked up speed as we headed along a wider road, to the new town of Tel Aviv. Opposite a clock tower and several Arabian coffee-*

*houses was the Anglo-Palestine Bank, where I was supposed to meet the manager and give him the letters of introduction from Begelmann, and from the Wassermann Bank, not to mention the camel-back trunk Begelmann had given me to take out of Germany. I had no idea what was in it, but from the weight I didn't think it was his stamp collection. I could see no advantage in delaying my going into the bank. Not in a place like Jaffa, which seemed full of hostile-looking Arabs. (Possibly they thought we were Jews, of course. There was little liking for Jews among the local Palestinian population.) So I told the driver to stop and, with the trunk under my arm, and the letters in my pocket, I got out, leaving Eichmann and Hagen to carry on to the hotel with the rest of my luggage.*

*The bank manager was an Englishman named Quinton. His arms were too short for his jacket and his fair hair was so fine it was hardly there at all. He had a snub nose that was surrounded by freckles and a smile like a young bulldog. Meeting him I couldn't help but picture Quinton's father, paying close attention to his son's German teacher. I suspected he would have been a good one because young Mr. Quinton spoke excellent German, with many enthusiastic inflections, as if he had been reciting Goethe's "The Destruction of Magdeburg."*

*Quinton took me into his office. There was a cricket bat on the wall and several photographs of cricket teams. A fan turned slowly on the ceiling. It was hot. Outside the office window was a fine view of the Mohammedan Cemetery and, beyond, the Mediterranean Sea. The clock on the nearby tower struck the hour, and the muezzin at the mosque on the other side of Howard Street called the faithful to prayer. I was a long way from Berlin.*

*He opened the envelopes with which I had been entrusted with a paper knife shaped like a little scimitar. "Is it true that Jews in Germany are not allowed to play Beethoven or Mozart?" he asked.*

*"They are forbidden to play music by those composers at Jewish*

*cultural events," I said. "But don't ask me to justify it, Mr. Quinton. I can't. If you ask me, the whole country has gone insane."*

*"You should try living here," he said. "Here, Jew and Arab are at each other's throats. With us in the middle. It's an impossible situation. The Jews hate the British for not allowing more of them to come and live in Palestine. And the Arabs hate us for allowing any Jews here at all. Right now, it's lucky for us they hate each other more than they hate us. But one day this whole country is going to blow up in our faces, and we'll leave and it'll be worse than ever before. You mark my words, Herr Gunther."*

*While he had been speaking, he'd been reading the letters and sorting out various sheets of paper, some of them blank but for a signature. And now he explained what he was doing:*

*"These are letters of accreditation," he said. "And signature samples for some new bank accounts. One of these accounts is to be a joint account for you and Dr. Six. Is that right?"*

*I frowned, hardly liking the idea of sharing anything with the head of the SD's Jewish Department. "I don't know," I said.*

*"Well, it's from this account that you are to take the money to buy the lease on a property here in Jaffa," he explained. "As well as your own fee and expenses. The balance will be payable to Dr. Six on presentation of a passbook that I will give to you to give to him. And his passport. Please make sure he understands that. The bank insists on the passbook holder identifying himself with a passport, if money is to be handed over. Clear?"*

*I nodded.*

*"May I see your own passport, Herr Gunther?"*

*I handed it over.*

*"The best person to help you find commercial property in Jaffa is Solomon Rabinowicz," he said, glancing over my passport and writing down the number. "He's a Polish Jew, but he's quite the*

*most resourceful fellow I think I've met in this infuriating country. He has an office in Montefiore Street. In Tel Aviv. That's about half a mile from here. I'll give you his address. Always assuming that your client won't want premises in the Arab quarter. That would be asking for trouble."*

*He handed back my passport and nodded at Mr. Begelmann's trunk. "I take it those are your client's valuables?" he said. "The ones he wishes to store in our vault, pending his arrival in this country."*

*I nodded again.*

*"One of these letters contains an inventory of the property contained in that trunk," he said. "Do you wish to check the inventory before handing it over?"*

*"No," I said.*

*Quinton came around the desk and collected the trunk. "Christ, it's heavy," he said. "If you would wait here, I'll have your own passbook prepared. May I offer you some tea? Or some lemonade, perhaps?"*

*"Tea," I said. "Tea would be nice."*

*My business at the bank concluded, I walked on to the hotel and found Hagen and Eichmann had already gone out. So, I had a cool bath, went to Tel Aviv, met Mr. Rabinowicz, and instructed him to find a suitable property for Paul Begelmann.*

*I did not see the two SD men until breakfast the next morning when, slightly the worse for wear, they came down to look for some black coffee. They had made a night of it at a club in the old town. "Too much arak," whispered Eichmann. "It's the local drink. A sort of aniseed-flavored grape spirit. Avoid it if you can."*

*I smiled and lit a cigarette but waved the smoke away when it seemed to nauseate him. "Did you get hold of Reichert?" I asked.*

*"Yes. As a matter of fact he was with us last night. But not Polkes. So he's liable to turn up here looking for us. Would you mind seeing him, just for five or ten minutes and explaining the situation?"*

*"What is the situation?"*

*"Our plans are changing by the minute, I'm afraid. We may not be coming back here after all. For one thing, Reichert seems to think we won't have any better luck getting a visa in Cairo than we've had here."*

*"I'm sorry to hear that," I said. I was not sorry at all.*

*"Tell him we've gone to Cairo," said Eichmann. "And that we'll be staying at the National Hotel. Tell him to come and meet us there."*

*"I don't know," I said. "I really don't want to get involved in any of this."*

*"You're a German," he said. "You're involved whether you like it or not."*

*"Yes, but you're the Nazi, not me."*

*Eichmann looked shocked. "How can you be working for the SD and not be a Nazi?" he asked.*

*"It's a funny old world," I said. "But don't tell anyone."*

*"Look, please see him," said Eichmann. "If only for courtesy's sake. I could leave a letter for him, but it would look so much better if you told him in person."*

*"Who is this Fievel Polkes, anyway?" I asked.*

*"A Palestinian Jew who works for the Haganah."*

*"And who are they?"*

*Eichmann smiled wearily. He was pale and sweating profusely. I almost felt sorry for him. "You really don't know very much about this country, do you?"*

*"I know enough to get a thirty-day visa," I said, pointedly.*

*"Haganah is a Jewish militia group and intelligence service."*

*"You mean, they're a terrorist organization."*

*"If you like," agreed Eichmann.*

*"All right," I said. "I'll see him. For courtesy's sake. But I'll need to know everything. I'm not meeting any of these murdering bastards with only half the story."*

*Eichmann hesitated. I knew he didn't trust me. But either he was too hung over to care, or he now realized he had no choice but to level with me.*

*"The Haganah want us to supply them with guns to use against the British here in Palestine," he said. "If the SD continues to promote Jewish emigration from Germany, they're also proposing to supply us with information on British troop and naval movements in the eastern Mediterranean."*

*"The Jews helping their own persecutors?" I laughed. "But that's preposterous." Eichmann wasn't laughing. "Isn't it?"*

*"On the contrary," said Eichmann. "The SD has already financed several Zionist training camps in Germany. Places where young Jews can learn the agricultural skills they will need to farm this land. Palestinian land. A National Socialist–financed Haganah is just one possible extension of that same policy. And that's one of the reasons I came here. To get the measure of the people in command of Haganah, the Irgun, and other Jewish militia groups. Look, I know it's hard to believe, but they dislike the British even more than they seem to dislike us."*

*"And where does Haj Amin fit into these plans?" I asked. "He's an Arab, isn't he?"*

*"Haj Amin is the other side of the coin," said Eichmann. "In case our pro-Zionist policy doesn't work out. We had planned to meet the Arab High Committee and some of its members—principally, Haj Amin—here, in Palestine. But it seems that the British have ordered the dissolution of the committee and the arrest of its members. Apparently the assistant district commissioner of Galilee was murdered in Nazareth a few days ago. Haj Amin is now in hiding,*

*in Jerusalem's old city, but he's going to try to slip out and meet us in Cairo. So, as you can see, there's just Polkes to worry about here in Jaffa."*

*"Remind me never to play cards with you, Eichmann," I said. "Or, if I do, to make sure you take off your coat and roll up your sleeves."*

*"Just tell Fievel Polkes to come to Cairo. He'll understand. But don't, for Christ's sake, mention the Grand Mufti."*

*"The Grand Mufti?"*

*"Haj Amin," said Eichmann. "He's the Grand Mufti of Jerusalem. He's the highest official of religious law in Palestine. The British appointed him in 1921. Which makes him the most powerful Arab in the country. He's also a rabid anti-Semite who makes the Führer seem like a Jew lover. Haj Amin has declared jihad on the Jews. Which is why the Haganah and the Irgun would like to see him dead. And which is why it's best Fievel Polkes doesn't know we're planning to see him. He'll suspect it's happening, of course. But that's his problem."*

*"I just hope it doesn't become mine," I said.*

*The day after Eichmann and Hagen left on the boat for Alexandria, Fievel Polkes turned up at the Jerusalem Hotel looking for them. Polkes was a chain-smoking Polish Jew in his mid-thirties. He wore a crumpled, tropical-weight suit and a straw hat. He needed a shave, but not as badly as the chain-smoking Russian Jew accompanying him. He was in his mid-forties, with a couple of boulders for shoulders and a weathered sort of face like something carved on a flying buttress. His name was Eliahu Golomb. Their jackets were buttoned, although it was, as usual, a baking-hot day. When a man keeps his jacket buttoned on a hot day, it usually means one thing. After I had explained the situation, Golomb swore in Russian, and in an effort to smooth things over—these men were terrorists, after all—I pointed at the bar and offered to buy them a drink.*

*"All right," said Polkes, who spoke good German. "But not in here. Let's go somewhere else. I have a car outside."*

*I almost said no. It was one thing to drink with them in the hotel bar. It seemed quite another thing to go somewhere in a car with men whose buttoned-up jackets told me they were armed, and probably dangerous. Seeing my hesitation, Polkes added, "You'll be safe enough, my friend. It's the British we're fighting, not the Germans."*

*We went outside and climbed inside a two-tone Riley saloon. Golomb drove slowly away from the hotel, like a man who didn't want to attract attention to himself. We went north and east, through a German colony of smart white villas known as Little Valhalla, and then left across the railway line, onto Hashachar Herzl. Left again onto Lilien Blum, and then we stopped at a bar next to a cinema. We were, said Polkes, in the center of the garden suburb of Tel Aviv. The air smelled of orange blossoms and the sea. Everything looked neater and cleaner than Jaffa. More European, anyway. And I remarked upon it.*

*"Naturally you feel at home here," said Polkes. "Only Jews live here. If it was up to the Arabs, this whole country would be little better than a pissing place."*

*We went into a glass-fronted café with Hebrew words painted on the window. It was called Kapulski's. The radio was playing what I would have described as Jewish music. A dwarfish woman was mopping the checkered floor. On the wall was a picture of a wild-haired old man wearing an open-necked shirt who looked like Einstein, but without the soup-straining mustache. I had no idea who he was. Beside this picture was one of a man who looked like Marx. I recognized this man as Theodor Herzl only because Eichmann had a picture of him in what he called his Jew file. The barman's eyes followed us as we passed through a beaded curtain and into a sweaty back room that was full of beer crates and chairs stacked on top of tables. Polkes took down three chairs and placed them on the floor. Meanwhile, Golomb helped himself to three beers from a crate, prized the tops off with his thumbs, and set them down on the table.*

*"That's a neat trick," I observed.*

*"You should see him open a tin of peaches," said Polkes.*

*It was hot. I took off my jacket and rolled up my sleeves. Both Jews kept their lightweight jackets buttoned. I nodded at their bulky armpits. "It's okay," I told Polkes. "I've seen a gun before. I won't get nightmares if I see yours."*

*Polkes translated into Hebrew and, smiling, Golomb nodded. His teeth were big and yellow, as if he usually ate grass for dinner. Then he took off his jacket. So did Polkes. Each of them was carrying a British Webley, as big as a dog's hind leg. We all lit cigarettes, tasted our warm beers, and looked one another over. I paid more attention to Golomb since he seemed to be the one in charge. Eventually, Polkes said:*

*"Eliahu Golomb is on the Command Council of Haganah. He's in favor of your government's radical Jewish policy, since it is the belief of Haganah that this will only increase the strength of the Jewish population in Palestine. In time, this can only mean that Jews will outnumber Arabs, after which the country will be ours for the taking."*

*I always hated warm beer. I hate drinking it from a bottle. I get mad when I have to drink it from a bottle. I'd rather not drink it at all.*

*"Let's get something clear," I said. "It's not my government. I hate the Nazis, and if you had any sense, you would, too. They're a bunch of goddamn liars and you can't believe a word they say. You believe in your cause. That's fine. But there's very little in Germany*

*that's worth believing in. Except perhaps that a beer should always be served cold and with a decent head on it."*

*Polkes translated all that I had said and when he finished, Golomb shouted something in Hebrew. But I hadn't finished my diatribe.*

*"You want to know what they believe in? The Nazis? People like Eichmann and Hagen? They believe that Germany is a thing worth cheating for. Worth lying for. And you're a pair of goddamn fools if you think any different. Even now those two Nazi clowns are preparing to meet your friend, the Grand Mufti, in Cairo. They'll make a deal with him. And then the next day they'll make a deal with you. And then they'll go back to Germany and wait to see which one Hitler will go for."*

*The barman arrived carrying three cold beers in glasses and put them on the table. Polkes smiled. "I think Eliahu likes you," he said. "He wants to know what you're doing in Palestine. With Eichmann and Hagen."*

*I told them that I was a private detective and about Paul Begelmann. "And just so you know there's nothing noble about it," I added, "I'm being paid quite handsomely for my trouble."*

*"You don't strike me as a man who's entirely motivated by money," said Golomb, through Polkes.*

*"I can't afford to have principles," I said. "Not in Germany. People with principles end up at Dachau concentration camp. I've been to Dachau. I didn't like it."*

*"You've been to Dachau?" said Polkes.*

*"Last year. A flying visit, you might say."*

*"Were there many Jews there?"*

*"About a third of the prisoners were Jewish," I said. "The rest were communists, homosexuals, Jehovah's Witnesses, a few Germans with principles."*

*"And which were you?"*

*"I was a man doing a job," I said. "Like I told you, I'm a private detective. And sometimes it takes me way out of my depth. It can happen very easily in Germany right now. I forget that myself sometimes."*

*"Maybe you would like to work for us?" said Golomb. "It would be useful to know the minds of these two men we were supposed to meet. Especially useful to know what they agree to with Haj Amin."*

*I laughed. It seemed that everyone these days wanted me to spy on someone else. The Gestapo wanted me to spy on the SD. And now Haganah wanted me to spy on them. There were times when I thought I'd joined the wrong profession.*

*"We could pay you," said Golomb. "Money's not something we're short of. Fievel Polkes here is our man in Berlin. From time to time you two could meet up, and exchange information."*

*"I wouldn't be worth anything to you," I said. "Not in Germany. Like I said, I'm just a private detective trying to make a living."*

*"Then help us here in Palestine," said Golomb. He had a deep gravelly voice that was entirely in keeping with the amount of hair on his body. He looked like a house-trained bear. "We'll drive you to Jerusalem from where you and Fievel can catch a train to Suez, and then to Alexandria. We'll pay you whatever you want. Help us, Herr Gunther. Help us to make something of this country. Everyone hates the Jews, and rightly so. We know no order or discipline. We've looked after ourselves for too long. Our only hope of salvation lies in a general immigration to Palestine. Europe is finished for the Jew, Herr Gunther."*

*Polkes finished the translation and shrugged. "Eliahu is quite an extreme Zionist," he added. "But his is not an uncommon opinion among members of the Haganah. I myself don't accept what he says about Jews deserving hatred. But he's right about our needing your help. How much do you want? Sterling? Marks? Gold sovereigns, perhaps."*

*I shook my head. "I won't help you for money," I said. "Everyone offers me money."*

*"But you are going to help us," said Polkes. "Aren't you?"*

*"Yes, I'll help you."*

*"Why?"*

*"Because I've been to Dachau, gentlemen. I can't think of a better reason to help you than that. If you'd seen it you would understand. That's why I'm going to help you."*

*Cairo was the diamond stud on the handle of the fan of the Nile delta. That was what my Baedeker said, anyway. To me it looked like something much less precious—more like the teat under a cow's belly that fed a representative of every tribe in Africa, of which continent it was the largest city. "City" seemed too small a word for Cairo, however. It seemed something much more than mere metropolis. It was like an island—a historical, religious, and cultural heartland, a city that was the model for every city that had come after it, and also its opposite. Cairo fascinated and alarmed me at the same time.*

*I checked into the National Hotel in the Ismailiyah Quarter, which was less than half a mile east of the Nile and the Egyptian Museum. Fievel Polkes stayed at the Savoy, which was at the southern end of the same street. The National was not much smaller than a decent-size village, with rooms as big as bowling alleys. Some of these were used as pungent-smelling hookah dens where as many as a dozen Arabs would sit, cross-legged on the floor, smoking pipes that were the size and shape of retort stands in a laboratory. A large Reuters notice board dominated the hotel lobby and, entering the guest lounge, you might have expected to see Lord Kitchener sitting in an armchair, reading his newspaper and twisting his waxed mustaches.*

*I left a message for Eichmann and, later on, met up with him and Hagen in the hotel bar. They were accompanied by a third German, Dr. Franz Reichert, who worked for the German News Agency in Jerusalem, but who quickly excused himself from our company, pleading an upset stomach.*

*"Something he ate, perhaps," said Hagen.*

*I slapped at a fly that had settled on my neck. "Just as likely it was something that ate him," I said.*

*"We were at a Bavarian restaurant last night," explained Eichmann. "Near the Central Station. I'm afraid it wasn't very Bavarian. The beer was all right. But the Wiener schnitzel was horse, I think. Or even camel."*

*Hagen groaned and held his stomach for a moment. I told them I had brought Fievel Polkes with me and that he was staying at the Savoy. "That's where we should have stayed," complained Hagen. And then: "I know why Polkes came to Cairo. But why did you come, Papi?"*

*"For one thing, I don't think our Jewish friend quite believed you really were here," I said. "So you can call it a sign of good faith, if you like. But for another, my business was concluded sooner than I had expected. And I decided that I might never have a better chance to see Egypt than this. So here I am."*

*"Thanks," said Eichmann. "I appreciate your bringing him down here. Otherwise we very probably wouldn't have met him at all."*

*"Gunther's a spy," insisted Hagen. "Why listen to him?"*

*"We applied for a Palestinian visa," said Eichmann, ignoring the younger man. "And were turned down again. We're applying again tomorrow. In the hope we can get a consular official who doesn't dislike Germans."*

"It's not Germans the British don't like," I told him. "It's Nazis." I paused for a moment. Then, realizing that this was a good opportunity to ingratiate myself with them, said, "But who knows? Maybe the official you got last time was a yid."

"Actually," said Eichmann, "I think he was Scottish."

"Look here," I said, affecting a tone of weary honesty. "I might as well level with you. It wasn't your boss, Franz Six, who asked me to spy on you. It was Gerhard Flesch. From the Gestapo's Jewish Department. He threatened to investigate my racial origins if I didn't. Of course, it's all a bluff. There are no kikes in my family. But you know what the Gestapo are like. They can put you through all sorts of hoops in order to prove that you're not a yid."

"I can't imagine anyone who could look less Jewish than you do, Gunther," said Eichmann.

I shrugged. "He's after proof that your department is corrupt," I said. "Well, of course, I could have told him that before we left Germany. I mean about my meeting with Six and Begelmann. But I didn't."

"So what are you going to tell him?" asked Eichmann.

"Not much. That you didn't get your visa. That I didn't have a proper opportunity to see much more than that you cheated on your expenses. I mean, I'll have to tell him something."

Eichmann nodded. "Yes, that's good. It's not what he's looking for, of course. He wants something more. To take over all the functions of our department." He clapped me on the shoulder. "Thanks, Gunther. You are a real mensch, do you know that? Yes. You can tell him I bought a nice new tropical suit, on expenses. That will piss him off."

"You did buy it on expenses," said Hagen. "Not to mention a whole load of other stuff besides. Solar topees, mosquito nets, walking boots. He's brought more kit than the Italian army. Except *for the one thing we really need. We don't have any pistols. We're about to meet some of the most dangerous terrorists in the Middle East and we don't have any means of protecting ourselves."*

*Eichmann pulled a face, which wasn't difficult. His normal expression was a sort of grimace and his mouth was usually a cynical rictus. Whenever he looked at me I thought he was going to tell me he didn't like my tie. "I'm sorry about that," he told Hagen. "I told you. It wasn't my fault. But I don't know what we can do about it now."*

*"We've been to the German embassy and asked them for some weapons," Hagen told me. "And they won't give us any without proper authorization from Berlin. And if we asked for that it would make us look like a couple of amateurs."*

*"Can't you go to a gunsmith and buy one?" I asked.*

*"The British are so alarmed about the situation in Palestine that they've stopped the sale of weapons in Egypt," said Hagen.*

*I had been looking for a way to insinuate myself into their meeting with Haj Amin. And I now saw how I might do it. "I can get a gun," I said. I knew the very man who would lend me one.*

*"How?" asked Eichmann.*

*"I used to be a cop, at the Alex," I said smoothly. "There are always ways of getting guns. Especially in a city as big as this. You just have to know where to look. Low life is the same the world over."*

*I went to see Fievel Polkes in his room at the Savoy.*

*"I've found a way to get into their meeting with Haj Amin," I explained. "They're scared of Al-Istiqlal and the Young Men's Muslim Brotherhood. And they're scared of the Haganah. Somehow they managed to leave their guns back in Germany."*

*"They're right to be scared," said Polkes. "If you hadn't agreed to spy on them we might have tried to assassinate them. And then blame it on the Arabs. We've done that before. Very possibly the Grand Mufti might have a similar idea about blaming something on us. You should be careful, Bernie."*

*"I've offered to buy a gun in Cairo's underworld," I said. "And offered them my services as a bodyguard."*

*"Do you know where to buy a gun?"*

*"No. I was rather hoping I might borrow that Webley you're carrying."*

*"No problem," said Polkes. "I can always get another." He took off his jacket, unbuckled the shoulder holster, and handed over his rig. The Webley felt as heavy as an encyclopedia and almost as unwieldy. "It's a top-break double-action forty-five," he explained. "If you do have to shoot it, just remember two things. One, it's got a kick like a mule. And two, it's got a bit of history attached to it, if you know what I mean. So make sure you throw it in the Nile, if you can. One more thing. Be careful."*

*"You already told me that."*

*"I mean it. These are the bastards who murdered Lewis Andrews, the acting high commissioner of Galilee."*

*"I thought that was your lot."*

*Polkes grinned. "Not this time. We're in Cairo now. Cairo is not Jaffa. The British tread more carefully here. Haj Amin won't hesitate to kill all three of you if he thinks you might make a deal with us, so even if you don't like what he says, pretend you do. These people are crazy. Religious fanatics."*

*"So are you, aren't you?"*

*"No, we're just fanatics. There's a difference. We don't expect God to be pleased if we blow someone's head off. They do. That's what makes them crazy."*

---

*The meeting took place in the vast suite Eichmann had reserved for himself at the National Hotel.*

*Shorter by a head than any man in the room, the Grand Mufti of Jerusalem wore a white turban and a long black cassock. He was a man quite without humor and had an air of self-importance that was doubtless helped by the fawning way his followers behaved around him. Most curious to me was the realization of how much he looked like Eichmann. Eichmann with a graying beard, perhaps. Maybe that explained why they got on so well.*

*Haj Amin was accompanied by five men wearing dun-colored tropical suits and the tarboosh, which is the Egyptian version of the fez. His interpreter was a man with a gray Hitler-style mustache, a double chin, and an assassin's eyes. He carried a thick carved walking stick, and like the other Arabs—with the exception of Haj Amin himself—he was wearing a shoulder holster.*

*Haj Amin, who was in his early forties, spoke only Arabic and French, but his interpreter's German was good. The German newspaperman, Franz Reichert, who was now recovered from his earlier stomach upset, translated into Arabic for the two SD men. I sat near the door, listening to the conversation and affecting a vigilance that seemed appropriate given my self-appointed role as SD bodyguard. Most of what was said came from Haj Amin himself, and was deeply disturbing—not least because of the profound shock I experienced at the depth of his anti-Semitism. Hagen and Eichmann disliked the Jews. That was common enough in Germany. They made jokes about them and wanted to see them excluded from German public life, but, to me, Hagen's anti-Semitism seemed naïve and Eichmann's, little more than opportunism. Haj Amin, on the other hand, hated Jews as a dog might have hated a rat.*

*"The Jews," said Haj Amin, "have changed life in Palestine in*

*such a way that, if it goes unchecked, it must inevitably lead to the destruction of the Arabs in Palestine. We do not mind people coming to our country as visitors. But the Jew comes to Palestine as an alien invader. He comes as a Zionist and as someone equipped with all the trappings of modern European life, which are themselves an affront to the most sacred concepts of Islam. We are not accustomed to European ways. We do not want them. We wish our country to remain just as it was before the Jews started coming here in large numbers. We want no progress. We want no prosperity. Progress and prosperity are the enemies of true Islam. And there has already been enough talk. Talk with the British, with the Jews, with the French. Now we are talking with the Germans. But I tell you this, nothing but the sword will decide the fate of this country now. If it is the policy of Germany to support Zionism, then you should be aware of this. It is our policy that all Zionists and those who support Zionism will be massacred to the last man.*

*"But I have not come here to threaten your Führer, Herr Eichmann. Germany is not an imperialistic country like Great Britain. It has not harmed a single Arab or Muslim state in the past. It was allied to the Ottoman Empire during the war. I myself served in the Ottoman army. Germany has only ever fought our imperialistic and Zionist enemies. The French. The British. The Russians. The Americans. For which your people have our gratitude and admiration. Only, you must not send us any more Jews, Herr Eichmann.*

*"I have read the Führer's great book. In translation only. However, I believe I may flatter myself that I know the Führer's mind, gentlemen. He hates the Jews because of the defeat they brought upon Germany in 1918. He hates the Jews because it was the Jew, Chaim Weizmann, who invented the poison gas that injured him during the war, and caused him temporary blindness. For his delivery we give thanks to God. He hates the Jew because it was the Jew who brought America into the war on the side of the British*

*Zionists, and helped to defeat Germany. I understand all of this only too well, gentlemen, since I hate the Jew, too. I hate the Jew for any number of reasons. But most of all I hate the Jew for his persecution of Jesus, who was a prophet of God. Because of that, for a Muslim to kill a Jew ensures him an immediate entry into heaven and into the august presence of Almighty God.*

*"And so, my message to the Führer is this. Jews are not just the most fierce enemies of Muslims, they are also an ever-corrupting element in the world. Recognizing this has been the Führer's greatest revelation to the world. Acting upon this revelation will, I believe, be his greatest legacy to the world. Acting decisively. For it is no solution to the Jewish problem in Germany and Europe to keep exporting them to Palestine. Another solution must be found, gentlemen. A solution to end all solutions. This is the message you must give your superiors. That the best way to deal with the Jewish problem is to dry up the source in Europe. And I make the Führer this solemn pledge. I will help him to destroy the British empire if he promises to liquidate the entire Jewish population of Palestine. All Jews, everywhere, must be killed."*

*Even Eichmann seemed a little shocked at the Grand Mufti's words. Hagen, who took notes, was left openmouthed with astonishment at the cold simplicity of what the Mufti proposed. Reichert, too, was taken aback. Nevertheless, they managed to gather themselves sufficiently to promise the Mufti that they would convey his exact thoughts to their superiors in Berlin. Formal letters were exchanged. After which Eichmann concluded the meeting with an assurance for Haj Amin that now that they had met, they would surely meet again. Nothing of any real import had been agreed upon, and yet I had the sense that the Mufti's words had made a real impression on the two SD men.*

*When the meeting was concluded and the Grand Mufti and his entourage had left Eichmann's suite at the National—his Arab translator making a joke about how the British believed they still had Haj Amin cooped up somewhere within the Muslim holy places in Jerusalem (which, of course, they did not dare violate by entering to search for him)—the four of us looked at one another, lit cigarettes, and shook our heads in yet more wonder.*

*"I never heard such madness," I said, hiking over to the window and watching the street below as Haj Amin and his men climbed into an anonymous-looking van with hard panel sides. "Utter madness. The fellow is a complete spinner."*

*"Yes," agreed Hagen. "And yet there was a certain cold logic to his madness, wouldn't you say?"*

*"Logic?" I repeated, slightly incredulous. "How do you mean 'logic'?"*

*"I agree with Gunther," said Reichert. "It all sounded like complete madness to me. Like something from the First Crusade. I mean, don't get me wrong, I'm no Jew lover, but, really, you can't just liquidate a whole race of people."*

*"Stalin liquidated a whole class of people in Russia," said Hagen. "Two or three if you stop to think about it. He might just as easily have fixed on the Jews as on peasants, kulaks, and the bourgeoisie. And liquidated them instead. He's spent the last five years starving the Ukrainians to death. There's nothing to say you couldn't starve the Jews to death in just the same way. Of course, that kind of thing presents enormous practical problems. And essentially my opinion remains unchanged. We should try to send them to Palestine. What happens when they get here is hardly our concern."*

*Hagen came over to the window and lit a cigarette.*

*"Although I do think that the establishment of an independent Jewish state in Palestine must be resisted at all costs. That's something I've realized since we got here. Such a state might actually be*

capable of diplomatic lobbying against the German government. Of suborning the United States into a war against Germany. That possibility ought to be resisted."

"But surely you haven't changed your opinion about de facto Zionism," said Eichmann. "I mean, clearly, we're going to have to send the bastards somewhere. Madagascar makes no sense. They'd never go there. No, it's here, or the other—what Haj Amin was talking about. And I can't see anyone in the SD agreeing with that solution. It's too far-fetched. Like something out of Fritz Lang."

Reichert picked up the Mufti's letter. There were two words on the envelope: Adolf Hitler. "Do you suppose he's said any of that in his letter?" he asked.

"I don't think there's any doubt of it," I said. "The question is, what are you going to do with it?"

"There can be no question of not handing this letter to our superiors." Hagen sounded shocked at the very idea of not delivering the Mufti's letter—more shocked at my implied suggestion than anything the Grand Mufti had said. "That wouldn't do at all. This is diplomatic correspondence."

"It didn't sound all that diplomatic to me," I said.

"Perhaps not. Nevertheless the letter still has to go back to Berlin. This is part of what we came for, Gunther. We have to have something to show for our mission here. Especially now that we know we're being watched by the Gestapo. Fiddling expenses is one thing. Coming down here on a wild-goose chase is something else. That would make us look ridiculous in the eyes of General Heydrich. Our careers in the SD can't afford that."

"No, I hadn't thought of that," said Eichmann, whose sense of career was as developed as Hagen's.

"Heydrich may be a bastard," I said. "But he's a clever bastard. Too clever to read that letter and not know the Mufti is a complete spinner."

*"Maybe," said Eichmann. "Maybe, yes. Fortunately the letter isn't addressed to Heydrich, is it? Fortunately the letter's addressed to the Führer. He'll know best how to respond to what—"*

*"From one madman to another," I said. "Is that what you're suggesting, Eichmann?"*

*Eichmann almost choked with horror. "Not for one moment," he spluttered. "I wouldn't dream—" Blushing to the roots of his hair, he glanced uncomfortably at Hagen and Reichert. "Gentlemen, please believe me. That's not what I meant at all. I have the greatest admiration for the Führer."*

*"Of course you do, Eichmann," I said.*

*Finally, Eichmann looked at me. "You won't tell Flesch about this, will you, Gunther? Please say you won't tell the Gestapo."*

*"I wouldn't dream of it. Look, forget about that. What are you going to do about Fievel Polkes? And Haganah?"*

*Eliahu Golomb joined Polkes in Cairo for the meeting with Eichmann and Hagen. He only just made it before the British closed the border after a number of bomb attacks in Palestine by Arabs and Jews. Before the meeting, I met with Golomb and Polkes at their hotel and told them everything that had been said at the meeting with Haj Amin. For a while Golomb called down plagues from heaven on the Mufti's head. Then he asked for my advice on how to handle Eichmann and Hagen.*

*"I think you should make them believe that in any civil war with the Arabs, it's Haganah that will win," I said. "Germans admire strength. And they like winners. It's only the British who like the underdog."*

*"We will win," insisted Golomb.*

*"They don't know that," I said. "I think it would be a mistake to ask them for military aid. It would look like a sign of weakness.*

*You must convince them that, if anything, you're actually much better armed than you are. Tell them you have artillery. Tell them you have tanks. Tell them you have planes. They've no way of finding out if that's true or not."*

*"How does that help us?"*

*"If they think you will win," I said, "then they'll believe that their continued support of Zionism is the right policy. If they think you'll lose, then frankly there's no telling where they might send Germany's Jews. I've heard Madagascar mentioned."*

*"Madagascar?" said Golomb. "Ridiculous."*

*"Look, all that matters is that you convince them that a Jewish state can exist and that it would be no threat to Germany. You don't want them going back to Germany thinking the Grand Mufti is right, do you? That all the Jews in Palestine should be massacred?"*

*When it eventually took place, the meeting went well enough. To my ears, Golomb and Polkes sounded like fanatics. But as they had pointed out earlier, they didn't sound like crazy, religious fanatics. After the Grand Mufti, anyone would have sounded reasonable.*

*A few days later, we sailed from Alexandria, on the Italian steamer* Palestrina, *for Brindisi, stopping at Rhodes and Piraeus on the way. From Brindisi, we caught a train and were back in Berlin by October 26.*

*I hadn't seen Eichmann for nine months when, while working on a case that took me to Vienna, I bumped into him on Prinz-Eugen-Strasse, in the Eleventh District, just south of what later became Stalin Platz. He was coming out of the Rothschild Palais, which (after the Wehrmacht's popular invasion of Austria in March 1938) had been seized from the eponymous Jewish family that owned it, and was now the headquarters of the SD in Austria. Eichmann was no longer a lowly noncommissioned officer, but a second lieutenant—an Untersturmführer. There seemed to be a spring in his step. Jews were already fleeing the country. For the first time in his life, Eichmann had real power. Whatever he had said to his superiors upon his return from Egypt had obviously made an impression.*

*We only spoke for a minute or two before he stepped into the back of a staff car and drove away. I remember thinking, there goes the most Jewish-looking man who ever wore an SS uniform.*

*After the war, whenever I saw his name appear in a newspaper, that was always how I thought of him. The most Jewish-looking man who ever wore an SS uniform.*

*There's one more thing I always remembered about him. It was something he told me on the boat from Alexandria. When he wasn't being seasick. It was something of which Eichmann was very proud. When he lived in Linz, as a boy, Eichmann had gone to the same school as Adolf Hitler. Maybe it explains something of what he was to become. I don't know.*

# ONE

## *Munich 1949*

We were just a stone's throw from what had once been the concentration camp. But when we were handing out directions, we tended not to mention that, unless it was absolutely necessary. The hotel, on the east side of the medieval town of Dachau, was down a cobbled, poplar-lined side road, separated from the former KZ—now a residential settlement camp for German and Czech refugees from the communists—by the Würm River canal. It was a half-timbered affair, a three-story suburban villa with a steep saddle roof made of orange tiles, and a wraparound first-floor balcony overflowing with red geraniums. It was the kind of place that had seen better days. Since the Nazis and then the German prisoners of war had left Dachau, nobody came to the hotel anymore, except perhaps the odd construction engineer helping to supervise the partial erasure of a KZ where, for several very unpleasant weeks in the summer of 1936, I myself had been an inmate. The elected representatives of the Bavarian people saw no need to preserve the remnants of the camp for present or future visitors. Most residents of the town, including myself, were of the opinion, however, that the camp presented the only opportunity for bringing money into Dachau. But there was little chance of that happening so long as the memorial temple remained unbuilt and a mass grave, where more than five thousand were buried, unmarked. The visitors stayed away, and despite my efforts with the geraniums, the hotel began to die. So when a new two-door Buick Roadmaster pulled up on our little brick driveway, I told myself that the two men were most probably lost and had stopped to ask directions to the U.S. Third Army barracks, although it was hard to see how they could have missed the place.

The driver stepped out of the Buick, stretched like a child, and looked up at the sky as if he was surprised that birds could be heard singing in a place like Dachau. I often had the same thought myself. The passenger stayed in his seat, staring straight ahead, and probably wishing he was somewhere else. He had my sympathies, and possessed of the shiny green sedan, I would certainly have kept on driving. Neither man was wearing a uniform but the driver was altogether better dressed than his passenger. Better dressed, better fed, and in rather better health, or so it seemed to me. He tap-danced up the stone steps and through the front door like he owned the place, and I found myself nodding politely at the hatless, tanned, bespectacled man with a face like a chess grandmaster who had considered every possible move. He didn't look lost at all.

"Are you the owner?" he asked as soon as he came through the door, without making much of an effort at a good German accent and without even looking at me while he awaited an answer. He glanced idly around at the hotel decor which was supposed to make the place feel more homey, but only if you roomed with a milkmaid. There were cowbells, spinning wheels, hemp combs, rakes, sharpening stones, and a big wooden barrel on top of which lay a two-day-old *Süddeutsche Zeitung* and a truly ancient copy of the *Münchener Stadtanzeiger.* On the walls were some watercolors of local rural scenes from a time when painters better than Hitler had come to Dachau, attracted by the peculiar charm of the Amper River and the Dachauer Moos—an extensive marsh now mostly drained and turned into farmland. It was all as kitsch as an ormolu cuckoo clock.

"You could say that I'm the owner," I said. "At least while my wife is indisposed. She's in the hospital. In Munich."

"Nothing serious, I hope," said the American, still not looking at me. He seemed more interested in the watercolors than in the health of my wife.

"I imagine you must be looking for the U.S. military barracks, at the old KZ," I said. "You turned off the road when you should have just driven across the bridge, over the river canal. It's less than a hundred yards from here. On the other side of those trees."

Now he looked at me and his eyes became playful, like a cat's. "Poplars, aren't they?" He stooped to stare out of the window in the direction of the camp. "I bet you're glad of them. I mean, you'd hardly know the camp was there at all, would you? Very useful."

Ignoring the implied accusation in his tone, I joined him at the window. "And here I was thinking you must be lost."

"No, no," said the American. "I'm not lost. This is the place I'm looking for. That is, if this is the Hotel Schroderbrau."

"This is the Hotel Schroderbrau."

"Then we are in the right place." The American was about five-feet-eight, with smallish hands and feet. His shirt, tie, pants, and shoes were all varying shades of brown, but his jacket was made of a light-colored tweed and nicely tailored, too. His gold Rolex told me there was probably a better car than the Buick in his garage back home in America. "I'm looking for two rooms, for two nights," he said. "For me and my friend in the car."

"I'm afraid we're not a hotel that is approved for Americans," I said. "I could lose my license."

"I won't tell if you don't," he said.

"Don't think I'm being rude, please," I said, trying out the English I'd been teaching myself. "But to be honest, we are almost closing. This was my father-in-law's hotel, until he died. My wife and I have had very little success in running it. For obvious reasons.

And now that she's ill—" I shrugged. "I'm not much of a cook, you see, sir, and I can tell you're a man who enjoys his comfort. You would be better off at another hotel. Perhaps the Zieglerbrau or the Hörhammer, on the other side of town. They are both approved for Americans. And they both have excellent cafés, too. Especially the Zieglerbrau."

"So am I to take it that there are no other guests in the hotel?" he asked, ignoring my objections and my attempts to speak English. His German accent may have been nonexistent, but there was nothing wrong with his grammar or his vocabulary.

"No," I said. "We're empty. As I said, we're on the verge of closing."

"I only asked because you keep on saying 'we,'" he said. "Your father-in-law is dead and you said your wife is in the hospital. But you keep on using the word 'we.' As if there's someone else here."

"Hotelier's habit," I said. "There's just me and my impeccable sense of service."

The American pulled a pint of rye out of his jacket pocket and held it so I could see the label. "Might that impeccable sense of service run to a couple of clean glasses?"

"A couple of glasses? Sure." I couldn't guess what he wanted. He certainly didn't look like he needed a deal on two rooms. If there was a rat crawling over his well-polished wingtips, I couldn't yet smell it. Besides, there was nothing wrong with the label on his rye. "But what about your friend in the car? Won't he be joining us?"

"Him? Oh, he doesn't drink."

I stepped into the office and reached down a couple of glasses. Before I could ask if he wanted any water with his whiskey, the American had filled both glasses to the brim. He held his glass against the light and said, slowly: "You know, I wish I could remember who it is that you remind me of."

I let that one go. It was a remark only an American, or an Englishman, could have made. In Germany today nobody wants to remember anything or anyone. The privilege of defeat.

"It'll come to me," he said, shaking his head. "I never forget a face. But it's not important." He drank his whiskey and pushed the glass to one side. I tasted mine. I was right. It was good whiskey, and I said so.

"Look here," he said. "It so happens that your hotel suits my purposes very well. As I said, I need two rooms for one or two nights. Depends. Either way I have money to spend. Cash money." He took a fold of very new deutschmarks from his back pocket, slipped off a silver money clip, and counted five twenties on the desk in front of me. It was about five times the going rate on two rooms for two nights. "The kind of money that's a little shy of too many questions."

I finished my drink and allowed my eyes to drift to the passenger still seated in the Buick outside and felt them narrow as, a little shortsighted these days, I tried to size him up. But the American was there ahead of me.

"You're wondering about my friend," he said. "If perhaps he's the lemon-sucking type." He poured another couple of drinks and grinned. "Don't worry. We're not warm for each other if that's what you were thinking. Anything but, as a matter of fact. If you ever asked him his opinion of me, I should imagine he would tell you that he hates my guts, the bastard."

"Nice traveling companion," I said. "I always say, a trip that's shared provides twice the happy memories." I took my second drink. But for the moment I left the hundred marks untouched, at least by my hand. My eyes were on and off the five notes, however, and the American saw it and said:

"Go ahead. Take the money. We both know you need it. This

hotel hasn't seen a guest since my government ended the prosecution of war criminals at Dachau last August. That's almost a year, isn't it? No wonder your father-in-law killed himself."

I said nothing. But I was starting to smell the rat.

"It must have been tough," he continued. "Very tough. Now that the trials are over, who wants to come and take a vacation here? I mean, Dachau's not exactly Coney Island, is it? Of course, you could get lucky. You might get a few Jews who want to take a stroll down memory lane."

"Get to the point," I said.

"All right." He swallowed his drink and palmed a gold cigarette case from the other pocket. "Herr Kommissar Gunther."

I took the offered cigarette and let him light me with a match he snapped into life with a thumbnail while it was still only halfway up to my face.

"You want to be careful doing that," I said. "You could spoil your manicure."

"Or you could spoil it for me? Yes?"

"Maybe."

He laughed. "Don't get hard-boiled with me, pal," he said. "It's been tried. The krauts who tried it are still picking pieces of shell out of their mouths."

"I don't know," I said. "You don't look like a tough guy. Or is that just this season's look for tough guys?"

"What you know is of incidental importance to me, Bernie, old boy," he said. "Let me tell you what I know, for a minute. I know a lot. How you and your wife came here from Berlin last fall, to help her old man run this hotel. How he killed himself just before Christmas and how she cracked up because of that. How you used to be a Kriminal Kommissar at the Alex in Berlin. A cop. Just like me."

"You don't look like a cop."

"Thanks, I'll take that as a compliment, Herr Kommissar."

"That was ten years ago," I said. "Mostly I was just an inspector. Or a private detective."

The American jerked his head at the window. "The guy in the car is handcuffed to the steering wheel. He's a war criminal. What your German newspapers would call a Red Jacket. During the war he was stationed here, at Dachau. He worked at the crematorium, burning bodies, for which he received a twenty-year sentence. You ask me, he deserved to hang. They all did. Then again, if he had been hanged he wouldn't be outside now, helping me with my inquiries. And I wouldn't have had the pleasure of meeting you."

He blew some smoke at the carved wooden ceiling and then picked a piece of tobacco off his eloquent pink tongue. I might have given him a short uppercut and then he'd have lost the tip of it. I was with the guy in the car. The one who hated the Ami's guts. I disliked the Yank's manner and the advantage he seemed to think he held over me. But it wasn't worth punching him out. I was in the American Zone, and we both knew they could make trouble for me. I didn't want trouble with the Americans. Especially after the trouble I'd had with the Ivans. So I kept my fists by my side. Besides, there was still the small matter of a hundred marks. A hundred marks was a hundred marks.

"It seems the guy in the car was a friend of your wife's father," said the American. He turned and walked into the hotel bar. "I expect he and some of his SS pals were in and out of this place a lot." I saw his eyes take in the dirty glasses on the bar top, the overflowing ashtrays, the beer spills on the floor. They were all mine. That bar was the one place in the hotel where I felt truly at home. "I guess those were better days, huh?" He laughed. "You know, you should go back to being a cop, Gunther. You're no hotelier, that's for sure. Hell, I've seen body bags that were more welcoming than this place."

"No one's asking you to stay and fraternize," I said.

"Fraternize?" He laughed. "Is that what we're doing? No, I don't think so. Fraternize implies something brotherly. I just don't feel that way about anyone who could stay in a town like this, bud."

"Don't feel bad about it," I said. "I'm an only child. Not the brotherly kind at all. Frankly, I'd rather empty the ashtrays than talk to you."

"Wolf, the guy in the car," said the American, "he was a real enterprising sort of guy. Before he burned the bodies, he used to take out any gold teeth with a pair of pliers. He had a pair of pruning shears to cut off fingers for the wedding rings. He even had this special pair of tongs so he could search the private parts of the dead looking for rolls of banknotes, jewels, and gold coins. It's amazing what he used to find. Enough to fill an empty wine box, which he buried in your father-in-law's garden before the camp was liberated."

"And you want to dig it up?"

"I'm not going to dig anything up." The American jerked his thumb at the front door. "He is, if he knows what's good for him."

"What makes you think the box is still there?" I asked.

He shrugged. "It's a safe bet that Herr Handlöser, your father-in-law, didn't find it. If he had, this place would be in a lot better shape. And probably he'd never have put his head on the Altomünster railway line, just like Anna Karenina. I bet he had less time to wait than she did. That's the one thing you krauts do really well. The trains. I gotta hand it to you. Everything still runs like clockwork in this damned country."

"And the hundred marks are for what? To keep my mouth shut?"

"Sure. But not the way you think. You see, I'm doing you a favor. You and everyone else in town. You see, if it ever gets out that someone dug up a box of gold and jewels in your back garden, Gunther, then everyone in town is going to have a problem with other people looking for treasure. Refugees, British and American soldiers, desperate Germans, greedy Ivans, you name it. That's why this is being handled unofficially. Simple as that."

"Talk of treasure might be good for business," I said, heading back to the front desk. The money was still there. "It could bring people back to this town in a big way."

"And when they don't find anything? Think about it. Things could get nasty. I've seen it happen."

I nodded. I can't say I wasn't tempted to take his money. But the truth was I didn't want any part of anything connected with gold that had come out of someone's mouth. So I pushed the banknotes back toward him. "You're welcome to dig," I said. "And you can do what the hell you like with whatever you find. But I don't like the smell of your money. It feels too much like a share of the loot. I didn't want any part of it then, and I certainly don't want any part of it now."

"Well, well," said the American. "Isn't that something? A kraut with principles. Hell, I thought Adolf Hitler killed all of you guys."

"It's three marks a night," I said. "Each. In advance. There's plenty of hot water, day and night, but if you want more than a beer or a cup of coffee, that's extra. Food is still rationed, for Germans."

"Fair enough," he said. "For what it's worth, I'm sorry. I was wrong about you."

"For what it's worth, I'm sorry, too." I poured myself some more of his rye. "Every time I look at that line of trees, I remember what happened on the other side."

## TWO

The man from the car was of medium height, dark-haired with protruding ears, and shadowy, downcast eyes. He wore a thick tweed suit and a plain white shirt, but without a necktie, no doubt in case he tried to hang himself. He didn't speak to me and I didn't speak to him. When he came into the hotel his head seemed to shrink into his narrow shoulders as if—I can think of no other explanation—he was burdened with a sense of shame. But perhaps I'm just being fanciful. Either way I felt sorry for him. If the cards had been dealt differently it might have been me in the American's Buick.

There was another reason I felt sorry for the man. He looked feverish and ill. Hardly equal to the task of digging a hole in my garden. I said as much to the American as he fetched some tools from the cavernous trunk of the Buick.

"He looks like he should be in hospital," I said.

"And that's where he's going after this," said the American. "If he finds the box, then he'll get his penicillin." He shrugged. "He wouldn't have cooperated at all if I didn't have that kind of leverage."

"I thought you Amis were supposed to pay attention to the Geneva Conventions," I said.

"Oh we do, we do," he said. "But these guys are not ordinary soldiers, they're war criminals. Some of them have murdered thousands of people. These guys put themselves outside the protection of Geneva."

We followed Wolf into the garden, where the American threw the tools down on the grass and told him to get on with it. The day was a hot one. Too hot to be digging anywhere but in your pockets. Wolf leaned on a tree for a moment as he tried to get his bearings, and let out a sigh. "I think this is the spot, right here," he whispered. "Could I have a glass of water?" His hands were shaking and there was sweat on his forehead.

"Get him a glass of water, will you, Gunther?" said the American.

I fetched the water, and returned to find Wolf, pickax in hand. He took a swing at the lawn and almost fell over. I caught him by the elbow and helped him to sit down. The American was lighting a cigarette, apparently unconcerned. "Take your time, Wolf, my friend," he said. "There's no hurry. That's why I figured on two nights, see? On account of how he's not exactly in the best of shape for gardening duty."

"This man is in no condition for any kind of manual work," I said. "Look at him. He can hardly stand."

The American flicked his match at Wolf and snorted with derision. "And do you imagine he ever said that to any of the people who were imprisoned in Dachau?" he said. "Like hell he did. Probably shot them in the head where they fell. Not a bad idea at that. Save me the trouble of taking him back to the prison hospital."

"That's hardly the point of this exercise, is it? I thought you just wanted what's buried here."

"Sure, but I'm not going to dig. These shoes are from Florsheim."

I took the pickax from Wolf, angrily. "If there's half a chance of getting rid of you before this evening," I said, "I'll do it myself." And I sank the point of the pick into the grass as if it had been the American's skull.

"It's your funeral, Gunther."

"No, but it will be his if I don't do this." I wielded the pick again.

"Thanks, comrade," whispered Wolf, and sitting underneath the tree, he leaned back and closed his eyes weakly.

"You krauts." The American smiled. "Stick together, don't you?"

"This has got nothing to do with being German," I said. "I'd probably have done it for anyone I didn't much like, including you."

I was at it for about an hour with the pick and then the shovel until, about three feet down, I hit something hard. It sounded and felt like a coffin. The American was quickly over to the side of the hole, his eyes searching the earth. I kept on digging and finally levered out a box that was the size of a small suitcase and placed it on the grass at his feet. It was heavy. When I looked up, I saw that he was holding a thirty-eight in his hand. A snub-nosed police special.

"This is nothing personal," he said. "But a man who's digging for treasure is just liable to think he deserves a share. Especially a man who was noble enough to turn down a hundred marks."

"Now that you mention it," I said, "the idea of beating your face to a pulp with the flat of a spade is rather tempting."

He waved the gun. "Then you'd best throw it away, just in case."

I bent over, picked up the spade, and launched it into the flower bed. I put my hand in my pocket and, seeing him stiffen a little, laughed. "Kind of nervous for a tough guy, aren't you?" I brought out a packet of Luckies, and lit one. "I guess maybe those krauts who are still picking pieces of shell from their mouths were just careless with their eggs. Either that, or you tell a good story."

"Now, here's what I want you to do," he said. "Climb out of that hole, pick up the box, and carry it to the car."

"You and your manicure," I said.

"That's right," he said. "Me and my manicure."

I climbed out of the hole and stared at him, then down at the box. "You're a bastard, all right," I said. "But I've met a lot of bastards in my time—some of the biggest, bigger than you—and I know what I'm talking about. There are lots of reasons to shoot a man dead in cold blood, but refusing to carry a box to a car isn't one of them. So I'm going into the house to wash up and fetch myself a beer, and you can go to hell."

I turned and walked back to the house. He didn't pull the trigger.

About five minutes later I looked out my bathroom window and saw Wolf carrying the box slowly to the Buick. Still holding his gun, and glancing nervously up at the windows of the hotel as if I might have a rifle, the American opened the trunk and Wolf dropped the box inside. Then the two of them got into the car and drove quickly away. I went downstairs, fetched a beer from the bar, and then locked the front door. The American had been right about one thing. I was a lousy hotel-keeper. And it was high time I recognized that in some practical way. I found some paper and, in large red letters, wrote on it "CLOSED UNTIL FURTHER NOTICE." Then I taped the sign to the glass in the door and went back into the bar.

A couple of hours, and twice as many beers later, I caught one of the new electric trains into Munich's main railway station. From there I walked through the bomb-damaged city center to the corner of Ludwigstrasse, where, in front of the charred ruins of the Leuchtenberg Palais and the Odeon, once the best concert halls in Munich, I took a tram north, in the direction of Schwabing. Here, nearly all of the buildings reminded me of myself, with only the housefronts standing, so that while the general appearance of the street seemed hardly impaired, everything was in reality badly damaged and burned out. It was high time I made some repairs. But I didn't see how that was possible doing what I was doing. Working as the Adlon house detective in the early thirties, I had learned a little about running a grand hotel, but this had been very poor preparation for running a small one. The Ami was right. I had to go back to what I knew best. I was going to tell Kirsten that I intended to put the hotel up for sale, and that I planned to become a private detective again. Of course, telling her was one thing; expecting her to register any sign of comprehension was quite another. And whereas I still had a façade, Kirsten seemed like a complete ruin of her former self.

On the north edge of Schwabing was the main state hospital. It was used as the American military hospital, which meant that Germans had to go somewhere else. That is, all except the lunatics, who went to the hospital's Max Planck Institute of Psychiatry. This was just around the corner from the main hospital, in Kraepelinstrasse. I visited her as often as I could given that I was running a hotel, which meant that lately I'd been coming only every other day.

Kirsten's room enjoyed a view of Prinz Luitpold Park to the southeast, but I could not have described her condition as comfortable. There were bars on the windows of the room and the three other women she shared it with were all severely disturbed. The room stank of urine and, from time to time, one of the other women would scream out loud, laugh hysterically, or throw something unspeakable in my direction. Also, the beds were verminous. There were bite marks on Kirsten's thighs and arms, and on one occasion, I had been bitten myself. Kirsten herself was hardly recognizable as the woman I had married. In the ten months since leaving Berlin she had aged ten years. Her hair was long and gray and unwashed. Her eyes were like two spent lightbulbs. She sat on the edge of her iron bedstead and stared at the green linoleum floor as if it had been the most fascinating thing she had ever seen. She looked like some poor stuffed animal in the anthropological collection at the museum on Richard-Wagner-Strasse.

After her father had died, Kirsten had fallen into a state of general depression and started drinking a lot and talking to herself. At first I had assumed she thought I was listening, but it was soon painfully clear to me that this was not the case. So I was actually pleased when she stopped talking to herself. The only trouble was that she stopped talking completely, and when it became apparent that she had withdrawn into herself, I summoned the doctor, who recommended immediate hospitalization.

"She's suffering from acute catatonic schizophrenia," was what

Dr. Bublitz, the psychiatrist treating Kirsten, had told me, about a week after her admission. "It's not all that uncommon. After what Germany has been through, who can be surprised? Almost a fifth of our inpatients are suffering from some kind of catatonia. Nijinsky, the dancer and choreographer, suffered from the same condition as Frau Handlöser."

Because Kirsten's family doctor had been treating her since she was a little girl, he had booked her into the Max Planck under her maiden name. (Much to my annoyance, it was a mistake that showed no sign of being rectified. And I had given up correcting the doctor when he called her Frau Handlöser.)

"Will she get better?" I had asked Dr. Bublitz.

"That's a little hard to say," he said.

"Well, how is Nijinsky these days?"

"There was a rumor that he had died. But that was false. He's still alive. Although he remains in psychiatric care."

"I guess that answers my question."

"About Nijinsky?"

"About my wife."

These days I rarely ever saw Dr. Bublitz. Mostly I sat beside Kirsten and brushed her hair and sometimes lit her a cigarette that I fixed in the corner of her mouth, where it stayed until I took it out, unsmoked. Sometimes the smoke trailing up her face made her blink, which was the only sign of life she ever showed, which was half of the reason I did it. Other times I read the paper to her, or a book; and once or twice, because her breath was so rank, I even cleaned her teeth. On this particular occasion I told her the plans I had for the hotel and myself.

"I have to do something with my life," I said. "I can't stay at that hotel any longer. Otherwise we'll both end up in here. So, after I leave here today, I'm going to see your family lawyer, and I'm going to put the place up for sale. Then I'm going to borrow a little money against it from Herr Kohl at Wechselbank, so I can start a little business of my own. As a private detective, of course. I've got no talent whatsoever for running a hotel. Police work is the only work I know. I'll rent an office and a small apartment here, in Schwabing, so I can be near you. As you know this part of Munich always reminds me a little of Berlin. And it's cheap, of course. Because of the bomb damage. Somewhere close to Wagmullerstrasse, at the south end of Englischerstrasse would be ideal. The Bavarian Red Cross has its offices there and that's where everyone goes first when they're looking for a missing person. I think there's probably quite a decent living to be made specializing in that end of the business."

I didn't expect Kirsten to say anything, and she certainly didn't disappoint me in that respect. She stared at the floor as if my news was the most depressing thing she had heard in months. As if selling a failing hotel in Dachau was the worst business decision anyone could make. I paused and put her cigarette in my mouth and took a drag of it before stubbing it out on the sole of my shoe and dropping the butt into my jacket pocket—the room was dirty enough without my adding a cigarette end to the filth.

"There are lots of people missing in Germany," I added. "Just like when the Nazis were still in power." I shook my head. "But I can't go on in Dachau. Not on my own. I've had enough of that, forever. The way I feel right now, it's me who should be in here, not you."

I jumped out of my skin as one of the other women let out a screech of laughter and then went to face the wall where she remained for the rest of my visit, rocking on her feet like some old rabbi. Maybe she knew something I didn't. They say that insanity is merely the ability to see into the future. And if we knew now what we'll know then, it would probably be enough to make any of us scream. In life the trick is all about keeping the two separate for as long as possible.

# THREE

I had to get a denazification certificate from the Ministry of the Interior, on Prinzregentenstrasse. Since I had never actually been a member of the Nazi Party, this didn't present too much of a problem. There were plenty of bulls at the Police Praesidium on Ettstrasse (where I had to have the certificate countersigned) who, like me, had been SS, not to mention quite a few who had been in the Gestapo or the SD. Fortunately for me, the occupation authorities did not hold the view that ex officio transfers from KRIPO, the criminal police, or ORPO, the uniformed police, into these Nazi police organizations were enough to disqualify a man from being a police officer in the fledgling Federal Republic of Germany. It was only younger men who had started their careers in the SS, the Gestapo, or the SD who faced any real difficulties. But even here there were ways around the Liberation Law of 1946, which, if it had ever been as rigidly enforced as had been intended, would have resulted in Germany having no policemen at all. A good cop is still a good cop even if he was a Nazi bastard.

I found a small office in Galeriestrasse, which ran west off Wagmullerstrasse. It seemed just what I had been looking for. My premises were opposite a small post office and above an antiquarian bookshop; and they shared a floor with a dentist and a coin dealer. I felt about as respectable as it was possible to feel in a building that still had its camouflage painting against Allied air attacks. The building had been some minor outpost of the War Office on Ludwigstrasse and, in an old cupboard, I found mildewed portraits of Hitler and Göring, an empty grenade bag, a rifle bandolier, and an M42 "razor edge" helmet that happened to be my size (sixty-eight).

Outside the front door were a cabstand and a kiosk selling newspapers and tobacco. I had my name on a brass plate and a mailbox mounted on the wall on the ground floor. I was set.

I walked around central Munich leaving my new business cards with offices and people who might conceivably put some business my way. The Red Cross, the German Information Bureau on Sonnenstrasse, the Israel Cultural Institute on Herzog-Max-Strasse, the American Express Company on Brienner Strasse, and the Lost Property Office at police headquarters. I even looked up a few old comrades. There was an ex-cop called Korsch who was working as a senior reporter at *Die Neue Zeitung,* an American newspaper; and a former secretary of mine called Dagmarr who helped look after the city archives on Winzererstrasse. But mostly I hit the offices of Munich's many lawyers in and around the Justice Palace. If there was anyone doing well under the American occupation it was the lawyers. The world might end one day but there will still be lawyers to process the documents.

My first Munich case was from a lawyer and, by a strange coincidence, it involved the Red Jackets at Landsberg. As it happened, so did the next case, which probably wasn't a coincidence at all. And maybe even the one after that. Any one of them could have taken over my life, but only one of them did. And even now I find it a little hard to say that none of them were connected.

Erich Kaufmann was a lawyer, a neoconservative, and a member of the so-called Heidelberg Circle of Jurists, which was the central coordinating body for freeing the prisoners at Landsberg. On September 21, 1949, I went to Kaufmann's plush office near the Justice Palace on Karlsplatz, which was another public building under repair. The sound of cement mixers, hammers, saws, and empty hoist containers hitting the ground made Karlsplatz as noisy as any battlefield. I remember the date because it was the day after the right-wing populist Alfred Loritz had stood up in the new Parliament, demanding an immediate and general amnesty for all but the most serious war criminals—by which he meant those who were already dead or on the run. I was reading about it in the *Süddeutsche Zeitung* when Kaufmann's sirenlike secretary came to fetch me into the palatial suite he modestly called an office. I don't know what surprised me more: the office, the story in the paper, or the secretary; it had been quite a while since anyone as attractive as that little fräulein had caressed me with her eyelashes. I put it down to the new suit I had bought at Oberpollinger. It fit me like a glove. Kaufmann's suit was better. It fit him like a suit.

I guessed that he was about sixty. But I didn't have to guess very hard to know that he was a Jew. For one thing, there was something written in Hebrew on a little plaque by the door. I felt pleased about that. Things in Germany were getting back to normal. It made a very pleasant change from a yellow Star of David daubed on his window. I had no idea what had happened to him under the Nazis, and it wasn't the kind of thing you asked. But in the few years since they'd been gone it was plain he'd done very well for himself. It wasn't just his suit that was better than mine, it was everything else as well. His shoes looked handmade, his fingernails were beautifully manicured, and his tie pin looked like a birthday gift from the Queen of Sheba. Even his teeth were better than mine. He was holding my card in his chubby fingers. And he came straight to the point without any of the time-wasting courtesies that can plague Munich business life. I didn't mind that one bit. I'm not big on courtesies. Not since my time in a Russian POW camp. Besides, I was in a hurry to be in business myself.

"I want you to interview an American soldier," said Kaufmann. "A private in the U.S. Third Army. His name is John Ivanov. He's a guard in War Crimes Prison Number One. You know where that is?"

"Landsberg, I imagine," I said

"That's right. That's exactly where it is. Landsberg. Check him out, Herr Gunther. Find out what kind of character he is. Reliable or not reliable. Honest or dishonest. An opportunist or sincere. I take it you respect the confidentiality of your clients?"

"Of course," I said. "I couldn't be more close-lipped if I were Rudolf Hess."

"Then in confidence I tell you that PFC Ivanov has made a number of allegations regarding the treatment of Red Jackets. Also that the executions of so-called war criminals in June of last year were deliberately botched by the hangman so that it would take longer for the men to die. I'll give you an address where you can make contact with Ivanov." He unscrewed a gold fountain pen and started to write on a piece of paper. "By the way, à propos of your remark about Hess. I don't have a sense of humor, Herr Gunther. It was beaten out of me by the Nazis. Quite literally, I can assure you."

"Frankly, my own sense of humor isn't up to much, either," I said. "Mine was beaten out of me by the Russians. That way you'll know I'm not joking when I tell you my fees are ten marks a day, plus expenses. Two days in advance."

He didn't bat an eyelid. The Nazis had probably done quite a bit of that to him. They were good at batting eyelids. But it was enough to persuade me that I might have priced myself too low. Back in Berlin I had always preferred it when people complained a little about my fees. That way I avoided the clients who wanted me to go on fishing trips. He tore the page off his pad and handed it to me.

"It says on your card that you speak some English, Herr Gunther. You do speak some English?"

"Yes," I said, in English.

"The witness speaks basic German, I believe, so some English might help you to get to know him better. To gain his confidence, perhaps. Americans are not great linguists. They have an island mentality, like the English. The English speak good German when they speak it at all. But the Americans regard learning all foreign languages as essentially a waste of time. Akin to playing football when they themselves play a strange variety of catch."

"Ivanov sounds like a Russian name," I said. "Maybe he speaks Russian. I speak excellent Russian. I learned it in the camp."

"You were one of the lucky ones," he said. "I mean, you came home." He looked at me for a long moment, as if sizing me up. "Yes, you've been lucky."

"Definitely," I said. "My health is good although I took a piece of shrapnel in the leg. And I had a bump on the head a couple of years ago. It gives me an itchy scalp sometimes. Usually when something doesn't make sense. Like now, for example."

"Oh? What doesn't make sense?"

"Why a Jew cares what happens to a few lousy war criminals?"

"That's a fair question," he said. "Yes, I'm a Jew. But that doesn't mean I'm interested in taking revenge, Herr Gunther." He got out of his chair and went over to the window, summoning me to his side with a peremptory nod of the head.

On my way over I took in the photograph of Kaufmann in the uniform of a German soldier in the first war, and a framed doctorate from the University of Halle. Standing beside him I saw that his light gray pinstripe suit was even better than I had imagined. It rustled silkily as he removed his light tortoiseshell-framed glasses and polished them vigorously on a white handkerchief that was as immaculate as his shirt collar. I was more interested in him than in the bird's-eye view of Karlsplatz his office window afforded him. I felt like Esau standing next to his smoother brother, Jacob.

"That's the Justice Palace and the New Law Courts," he said. "In a year or two—maybe less, God willing, because the noise drives me mad—they'll be just like they were before. You'll be able to walk in there and see a trial and not know that the building was ever destroyed by Allied bombs. That might be okay for a building. But the law is something different. It grows out of people, Herr Gunther. Placing mercy ahead of justice, with an amnesty for all war criminals, will foster a new beginning for Germany."

"Does that include war criminals like Otto Ohlendorf?"

"It includes all prisoners," he said. "I'm just one of a number of people, Jews included, who believe that the political purge imposed upon us by the occupation authorities has been unjust in virtually every respect, and has failed monstrously. The pursuit of so-called fugitives needs to be ended as quickly as possible, and the remaining prisoners released so that we can all draw a line through the sad events of an unfortunate era. I and a group of like-minded lawyers and church leaders intend to petition the American high commissioner regarding these prisoners at Landsberg. Gathering any evidence of prisoner ill-treatment is a necessary prelude to our doing so. And my being Jewish has absolutely nothing to do with anything. Do I make myself clear?"

I liked the way he cared enough to give me a little lecture on the new Federal Republic. It had been a while since anyone had taken that kind of trouble with my education. Besides, it was a little early in our professional relationship to get smart with him. He was a lawyer, and sometimes, when you get smart with a lawyer, they call it contempt and throw you in jail.

So I went to Landsberg and met PFC Ivanov and came back to meet Kaufmann again, and as it happened, that was time and opportunity enough to work in every smart remark I could think of. He had to sit there and take it, too. Because it was what we private detectives call a report, and coming from me a report can sound a lot like contempt if you're not used to my manner. Especially when none of it was what he really wanted to hear. Not if he was ever going to save the likes of Otto Ohlendorf from hanging. Because Ivanov was a liar and a cheat and, worst of all, a doper—a worthless gorilla who was looking to settle a cheap score with the U.S. Army and get paid for it in the bargain.

"For one thing I'm not convinced he's ever worked in Landsberg," I said. "He didn't know that Hitler had been imprisoned there in 1924. Or that the castle had been built as recently as 1910. He didn't know that the seven men hanged at Landsberg in June 1948 were Nazi doctors. Also, he said the hangman was a guy named Joe Malta. In fact, Malta left the army in 1947. They have a new hangman at Landsberg and his identity is kept a secret. Also, he said the gallows is located indoors. In fact it's outside, near the rooftop. These are the kind of things you'd know if you really did work there. My guess is that he's only ever worked at the displacement camp."

"I see," said Kaufmann. "You've been very thorough, Herr Gunther."

"I've met more dishonest men than him," I told Kaufmann, concluding my report with just a lick of relish. "But only in prison. The only way Ivanov would make a convincing witness was if you made sure there was a hundred dollars inside the Bible when he took the oath."

Kaufmann was silent for a moment. Then he opened his desk drawer and took out a cash box from which he paid me the balance of what he owed, in cash. Finally, he said, "You look pleased with yourself."

"I'm always pleased when I've done a good job," I said.

"You're being disingenuous," he said. "Come now. We both know it's more than that."

"Maybe I am a little pleased with myself at that," I admitted.

"Don't you believe in a fresh start for Germany?"

"For Germany, yes. Not for people like Otto Ohlendorf. Being a bastard wasn't a necessary condition of joining the SS, although it certainly helped. I should know. For a while, I was in the SS myself. Maybe that's part of the reason why I'm out of step with your new Federal Republic. And maybe it's just that I'm a bit old-fashioned.

But you see, there's something about a man who massacred a hundred thousand men, women, and children that I just don't like. And I tend to think that the best way of getting the new Germany off to a flying start is if we just get on and hang him and his ilk."

## FOUR

Kaufmann didn't strike me as spiteful man at all. Merely a pompous one, and I think it irked him a little that I ticked him off about helping the Red Jackets. So I suspected it was he who steered my next client to me, knowing that I would dislike him, and knowing also that I couldn't afford to turn him away. Not when I was just getting started in business again. Maybe he even hoped to change my mind about how we were going to ensure the best beginning for the Federal Republic.

The phone call told me to catch a train to Starnberg, where a car would pick me up. All I knew about the client was that he was the Baron von Starnberg, that he was extremely rich, and that he was the retired director of I. G. Farben, once the largest chemical manufacturing company in the world. Some of directors of I. G. Farben had been put on trial at Nuremberg for war crimes, but von Starnberg wasn't one of them. I had no idea of the job he wanted me to do.

The train climbed through the Würm Valley and some of the loveliest countryside in Bavaria before arriving after thirty minutes in Starnberg. It made a very pleasant change from breathing the builder's dust of Munich. Starnberg itself was a smallish town built in terraces at the north end of the Würmsee, a lake twelve miles long and a mile wide. The sapphire blue water was studded with yachts that shone like diamonds in the morning sunlight. It was overlooked by the ancient castle of the dukes of Bavaria. "Scenic" hardly covered it. After only a minute looking at Starnberg, I wanted to lift the lid and eat the strawberry crème.

There was an old Maybach Zeppelin at the station to collect me. The chauffeur was kind enough to put me in the backseat instead of the trunk, which was probably his first inclination with someone getting off a train. After all, there was enough silver in the back to keep the Lone Ranger in bullets for the next hundred years.

The house was about a five-minute drive west of the station. A brass plaque on one of the obelisk-shaped gateposts said it was a villa, but probably only because they were a little shy about using a word like "palace." It took me a whole minute to climb the steps to the front door, where a fellow dressed to go cheek-to-cheek with Ginger Rogers was waiting to take my hat and act as my scout across the marble plains that lay ahead. He stayed with me as far as the library, then wheeled around silently and set off for home again before it started to get dark.

In the library was a small man who turned out to be quite tall by the time I got near enough to hear him shouting an offer of schnapps at me. I said yes and got a better look at him while he fussed with a huge decanter of glass and gold that was so big it looked like it was guarded by seven dwarfs. He wore glasses and an eccentric sort of white beard that made me suspect I might have to drink my schnapps in a test tube.

"The old parish church in our town," he was saying, in a voice with about a half ton of gravel heaped on top of his larynx, "has a late-rococo high altar by an Ignaz Gunther. Would he be a relation of yours?"

"Ignaz was the black sheep of the family, Herr Baron," I said brightly. "We never talk about him in polite society."

The baron chuckled his way up into a cough that lasted only until he had lit a cigarette and got his breath. Along the way he somehow managed to shake my hand with only his fingertips, offer me a nail from a gold box as big as a dictionary on the library table, toast me, sip his schnapps, and draw my attention to the studio photograph of a baby-faced young man in his early thirties. He looked more like a movie star than an SS Sturmbannführer. The smile was pure porcelain. The frame was solid silver, which, next to the gold cigarette box, made me suspect that someone had been forcing some economies on the Starnberg household.

"My son, Vincenz," said the baron. "In that uniform it would be all too easy to think of him as my own black sheep. But he's anything but, Herr Gunther. Anything but. Vincenz was always such a gentle boy. In the choir at school. So many pets when he was young you'd have thought his rooms were a zoo."

I liked that: room*s*. It said a lot about the childhood of Vincenz von Starnberg. And I liked the way the baron talked German the way people used to talk German before they started using words like "Lucky Strike," "Coca-Cola," "okay," "jitterbug," "bubble gum," and, worst of all, "buddy."

"Are you a father, Herr Gunther?"

"No, sir."

"Well, what's a father supposed to say about his only son? I know this much: He's not nearly as black as he's been painted. I'm sure you of all people would understand that, Herr Gunther. You were an SS man yourself, were you not?"

"I was a policeman, Herr Baron," I said, smiling thinly. "In the KRIPO until 1939 when, in order to increase efficiency—at least that's what they told us—we were combined with the Gestapo and the SD into a new office of the SS called the RSHA—the Main Office of Government Security. I'm afraid none of us had much choice in the matter."

"No, indeed. Giving people choice was not something Hitler was good at. We all had to do things we didn't much care for, perhaps.

My son, too. He was a lawyer. A promising lawyer. He joined the SS in 1936. Unlike you, it was by his own choice. I counseled caution, but it is the privilege of being a son to pay no attention to his father's advice until it's too late. We fathers expect that of our sons. Indeed, it is why we grow old and gray. In 1941, he became the deputy leader of a mobile killing unit in Lithuania. There. I've said what it was. They called it something else. Special Action, or some such nonsense. But mass murder was what it was charged with. In all normal circumstances Vincenz would have had nothing to do with such a terrible thing. But like many others, he felt duty-bound by reason of the oath he had taken to the person of the Führer as the highest organ of the German state. You must understand that he did what he did out of respect for that oath and the state, but always with acute inner disapproval."

"You mean he was only obeying orders," I said.

"Exactly so," said the baron, ignoring or just not noticing the sarcasm that was carried in my voice. "Orders are orders. You can't get away from that fact. People like my son are the victims of historical value judgments, Herr Gunther. And nothing besmirches the honor of Germany more profoundly than these prisoners at Landsberg. Of whom my son is one. These Red Jackets, as the newspapers call them, present the greatest obstacle to the restoration of our national sovereignty. Which we must have if we are ever going to contribute, as the Americans want, to the cause of Western defense. I am referring, of course, to the forthcoming war against communism."

I nodded politely. It was my second lecture in as many weeks. But this one was easier to understand. Baron von Starnberg didn't like the communists. That much was plain from our surroundings. If I'd lived there I wouldn't have liked the communists either. Not that I did like the communists. But having very little myself, I had more in common with them than with the baron, who had so much. And who wasn't about to put his hand in his pocket and help win America's war on communism as long as America treated his son like some common criminal.

"Has he been tried yet?" I asked.

"Yes," said the Baron. "He was sentenced to death, in April 1948. But following a petition to General Clay, that sentence was commuted to life imprisonment."

"Then I really don't see what I can do," I said politely, neglecting to add that, as far as I was concerned, the baron's "black sheep" had already been luckier than he could ever have reasonably expected. "After all, it's not as if he denies doing what he did. Does he?"

"No, not at all," said the baron. "As I have explained, his defense was based on force majeure. That he could not act but as he did act. We now wish to draw the governor's attention to the fact that Vincenz had nothing personal against the Jews. You see, after graduating, Vincenz became a reader in law at the University of Heidelberg. And in 1934, he saw to it that measures taken by the Gestapo against a student who had been sheltering Jews at his home were brought to a halt. His name was Wolfgang Stumpff, and I want you to find him, Herr Gunther. You must find him so that we might attach his testimonial regarding the Heidelberg Jewish affair to a petition for Vincenz's early release." The baron sighed. "My son is only thirty-seven, Herr Gunther. He still has his whole life in front of him."

I helped myself to some more of the baron's excellent schnapps to take away the taste in my mouth. It also helped to prevent me from making the tactless remark that at least Vincenz still had a life to have in front of him, unlike the many Lithuanian Jews whose deaths he had overseen, albeit only out of respect for his oath as an SS officer. By now I had little doubt that Erich Kaufmann was the author of this new client relationship.

"You say this happened in 1934, Baron?" I asked. He nodded. "That's a lot of water under the bridge. How do you know this fellow Stumpff is still alive?"

"Because a couple of weeks ago my daughter, Helene Elisabeth, saw Wolfgang Stumpff on a tram in Munich."

I tried my best to eliminate a note of surprise from my voice. "Your daughter was on a tram?"

The baron smiled weakly as if perceiving the absurdity of such an idea. "No, no," he said. "She was in her car. Leaving the Glyptothek, the Sculpture Gallery. She was at a traffic light and she looked up and saw him at the window of a tram. She's quite certain of it."

"The Glyptothek," I said. "That's in the Museum Quarter, isn't it? Let's see now. A number eight from Karlsplatz to Schwabing. A number three and a number six, also to Schwabing. And a number thirty-seven from the Hohenzollernstrasse to the Max Monument. I don't suppose she remembers which number it was?" The baron shook his head, and I did the same. "No matter. I'll find him."

"I'll pay you a thousand marks if you do," he said.

"Fine, fine, but after I find him it's down to you and your lawyers, Baron. I won't play advocate for your son. It's better that way. Better for your son but, more importantly, better for me. I'm finding it hard enough to sleep at night as it is without speaking up for a mass murderer."

"People don't talk to me that way, Herr Gunther," he said stiffly.

"You'd better get used to it, Baron," I said. "This is a republic now. Or did you forget? Besides, I'm the fellow who knows exactly how to find your son's ace in the hole." That was just a bluff, to stop his fine nostrils from looking any more pinched than they already were. I had gone too far, waving my conscience in front of him like a matador's cape. Now I had to convince him that being blunt was just an idiosyncrasy of mine and that I was more than equal to the job. "I'm glad you offered that bonus because this won't take more than a few days, and at ten marks a day, plus expenses, it might be hardly worth my while otherwise."

"But how? I've already made a few inquiries of my own."

"I could tell you. But then I'd be out of a job. Of course, I'll need to speak to your daughter."

"Of course, of course. I'll tell her to expect you."

The truth was that I had no idea where I was going to start. There were 821,000 people in Munich. Most of them were Roman Catholics and were pretty tight-lipped about everything, even in the confessional.

"Is there anything else you need?" he asked. By now my insolence was quite forgotten.

"You could pay me something in advance," I said. "For thirty marks, you get the rest of my week and the comfort of knowing that the petition for your son's release is as good as on the train to Landsberg."

## FIVE

In Germany there is a record of almost everything. We are a meticulous, observant, and bureaucratic people, and sometimes behave as if documentation and memorandum were the identifying hallmarks of true civilization. Even when it involved the systematic murder of an entire race of people, there were statistics, minutes, photographs, reports, and transcripts. Hundreds, possibly thousands, of war criminals might successfully have resisted conviction but for our very German obsession with numbers, names, and addresses. Many records had been destroyed in Allied air raids, it was true, but I was certain that somewhere I would find Wolfgang Stumpff's name and address.

I started at police headquarters, visiting both the Registration of Address section and the Passport Office, but found no trace of him there. Then I checked at the Ministry of the Interior on Prinzregentenstrasse. I even looked for his name at the Society of German Jurists. I knew that Stumpff was from Munich and that he had studied to be a lawyer. The baron had told me that much himself. And reasoning that it was highly unlikely he could have come through the war without doing military service, my next port of call was the Bavarian State Archives on Arcisstrasse, where there were records going back as far as 1265. These had suffered no damage at all. But I had no luck there either, except to discover that the archives of the Bavarian army had been moved, to Leonrodstrasse, and it was here, finally, that I found what I was looking for, in the Rank Lists—the officer rolls for Bavaria. Alphabetically listed, year on year. It was a beautiful bit of record-keeping, handwritten, in purple ink. Hauptmann Wolfgang Stumpff of the 1st Gebirgsdivision, which was formerly the Bavarian Mountain Division. I now had a name, an address, the name of Stumpff's regimental commander—I even borrowed his photograph.

The address in the Haidhausen district of East Munich was no more, having been completely destroyed on July 13, 1944. At least, that's what the sign on the ruins told me. And temporarily bereft of ideas, I decided to spend an afternoon riding the trams—specifically the three, six, eight, and thirty-seven, with the photograph of Stumpff I had borrowed from his file. But before I did I had an appointment to meet the baron's daughter outside the Glyptothek.

Helene Elisabeth von Starnberg was wearing a knee-length beige skirt, a yellow sweater that was just clingy enough to let you know she was a woman, and a pair of pigskin leather driving gloves. We had a pleasant conversation. I showed her the picture I had purloined from the army archives.

"Yes, that's him," she said. "Of course he was much younger when this picture was taken."

"Didn't you know? This is at least a thousand years old. I know because that's how long Hitler said the Third Reich would last."

She smiled and, for a moment, it was hard to believe she had a brother who had lived and worked in the lowest pit in hell. Blond, of course. Like she'd stepped down from the Berchtesgaden. It was easy to see where Hitler had developed his taste for blondes if he'd ever met a blonde like Helene Elisabeth von Starnberg. Either way she was a creature from another world. I might have misjudged her, but my first thought about her, that she'd never been on a tram, was not one I was able to dislodge. I tried to picture it, but the image wouldn't stick. It always came off looking like a tiara in a biscuit tin.

"Are you any relation to Ignaz Gunther?" she asked me.

"My great-great-grandfather," I said. "But please don't tell anyone."

"I won't," she said. "He sculpted a lot of angels, you know. Some of them are rather fine. Who knows? Maybe you'll turn out to be our angel, Herr Gunther."

By which I assumed she meant the von Starnberg family's angel. Maybe it was lucky it was a fine day and I was in a good mood, but I didn't reply with a rude remark about how, if I was going to help her brother, I'd have to be a black angel, which, of course, was what people used to call the SS. Maybe. More likely I just let that one slide by me because she was what people used to call a peach, in the days before they'd forgotten what one looked and tasted like.

"There's a fine group of guardian angels sculpted by Ignaz Gunther in the Burgersaal," she said, pointing across Königsplatz. "Somehow they survived the bombing. You should take a look at them sometime."

"I'll do that," I said, and stepped back as she opened the door of her Porsche and climbed inside. She waved a neatly gloved hand from behind the split windshield, fired up the flat-four engine, and then sped away.

I walked south across Karlsplatz and the "Stachus," which was Munich's main traffic center, named after an inn that had once stood there. I walked along Neuhauser Strasse to Marienplatz, both of them badly damaged during the war. Special passages had been constructed for pedestrians beneath the scaffolding, and the many gaps between bomb-damaged buildings were filled with one-storied temporary shops. Scaffolding made the Burgersaal as inconspicuous as an empty beer bottle. Like everywhere else in that part of Munich, the chapel was being restored. Every time I walked around the city I congratulated myself for being lucky enough to spend most of 1944 with General Ferdinand Schorner's army in White Russia. Munich had been hit hard. April 25, 1944, had been one of the worst nights in the city's history. Most of the chapel had been burned out. The high altar had perished, yet Gunther's sculptures had survived. But with their pink cheeks and delicate hands these were hardly my idea of guardian angels. They looked like a couple of rent boys from a bathhouse in Bogenhausen. I didn't think I was descended from Ignaz, but after two hundred years who can be sure of anything like that? My father had never been entirely certain who his mother was, let alone his own father. Either way, I'd have sculpted the group differently. My idea of a guardian angel involved being armed with something more lethal than a supercilious smile, an elegantly cocked little finger, and one eye on the Pearly Gates for backup. But that's me. Even now, four years after the war ended, my first thought when I wake up is to wonder where I left my KAR 98.

I came out of the church and stepped straight onto a number six heading south down Karlsplatz. I like trams. You don't have to worry about filling them up with gasoline, and it's safe to leave them parked down some insalubrious backstreet. They're great if you can't afford a car, and in the summer of 1949, there were few people, other than Americans and the Baron von Starnberg, who could. Also, trams go exactly where you want them to go, provided you're wise enough to choose a tram that's going somewhere near where you're going. I didn't know where Wolfgang Stumpff was going, or where he was coming from, but I figured there was a better chance of seeing him on one of those trams instead of some others. Detective work doesn't always require a brain the size of Wittgenstein's. I rode the number six as far as Sendlinger-Tor-Platz, where I got off and caught a number eight going the opposite way. It went up Barer Strasse, to Schwabing and I rode this one as far as Kaiserplatz and the Church of St. Ursula. For all I knew, there were more sculptures by Ignaz Gunther in there, too, but seeing a thirty-seven coming along Hohenzollernstrasse, I hopped on that one.

I told myself there was no point in riding each tram to its terminus. My chances of spotting Wolfgang Stumpff were improved by riding them around the center of Munich, where there were many more people getting on and off. Sometimes being a detective involves playing statistician and figuring out the probabilities. I rode them on top and I rode them down below. Up top was better because you could smoke, but it meant you couldn't see who was getting on and off inside, which was what people called that part of a tram that wasn't upstairs. It was nearly all men on top because nearly all men were smokers, and if women did smoke they preferred not to do it on a tram. Don't ask me why. I'm a detective, not a psychologist. I didn't want to take a chance that Stumpff wasn't a smoker, but I figured the baron's daughter would never have seen Stumpff if he had been upstairs on a tram. Not from the window of a Porsche 356—it was too low. She might have seen him on the top deck if she had been in a cabriolet, but never from a coupe.

Why am I going into such detail? Because it was these little, routine things that made me remember what it was like to be a cop.

Sore feet, some sweat in the small of my back and on the inside of my hat, and exercising my peeper's eye. I had started to look at faces again. Searching apparently standard faces on the seat opposite for a distinguishing characteristic. Most people have one if you look hard enough.

I almost missed him coming downstairs. The tram had been full inside. He had intense dark eyes, a high forehead, thin mouth, chin dimple, and a canine nose that he carried in a way that made you think he was on the scent of something. He reminded me a lot of Georg Jacoby, the singer, and, for a brief moment I half expected him to break into "The Woman Who's My Dream." But Wolfgang Stumpff's distinguishing characteristic was easy. He was missing an arm.

I followed him off the tram and into Holzkirchner railway station. There he caught a suburban train south to München-Mittersendling. So did I. Then he walked about a mile west along Zielstattstrasse to a pleasant, modern little villa on the edge of some trees. I watched the house for a moment and then saw a light go on in an upstairs room.

I didn't care if Vincenz von Starnberg spent twenty years in Landsberg or not. I didn't care if they hanged him in his cell with weights tied to his ankles. I didn't care if his father died of a broken heart. I didn't care if Stumpff was inclined to give his old university comrade a character reference or not. But I rang the doorbell all the same, even though I had told myself I wouldn't. I wasn't going to make a pitch for the sake of SS Sturmbannführer von Starnberg, or for his father the baron. No, not even for a thousand marks. But I didn't mind making a pitch for the sake of the peach. Being considered as some kind of angel in the pale blue eyes of Helene Elisabeth von Starnberg was something I could live with.

# SIX

Three days later I received a certified check drawn against the baron's personal account at Delbrück & Co. for one thousand deutschmarks. It had been a while since I'd made any real money of my own, and for a while I just left the check on my desk so I could keep my eye on it. From time to time I picked it up and read it again, and told myself I was really back in business. Feeling good about myself lasted for the whole of one hour.

The telephone rang. It was Dr. Bublitz at the Max Planck Institute of Psychiatry. He told me that Kirsten was ill. After developing a fever her condition had worsened and she had been transferred to the city's General Hospital, near Sendlinger-Tor-Platz.

I ran out of the office, jumped on a tram, then hurried across Nussbaum Gardens to the Women's Clinic on Maistrasse. Half of it looked like a building site; the other half looked like a ruin. I walked through a gauntlet of cement mixers, around a redoubt of new bricks and timber, and up the stone stairs. Builder's dust ground under the soles of my shoes like spilled sugar. Hammering echoed loudly in the hospital stairwell with monotonous force, as if some prehistoric woodpecker was making a hole in an even larger tree. Outside, a pair of jackhammers were finishing a battle for the last foxhole in Munich. And someone was drilling the teeth of a very long-suffering giant while someone else was sawing off the leg of his even more long-suffering wife. Water was splashing into the courtyard outside, as if in some subterranean cavern. A sick coal miner or injured steelworker would have appreciated the peace and quiet of that place, but for anyone else with eardrums, the Women's Clinic sounded like hell with all the windows open.

Kirsten was in a small private room off the main ward. She was feverish and yellow. Her hair was matted against her head as if she had just washed it. Her eyes were closed and her breathing rapid and shallow. She looked extremely ill. The nurse with her was wearing a face mask. From what I could see of her face it looked like a good idea. A man in a white coat appeared at my elbow.

"Are you the next of kin?" he barked. He was stout, with a center part in his fair hair, rimless glasses, a Hindenburg-size mustache, a stiff collar you could have cut corns with, and a bow tie off a box of chocolates.

"I'm her husband," I said. "Bernhard Gunther."

"Husband?" He searched his notes. "Fräulein Handlöser is married? There's no record of that here."

"When her family doctor referred her to the Max Planck, he forgot about it," I said. "Maybe we didn't invite him to the wedding, I don't know. These things happen. Look, can we forget all that? What's wrong with her?"

"I'm afraid we can't forget it, Herr Gunther," said the doctor. "There are regulations to be considered. I can only discuss Fräulein Handlöser's condition with her next of kin. Perhaps you have your wedding certificate with you?"

"Not with me, no," I said, patiently. "But I'll bring it with me next time I come here. How's that?" I paused and endured the doctor's indignant scrutiny for a moment or two. "There's no one else but me," I added. "No one else will be visiting her, I can assure you of that." I waited. Still nothing. "And if all that leaves you uncomfortable then answer me this. If she's unmarried, why is she still wearing a wedding ring?"

The doctor glanced around my shoulder. Upon seeing Kirsten's wedding ring still on her finger, he searched his notes again as if there might be some clue as to the proper course of action to be taken. "Really, this is most irregular," he said. "However, given her condition, I suppose I will have to take your word for it."

"Thank you, Doctor."

His heels came together and he nodded curtly back at me. I was quickly getting the impression that he had obtained his medical degree at a hospital in Prussia, somewhere they gave out jackboots instead of stethoscopes. But in truth it was a common enough scene in Germany. German doctors have always regarded themselves as being as important as God. Indeed, it's probably worse than that. God probably thinks he's a German doctor.

"My name is Dr. Effner," he said. "Your wife—Frau Gunther—she is extremely ill. Gravely ill. Not doing well. Not doing well at all, Herr Gunther. She was transferred here during the night. And we're trying our best, sir. You may be assured of that. But it's my opinion that you must prepare yourself, sir. Prepare yourself for the worst. She may not survive the night." He spoke like a cannon, in short, fierce bursts of speech, as if he had learned his bedside manner in a Messerschmitt 109. "We will make her comfortable, of course. But everything that can be done, has been done. You understand?"

"Are you saying she might die?" I asked, when, at last, I was able to get a shot back at him.

"Yes, Herr Gunther," he said. "I am saying that. She is critically ill as you can see for yourself."

"What on earth's wrong with her?" I asked. "I mean, I saw her only a few days ago and she seemed fine."

"She has a fever," he said, as if this was all the explanation that was required. "A high fever. As you can see, although I don't advise you to get too close to her. Her pallor, her shortness of breath, her anemia, her swollen glands—these all lead me to suppose that she has a bad case of influenza."

"Influenza?"

"The old, the homeless, prisoners, and people who are institutionalized or mentally retarded, such as your wife, are especially vulnerable to the influenza virus," he said.

"She's not mentally retarded, " I said, frowning fiercely at him. "She's depressed. That's all."

"These are facts, sir, facts," said Dr. Effner. "Respiratory disease is the most common cause of death among individuals who are mentally retarded. You can't argue with the facts, Herr Gunther."

"I'd argue with Plato, Herr Doktor," I said, biting my lip. It helped stop me from biting Effner on the neck. "Especially if the facts were wrong. And I'll thank you not to mention death with such alacrity. She's not dead yet. In case you hadn't noticed. Or maybe you're the kind of doctor who prefers to study patients instead of trying to cure them."

Dr. Effner took a deep breath through flaring nostrils, came to attention even more—if such a thing were possible—and climbed into the saddle of a horse that was at least seventeen hands high. "How dare you suggest such a thing," he said. "The very idea that I don't care about my patients. It's outrageous. Outrageous. We're doing everything we can for—*Fräulein Handlöser.* Good day to you, sir." He glanced at his wristwatch, turned smartly on his heel, and cantered away. Throwing a chair after him might have made me feel better, but it wouldn't have helped Kirsten, or any of the other patients. There was enough noise already in that builder's yard.

## SEVEN

I stayed at the hospital for several hours. The nurse told me she'd call if there was any change for the worse, and since the only telephone was in my office, this meant going there instead of my apartment. Besides, Galeriestrasse was nearer to the hospital than Schwabing. It was twenty minutes by foot. Half that when the trams were running.

On my way back I stepped into the Pschorr beer house on Neuhauser Strasse for a beer and a sausage. I wasn't in the mood for either, but it's an old cop's habit to eat and drink when you can, instead of when you're hungry. Then I bought a quarter-liter of Black Death across the bar, holstered it, and left. The anesthetic was for what I guessed lay ahead. I'd lost one wife to influenza before, in the great pandemic of 1918. And I'd seen enough men dying in Russia to recognize all the signs. The hands and feet turning quietly blue. The spit in the throat that she couldn't get rid of. The fast breathing followed by the holding of her breath, and then the fast breathing again. A slight smell of decay. The truth was I didn't want to sit there and watch her die. I didn't have the guts for it. I told myself I wanted to remember Kirsten full of life, but I knew the truth was different. I was a coward. Too yellow to see it through at her side. Kirsten could have expected more from me. I was certain I had expected a little more from myself.

I entered my office, switched on the desk lamp, placed the bottle beside the telephone, and then lay down on a creaking, green leather sofa I had brought from the bar at the hotel. Next to the sofa stood a matching button-back library chair with scabrous cracked-leather armrests. Beside the chair was a single pedestal rolltop desk and, on the floor, a threadbare green Bokhara, both of these from the office at the hotel. A conference table and four chairs took up the other half of my suite. On the wall were two framed maps of Munich. There was a small bookshelf with telephone directories, railway timetables, and various pamphlets and booklets I'd picked up at the German Information Bureau on Sonnenstrasse. It all looked a little better than it was, but not much. Just the kind of place you'd find the kind of man who didn't have the nerve to sit beside his wife and wait for her to die.

After a while I got up, poured myself a shot of Black Death, drank it, and dropped back onto the sofa. Kirsten was forty-four years old. Much too young to die of anything. The injustice of it seemed quite overwhelming, and it would have been enough to shatter my belief in God, assuming I still had one. Not many people came back from a Soviet POW camp believing in anything much other than the human propensity to be inhumane. But it wasn't only the injustice of her premature death that grated on my mind. It was also the downright bad luck of it. To lose two wives to influenza was more than just unlucky. It felt more like perdition. Surviving a war like the one we had just come through, when so many German civilians had died, only then to die of influenza seemed improbable somehow. More so than in 1918, when so many others had died of it, too. But then these things always seemed unjust when seen from the perspective of those who were left behind.

There was a knock at the door. I opened it to reveal a tall, good-looking woman. She smiled uncertainly at me and then at the name on the frosted glass in the door. "Herr Gunther?"

"Yes."

"I saw the light on in the street," she said. "I telephoned earlier but you were out." But for the three small, semicircular scars on her right cheek, she would have been quite beautiful. They reminded me of the three little kiss curls worn by Zarah Leander in some old film about a bullfighter that had been a favorite of Kirsten's. *La Habanera*. It must have been 1937. A thousand years ago.

"I haven't yet managed to find myself a secretary," I said. "I've not been in business that long."

"You're a private detective?" She sounded a little surprised and stared hard at me for several seconds, as if she was trying to gauge what kind of man I was and whether or not she could depend on me.

"That's what it says on the door," I said, acutely aware that I wasn't looking my dependable best.

"Perhaps I've made a mistake," she said, with one eye on the bottle open on the desktop. "Forgive me for disturbing you."

At any other time I'd have remembered my manners and my lessons from charm school and ushered her into a chair, put away the bottle, and asked her, politely, what seemed to be the trouble. Maybe even offered her a drink and cigarette to calm her nerves. It wasn't uncommon for clients to get cold feet standing on the threshold of a private detective's office. Especially the women. Meeting a detective—seeing his cheap suit and getting a noseful of his body odor and heavy cologne—can be enough to persuade a potential client that sometimes it's better not to know what they thought they wanted to know. There's too much truth in the world. And too many bastards who are ready to give it to you, right between the eyes. But I was a little short on manners and all out of charm. A dying wife will do that to you. Out of habit, I stood aside, as if silently inviting her to change her mind and come inside, but she stayed put. Probably she had caught the liquor on my breath and the watery, self-pitying look in my eyes, and decided that I was a drunk. Then she turned away on one of her elegant high heels.

"Good night," she said. "I'm sorry."

I followed her out onto the landing and watched her clip-clop across the linoleum floor to the top of the stairs. "Good night yourself," I said.

She didn't look back. She didn't say anything else. And then she was gone, leaving a trail of something fragrant in her wake. I hoovered the last traces of her into my nostrils and then breathed her into the pit of my stomach and all the important places that made me a man. The way I was supposed to. It made a very pleasant change from the smell at the hospital.

## EIGHT

Kirsten died just after midnight, by which time I'd had enough anesthetic for it to feel just about bearable. The trams weren't running so I walked back to the hospital, just to prove that I could do it like a regular guy. I'd seen her alive; I didn't need to see her dead, but the hospital wanted it that way. I even took our marriage certificate. I figured it was better to get it over with before she stopped looking like a human being. It always amazes me how quickly that happens. One minute a man is as full of life as a basketful of kittens, and a few hours later he looks like an old waxwork at the Hamburg Panoptikum.

A different nurse met me, and a different doctor, too. Both of them were an improvement on the day shift. The nurse was slightly better-looking. The doctor was recognizably human, even in the dark.

"I'm very sorry about your wife," he whispered with what seemed like a very proper show of respect, until I realized that we were standing in the middle of the ward, beside the night nurse's desk, and surrounded by sleeping women who weren't quite as sick as my wife had been. "We did everything we could, Herr Gunther. But she was really very ill."

"Flu was it?"

"It seems so." In the light of the desk lamp he came up very thin, with a round white face and pointy red hair. He looked like a one-man coconut shy.

"Kind of odd, though, wouldn't you say?" I remarked. "I mean, I haven't heard of anyone else who's got the flu."

"As a matter of fact," he said, "we've had several cases. There's a case on the next ward. We're very concerned that it will spread. I'm sure I don't have to remind you of the last serious outbreak of flu, in 1918. And of how many died. You remember that, don't you?"

"Better than you," I said.

"For that reason alone," he said, "the occupation authorities are anxious to contain the possible spread of any infection. Which is why we'd like to seek your permission to order an immediate cremation. In order to prevent the virus from spreading. I appreciate that this is a very difficult time for you, Herr Gunther. Losing your wife at such a young age must be dreadful. I can only guess what you must be going through right now. But we wouldn't ask for your full cooperation in this matter unless we thought it important."

He was giving it plenty of choke, as well he needed to after the master class in cold-blooded indifference exhibited by his stiff-necked colleague, Dr. Effner. I let him rev some more, hardly liking to intercept his continuing effusions of sympathy with what I was really thinking, which was that before being a spinner in the Max Planck, Kirsten had been a real blue, always drunk, and before then, something of a slut, especially with the Americans. In Berlin, immediately after the war, I had suspected that she was little more than a snapper, doing it for chocolate and cigarettes. So many others had done the same, of course, although perhaps with a little less obvious enjoyment. Somehow it seemed only appropriate that the Americans should have their way with Kirsten in death. After all, they'd had their way with her often enough while she had been alive. So when the doctor had finished whispering his pitch, I nodded and said, "All right, we'll play it your way, Doc. If you think it's really necessary."

"Well, it's not so much me as the Amis," he said. "After what happened in 1918, they're really worried about an epidemic in the city."

I sighed. "When do you want to do it?"

"As soon as possible," he said. "That is, immediately. If you don't mind."

"I'd like to see her first," I said.

"Yes, yes, of course," he said. "But try not to touch her, okay? Just in case." He found me a surgical mask. "You'd better wear this," he added. "We've already opened the windows to help air the room, but there's no point in taking any risks."

# NINE

The next day I traveled out to Dachau to see Kirsten's family lawyer and give him the news. Krumper had been handling the sale of the hotel, but so far without success. It seemed that nobody wanted to buy a hotel in Dachau any more than he wanted to stay in one. Krumper's offices were above the marketplace. From the window behind his desk there was a fine view of St. Jakob's and the town hall and the fountain in front of the town hall that always put me in mind of a urinal. His office was very like a building site except that there were piles of files and books on the floor instead of bricks and planks.

Krumper was bound to a wheelchair because of a hip injury he had received during one of Munich's many air raids. Monocled and grouchy, with a cartoon voice and a pipe to match, he was shabby but competent. I liked him in spite of the fact that he had been born in Dachau and lived there all his life without ever having thought to inquire what was happening east of the town. Or so he said. He was very sorry to hear the news of Kirsten's death. Lawyers are always sorry to lose a good client. I waited for the expressions of sympathy to subside and then asked if he thought I should drop the price of the hotel.

"I don't think so," he said carefully. "I'm sure somebody will buy it, although perhaps not as a hotel. As a matter of fact there was a woman here just yesterday asking about the place. She had some questions I wasn't able to answer, and I took the liberty of giving her your business card. I hope that was all right, Herr Gunther."

"Did she have a name?"

"She said her name was Frau Schmidt." He put aside his pipe, flipped open the cigarette box on his desk, and invited me to take one. I lit us both as he continued. "A good-looking woman. Tall. Very tall. With three little scars on the side of her face. Shrapnel scars probably. Not that she seemed at all self-conscious of them. Most women would have grown their hair a bit so that you wouldn't notice. Not her, though. And not that it really spoiled her looks at all. But then it's not every woman who would feel confident of that, is it?"

Krumper had just described the woman who had turned up at my office the previous evening. And I had an idea that she wasn't interested in buying a hotel.

"No indeed," I said. "Maybe she's in a dueling society, like the Teutonia Club. Bragging scars to make her more attractive to some lout with a rapier in his hand. What was that crap the kaiser used to say about those old clubs? The best education a young man can get for his future life."

"You paint a very vivid picture, Herr Gunther," said Krumper, fingering a small scar on his cheekbone as if he, too, had enjoyed the kind of education favored by the kaiser. For a moment or two he was silent, opening a file that lay on his overcrowded desk. "Your wife left a will," he said. "Leaving everything to her father. She hadn't made a new will since his death. But as her next of kin you inherit everything anyway. The hotel. A few hundred marks. Some pictures. And a car."

"A car?" This was news to me. "Kirsten owned a car?"

"Her father's. He kept it hidden throughout the war."

"I think he was probably quite good at keeping things hidden," I said, thinking of the box his SS friend had buried in the garden. I was certain he must have known about it, contrary to what the American who dug it up had believed.

"In a garage on Donauwörther Landstrasse."

"You mean that old Fulda tire place on the road to Kleinberghofen?" Krumper nodded. "What kind of a car?"

"I don't know much about cars," said Krumper. "I saw him in it before the war. Very proud of it, he was. Some sort of duo-tone cabriolet. Of course, business was better then and he could afford to run it. At the beginning of the war he even buried the wheels to stop anyone requisitioning it." Krumper handed me a set of car keys. "And I know he looked after it, even though he didn't drive it. I'm sure it will be in good running order."

A few hours later I was driving back to Munich in a handsome-looking two-door Hansa 1700 that looked as good as it had the day it left the Goliath works in Bremen. I went straight to the hospital, collected Kirsten's ashes, and then drove all the way back to Dachau and the Leitenberg Cemetery, where I had arranged to meet the local undertaker, Herr Gartner. I handed over her cremains and arranged for a short service of remembrance the following afternoon.

When I got back to my apartment in Schwabing, I tried some of the anesthetic again. This time it didn't work. I felt as lonely as a fish in a toilet bowl. I had no relations and no friends to speak of other than the guy in the bathroom mirror, who used to say hello in the morning. Lately even he had stopped speaking to me and seemed, more often than not, to greet me with a sneer, as if I had become obnoxious to him. Maybe we had all become obnoxious. All of us Germans. There were none of us the Americans looked at with anything other than quiet contempt, except perhaps the party-girls and the snappers. And you didn't need to be Hanussen the clairvoyant to read the minds of our new friends and protectors. How could you let it happen? they asked. How could you do what you did? It's a question I had often asked myself. I didn't have an answer. I don't think any of us will ever have an answer. What possible answer could there ever be? It was just something that happened in Germany once, about a thousand years ago.

## TEN

About a week later she came back. The tall one. Tall women are always better than short ones, especially the kind of tall women that short men seem to favor, who really aren't that tall, they just seem that way. This one wasn't quite as tall as the hoop on a basketball court, but a lot of her was just hair and a hat and high heels and hauteur. She had plenty of that. She looked as if she needed help as much as Venice needed rain. That's something I appreciate in a client. I enjoy being pitched at by someone who's not used to words like "please" and "thank you." It brings out the 'forty-eighter in me. Sometimes even the Spartacist.

"I need your help, Herr Gunther," she said, sitting down very carefully on the edge of my creaking green leather sofa. She kept hold of her briefcase for a moment, hugging it to her ample chest like a breastplate.

"Oh? What makes you think so?"

"You're a private detective, aren't you?"

"Yes, but why me? Why not use Preysings in Frauenstrasse? Or Klenze on Augustinerstrasse? They're both bigger than me."

She looked taken aback, as if I'd asked what color underwear she had on. I smiled encouragingly and told myself that so long as she was sitting on the edge of the sofa, I would just have to guess.

"What I'm trying to find out, Fräulein, is if someone recommended me. In this business, it's the sort of thing you like to know."

"Not Fräulein. It's Frau Warzok. Britta Warzok. And yes, you were recommended to me."

"Oh? By whom?"

"If you don't mind, I'd rather not say."

"But you were the lady who turned up at Herr Krumper's last week. My lawyer. Asking about my hotel? Only you were calling yourself Schmidt then, I believe."

"Yes. Not very original of me, I know. But I wasn't sure whether I wanted to hire you or not. I had been here a couple of times and you were out and I didn't care to leave a message in your mailbox. The concierge said that he thought you owned a hotel in Dachau. I thought I might find you there. I saw the 'For Sale' sign and then I went to Krumper's office."

Some of that might have been true, but I let it go, for now. I was enjoying her discomfort and her elegant long legs too much to scare her off. But I didn't see any harm in teasing her a little.

"And yet when you came in here the other night," I said, "you said you'd made a mistake."

"I changed my mind," she said. "That's all."

"You changed it once, you could do it again. Leave me out on a limb. In this business that can be awkward. I need to know that you're committed to this, Frau Warzok. It won't be like buying a hat. Once an investigation is under way it's not something you can return. You won't be able to take it back to the shop and say you don't like it."

"I'm not an idiot, Herr Gunther," she said. "And please don't speak to me as if I haven't given any thought to what I'm doing. It wasn't easy coming here. You've no idea how difficult this is. If you did you might be a little less patronizing." She spoke coolly and without emotion. "Is it the hat? I can take the hat off if it bothers you." Finally she let go of her briefcase, placing it on the floor by her feet.

"I like the hat." I smiled. "Please, keep it on. And I'm sorry if my manner offends you. But to be frank, there are a lot of time-wasters in this business and my time is precious to me. I'm a one-man operation, and if I'm working for you I can't be working for someone else. Someone whose need might conceivably be greater than yours, perhaps. That's just how it is."

"I doubt there is anyone who needs you more than I do, Herr Gunther," she said, with just enough tremor in her voice to tug at the softer end of my aorta. I offered her a cigarette.

"I don't smoke," she said, shaking her head. "My . . . doctor says they're bad for you."

"I know. But the way I figure it, they're one of the more elegant ways to kill yourself. What's more, they give you plenty of time to put your affairs in order." I lit my cigarette and gulped down a mouthful of smoke. "Now, what seems to be the trouble, Frau Warzok?"

"You sound like you mean that," she said. "About killing yourself."

"I was on the Russian front, lady. After something like that, every day seems like a bonus." I shrugged. "So eat, drink, and be merry for tomorrow we might get invaded by the Ivans, and then we'll wish we were dead even if we're not, although of course we will be, because this is an atomic world we live in now and it takes just six minutes not six years to kill six million people." I pinched the cigarette from between my lips and grinned at her. "So what's a few smokes beside a mushroom cloud?"

"You've been through it, then?"

"Sure. We've all been through it." I couldn't see them, but I knew they were there. The little piece of black fishnet on the side of her hat was covering the three scars on her cheek. "You, too, by the look of things."

She touched her face. "Actually, I was quite lucky," she said.

"That's the only way to look at it."

"There was an air raid on the twenty-fifth of April 1944," she said. "They say that forty-five high-explosive and five thousand incendiary bombs fell on Munich. One of the bombs shattered a water pipe in my house. I got hit by three red-hot copper rings that were blown off my boiler. But it could just as easily have been my eyes. It's amazing what we can come through, isn't it?"

"If you say so."

"Herr Gunther, I want to get married."

"Isn't this a little sudden, dear? We've only just met."

She smiled politely. "There's just one problem. I don't know if the man I married is still alive."

"If he disappeared during the war, Frau Warzok," I said, "you would be better off inquiring about him at the Army Information Office. The Wehrmacht Dienststelle is in Berlin, at 179 Eichborndamm. Telephone 41904."

I knew the number because when Kirsten's father had died, I had tried to find out if her brother was alive or dead. The discovery that he had been killed, in 1944, had hardly helped her deteriorating mental condition.

Frau Warzok was shaking her head. "No, it's not like that. He was alive at the end of the war. In the spring of 1946 we were in Ebensee, near Salzburg. I saw him for only a short while, you understand. We were no longer living together as man and wife. Not since the end of the war." She tugged a handkerchief down the sleeve of her tailored suit jacket and held it crushed in the palm of her hand, expectantly, as if she was planning to cry.

"Have you spoken to the police?"

"The German police say it's an Austrian matter. The Salzburg police say I should leave it to the Americans."

"The Amis won't look for him either," I said.

"Actually, they might." She swallowed a bolus of raw emotion and then took a deep breath. "Yes, I think they might be interested enough to look for him."

"Oh?"

"Not that I have told them anything about Friedrich. That's his name. Friedrich Warzok. He's Galician. Galicia was part of Austria until the Austro-Prussian War of 1866, after which it was allowed its autonomy. Then, after 1918, it became part of Poland. Friedrich was born in Kraków in 1903. He was a very Austrian sort of Pole, Herr Gunther. And then a very German one, after Hitler was elected."

"So why would the Americans be interested in him?" I was asking the question, but I was beginning to have a shrewd idea.

"Friedrich was an ambitious man, but not a strong one. Not intellectually strong, anyway. Physically he was very strong. Before the war he was a stonemason. Rather a good one. He was a very virile man, Herr Gunther. I suppose that was what I fell for. When I was eighteen, I was quite vigorous myself."

I didn't doubt it for a moment. It was all too easy to imagine her wearing a short, white slip and a laurel wreath in her hair and doing interesting things with a hoop in a nice propaganda film from Dr. Goebbels. Female vigor never looked so blond and healthy.

"I'll be honest with you, Herr Gunther." She dabbed her eye with the corner of her handkerchief. "Friedrich Warzok was not a good man. During the war, he did some terrible things."

"After Hitler there's none of us can say he has a clear conscience," I said.

"It's very good of you to say so. But there are things that one has to do to survive. And then there are other things that don't involve survival at all. This amnesty that's being discussed in the Parliament. It wouldn't include my husband, Herr Gunther."

"I wouldn't be too sure about that," I said. "If someone as bad as Erich Koch is prepared to risk coming out of hiding to claim the protection of the new Basic Law, then anyone might do the same. No matter what he had done."

Erich Koch had been the gauleiter of East Prussia and the Reich commissioner for the Ukraine, where some dreadful things had been done. I knew that because I'd seen quite a few of them myself. Koch was banking on receiving the protection of the Federal Republic's new Basic Law, which forbade both the death penalty and extradition for all new cases of war crimes. Koch was currently being held in a prison in the British Zone. Time would tell if he had made a shrewd decision or not.

I was beginning to see where this case, and my new business, were headed. Frau Warzok's husband was my third Nazi in a row. And thanks to the likes of Erich Kaufmann and the Baron von Starnberg, from whom I had received a personal letter of thanks, it looked as if I was turning out to be the man to turn to if your problem involved a Red Jacket or a fugitive war criminal. I didn't much like that. It wasn't why I had gone back to being a private detective. And I might have brushed Frau Warzok off if she had been there telling me that her husband had nothing personal against the Jews, or that he was merely the victim of "historical value judgments." But so far, she wasn't telling me that. Quite the contrary, as she now proceeded to underline.

"No, no, Friedrich is an evil man," she said. "They could never grant amnesty to a man like that. Not after what he did. And he deserves whatever is coming to him. Nothing would please me more than to know he's dead. Believe me."

"Oh, I do, I do. Why don't you tell me what he did?"

"Before the war he was in the Freikorps, and then the Party. Then he joined the SS, and rose to the rank of Hauptsturmführer. He was transferred to the Lemberg-Janowska camp in Poland. And that was the end of the man I had married."

I shook my head. "I haven't heard of Lemberg-Janowska."

"Be glad of that, Herr Gunther," she said. "Janowska wasn't like the other camps. It started out as a network of factories that were part of the German Armament Works, in Lvov. It used forced labor, Jews and Poles. About six thousand of them in 1941. Friedrich went there in early 1942 and, for a few days at least, I went with him. The commander was a man named Wilhaus, and Friedrich became his assistant. There were about twelve or fifteen German officers, like my husband. But most of the SS, the guards, were Russians who had volunteered for service with the SS as a way of escaping a prisoner of war camp." She shook her head and tightened her grip on the handkerchief, as if squeezing tearful memories out of the cotton. "After Friedrich got to Janowska, more Jews arrived. Many more Jews. And the ethos—if I can use such a word about Janowska—the ethos of the camp changed. Making Jews produce munitions became of much less importance than simply killing them. It wasn't systematic killing of the kind that went on at Auschwitz-Birkenau. No, this was just murdering them individually in whatever way an SS man felt like. Each SS man had his own favorite way of dispatching a Jew. And every day there were shootings, hangings, drownings, impalements, disembowelings, crucifixions—yes, crucifixions, Herr Gunther. You can't imagine it, can you? But it's true. Women were stabbed to death with knives, or chopped to pieces with hatchets. Children were used for target practice. I heard a story that bets were made as to whether a child could be cleaved in two with a single blow from an ax. Each SS man was obliged to keep a tally of how many he had killed, so that a list might be compiled. Three hundred thousand people were killed like this, Herr Gunther. Three hundred thousand people brutally murdered, in cold blood, by laughing sadists. And my husband was one of them."

While she spoke she looked not at me but at the floor, and it wasn't long before a tear rolled down the length of her fine nose and hit the carpet. Then another.

"At some stage—I'm not sure when, because Friedrich stopped writing to me after a while—he assumed command of the camp. And it's safe to say he kept things going just as they were. He did write to me once, to say Himmler had visited and how happy he was with the way things were progressing at Janowska. The camp was liberated by the Russians in July 1944. Wilhaus is dead now. I think the Russians killed him. Fritz Gebauer, who had been camp commandant before Wilhaus, was tried at Dachau and sentenced to life imprisonment. He's in Landsberg Prison. But Friedrich escaped to Germany, where he stayed until the end of the war. We had some contact during this time. But the marriage was over, and had it not been for the fact that I am a Roman Catholic, I would certainly have divorced him.

"In late 1945, he disappeared from Munich and I didn't hear from him again until March 1946. He was on the run. He contacted me and asked for money, so that he could go away. He was in contact with an old comrades' association—the ODESSA. And he was awaiting a new identity. I have money of my own, Herr Gunther. So I agreed. I wanted him out of my life, forever. At the time, it did not occur to me that I would marry again. My scars were not as you see them now. A surgeon has worked hard to make my face more presentable. I spent most of my remaining fortune paying him."

"It was worth it," I observed. "He did a good job."

"It's kind of you to say so. And now I've met someone. A decent man whom I should like to marry. So I want to know if Friedrich is dead or alive. You see, he said he'd write to me when he got to South America. That's where he was going. That's where most of them go. But he never did. There were others escaping with Friedrich who did contact their families and who are now safe in Argentina and Brazil. But not my husband. I've taken advice from Cardinal Josef Frings, in Cologne, and he tells me that there can be no remarriage in the Roman Catholic Church without there being some evidence of Friedrich's death. And I thought, you having been in the SS yourself, you might have a better chance of finding out if he's alive or dead. If he's in South America."

"You're well informed," I said.

"Not me," she said. "My fiancé. That's what he told me, anyway."

"And what does he do?"

"He's a lawyer."

"I might have known."

"What do you mean?"

"Nothing," I said. "You know, Frau Warzok, not everyone who was in the SS is as warm and cuddly as I am. Some of these old comrades don't like questions, even from people like me. What you're asking me to do could be dangerous."

"I appreciate that," she said. "We'll make it worth your while. I have some money left. And my fiancé is a rich lawyer."

"Is there any other kind? In the future I've an idea that everyone will be a lawyer. They'll have to be." I lit another cigarette. "A case like this, it might take a bit of money at that. Expenses. Talking money."

"Talking money?"

"A lot of people won't say or do anything until they see a picture of Europa and her bull." I took out a banknote and showed her the picture I was talking about. "This picture."

"I suppose that includes you."

"Me, I'm coin-operated, like everything and everyone else these days. Lawyers included. I get ten marks a day plus expenses. No receipts. Your accountant won't like that but it can't be helped. Buying information isn't like buying stationery. I get something in advance. That's for your inconvenience. You see, I might draw a blank and it always inconveniences a client when he finds himself paying for nothing very much."

"How does two hundred in advance sound?"

"Two hundreds are better than one."

"And a substantial bonus if you find any evidence that Friedrich is alive or dead."

"How substantial?"

"I don't know. I hadn't given it much thought."

"Might be a good idea if you did. I work better that way. How much would it be worth to you if I did find something out? If you could marry, for example."

"I'd pay five thousand marks, Herr Gunther."

"Have you thought of offering that much to the cardinal?" I asked.

"You mean like a bribe?"

"No, not *like* a bribe, Frau Warzok. I mean a *bribe,* pure and simple. Five thousand marks buys an awful lot of rosaries. Hell, that's how the Borgias made their fortune. Everyone knows that."

Frau Warzok seemed shocked. "The Church is not like that anymore," she said.

"No?"

"I couldn't," she said. "Marriage is a sacrament that is indissoluble."

I shrugged. "If you say so. Do you have a photograph of your husband?"

From an envelope in her briefcase she handed me three photographs. The first was a standard studio portrait of a man with a twinkle in his eye and a large grin on his face. The eyes were a little too close together, but apart from that there was nothing about it that might have led you to suppose that this was the face of a psychopathic murderer. He looked like a regular nine-to-five guy. That was the frightening thing about the concentration camps and the special action groups. It had been the regular guys—the lawyers, the judges, the policemen, the chicken farmers, and the stonemasons—who had done all the killing. In the second picture, things were clearer cut: a slightly tubbier Warzok, his chins bulging over his tunic collar, was standing stiffly to attention, his right hand held in the clasp of a beaming Heinrich Himmler. Warzok was about an inch shorter than Himmler, who was accompanied by an SS Gruppenführer I didn't recognize. The third picture was a wider shot, taken the same day, of about six SS officers, including Warzok and Himmler. There were shadows on the ground and it looked like the sun had been shining.

"Those two were taken in August 1942," explained Frau Warzok. "As you can see, Himmler was being shown around Janowska. Wilhaus was drunk, and things were slightly less cordial than it seems. Himmler didn't really approve of wanton cruelty. Or so Friedrich told me."

She reached into her briefcase and took out a typewritten sheet of paper. "This is a copy of some details that were on his SS record," she said. "His SS number. His NSDAP number. His parents—they're both dead, so you can forget any leads from that direction. He had a girlfriend, a Jewess called Rebecca, whom he murdered just before the camp was liberated. It's possible you might get something out of Fritz Gebauer. I haven't tried."

I glanced over the paper she had prepared. She'd been very thorough, I had to give her that much. Or perhaps her lawyer fiancé had. I looked at the photographs again. Somehow it was a little hard to imagine her in bed with the man shaking hands with Himmler, but I'd seen more unlikely-looking couples. I could see what Warzok got out of it. He was short, she was tall. In that he was conforming to type, at least. It was harder to see what had been in it for her. Tall women usually married short men because it wasn't money the men were short of, just inches. Stonemasons didn't make a lot of money. Not even in Austria, where the tombs are fancier than almost anywhere else in Europe.

"I don't get it," I said. "Why did a woman like you marry a squirt like him in the first place?"

"Because I got pregnant," she said. "I wouldn't have married him otherwise. After we married, I lost the child. And I told you. I'm a Catholic. We mate for life."

"All right. I'll buy that. But suppose I do find him. What happens then? Have you thought about that?"

Her nostrils narrowed and her face took on a hard aspect that hadn't been there before. She closed her eyes for a moment, removed the velvet glove she'd been wearing, and let me see the steel hand that had been there all along.

"You mentioned Erich Koch," she said. "It's my fiancé's understanding that since he came out of hiding, in May, the British—in whose zone of occupation he is now imprisoned—are considering the extradition requests of Poland and the Soviet Union, in whose countries Koch's crimes were committed. Despite the Basic Law, and any amnesties the Federal Republic might push through, it is my fiancé's opinion—his well-informed opinion—that the British will approve his extradition to the Russian Zone. To Poland. Should he be found guilty in a Warsaw court, he will undoubtedly face the maximum punishment under Polish law. A sentence that Germany is judicially inclined to disapprove of. We anticipate the same fate for Friedrich Warzok."

I grinned at her. "Well, that's more like it," I said. "Now I can see what you two had in common. You're really quite a ruthless woman, aren't you? Kind of like one of those Borgias I was talking about. Lucrezia Borgia. Ruthless, and beautiful with it."

She blushed.

"Do you really care what happens to a man like that?" she said, brandishing her husband's photograph.

"Not particularly. I'll help you to look for your husband, Frau Warzok. But I won't help you put a noose around his neck—even if he does deserve it several thousand times over."

"What's the matter, Herr Gunther? Are you squeamish about such things?"

"It could be," I said. "If I am it's because I've seen men hanged and I've seen them shot. I've seen them blown to pieces and starved to death, and toasted with a flamethrower, and crushed underneath the tracks of a Panzer tank. It's a funny thing, but after a while you realize you've seen too much. Things you can't pretend you didn't see because they're always on the insides of your eyelids when you go to sleep at night. And you tell yourself that you'd rather not see any more. Not if you can help it. Which of course you can because none of the old excuses are worth a damn anymore. And it's simply not good enough to say we can't help it and orders are orders and expect people to swallow that the way they used to. So yes, I suppose I am a little squeamish. After all, just look where ruthless has gotten us."

"You're quite the philosopher, aren't you?" she said. "For a detective."

"All detectives are philosophers, Frau Warzok. They have to be. That way they can recognize how much of what a client tells them they can swallow safely and how much they can flush. Which of them is as mad as Nietzsche and which of them is only as mad as Marx. The clients, I mean. You mentioned two hundred in advance."

She reached down for her briefcase, took out her wallet, and counted out four seated ladies into my hand. "I also brought some hemlock," she said. "If you didn't take the case, I was going to threaten to drink it. But if you do find my husband, maybe you could give it to him instead. Sort of a good-bye present."

I grinned at her. I liked grinning at her. She was the type of client who needed to see my teeth, just to remind her that I might bite. "I'll write you a receipt," I said.

Our business concluded she stood up, shifting some of her perfume off her delectable body and up my airways. Without the heels and the hat, I figured she was probably only as tall as I was. But while she was wearing them I felt like her favorite eunuch. I imagined it was the effect she was looking for.

"Look after yourself, Herr Gunther," she said, reaching for the door handle. Mr. Manners got there first.

"I always do. I've had an awful lot of practice."

"When will you start to look for him?"

"Your two hundred says right now."

"And how and where will you go about it?"

"I'll probably lift some rocks and see what crawls out from underneath. With six million Jews murdered, there are plenty of rocks in Germany to choose from."

## ELEVEN

Detective work is a little like walking into a movie that's already started. You don't know what's happened already and, as you try to find your way in the dark, it's inevitable that you're going to stand on someone's toes, or get in their way. Sometimes people curse you, but mostly they just sigh or tut loudly and move their legs and their coats, and then do their best to pretend you're not there. Asking questions of the person seated next to you can result in anything from a full plot and cast list to a slap in the mouth with a rolled-up program. You pay your money and you take your chances.

Chance was one thing. Pushing my luck was quite another. I wasn't about to go asking questions about old comrades without a friend to keep me company. Men who are facing the gallows are apt to be a little jealous about their privacy. I hadn't owned a gun since leaving Vienna. I decided that it was time I started to dress for all occasions.

Under National Socialism's law of 1938, handguns could be purchased only on submission of a Weapons Acquisitions Permit, and most men of my acquaintance had owned some kind of firearm. But at the end of the war General Eisenhower had ordered all privately owned firearms in the American Zone to be confiscated. In the Soviet Zone things were even stricter: A German in possession of so much as a single cartridge was likely to be summarily shot. A gun was as difficult to get hold of in Germany as a banana.

I knew a fellow named Stuber—Faxon Stuber—who drove an export taxi, who could get hold of all kinds of things, mostly from American GIs. Marked with the initials E.T., export taxis were reserved for the exclusive use of people in possession of foreign exchange coupons, or FECs. I wasn't sure how he had got hold of them, but I had found some FECs in the glove box of Kirsten's father's Hansa. I supposed he had been saving them to buy gasoline on the black market. I used some of them to pay Stuber for a gun.

He was a small man in his early twenties, with a mustache like a line of ants, and, on his head, an SS officer's black service cap from which all the insignia and cap cords had been removed. None of the Americans getting into Stuber's E.T. would ever have recognized his cap for what it was. But I did. I'd damn near had to wear a black cap myself. As it was, I'd been obliged to wear the field gray version only as part of the M37 SS uniform, which came along after 1938. I figured

Stuber had found the cap or someone had given it to him. He was too young to have been in the SS himself. He looked too young to be driving a cab. In his small white hand the weapon he'd brought me was recognizably a firearm, but in my own sixteen-ounce glove it looked more like a water pistol.

"I said a firearm, not a spud gun."

"What are you talking about?" he said. "That's a twenty-five-caliber Beretta. That's a nice little gun. There's eight in the clip and I got you a box of pills to go with it. It's got a hinged barrel so you can slide the first one in, or take it out with ease. Five inches long and just eleven ounces in weight."

"I've seen bigger lamb chops."

"Not on your ration card, Gunther," said Stuber. He grinned as if he ate steak every night of the week. Given his passengers, he probably did. "That's all the gun you'll need around this city, unless you're planning a trip to the O.K. Corral."

"I like a gun people can see," I said. "The sort of gun that gives a man some pause for thought. With this little popgun no one will take me seriously unless I shoot them first. Kind of defeats the purpose."

"That little gun packs more of a punch than you might think," he insisted. "Look, if you want something bigger, I can get it. But it's going to take more time. And I got the impression that you were in a hurry."

We drove around for a few minutes while I thought about it. He was right about one thing. I was in a hurry. Eventually, I sighed and said, "All right, I'll take it."

"You ask me, that's a perfect town gun," he said. "Businesslike. Convenient. Discreet." He made it sound more like a membership of the Herrenklub than a snapper's rattle. Which was what it was. The rhinestone holster it came in told me that much. Some GI had very likely confiscated it from the slot he'd been feeding. Maybe she'd got him on the trap with it, intending to drop him for a few extra marks and he'd wrestled it off her. I just hoped it wasn't a gun that the ballistics boys at the Praesidium were looking for. I tossed the holster back at Stuber and got out of his cab on Schellingstrasse. I figured a free ride to my next port of call was the least he could do after selling me some party-girl's belly gun.

I went through the doors of *Die Neue Zeitung* and had the hatchet-faced redhead behind the desk call up Friedrich Korsch. I glanced over the front page while I waited for him to come down. There was a story about Johann Neuhausler, the Protestant auxiliary bishop of Munich who was involved with the various groups that were trying to free the Red Jackets in Landsberg. According to the bishop, the Americans "did not lag behind the Nazis in sadism," and he spoke about an American prison guard—not named—whose description of conditions at Landsberg "beggared belief." I had a shrewd idea of who this American soldier was, and it infuriated me to see, of all people, a bishop repeating the lies and half-truths of PFC John Ivanov. Evidently my efforts on behalf of Erich Kaufmann had been wasted.

Friedrich Korsch had been a young Kriminalassistent with KRIPO when I had been a Kommissar at the Alex, in Berlin, back in 1938–39. I hadn't seen him in almost ten years until, one day the previous December, I had bumped into him coming out of Spöckmeier, a *Bierkeller* on Rosenstrasse. He hadn't changed a bit, apart from the leather eye patch. With his long chin and Douglas Fairbanks–style mustache, he looked like a swashbuckling buccaneer, which might have been a good thing in a journalist working for an American newspaper.

We went to the Osteria Bavaria—once Hitler's favorite restaurant—and argued about who was going to pick up the bill while at the same time we reminisced about old times and made a tally of who was dead and who was alive. But after I had told him of how I suspected Bishop Neuhausler's source inside Landsberg Prison was a liar and a crook, Korsch refused to hear any more talk of me paying. "For a story like that, the paper will cover lunch," he said.

"That's too bad," I said. "Because I was hoping to get some information out of you. I'm looking for a war criminal."

"Isn't everyone?"

"Name of Friedrich Warzok."

"Never heard of him."

"He was the sometime commander of a labor camp near the ghetto at Lvov. A place called Lemberg-Janowska."

"It sounds more like a type of cheese."

"It's in southeastern Poland, near the Ukrainian border."

"Miserable country," said Korsch. "I lost my eye there."

"How does one go about it, Friedrich? How do you set about trying to find such a man?"

"What's your angle?"

"My client is the wife. She wants to get married again."

"Can't she just obtain a declaration from the Wehrmacht Information Office? They're quite obliging, really. Even for ex-SS."

"He was seen alive in March 1946."

"So you want to know if there's been some kind of investigation."

"That's right."

"All war crimes committed by our old friends and superiors are currently investigated by the Allies. Although there is some talk that in the future they will be investigated by the state attorneys general offices. However, right now, the best place to start is with the Central Registry of War Criminals and Security Suspects, set up by SHAEF. The so-called CROWCASS registers. There are about forty of them. But those are not open to the public. Actual investigative responsibility lies with the Directorate of Army Legal Services, which deals with offenses committed in all military theaters during the war. Then there's the CIA. They have some sort of central registry. But neither Army Legal Services nor the CIA are readily available to a private individual like yourself, I'm afraid. There is the American Documents Center, in West Berlin, of course. I believe it is possible for a private person to get access to documents there. But only by permission of General Clay."

"No, thanks," I said. "The blockade may be over, but I'd rather keep away from Berlin if possible. Because of the Russians. I had to leave Vienna to get away from a Russian intelligence colonel who had his eye on recruiting me to the MVD, or whatever it is they call the Soviet Secret Police these days."

"It's called the MVD," said Korsch. "Of course, if you don't want to go to Berlin there's always the Red Cross. They run an international tracing service. But that's for displaced persons. They might know something. Then there are the Jewish organizations. The Brichah, for example. It started out as a refugee-smuggling organization but, since the establishment of the State of Israel, they've become much more active in the hunt for old comrades. It seems they don't trust the Germans or the Allies to do the job. Can't say I blame them. Oh yes, and there's some chap in Linz who runs his own Nazi-hunting operation with private American money. Name of Wiesenthal."

I shook my head. "I don't think I'll be troubling any Jewish organizations," I said. "Not with my background."

"That's probably wise," said Korsch. "I can't imagine a Jew wanting to help someone who was in the SS, can you?" He laughed at the very thought of it.

"No, I'll stick to the Allies for now."

"Are you absolutely sure Lvov is in Poland? I think you'll find it used to be in Poland but now it's part of the Ukraine. Just to make things a little more complicated for you."

"What about the paper?" I asked. "You must have some sort of access to the Amis. Couldn't you find out something?"

"I suppose I could," said Korsch. "Sure, I'll take a look."

I wrote Friedrich Warzok's name on a piece of paper and, underneath it, the name of the labor camp at Lemberg-Janowska. Korsch folded it and slipped it into his pocket.

"Whatever happened to Emil Becker?" he asked. "Remember him?"

"The Amis hanged him in Vienna about two years ago."

"War crimes?"

"No. But as it happens, if they'd looked they'd have certainly found evidence of some war crimes."

Korsch shook his head. "We've all got some kind of dirty mark on our faces, if you look closely enough."

I shrugged. I hadn't asked what Korsch had done during the war. I only knew that he'd come out of the war as a Kriminalinspektor in the RSHA, which meant he'd had something to do with the Gestapo. There seemed no point in spoiling a perfectly affable lunch by asking him about all that now. Nor did he exhibit any curiosity about what I had done.

"So what was it?" he asked. "What did they hang him for?"

"For murdering an American officer," I said. "I heard he was heavily involved in the black market."

"That much I can believe," he said. "That he was into the black market." Korsch raised a glass of wine. "Here's to him, anyway."

"Yes," I said, picking up my glass. "Here's to Emil. The poor bastard." I drained the glass. "As a matter of curiosity, how is it that a bull like you turns into a journalist, anyway?"

"I got out of Berlin just before the blockade," he said. "Had a tip from an Ivan who owed me a favor. So I came down here. And got offered a job as a crime correspondent. The hours are much the same, but the pay is a lot better. I've learned English. Got myself a wife and son. Nice house in Nymphenburg." He shook his head. "Berlin is finished. It's only a matter of time before the Ivans take it over. The war seems like a thousand years ago, quite frankly. And if you don't mind my saying so, all this war crimes stuff, soon it won't matter a damn. Any of it. Not when the amnesty kicks in. That's what everyone wants now, isn't it?"

I nodded. Who was I to argue with what everyone wanted?

## TWELVE

I drove west out of Munich, toward the medieval town of Landsberg. With its town hall, Bavarian Gothic gate, and famous fortress, it was a historic place, and largely undamaged because, during the war, Allied bombers had given it a wide berth, to avoid killing thousands of foreign workers and Jews held in as many as thirty-one concentration camps in the surrounding area. After the war these same camps had been used by the Americans to take care of displaced persons. The largest of these was still in existence with over a thousand Jewish DPs. Although it was much smaller than Munich and Nuremberg, the Nazi Party had considered Landsberg one of the three most significant towns in Germany. Before the war it had been a place of pilgrimage for German youth. Not for the architecture or religious reasons, unless you counted Nazism as a kind of religion, but because people were intent on seeing the cell in Landsberg where Adolf Hitler, imprisoned there for almost a year after the abortive Beer Hall Putsch of 1923, had written *Mein Kampf*. By all accounts Hitler had been very comfortable in Landsberg Prison. Built in 1910, within the walls of the medieval fortress, the prison had been one of the most modern in Germany, and Hitler seems to have been treated more like an honored guest than some dangerous revolutionary. The authorities had afforded him every opportunity to meet with friends and to write his book. Without his time in Landsberg, the world might never have heard of Hitler.

In 1946, the Americans had renamed Landsberg Prison War Criminal Prison Number One and, after Spandau in Berlin, it was the most important penal facility in Germany, with over one thousand war criminals from the Dachau trials, almost a hundred from the Nuremberg trials, and more than a dozen from the trials of Japanese POWs in Shanghai. Over two hundred war criminals had been hanged at WCP1 and many of their bodies were buried nearby in the cemetery of Spottingen Chapel.

It wasn't easy getting into Landsberg to see Fritz Gebauer. I'd had to telephone Erich Kaufmann and eat a couple of spoonfuls of humble pie in order to persuade him to contact Gebauer's lawyers and persuade them that I could be trusted.

"Oh, I think we can rely on you, Herr Gunther," Kaufmann had said. "That was a good job you did for Baron von Starnberg."

"What little I did I got paid for," I said. "And handsomely, too."

"You can take a certain amount of satisfaction in a job well done, can't you?"

"A certain amount, sometimes, yes," I said. "Not too much on this one, though. Not as much as I got from working your case."

"Proving the unreliability of PFC Ivanov? I'd have thought that being an ex–SS man yourself, you would be keen to see your old comrades out of prison."

This was the cue I had been waiting for. "It's true," I had told him, bowdlerizing the lecture he had given me in his office. "I was in the SS. But that doesn't mean I'm not interested in justice, Herr Doktor. Men who have murdered women and children deserve to be in prison. People need to know that doing wrong will be punished. That's my idea of a healthy Germany."

"Lots of people would say that many of these men were POWs who were only doing their duty, Herr Gunther."

"I know. I'm perverse that way. Contrarian."

"That sounds unhealthy."

"It could be," I said. "On the other hand, it's easy to ignore someone like me. Even when I'm right. But it's not so easy to ignore Bishop Neuhausler. Even when he's wrong. Imagine the hurt to my job satisfaction when I read what he had to say about the Red Jackets in the newspapers. It was like no one had told him that Ivanov was a chiseler and a thief with an ax to grind."

"Neuhausler is the creature of people much more unscrupulous than myself, Herr Gunther," said Kaufmann. "I hope you can appreciate that I had nothing to do with that."

"I'm doing my best."

"People like Rudolf Aschenauer, for one."

I had heard this name before. Aschenauer was the Nuremberg attorney and legal adviser to nearly seven hundred Landsberg prisoners, including the infamous Otto Ohlendorf, and a member of the right-wing German Party.

"As a matter of fact," said Kaufmann, "I'll have to speak to Aschenauer to get you into Landsberg, to see Gebauer. He is Gebauer's lawyer. He was the lawyer for all of the accused of the Malmedy massacre."

"Gebauer's one of them?"

"That's why we want him out of an American prison," said Kaufmann. "I'm sure you can imagine why."

"Yes," I said. "In this particular instance I probably can."

I parked my car and walked up the castle esplanade to the gatehouse of the fortress, where I showed my papers and a letter from Aschenauer's office to the black American GI on duty. While I waited for him to find my name on his clipboard, listing the day's visitors, I smiled amiably and tried to practice my English.

"It is a nice day, yes?"

"Fuck off, kraut."

I kept on smiling. I wasn't exactly sure what he had said but his expression told me he wasn't inclined to be friendly. After he had found my name on his list, he tossed my papers back at me and pointed to a white, four-story building with a mansard roof made of red tiles. From a distance it looked almost like a school. Up close, it looked exactly what it was: a prison. Inside was no different. All prisons smell of the same things. Cheap food, cigarettes, sweat, urine, boredom, and despair. Another stone-faced military policeman escorted me to a room with a view of the Lech Valley. It looked lush and green and full of the last days of summer. It was a terrible day to be in prison, assuming there's such a thing as a good day to be in prison. I sat down on a cheap chair at a cheap table and dragged a cheap ashtray toward me. Then the American went out, locking the door behind him, which gave me a nice warm glow in the pit of my stomach. And I imagined what it must have been like to be one of the Malmedy Unit, in WCP1.

Malmedy was the place in Belgium's Ardennes Forest where, during the winter of 1944, at the Battle of the Bulge, eighty-four prisoners of war had been massacred by a Waffen-SS unit. American POWs. The entire SS unit—seventy-five of them, anyway—were now in Landsberg, serving long terms of imprisonment. A lot of the men had my sympathy. It's not always possible to take a lot of men prisoner in the middle of a battle. And if you let a man go, there's always the chance that, later on, you might find yourself fighting him again. War wasn't some game played by gentlemen, where paroles were given and honored. Not the war we had fought. And inasmuch as these particular SS men had been fighting one of the most brutal battles of the Second World War, it hardly made sense to charge them with war crimes. To that extent Kaufmann was right. But I wasn't sure if my sympathy extended to Fritz Gebauer. Prior to his front-line service with the Waffen-SS, Obersturmbannführer Gebauer had been the commandant of Lemberg-Janowska. At some stage he must have volunteered to fight on the western front, which required a certain amount of courage—perhaps even a certain amount of distaste for his job at the labor camp.

The key scraped in the lock and the metal door opened. I turned around to see a strikingly good-looking man in his late thirties enter the room. Tall and broad-shouldered, Fritz Gebauer had a vaguely aristocratic bearing and, somehow, managed to make his prisoner's red jacket look more like a smoking jacket. He bowed slightly before sitting down opposite me.

"Thanks for agreeing to this meeting," I said, placing a packet of Lucky Strikes and some matches on the table between us. "Smoke?"

Gebauer glanced around at the soldier who remained with us. "Is it permitted?" he asked, in English.

The soldier nodded, and Gebauer took a nail from the packet and smoked it gratefully.

"Where are you from?" asked Gebauer.

"I live in Munich," I said. "But I was born in Berlin. I lived there until a couple of years ago."

"Me, too," he said. "I've asked to be moved to a prison in Berlin, so that my wife can visit me, but that doesn't appear to be possible." He shrugged. "But what do they care? The Amis. We're scum to them. Not soldiers at all. Murderers, that's what we are. It's fair to say that there are some murderers among us. The Jew killers. I never much cared for that kind of thing myself. I myself was on the western front, where Jew killing was of little importance."

"Malmedy, wasn't it?" I said, lighting one for myself. "In the Ardennes."

"That's right," he said. "It was a desperate fight. Our backs were really against the wall. It was all we could do to look after ourselves, let alone a hundred surrendering Amis." He inhaled deeply and looked up at the green ceiling. Someone had done a good job of matching the paint on the walls and the floor. "Of course, it doesn't matter to the Amis that we had no facilities for taking prisoners. And no one thinks for a minute to suggest that the men who surrendered were cowards. We wouldn't have surrendered. Not a chance. That's what the SS was all about, wasn't it? Loyalty is my honor, wasn't it? Not self-preservation." He took a hit on the cigarette. "Aschenauer says you were SS yourself. So you would understand what I'm talking about."

I glanced at our American guard, uncomfortably. I hardly wanted to talk about having been in the SS in front of an American MP. "I really wouldn't like to say," I said.

"You can speak quite freely in front of him," said Gebauer. "He doesn't speak a word of German. Few of the Amis in here do. Even the officers are too lazy to learn. From time to time you get the odd intelligence officer who speaks German. But mostly they don't see the point of it."

"I think they feel that it would demean their victory to learn our language," I said.

"Yes, that might be true," said Gebauer. "They're worse than the French in that respect. But my English is improving all the time."

"Mine, too," I said. "It's a sort of mongrel language, isn't it?"

"Hardly surprising when you see the miscegenation that's gone on," he said. "I've never seen such a racially diverse people." He shook his head wearily. "The Amis are a curious lot. In some ways, of course, they're quite admirable. But in others, they're completely stupid. Take this place. Landsberg. To put us here, of all places. Where the Führer wrote his great book. There's not one of us who doesn't take a certain amount of comfort in that. I myself came here before the war to look at his cell. They've removed the bronze plaque that was placed on the Führer's cell door, of course. But we all know exactly where it is. In the same way that a Muslim knows the direction of Mecca. It's something that helps to sustain us. To keep up our spirits."

"I was on the Russian front myself," I said. I was showing him some credentials. It didn't seem appropriate to mention my sometime service with the German War Crimes Bureau, in Berlin. Where we had investigated German atrocities as well as Russian ones. "I was an intelligence officer, with General Schorner's army. But before the war, I was a policeman, at the Alex."

"I know it well," he said, smiling. "Before the war I was a lawyer, in Wilmersdorf. I used to go to the Alex now and then to interview some rogue or other. How I wish I was back there now."

"Before you joined the Waffen-SS," I said, "you went to a labor camp. Lemberg-Janowska."

"That's right," he said. "With the DAW. The German Armament Works."

"It's your time there that I wanted to ask you about."

For a moment his face wrinkled with disgust as he recalled it. "It was a forced labor camp constructed around three factories in Lvov. The camp was named after the factory address: 133 Janowska Street. I went there in May 1942, to take command of the factories. Someone else was in charge of the residential camp where the Jews lived. And things were pretty bad there, I believe. But my responsibility was the factory only. This meant that there was a certain amount of friction between myself and the other commander, as to who was really in charge. Strictly speaking, it ought to have been me. At the time, I was a first lieutenant and the other fellow was a second lieutenant. However, it so happened his uncle was SS Major General Friedrich Katzmann, the police chief of Galicia and a very powerful man. He was part of the reason why I left Janowska. Wilhaus—that was the other commander's name—he hated me. Jealous, I suppose. Wanted control of everything. And he'd have done anything to get rid of me. It was only a matter of time before he made his move. Framed me for something I hadn't done. So I decided to get out while I could. And, after all, there was nothing worth staying for. That was the other reason. The place was ghastly. Really ghastly. And I didn't think I could stay there and serve with any honor to myself. So I applied to join the Waffen-SS, and the rest you know." He helped himself to another one of my cigarettes.

"There was another officer at the camp," I said. "Friedrich Warzok. Do you remember him?"

"I remember Warzok," he said. "He was Wilhaus's man."

"I'm a private detective," I explained. "I've been asked by his wife to see if I can find out if he's alive or dead. She wants to remarry."

"Sensible woman. Warzok was a pig. They all were." He shook his head. "She must be a pig, too, if she was ever married to that bastard."

"So you never met her."

"You mean she's not a pig?" He smiled. "Well, well. No, I never met her. I knew he was married. Matter of fact, he was always telling us how good-looking his wife was. But he never brought her to live there. At least not while I was there. Unlike Wilhaus. He had his wife and little daughter living there. Can you believe it? I wouldn't have had a wife and child of mine within ten miles of that place. Almost everything unpleasant you've heard about Warzok is likely to be true." He laid his cigarette in the ashtray, put his hands behind his head, and leaned back in his chair. "How can I help?"

"In March 1946, Warzok was living in Austria. His wife thinks he might have used an old comrades' network to get away. Since then, she's heard nothing."

"She should count herself lucky."

"She's a Roman Catholic," I said. "She's been told by Cardinal Josef Frings that she can't remarry without some evidence that Warzok is dead."

"Cardinal Frings, eh? He's a good man, that Cardinal Frings." He smiled. "You won't hear anyone in this place say anything bad about Frings. He and Bishop Neuhausler are the ones trying hardest to get us out of here."

"So I believe," I said. "All the same, I was hoping that I might get some information from you that might enable me to find out what happened to him."

"What sort of information?"

"Oh, I don't know. What kind of man he was. If you ever discussed what might happen after the war. If he'd ever mentioned what plans he had."

"I told you. Warzok was a pig."

"Can you tell me any more than that?"

"You want details?"

"Please. Anything at all."

He shrugged. "Like I said, when I was there, Lemberg-Janowska was just another labor camp. And there were only so many workers that I could use in the factory before they started to get in one another's way. Nevertheless they kept sending me more and more. Thousands of Jews. At first we transported our surplus Jews to Belzec. But after a while we were told that this couldn't happen anymore and that we'd have to deal with them ourselves. To me it was quite clear what this meant, and I tell you frankly that I wanted nothing to do with it. So I volunteered for front-line duty. But even before I had left, Warzok and Rokita—he was another of Wilhaus's creatures—were turning the place into an extermination camp. But nothing on the industrial scale of some other places, like Birkenau. There were no gas chambers at Janowska. Which left bastards like Wilhaus and Warzok with something of a problem. How to kill the camp's surplus Jews. So Jews were taken to some hills behind the residential camp and shot. You could hear the firing squads in the factory. All day that went on. And sometimes part of the night. They were the lucky ones. The ones who were shot. It soon turned out that Wilhaus and Warzok enjoyed killing people. And as well as killing large numbers of Jews by firing squads, these two started killing for their own amusement. Some people get up in the morning and exercise. Warzok's idea of exercise involved walking around the camp with a pistol and shooting people indiscriminately. Sometimes he hanged women up by their hair and used them for target practice. For him, killing was like lighting a cigarette, having a coffee, or blowing his nose. Something utterly commonplace. He was an animal. He hated me. They both did, he and Wilhaus. Wilhaus told Warzok to think up some new ways of killing Jews. So Warzok did just that. And after a while they all had their favorite ways of killing people. After I left, I believe they even had a hospital for medical experimentation. Using Jewish women for research into various clinical procedures.

"Anyway, what I heard was this. That the camp was liquidated in the last weeks of 1943. The Red Army didn't liberate Lvov until July 1944. Many of the people at Janowska were sent to the concentration camp at Majdanek. If you want to find out what happened to Warzok, you'll need to speak to some of the other men who worked at Janowska. Men like Wilhelm Rokita. There was a man called Wepke—I can't remember his Christian name—only that he was a Gestapo Kommissar and that he was friendly with Warzok. Warzok was also friendly with two fellows from the SD. A Scharführer Rauch and an Oberwachtmeister Kepich. They could be alive or dead. I have no idea."

"Warzok was last seen in Ebensee, near Salzburg," I said. "His wife says he was being helped to escape by the old comrades. The ODESSA."

Gebauer shook his head. "No, it wouldn't have been the ODESSA," he said. "The ODESSA and the Comradeship are two very different things. The ODESSA is largely an American-run organization, not German. At the bottom level, yes, it uses a lot of the same people who work for the Comradeship, but at the top it's

CIA. The CIA set it up to help some Nazis escape when they outlived their usefulness as anticommunist agents. And I can't see that Warzok would have been much good as a CIA agent. For a start, he knew nothing about intelligence matters. If he ever got away it's the Comradeship, or the Web as it's sometimes called, who would have helped. You'd have to ask one of the spiders where he might have gone."

I chose my next words carefully. "My late wife was always afraid of spiders," I said. "Really afraid. Every time she found one I would have to go and deal with it. The curious thing is that now she's gone, I never see a spider. I wouldn't know where to look for one. Would you?"

Gebauer grinned. "He really doesn't speak a word of German," he said, referring to the guard. "It's all right." Then he shook his head. "One hears things in here about the Comradeship. To be frank, I don't know how reliable any of this is. After all, none of us ever managed to escape. We got caught and banged up in this place. It also occurs to me that what you're doing could be dangerous, Herr Gunther. Very dangerous. It's one thing to avail yourself of a secret escape route, it's quite another to ask questions about such a thing. Have you considered the risks you are running? Yes, even you, a man who was in the SS himself. After all, you wouldn't be the first SS man to cooperate with the Jews. There's a fellow in Linz, a Nazi hunter by the name of Simon Wiesenthal, who uses an SS informer."

"I'll take my chances," I said.

"If you were looking to go missing in Germany," Gebauer said carefully, "the best thing to do would be to go and see the experts. The Bavarian Red Cross are very good at finding missing persons. I believe they also have some expertise in achieving the opposite result. Their offices are in Munich, are they not?"

I nodded. "Wagmullerstrasse," I said.

"There you will have to seek out a priest called Father Gotovina and show him a one-way ticket for any local destination with the letter S printed twice in a row. Peissenberg, perhaps. Kassel if you were near there. Or Essen, perhaps. You must cross out all of the other letters on the rail ticket so that SS are the only letters remaining. When you speak to this priest or anyone else in the Comradeship for the first time, you must hand this ticket over. At the same time, you need to ask if he can recommend anywhere to stay in the place you bought a ticket for. That's really all I know. Except for one thing: You will be asked some apparently innocent questions. If he asks what your favorite hymn is, you are to say 'How Great Thou Art.' I don't know the hymn myself, but I do know the tune. It's more or less the same tune as the Horst Wessel Song."

I started to thank him but he shrugged it off. "I might need your help some day, Herr Gunther."

I hoped he was wrong. But then again it's just a job, so maybe I would help him if he ever asked for my help. He'd been unlucky, that was all. For one thing, there was another officer, an SS Lieutenant Colonel Peiper, who had been in charge of that Waffen-SS unit at Malmedy. Executing the prisoners had been Peiper's call, not Gebauer's. For another—at least from what I'd read in the newspapers—the unit had already taken a lot of casualties and were under a lot of pressure. Under those circumstances, giving Fritz Gebauer a life sentence seemed a little harsh, to say the least. Gebauer was right. What choice did they have? Surrendering in a theater of war like the Ardennes was like asking a burglar to look after your house while you were on holiday. On the Russian front there was no one who expected to be take prisoner. Most of the time we shot theirs and they shot ours. I had been one of the lucky ones. Gebauer hadn't, and that was all there was to it. War was like that.

I skipped out of Landsberg feeling like Edmond Dantès after a thirteen-year stretch in the Château d'If, and drove quickly back to Munich as if a fortune in gold and jewels awaited me at my office.

Prisons affect me like that. Just a couple of hours in the cement and I'm looking for a hacksaw. I hadn't been back very long when the phone rang. It was Korsch.

"Where have you been?" he asked. "I've been ringing you all morning."

"It's a nice day," I said. "I thought I'd go to the English Garden. Have an ice cream. Pick some flowers." That was what I felt like doing. Something ordinary and innocent and outdoors where you didn't breathe the smell of men all day. I kept thinking about Gebauer, younger than me and facing life in prison, unless the bishop and the cardinal came through for him and the others. What wouldn't Fritz Gebauer have given for a fistful of ice cream and a walk to the Chinese pagoda? "How did you make out with the Amis?" I asked Korsch, stabbing a cigarette into my mouth, and scarping a match along the underside of my desk drawer. "Anything on Janowska and Warzok?"

"Apparently the Soviets set up a special commission of inquiry into the camp," he said.

"Isn't that a little unusual? Why'd they do something like that?"

"Because while there were German officers and NCOs running the camp," said Korsch, "it was largely Russian POWs who had volunteered for service with the SS who did most of the killing. I say most and I mean most. With them it was all about numbers. Killing as many as they could as quickly as possible because that's what they were told to do, on pain of death. But with our old comrades, the officers, it was something else. For them killing was a pleasure. There's very little in the file about Warzok. Most of the witness statements are about the camp's factory commandant, Fritz Gebauer. He sounds like a right bastard, Bernie."

"Tell me more about him," I said, feeling my stomach turn into a pit.

"This sweetheart liked to strangle women and children with his bare hands," said Korsch. "And he liked to tie people up and put them in barrels of water overnight, in winter. The only reason he's doing life for what happened at Malmedy is that the Ivans won't let the witnesses come to the American Zone for a trial. But for that, he'd probably have been hanged like Weiss and Eichelsdorfer, and some of those others."

Martin Weiss had been the last commandant at Dachau, and Johann Eichelsdorfer had been in charge at Kaufering IV—the largest of the camps near Landsberg. Knowing that the man I had spent the morning with, a man I had considered to be a decent sort of fellow, was, in reality, as bad as these two others left me feeling disappointed not just with him, but also with myself. I don't know why I was so surprised. If there was one thing I had learned in the war it was that decent, law-abiding family men were capable of the most bestial acts of murder and brutality.

"Are you still there, Bernie?"

"I'm still here."

"After Gebauer left Janowska in 1943, the camp was run by Wilhaus and Warzok, and any pretense that it was a labor camp was abandoned. Mass exterminations, medical experiments, you name it, they did it at Janowska. Wilhaus and some of the others were hanged by the Russians. As a matter of fact they filmed it. Sat them on a truck with halters around their necks and then drove the truck away. Warzok and some of the others are still at large. Wilhaus's wife, Hilde—she's wanted by the Russians. So is an SS captain called Gruen. A Gestapo Kommissar called Wepke. And a couple of NCOs, Rauch and Kepich."

"What did Wilhaus's wife do?"

"She murdered prisoners to amuse her daughter. When the Russians got close, Warzok and the rest moved to Plaszow, and then Gross-Rosen—a quarry camp near Breslau. Others went to Majdanek and Mauthausen. After that, who knows? If you ask me, Bernie, looking for Warzok will be like looking for a pin in a hayloft. If I were you, I'd be inclined to forget about it and get myself another client."

"Then it's lucky she asked me and not you."

"She must smell really nice."

"Better than you and me."

"It goes without saying, Bernie," said Korsch. "The federal government prefers us to keep downwind of the Amis. So as not to scare off the new investment that's coming here. That's why they want all these war crimes investigations to finish. So we can all get on and make some money. You know, I bet I could get you fixed up with something here at the paper, Bernie. They could use a good private investigator."

"For those undercover stories that won't spoil anyone's breakfast? Is that it?"

"Communists," said Korsch. "That's what people want to read about. Spy stories. Stories about life in the Russian Zone and how terrible it is. Plots to destabilize the new federal government."

"Thanks, Friedrich, but no," I said. "If that's really what they want to read about, I'd probably end up investigating myself."

I put the phone down and lit a cigarette with the butt of the one I was finishing, to help me think things over in detail. It's what I do when I work a case that starts to interest not just me but other people as well. People like Friedrich Korsch, for example. Some people smoke to relax. Others to stimulate their imaginations, or to concentrate. With me it was a combination of all three at once. And the more I thought about it the more my imagination was telling me not only that I'd just been warned off a case, but also that this had been swiftly followed up by an attempt to buy me off, with a job offer. I took another drag on the cigarette and then stubbed it out in the ashtray. Nicotine was a drug, wasn't it? I was smoking way too much. It was a crazy idea. Korsch trying to warn me and then buy me off? That was the drug talking, surely?

I went out to get a coffee and a cognac. They were drugs, too. Maybe that way I'd see things differently. It was worth a try.

## THIRTEEN

Wagmullerstrasse ran onto Prinzregentenstrasse, between the National Museum and the House of Art. On the English Garden side, the House of Art was now being used as an American Officers' Club. The National Museum had just reopened following extensive repairs and now, once again, it was possible to see the city treasures that no one really wanted to look at. Wagmullerstrasse was in a district of Munich called Lehel, which was full of quiet residential streets built for the well-to-do during Germany's industrial revolution. Lehel was still quiet but only because half of the houses were in ruins. The other half had been or were still being repaired and lived in by Munich's new well-to-do. Even out of uniform the new well-to-do were easily recognizable by their buzz-cut hairstyles; their busy, gum-chewing mouths; their loud braying laughs; their impossibly wide trousers; their handsome cigarette cases; their sensible English shoes; their Kodak folding Brownies; and, above all, their semi-aristocratic air—that sense of absolute precedence they all gave off like cheap cologne.

The Red Cross building was four stories of yellowish Danubian limestone set between a rather fancy-looking shop selling Nymphenburger porcelain and a private art gallery. Inside, everything was in motion. Typewriters were being punched, filing cabinets opened and closed loudly, forms being filled out, people coming down stairs, and people going up in an open-grille elevator. Four years after the end of the war the Red Cross was still dealing with the human fallout. Just to make things more interesting they had let the painters in, and I didn't have to look at the ceiling to know they were painting it white—there were spots of it all over the brown linoleum floor. Behind a desk that looked more like a counter in a beer hall, a woman with braids and a face as pink as a ham was brushing off an old man who might or might not have been a Jew. I never could tell the difference.

Most of her problem with him related to the fact that only half of what he was saying to her was in German. The rest, which was mostly spoken at the floor, just in case she understood the swear words, was in Russian. I buckled on my armor, mounted my white horse, and leveled my lance at the ham.

"Perhaps I can be of assistance," I said to her before speaking to the man in Russian. It turned out that he was looking for his brother who had been in the concentration camp at Treblinka, then Dachau, before finally ending up in one of the Kaufering camps. He'd run out of money. He needed to get to the DP camp at Landsberg. He had been hoping that the Red Cross would help him. The way the ham was looking at him I wasn't sure they would, so I gave the old man five marks and told him how to get to the railway station on Bayerstrasse. He thanked me profusely and then left me to be eaten by the ham.

"What was all that about?" she demanded.

I told her.

"Since 1945, a total of sixteen million tracing requests have been submitted to the Red Cross," she said, answering the accusation that lay behind my eyes. "One point nine million returnees have been interviewed about missing persons. We're still missing sixty-nine thousand prisoners of war, one point one million members of the Wehrmacht, and almost two hundred thousand German civilians.

That means there are proper procedures to be observed. If we gave five marks to every heel who walks in off the street with a sob story we'd be broke in no time. You'd be surprised how many walk in here looking for their long-lost brother when what they're really looking for is just the price of a drink."

"Then it's very lucky he took five marks from me instead of from the Red Cross," I said. "I can afford to lose it." I smiled warmly at her but she wasn't near being thawed.

"What can I do for *you*?" she asked coolly.

"I'm looking for Father Gotovina."

"Do you have an appointment?"

"No," I said. "I thought I'd save him the trouble of meeting me at the Praesidium."

"The Police Praesidium?" Like most Germans the ham was still apprehensive where the police were concerned. "On Ettstrasse?"

"With the stone lion in front of the entrance," I said. "That's right. Have you been there?"

"No," she said, keen to be rid of me now. "Take the elevator to the second floor. You'll find Father Gotovina in the Passport and Visa Section. Room twenty-nine."

At first glance the man operating the elevator looked not much older than me. It was only after the second glance, when you'd finished taking in the one leg and the scar on his face that the third glance told you he was probably not much more than twenty-five. I got in the car with him, and said "two" and he went into action with the well-practiced air and grim determination of a man operating a 20mm Flak 38—the gun with the foot pedals and the collapsing seat. Stepping out onto the second floor I almost glanced up to see if he'd hit anything. It was just as well I didn't, because if I had I'd have tripped over the man painting a skirting board that ran the length of a corridor as big as a bowling alley.

The Passport and Visa Section was like a state within a state.

More typewriters, more filing cabinets, more forms to be filled, and more meaty-looking women. Each of them looked like she ate a Red Cross parcel, including the wrapping paper and string, for breakfast. There was a guy standing around beside a 50mm camera with a trip and hood. Outside the window there was a good view of the Angel of Peace monument on the other side of the River Isar. Erected in 1899 to commemorate the Franco-Prussian War, it hadn't meant much then and it certainly didn't mean much now.

Being a detective I spotted Father Gotovina within a few seconds of going through the door. There were lots of things that gave it away. The black suit, the black shirt, the crucifix hanging around his neck, the little white halo of collar. His was not a face that made you think of Jesus so much as Pontius Pilate. The thick, dark eyebrows were the only hair on his head. The skull looked like the rotating dome roof on the Göttingen Observatory, and each lobeless ear resembled a demon's wing. His lips were as thick as his fingers, and his nose as broad and hooked as the beak on a giant octopus. He had a mole on his left cheek that was the size and color of a five-pfennig piece and walnut-brown eyes, like the walnut on the grip of a Walther PPK. One of them picked me out like a shoemaker's awl and he came over, almost as if he could smell the cop on my shoes. It could just as easily have been the cognac on my breath. But I didn't figure him for the teetotaler type any more than I could picture him singing in the Vienna Boys Choir. If the Medici had still been siring popes, Father Gotovina would have been what one looked like.

"Can I help you?" he asked in a voice like liquid furniture polish, with lips stretched tight across teeth that were as white as his collar in what, among the Holy Inquisition anyway, must have passed for a smile.

"Father Gotovina?" I asked.

He nodded, almost imperceptibly.

"I'm going to Peissenberg," I told him, showing the rail ticket I had bought earlier. "I wondered if you know anyone there I could stay with."

He glanced at my ticket for only a moment, but his eyes did not miss the way the name "Peissenberg" had been altered.

"I believe there's a very good hotel there," he said. "The Berggasthof Greitner. But it's probably closed right now. You're a little early for the ski season, Herr . . . ?"

"Gunther, Bernhard Gunther."

"Of course there's a fine church there which, incidentally, affords a remarkably extensive and panoramic view of the Bavarian Alps. As it happens the priest there is a friend of mine. He might be able to help you. If you come by the Holy Ghost Church at about five o'clock this afternoon, I'll provide you with a letter of introduction. But I warn you, he's a keen musician. If you spend any time in Peissenberg he'll dragoon you into the church choir. Have you singing hymns for your supper, so to speak. Do you have a favorite hymn, Herr Gunther?"

"A favorite? Yes, probably 'How Great Thou Art.' I think it's the tune I like more than anything."

He closed his eyes in a poor affectation of piety and added, "Yes, that is a lovely hymn, isn't it?" He nodded. "Until five o'clock, then."

I left him and walked out of the building. I went south and west, across the city center, vaguely in the direction of the Holy Ghost Church but more precisely in the direction of the Hofbrauhaus, in the Platzl. I needed a beer.

With its red mansard roof, pink walls, arched windows, and heavy wooden doors, the Hofbrauhaus had a folkish, almost fairytale air, and whenever I passed it, I half expected to see the Hunchback of Notre Dame swinging down from the roof to rescue some hapless Gypsy girl from the center of the cobbled square (assuming there were any Gypsies still left in Germany). But it could just as easily have been the Jew Süss swinging down into the medieval marketplace. Munich is that kind of a town. Small-minded. Even a bit rustic and primitive. It's no accident that Adolf Hitler got started here, in another beer hall, the Burgerbraukeller, just a few blocks away from the Hofbrauhaus on Kaufingerstrasse. But Hitler's echo was only part of the reason I seldom went to the Burgerbrau. The main reason was I didn't like Löwenbräu beer. I preferred the darker beer at the Hofbrauhaus. The food there was better, too. I ordered Bavarian potato soup, followed by pork knuckles with potato dumplings and homemade bacon-cabbage salad. I'd been saving my meat coupons.

Several beers and a sweet yeast pudding later, I went along to the Holy Ghost Church on Tal. Like everything else in Munich, it had taken a battering. The roof and vaulting had been completely destroyed and the interior decoration devastated. But the pillars in the nave had been re-erected, the church reroofed and repaired sufficiently for services to be resumed. There was one under way as I entered the half-empty church. A priest who wasn't Gotovina stood facing the still impressive high altar, his fluting voice echoing around the church's skeletal interior like Pinocchio's when he was trapped inside the whale. I felt my lip and nose curl with Protestant abhorrence. I disliked the idea of a God who could put up with being worshipped in this reedy, singsong, Roman way. Not that I ever called myself a Protestant. Not since I learned how to spell Friedrich Nietzsche.

I found Father Gotovina under what remained of the organ loft, next to the bronze tomb-slab of Duke Ferdinand of Bavaria. I followed him to a wooden confessional that looked more like an ornate photo booth. He swept aside a gray curtain and stepped inside. I did the same on the other side, sat down and knelt beside the screen, the way God liked it I presumed. There was just enough light in the confessional to see the top of the priest's billiard-ball head. Or at least a patch of it—a small, shiny square of skin that looked like the lid on a copper kettle. In the half darkness and close confines of the confessional his voice sounded particularly infernal. He probably laid it on a greased rack and left it to smoke over a hickory-wood fire when he went to bed at night.

"Tell me a little about you, Herr Gunther?" he said.

"Before the war I was a Kommissar in KRIPO," I told him. "Which is how I came to join the SS. I went to Minsk as a member of the special action group commanded by Arthur Nebe." I left out my service with the War Crimes Bureau and my time as an intelligence officer with the Abwehr. The SS had never liked the Abwehr. "I held the rank of SS Oberleutnant."

"There was a lot of good work done in Minsk," said Father Gotovina. "How many did you liquidate?"

"I was part of a police battalion," I said. "Our responsibility was dealing with NKVD murder squads."

Gotovina chuckled. "There's no reason to be coy with me, Oberleutnant. I'm on your side. And it makes no difference to me whether you killed five or five thousand. Either way, you were about God's work. The Jew and the Bolshevik will always be synonymous. It's only the Americans who are too stupid to see that."

Outside the booth, in the church, the choir started to sing. I'd judged them too harshly. They were much sweeter on the ear than Father Gotovina.

"I need your help, Father," I said.

"Naturally. That's why you're here. But we have to walk before we can run. I have to be satisfied that you are what you say you are, Herr Gunther. A few simple questions should suffice. Just to put my mind at rest. For example, can you tell me your oath of loyalty, as an SS man?"

"I can tell you it," I said. "But I never had to take it. As a member of KRIPO my membership in the SS was more or less automatic."

"Let me hear you say it, anyway."

"All right." The words almost stuck in my throat. "I swear to you, Adolf Hitler, as Führer and Reich Chancellor, loyalty and bravery. I vow to you, and to those you have named to command me, obedience unto death, so help me God."

"You say it so nicely, Herr Gunther. Just like a catechism. And yet you never had to take the oath yourself?"

"Things were always rather different in Berlin from the rest of Germany," I said. "People were always a little more relaxed about such matters. But I can't imagine I'm the first SS man to tell you he never took the oath."

"Perhaps I'm just testing you," he said. "To see how honest you're being. Honesty's best, don't you think? After all, we're in a church. It wouldn't do to lie in here. Think of your soul."

"These days I prefer not to think about it at all," I said. "At least not without a drink in my hand." That was being honest, too.

"*Te absolvo,* Herr Gunther," he said. "Feeling better now?"

"Like something just got lifted off my shoulders," I said. "Dandruff, probably."

"That's good," he said. "A sense of humor will be important to you in your new life."

"I don't want a new life."

"Not even through Christ?" He laughed again. Or perhaps he was just clearing his throat of some finer feelings. "Tell me more about Minsk," he said. His tone had changed. It was less playful. More businesslike. "When did the city fall to German forces?"

"June 28, 1941."

"What happened then?"

"Do you know, or do you want to know?"

"I want to know that *you* know," he said. "To make a little peephole into your persona to see if it is or it isn't non grata. Minsk."

"Do you want to know details or broad brushstrokes?"

"Paint the house, why don't you?"

"All right. Within hours of the occupation of the city, forty thousand men and boys were assembled for registration. They were kept in a field, surrounded by machine guns and floodlights. They were all races. Jews, Russians, Gypsies, Ukrainians. After a few days, Jewish doctors, lawyers, and academics were asked to identify themselves. Intelligentsia, so-called. Two thousand did. And I believe the same two thousand were then marched into a nearby wood and shot."

"And naturally you didn't play any part in that," said Father Gotovina. He spoke as if he had been speaking to a crybaby.

"As a matter of fact I was still in the city. Investigating another atrocity. This one committed by the Ivans themselves."

In the church service proceeding outside the confessional, the priest said "Amen." I muttered it myself. Somehow it seemed appropriate when I was talking about Minsk.

"How soon after your arrival was the Minsk ghetto established?" asked Gotovina.

"Less than a month," I said. "July 20."

"And how was the ghetto created?"

"There were about three dozen streets, I believe, including the Jewish cemetery. It was surrounded by thick rows of barbed wire and several watchtowers. And one hundred thousand people were transported there from places as far afield as Bremen and Frankfurt."

"In what way was Minsk an unusual ghetto?"

"I'm not sure I understand the question, Father. There was nothing usual about what happened there."

"What I mean to say is, where did most of the Jews in that ghetto meet their deaths? Which camp?"

"Oh, I see. No. I believe most of the people in Minsk were killed in Minsk. Yes, that's what made it unusual. When the ghetto was liquidated in October 1943, there were just eight thousand left. Of the original one hundred thousand. I'm afraid I have no idea what happened to the eight thousand."

This was all proving much more difficult than I could have supposed. Most of what I had told him about Minsk I knew from my service with the War Crimes Bureau and, in particular, the case of Wilhelm Kube. In July 1943, Kube, the SS general commissioner in charge of White Ruthenia, which included Minsk, had made a formal complaint to the Bureau, alleging that Eduard Strauch, commander of the local SD, had personally murdered seventy Jews who were employed by Kube, and pocketed their valuables. I was charged with the investigation. Strauch, who was certainly guilty of the murders—and many others besides—had made a counterallegation against Kube, that his boss had let more than five thousand Jews escape liquidation. Strauch turned out to be right but he had not expected to be vindicated. And probably he murdered Kube, with a bomb planted under his bed, in September 1943, before I had a chance actually to form any conclusions. Despite my best endeavors, the crime was quickly blamed on Kube's Russian maid, who was just as quickly hanged. Suspecting Strauch's complicity in Kube's murder I then started another investigation only to be ordered by the Gestapo to drop the case. I refused. Not long afterward I found myself transferred to the Russian front. But none of this I felt able to reveal to Father Gotovina. Certainly he did not want to hear of how I had sympathized with poor Kube. There but for the grace of God.

"Come to think of it," I said, "I do remember what happened to those eight thousand Jews. Six thousand went to Sobibor. And two thousand were rounded up and killed at Maly Trostinec."

"And we all lived happily ever after," said Gotovina. He laughed. "For someone who was only dealing with NKVD death squads, you seem to know an awful lot about what happened at Minsk, Herr Gunther. You know what I think? I think you're just being modest. For the last five years you've had to hide your lamp under a basket. Just like it says in Luke chapter eleven, verses thirty-three to thirty-six."

"So you *have* read the Bible," I said, more than a little surprised.

"Of course," he said. "And now I'm ready to play the Good Samaritan. To help you. Money. A new passport. A weapon if you need one. A visa to wherever you want to go, just as long as it's Argentina. That's where most of our friends are, these days."

"As I told you already, Father," I said. "I don't want a new life."

"Then exactly what is it you do want, Herr Gunther?" I could hear him stiffening as he spoke.

"I'll tell you. These days I'm a private detective. I have a client who's looking for her husband. An SS man. She ought to have had a postcard from Buenos Aires by now, but she's heard nothing in more than three and a half years. So she's hired me to help find out what happened to him. The last time she saw him was in Ebensee, near Salzburg, in March 1946. He was already on the Web. In a safe house. Waiting for his new papers and tickets. She doesn't want to spoil anything for him. All she wants to know is if he's alive or dead. She'd like to remarry if it's the second. But not if it's the first. You see, the trouble is she's like you, Father. A good Roman Catholic."

"That's a nice story," he said.

"I liked it."

"Don't tell me." The laugh took on an altogether different persona. This one sounded a little unbalanced. "You're the schmuck she wants to marry."

I waited for him to finish laughing. Probably it was just shock. It's not every day you meet a priest who peels his lips back and lets it go like Peter Lorre.

"No, Father, it's exactly the way I told you. In that respect at least, I'm like a priest. People bring me their problems and I try to sort them out. The only difference is that I don't get much help from the guy on the high altar."

"Does this housewife have a name?"

"Her name is Britta Warzok. Her husband's name is Friedrich Warzok." I told him what I knew about Friedrich Warzok.

"I like him already," said Father Gotovina. "Three years without a word? He could very well be dead."

"To be honest, I don't think she's looking for good news."

"So why not tell her what she wants to hear?"

"That would be unethical, Father."

"It took a lot of guts speaking to me like this," he said quietly. "I admire that in a man. The Comradeship is, shall we say, easily alarmed. This business at Landsberg with the Red Jackets. It doesn't help. Not to mention the prospect of yet more executions. The war's been over for four years and the Amis are still trying to hang people, like some stupid sheriff in a cheap Western."

"Yes, I can see why that would make some of my old comrades nervous," I said. "There's nothing quite like the gallows to make a man swallow his scruples."

"I'll see what I can find out," he said. "Meet me at the art gallery next to the Red Cross the day after tomorrow. At three p.m. If I'm late you'll have something to occupy your attention."

People started to walk by the confessional. Father Gotovina drew back the curtain and went out, mingling with the faithful. I waited for a minute and then followed, crossing myself for no other reason than a wish not to be noticed. It felt silly. One more type of peculiar human behavior for the anthropology textbooks. Like rocking in front of a wall, kneeling down in the direction of a Middle Eastern city, or sticking your arm straight out in front of you and shouting "Hail Victory." None of it meant anything except a lot of trouble for someone else. If there's one thing history has taught me to believe it is that it's dangerous to believe in anything very much. Especially in Germany. The trouble with us is that we take belief much too seriously.

# FOURTEEN

A couple of days went by. A southerly wind bearing an area of intense high pressure started to bear down on the city. At least that's what the weather man on Radio Munich said. He said it was the Föhn, which meant the wind was charged with a lot of static electricity, on account of it having already blown across the Alps before it got to us. Walking around Munich you could feel the warm, dehydrated wind drying your face and making your eyes water. Or maybe I was just hitting the bottle too much.

Americans took the Föhn more seriously than anyone, of course, and kept their children indoors to avoid it, almost as if it had been carrying something more lethal than a few positively charged ions. Maybe they knew something the rest of us didn't. Anything was possible now that the Ivans had exploded their atomic bomb the previous month. Possibly there were all sorts of things in the Föhn to really worry about. Either way, the Föhn served a very useful purpose. Müncheners blamed the Föhn for all kinds of things. They were always grousing about it. Some claimed it made their asthma worse, others that it gave them rheumatic pains, and quite a few that it caused them to have headaches. If the milk tasted funny, that was the Föhn. And if the beer came out flat, that was the Föhn, too. Where I lived, in Schwabing, the woman downstairs claimed that the Föhn interfered with the signal on her wireless radio. And on the tram I even heard a man claim he'd got into a fight because of the

Föhn. It made a change from blaming things on the Jews, I suppose. The Föhn certainly made people seem cranky and more irritable than usual. Maybe that's how Nazism got started here in the first place. Because of the Föhn. I never heard of people trying to overthrow a government who weren't cranky and irritable.

That was the kind of day it was when I went back to Wagmullerstrasse and stood in front of the art gallery window next door to the offices of the Red Cross. I was earlier than the appointed time. I'm usually early for things. If punctuality is the virtue of kings then I'm the kind of person who likes to get there an hour or two before, to look for a landmine underneath the red carpet.

The gallery was called Oscar & Shine. Most of the city's art dealers were in the Brienner Strasse district. They bought and sold Secessionists and Munich Post-Impressionists. I know that because I read it on a Brienner Strasse gallery window, once. This particular gallery looked a little different from those others. Especially inside. Inside it looked like one of those Bauhaus buildings the Nazis used to frown upon. Of course it wasn't just the open staircase and the freestanding walls that looked futuristic. The paintings on exhibition were similarly modern-looking, which is to say they were as easy on the eye as a sharp stick.

I know what I like. And most of what I like isn't art at all. I like pictures and I like ornaments. Once I even owned a French Spelter banjo-lady. It wasn't a sculpture, just a piece of junk that sat on my mantelpiece next to a photograph of Gath, my hometown in the land of the Philistines. If I want a picture to speak to me, I'll go watch Maureen O'Sullivan in a Tarzan movie.

While I shambled around the gallery I was closely tracked by the periscope eye of a woman in a wool black tailor-made, which, thanks to the Föhn, she was probably regretting having worn. She was thin, a little too thin, and the long, ivory cigarette-holder she was carrying might just as easily have been one of her bony, ivory-colored fingers. Her hair was long and brown and bushy, and it was gathered up at the back of her fine head in what looked like a twenty-five-pfennig loaf. She came up to me, her arms folded defensively in front of her, in case she needed to run me through with one of her pointy elbows, and nodded at the painting I was appraising with careful discrimination and good taste, like some queeny connoisseur.

"What do you think?" she asked, waving her cigarette holder at the wall.

I tilted my head to one side in the vague hope that a slightly different perspective on the picture might let me ante up like Bernard Berenson. I tried to picture the crazy sonofabitch painting it but kept on thinking of a drunken chimpanzee. I opened my mouth to say something. Then closed it again. There was a red line going one way, a blue line going the other, and a black line trying to pretend it had nothing much to do with either of them. It was a work of modern art all right. That much I could see. What's more, it had obviously been executed with the craft and skill of one who had studied licorice-making carefully. Putting it on the wall probably gave the flies escaping the Föhn through the open window something to think about. I looked again and found that it really spoke to me. It said, "Don't laugh, but some idiot will pay good money for this." I pointed at the wall and said, "I think you should get that patch of damp seen to, before it spreads."

"It's by Kandinsky," she said, without batting a garden rake of an eyelash. "He was one of the most influential artists of his generation."

"And who were his influences? Johnnie Walker? Or Jack Daniel's?"

She smiled.

"There," I said. "I knew you could do it if you tried. Which is more than I can say for Kandinsky."

"Some people like it," she said.

"Well, why didn't you say so? I'll take two."

"I wish you *would* buy one," she said. "Business has been a little slow today."

"It's the Föhn," I told her.

She unbuttoned her jacket and flapped herself with half of it. I sort of enjoyed that myself. Not just the perfumed breeze she made for us but also the low-cut silk blouse she was wearing underneath. If I'd been an artist I'd have called it an inspiration. Or whatever artists call it when they see a girl's nipples pressing through her shirt like two chapel hat-pegs. She was worth a bit of charcoal and paper anyway.

"I suppose so," she said and blew a lipful of air and cigarette smoke at her own forehead. "Tell me, did you come in here to look or just to laugh?"

"Probably a bit of both. That's what Lord Duveen recommended, anyway."

"For an artless vulgarian, you're quite well informed, aren't you?"

"True decadence involves taking nothing too seriously," I said. "Least of all, decadent art."

"Is that really what you think of it? That it's decadent?"

"I'll be honest," I said. "I don't like it one little bit. But I'm delighted to see it exhibited without any interference from people who know as little about art as I do. Looking at it is like looking inside the head of someone who disagrees with you about nearly everything. It makes me feel uncomfortable." I shook my head sadly and sighed, "That's democracy, I guess."

Another customer came in. A customer chewing gum. He was wearing a pair of enormous brogues and carrying a folding Kodak Brownie. A real connoisseur. Someone with lots of money, anyway. The girl went to squire him around the pictures. And a little after that Father Gotovina showed up and we went out of the gallery, to the English Garden, where we sat down on a bench beside the Rumford

Monument. We lit cigarettes and ignored the warm wind in our faces. A squirrel came bounding along the path, like an escaped fur tippet, and stopped near us in the hope of some morsel. Gotovina flicked his match and then the toe of a well-polished black boot at the furry oscillation. The priest was obviously not a nature lover.

"I made a few inquiries regarding your client's husband," he said, hardly looking at me at all. In the bright afternoon sunshine his head was amber-colored, like a good bock beer, or maybe a *Doppel*. While he spoke, the cigarette stayed in his mouth, jerking up and down like a conductor's baton bringing to order the riotous orchestra of hydrangeas, lavender, gentian, and irises that was arrayed in front of him. I hoped they would do what they were told, just in case he tried to kick them the way he had tried to kick the squirrel.

"At the Ruprechtskirche, in Vienna," he said, "there's a priest who performs a similarly charitable function for old comrades like you. He's an Italian. Father Lajolo. He remembers Warzok only too well. It seems he turned up with a rail ticket for Güssing just after Christmas 1946. Lajolo got him to a safe house in Ebensee while they waited for a new passport and visa."

"A passport from whom?" I asked, out of curiosity.

"The Red Cross. The Vatican. I don't know for sure. One of the two, you can bet on that. The visa was for Argentina. Lajolo or one of his people went to Ebensee, handed over the papers, some money, and a rail ticket to Genoa. That was where Warzok was supposed to get on the boat for South America. Warzok and another old comrade. Only they never showed up. No one knows what happened to Warzok, but the other guy was found dead in the woods near Thalgau, a few months later."

"What was his name? His real name."

"SS Hauptsturmführer Willy Hintze. He was the former deputy chief of the Gestapo in a Polish town called Thorn. Hintze was in a shallow grave. Naked. He'd been shot through the back of the skull while kneeling on the edge of his grave. His clothes were tossed in on top of him. He'd been executed."

"Were Warzok and Hintze in the same safe house?"

"No."

"Did they know each other from before?"

"No. The first time they ever met would have been on the boat to Argentina. Lajolo figured both safe houses had been blown and closed them down. It was decided that what happened to Hintze had been what happened to Warzok. The Nakam had got them."

"The Nakam?"

"After 1945, the Jewish Brigade—volunteers from Palestine who had joined a special unit of the British army—was ordered by the fledgling Jewish army, the Haganah, to form a secret group of assassins. One group of assassins, based in Lublin, took the name of Nakam, a Hebrew word meaning 'vengeance.' Their sworn purpose was to avenge the deaths of six million Jews."

Father Gotovina pulled the cigarette from his lips as if to more effectively give them up to a curling sneer that ended by including his nostrils and his eyes. I daresay if there had been any muscle groups to control the ears, he would have brought them into it, too. The Croatian priest's sneer had Conrad Veidt beat into a poor second, and Bela Lugosi a sly, broken-necked third.

"No good thing cometh out of Israel," he said, sulfurously. "Least of all the Nakam. An early plan of the Nakam was to poison the reservoirs of Munich, Berlin, Nuremberg, and Frankfurt and murder several million Germans. You look disbelieving, Herr Gunther."

"It's just that there have been stories about Jews poisoning Christian wells since the Middle Ages," I said.

"I can assure you I'm perfectly serious. This one was for real. Luckily for you and me, the Haganah command heard about the plan and, pointing out the number of British and Americans who would have been killed, the Nakam was forced to abandon the plan." Gotovina laughed his psychopathic laugh. "Maniacs. And they wonder why we tried to eliminate the Jew from decent society."

He flicked his cigarette end at a hapless pigeon, crossed his legs, and adjusted the crucifix around his muscular neck before continuing with his explanation. It was like having a chat with Tomás de Torquemada.

"But the Nakam were not quite ready to abandon their plans to use poison on a large number of Germans," he said. "They devised a plan to poison a POW camp near Nuremberg where thirty-six thousand SS were interned. They broke into a bakery supplying bread to the camp and poisoned two thousand loaves. Mercifully this was many fewer than they had planned to poison. Even so, several thousand men were affected and as many as five hundred died. You can take my word for that. It's a matter of historical record." He crossed himself and then looked up as, momentarily, a cloud crossed the sun, placing us both in a little pool of shadow, like some damned souls from the pages of Dante.

"After that they stuck to murder, pure and simple. With the help of Jews in British and American intelligence they set up a documents center in Linz and Vienna and started to track down so-called war criminals, using the Jewish emigration organization as a cover. At first they followed men as they were released from POW camps. They were easy to watch, especially with tip-offs from the Allies. And then, when they were ready, they started with the executions. In the beginning they hanged a few. But one man survived and after that it was always the same modus operandi. The shallow grave, the bullet in the back of the head. As if they were seeking to copy what all those Order battalions had done in eastern Europe."

Gotovina allowed himself a thin smile of something close to admiration. "They've been very effective. The number of old comrades assassinated by the Nakam is between one and two thousand. We know this because some of our Vienna group managed to catch one of them and, before he died, he told them what I just told you. So you see, it's the kikes you have to be careful of now, Herr Gunther. Not the Brits, or the Amis. All they care about is communism, and on occasion, they've even helped to get our people out of Germany. No, it's the Jew boys you have to worry about, these days. Especially the ones who don't look like Jew boys. Apparently the one they caught and tortured in Vienna, he looked like the perfect Aryan. You know? Like Gustav Froelich's better-looking brother."

"So where does all this leave my client?"

"Weren't you listening, Gunther? Warzok's dead. If he was still alive he'd be doing the tango and that's a fact. If he was there, she'd have heard, believe me."

"What I mean is, where does all that leave her in the eyes of the Roman Catholic Church?"

Gotovina shrugged. "She waits a while longer and then petitions for a formal judicial process, to determine whether or not she is considered free to enter into a second marriage."

"A judicial process?" I said. "You mean with witnesses and stuff like that?"

Gotovina looked away in disgust. "Forget it, Gunther," he said. "The archbishop would have my collar if he knew even a tenth of what I just told you. So there's no way I'm ever repeating any of this. Not to a tribunal of canon law. Not to her. Not even to you." He stood up and stared down at me. With the sun behind him he looked hardly there at all, like a silhouette of a man. "And here's some free advice. Drop it now. Drop the whole case. The Comradeship doesn't like questions and they don't like sniffers—even sniffers who think they can get away with it because they once had a tattoo under their arms. People who ask too many questions about the Comradeship end up dead. Do I make myself clear, sniffer?"

"It's been a while since I was threatened by a priest," I said. "Now I know how Martin Luther felt."

"Luther nothing." Gotovina was beginning to sound more irate. "And don't contact me again. Not even if David Ben-Gurion asks you to dig a hole in his garden at midnight. Got that, sniffer?"

"Like it came from the Holy Inquisition with a nice little ribbon and a lead seal with Saint Peter's face on it."

"Yeah, but will it stick?"

"That's why it's lead, isn't it? So people stay warned?"

"I hope so. But you've got the face of a heretic, Gunther. That's a bad look for someone who needs to keep his nose out of things he should leave alone."

"You're not the first person to tell me that, Father," I said, standing up. I'm more equal to the task of being threatened when I'm on my feet. But Gotovina was right about my face. Seeing his basilica-like head, and his cross, and his collar made me want to go straight home and type out ninety-five theses to nail on his church door. I tried to appear grateful for what he had told me, even a little contrite, but I knew it would just come out looking recusant and unfearing. "But thanks anyway. I appreciate all your help and good advice. A little spiritual guidance is good for us all. Even unbelievers like myself."

"It would be a mistake not to believe me," he said coldly.

"I don't know what I believe, Father," I said. Now I was just being willfully obtuse. "Really, I don't. All I know is that life is better than anything I've seen before. And probably better than anything I'll see when I'm dead."

"That sounds like atheism, Gunther. Always a dangerous thing in Germany."

"That's not atheism, Father. That's just what we Germans call a worldview."

"Leave such things to God. Forget the world and mind your own business, if you know what's good for you."

I watched him walk as far as the edge of the park. The squirrel came back. The flowers relaxed. The pigeon shook its head and tried to pull itself together. The cloud shifted and the grass brightened up. "Saint Francis of Assisi he is not," I told them all. "But you probably knew that already."

## FIFTEEN

I went back to the office and telephoned the number Frau Warzok had given me. A low, growling, possibly female voice that was a little less guarded than Spandau Prison, answered and said that Frau Warzok was not at home. I left my name and number. The voice repeated them back to me without a mistake. I asked if I was speaking to the maid. The voice said she was the maid. I put the phone down and tried to picture her in my mind's eye, and each time she came out looking like Wallace Beery in a black dress, holding a feather duster in one hand and a man's neck in the other. I'd heard of German women disguising themselves as men in order to avoid being raped by the Ivans. But this was the first time I ever had the idea that some queer wrestler might have disguised himself as a lady's maid for the opposite reason.

An hour went by like so much traffic outside my office window. Several cars. A few trucks. A USMP motorcycle. They were all going slowly. People went in and out of the post office on the other side of the street. There was nothing very quick about what was happening in there, either. Anyone who had ever waited for a letter in Munich knew that in spades. The cabbie at the cabstand out front was having an even slower time of it than I was. But unlike me he could at least risk going to the kiosk for some cigarettes and an evening newspaper. I knew that if I did that I'd miss her call. After a while I decided to make the phone ring. I put on my jacket and walked out of the door, left it open, and headed for the washroom. When I got to the washroom door, I paused for several seconds and only imagined myself doing what I would have done in there; and then the telephone started to ring. It's an old detective's trick, only for some reason you never see it in the movies.

It was her. After the maid, she sounded like a choirboy. Her breathing was a little loud, like she'd been running.

"Did you come up a flight of stairs?" I asked.

"I'm a little nervous, that's all. Did you find out something?"

"Plenty. Do you want to come here again? Or shall I come by your house?" Her business card was in my fingertips. I put it up to my nose. There was a faint scent of lavender water on it.

"No," she said firmly. "I'd rather you didn't do that, if you don't mind. We have decorators here. It's a little difficult, right now. Everything is covered in dust sheets. No, why don't you meet me in the Walterspiel at the Hotel Vier Jahreszeiten."

"Are you sure they take marks there?" I asked.

"As a matter of fact they don't," she said. "But I'm paying so that needn't concern you, Herr Gunther. I like it there. It's the only place in Munich where they can mix a decent cocktail. And I've a feeling I'm going to need a stiff drink regardless of what you tell me. Shall we say in one hour?"

"I'll be there."

I put the phone down and worried a little about the alacrity with which she had forbidden me to come to the house in Ramersdorf. I was a little worried that there might be another reason she didn't want me there that wasn't necessarily connected with what was under my fingernails. That maybe she was holding out on me in some way. I resolved to check out her address in Bad Schachener Strasse as soon as our meeting was concluded. Maybe I would even follow her.

The hotel was just a few blocks south of me, on Maximilianstrasse, near the Residenztheater, which was still under reconstruction. From the outside it was big but unremarkable, which was remarkable given that the hotel had almost completely burned down, following a bombing raid in 1944. You had to hand it to Munich's construction workers. With enough bricks and overtime they could probably have rebuilt Troy.

I walked through the front door ready to give the place the benefit of my extensive hotel-keeping experience. Inside was lots of marble and wood, which matched the faces and expressions of the penguins working there. An American in uniform was complaining loudly in English about something to the concierge, who caught my eye in the vain hope that I might sock the Ami in the ear and make him pipe down a bit. For what they charged a night I thought he would probably just have to put up with it. An undertaker type in a cutaway coat came alongside me like a pilot fish and, bowing slightly from the hip, asked if he could help me with something. It's what the big hotels call Service, but to me it just looked officious, as if he was wondering why someone with shoulders like mine would have the nerve to even think I could go rub them with the kind of people they had in there. I smiled and tried to keep the knuckles out of my voice.

"Yes, thank you," I said. "I'm meeting someone in the restaurant. The Walterspiel."

"A guest in the hotel?"

"I don't believe so."

"You're aware that this is a foreign currency hotel, sir."

I liked it that he called me sir. It was decent of him. He probably threw it in because I'd had a bath that morning. And probably because I was a little too large for him to throw his weight at.

"I am aware of it, yes," I said. "I don't like it, now that you mention it. But I am aware of it. The person I'm meeting is aware of it, too. I mentioned it to her when she suggested this place on the telephone. And when I objected and said I could think of a hundred better places, she said it wouldn't be a problem. By which I assumed she meant that she was in possession of foreign currency. I haven't actually seen the color of her money yet, but when she gets here, how about you and I search her handbag, just so you can have some peace of mind when you see us drinking your liquor?"

"I'm sure that won't be necessary, sir," he said stiffly.

"And don't worry," I said. "I won't order anything until she actually shows up."

"From February next year, the hotel will be accepting deutschmarks," he said.

"Well, let's hope she gets here before then," I said.

"The Walterspiel is that way, sir. To your left."

"Thank you. I appreciate your help. I used to be in the hotel business myself. I was the house bull at the Adlon in Berlin for a while. But you know what? I think this place has got it beat for efficiency. No one at the Adlon would ever have had the presence of mind to ask someone like me if he could have afforded it or not. Wouldn't have crossed their minds. Keep it up. You're doing a fine job."

I went through to the restaurant. There was another doorway out onto Marstallstrasse and a row of silk-covered chairs for people waiting for cars. I took one look at the menu and the prices and then sat down on one of the chairs to await my client's arrival with the dollars, or foreign exchange coupons or whatever else she was planning to use when she handed over the ransom-money rates they were asking in the Walterspiel. The maître d' flicked his gaze on me for a second and asked if I would be dining that night. I said I hoped so and that was the end of it. Most of the jaundice in his eye was reserved for a large woman sitting on one of the other chairs. I say large but I really mean fat. That's what happens when you've been married for a while. You stop saying what you mean. That's the only reason people ever stay married. All successful marriages are based on some necessary hypocrisies. It's only the unsuccessful ones where people always tell the truth to each other.

The woman sitting opposite me was fat. She was hungry, too. I could tell that because she kept eating things she brought out of her handbag when she thought the maître d' wasn't looking: a biscuit, an apple, a piece of chocolate, another biscuit, a small sandwich. Food came forth from her handbag the way some women bring out a compact, a lipstick, and an eyeliner. Her skin was very pale and white and loose on the pink flesh underneath and looked like it had just been plucked clean of feathers. Big amber earrings hung off her skull like two toffees. In an emergency she'd probably have eaten them as well. Watching her eat a sandwich was like watching a hyena devour a leg of pork. Things just seemed to gravitate toward her strudel hole.

"I'm waiting for someone," she explained.

"Coincidence."

"My son works for the Amis," she said, thickly. "He's taking me to dinner. But I don't like to go in there until he comes. It's so expensive."

I nodded, not because I agreed with her but just to let her know I could. I had the idea that if I stopped moving for a while she would have eaten me, too.

"So expensive," she repeated. "I'm eating now so that I don't eat too much when we go in. It's such a waste of money, I think. Just for dinner." She started to eat another sandwich. "My son is the director of American Overseas Airlines, on Karlsplatz."

"I know it," I said.

"What do you do?"

"I'm a private detective."

Her eyes lit up, and for a moment, I thought she was going to hire me to look for a missing pie. So it was fortunate that this was the moment Britta Warzok chose to come through the Marstall-strasse door.

She was wearing a black full-length skirt, a white tailored jacket gathered at the waist, long black gloves, white patent high-heeled shoes, and a white hat that looked like it had been borrowed from a well-dressed Chinese coolie. It shaded the scars on her cheek very effectively. Around her neck were five strings of pearls and hooked over her arm was a bamboo-handle handbag that she opened while she was still greeting me and retrieved a five-mark note. The note went to the maître d', who greeted her with a subservience worthy of a courtier at the court of the electress of Hannover. While he was abasing himself even further, I glanced over her forearm at the contents of her bag. It was just long enough to see a bottle of Miss Dior, a Hamburger Kreditbank checkbook, and a .25-caliber automatic that looked like the little sister of the one I had in my coat pocket. I wasn't sure which I was more concerned about—the fact she banked in Hamburg or the nickel-plated rattle she was carrying.

I followed her into the restaurant in a slipstream of perfume, deferential nods, and admiring glances. I didn't blame anyone for looking. As well as the Miss Dior, she gave off an air of perfect self-assurance and poise, like a princess on her way to being crowned. I supposed it was her height that made her the automatic center of attention. It's difficult to look regal when you're no higher than a door handle. But it could just as easily have been her careful dress sense that got their attention. That and her natural beauty. It certainly wasn't anything to do with the guy who was walking behind her and holding the brim of his hat like it was the train of her gown.

We sat down. The maître d', who seemed to have met her before, handed us menus the size of kitchen doors. She said she wasn't all that hungry. I was, but for her sake I said I wasn't hungry either. It's difficult to tell a client that her husband is dead when your mouth is full of sausage and sauerkraut. We ordered drinks.

"Do you come here very often?" I asked her.

"Quite often, before the war."

"Before the war?" I smiled. "You don't look old enough."

"Oh, but I am," she said. "Do you flatter all your clients, Herr Gunther?"

"Just the ugly ones. They need it. You don't. Which is why I wasn't flattering you. I was stating a matter of fact. You don't look like you're more than thirty."

"I was just eighteen when I married my husband, Herr Gunther," she said. "In 1938. There now. I've told you how old I am. And I hope you feel ashamed of yourself at having added a year to my age. Especially that age. For another four months, I'm still in my twenties."

The drinks came. She had a brandy Alexander that matched her hat and jacket. I had a Gibson so that I could eat the onion. I let her drink some of her cocktail before I told her what I'd discovered. I told it straight, without any euphemisms or polite evasions, right down to the details about the Jewish assassination squad forcing Willy Hintze to dig his own grave and kneel down on the edge before being shot in the back of the head. After what she had told me in my office—about how she and her fiancé were hoping that if Warzok was alive he might be caught and extradited to a country where they hanged most of their Nazi war criminals—I was quite sure she could take it.

"And you think that's what happened to Friedrich?"

"Yes. The man I spoke to is more or less certain of it."

"Poor Friedrich," she said. "Not a very pleasant way to die, is it?"

"I've seen worse," I said. I lit a cigarette. "I would say I'm sorry but it hardly seems appropriate. And for a number of reasons."

"Poor, poor Friedrich," she said again. She finished her drink and ordered another for us both. Her eyes were looking moist.

"You say that like you almost mean it," I said. "Almost."

"Let's just say that he had his moments, shall we? Yes, in the beginning, he very definitely had his moments. And now he is dead." She took out her handkerchief and, very deliberately, pressed it into the corner of each eye.

"Knowing it is one thing, Frau Warzok. Proving it to the satisfaction of a church court is quite another. The Comradeship—the people who tried to help your husband—are not the kind to swear on anything except perhaps an SS dagger. The man I met made that quite clear to me in no uncertain terms."

"Nasty, eh?"

"Like a common wart."

"And dangerous."

"I wouldn't be at all surprised."

"Did he threaten you?"

"Yes, I suppose he did," I said. "But I wouldn't let it concern you at all. Being threatened is an occupational hazard for someone like me. I almost didn't notice it."

"Please be careful, Herr Gunther," she said. "I would not like to have you on my conscience."

The second round of drinks arrived. I finished my first one and placed the empty on the waiter's tray. The fat lady and her son who worked for American Overseas Airline came in and sat at the next table. I ate my cocktail onion quickly before she could ask for it. The son was German. But the wine-colored gabardine suit he wore looked like something out of *Esquire* magazine. Or maybe a Chicago nightclub. The jacket was oversize, with wide lapels and even wider shoulders, and the trousers were baggy and low on the crotch and narrowed dramatically at the ankle, as if to accentuate his brown and white shoes. His shirt was plain white, his tie an electric shade of pink. The whole ensemble was made complete by a double key chain of exaggerated length that hung from a narrow leather belt. Assuming she wouldn't have eaten it I imagined that he was probably the apple of his mother's eye. Not that he would have noticed given that his own eye was already crawling over Britta Warzok like an invisible tongue. The next second he was pushing his chair back, putting down his pillowcase-size napkin, standing up, and coming over to our table like maybe he knew her. Smiling as if his life depended on it and bowing stiffly, which looked all wrong in the easygoing suit he was wearing, he said:

"How are you, dear lady? How are you enjoying Munich?"

Frau Warzok regarded him blankly. He bowed again almost as if he hoped that the movement might jog her memory.

"Felix Klingerhoefer? Don't you remember? We met on the plane."

She started to shake her head. "I think you must be mistaking me for someone else, Herr—?"

I almost laughed out loud. The idea that Britta Warzok could have been mistaken for anyone, except perhaps one of the three Graces, was too absurd. Especially with those three scars on her face. Eva Braun would have been more forgettable.

"No, no," insisted Klingerhoefer. "There's no mistake."

Silently I agreed with him, thinking it rather clumsy of her to pretend to have forgotten his name like that, especially since he had just finished mentioning it. I remained silent, waiting to see how this would play out.

Ignoring him altogether now, Britta Warzok looked at me and said, "What were we talking about, Bernie?"

I thought it odd that it should have been that particular moment she chose to use my Christian name for the first time. I didn't look at her. Instead, I kept my eyes on Klingerhoefer in the hope it might encourage him to say something else. I even smiled at him, I think. Just so he wouldn't get the idea I was going to get rough with him.

But he was stranded like a dog on an ice floe. And bowing a third time, he muttered an apology and went back to his own table with his face turning the color of his strange suit.

"I think I was telling you about some of the odd people this job brings me into contact with," I said.

"Doesn't it just?" she whispered, glancing nervously in Klingerhoefer's direction. "Honestly. I don't know where on earth he got the idea that we were acquainted. I've never seen him before."

*Honestly.* I just love it when clients talk like that. Especially the females. All my doubts about her veracity were instantly removed, of course.

"In that suit, I think I'd have remembered him," she added, quite redundantly.

"No doubt about it," I said, watching the man. "You certainly would."

She opened her bag and took out an envelope that she handed to me. "I promised you a bonus," she said. "And here it is."

I glanced inside the envelope at some banknotes. There were ten of them and they were all red. It wasn't five thousand marks. But it was still more than generous. I told her it was too generous. "After all," I said. "The evidence doesn't help your cause very much."

"On the contrary," she said. "It helps me a great deal." She tapped her forehead with an immaculate fingernail. "In here. Even if it doesn't help my cause, as you say, you've no idea what a load off my mind this is. To know that he won't be coming back." And taking hold of my hand, she picked it up and kissed it with what looked like real gratitude. "Thank you, Herr Gunther. Thank you, very much."

"It's been a pleasure," I said.

I put the envelope in my inside pocket and buttoned it down for safekeeping. I liked the way she had kissed my hand. I liked the bonus, too. I liked the fact that she'd paid it in hundred-mark notes.

Nice new ones with the lady reading a book beside a mounted terrestrial globe. I even liked her hat, and the three scars on her face. I liked pretty much everything about her except the little gun in her bag.

I dislike women who carry guns almost as much as I dislike men who carry them. The gun and the little incident with Herr Klingerhoefer—not to mention the way she had avoided having me back to her home—made me think there was much more to Britta Warzok than met the eye. And given that she met the eye like Cleopatra, that gave me a cramp in a muscle that suddenly I felt I just had to stretch.

"You're a pretty strict Roman Catholic, Frau Warzok," I said. "Am I right?"

"Unfortunately, yes. Why do you ask?"

"Only because I was speaking to a priest about your dilemma and he recommended that you employ the good old Jesuit device of equivocation," I said. "It means saying one thing while thinking quite another, in pursuit of a good cause. Apparently it's something that was recommended by the founder of the Jesuits, Ulrich Zwingli. According to this priest I was speaking to, Zwingli writes about it in a book called *Spiritual Exercises*. Maybe you should read it. Zwingli says that the greater sin than the lie itself would be the evil action that would result from not telling a lie. In this case, that you're a good-looking young woman who wants to get married and start a family. The priest I spoke to reckons that if you were to forget about the fact that you saw your husband alive in the spring of 1946, you would only have to get the Dienststelle to declare that he was dead, and then there would be no need to involve the church at all. And now that you know that he really is dead, where would the harm be in that?"

Frau Warzok shrugged. "What you say is interesting, Herr Gunther," she said. "Perhaps we will speak to a Jesuit and see what he recommends. But I couldn't lie about such a thing. Not to a priest. I'm afraid that, for a Catholic, there are no easy shortcuts." She finished her drink and then dabbed at her mouth with her napkin.

"It's just a suggestion," I said.

She dipped into her bag again, put five dollars on the table, and then made as if to go. "No, please don't get up," she said. "I feel awful having stopped you from having dinner. Do please stay and order something. There's enough there to cover more or less whatever you want. At least finish your drink."

I stood up, kissed her hand, and watched her go. She didn't even glance at Herr Klingerhoefer, who blushed again, fiddled with his key chain, and then forced a smile at his mother. Half of me wanted to follow her. Half of me wanted to stay and see what I could get out of Klingerhoefer. Klingerhoefer won.

All clients are liars, I told myself. I haven't yet met one who didn't treat the truth as if it was something on the ration. And the detective who knows that his client is a liar knows all the truth that need concern him, for he will then have the advantage. It was no concern of mine to know the absolute truth about Britta Warzok, assuming that such a thing existed. Like any other client she would have had her reasons for not telling me everything. Of course, I was a little out of practice. She was only my third client since starting my business in Munich. All the same, I told myself, I ought to have been a little less dazzled by her. That way I might have been less surprised, not to catch her lying so outrageously, but to find her lying at all. She was no more of a strict Roman Catholic than I was. A strict Roman Catholic would not necessarily have known that Ulrich Zwingli had been the sixteenth-century leader of Swiss Protestantism. But she would certainly have known that it was Ignatius of Loyola who had founded the Jesuits. And if she was prepared to lie about being a Roman Catholic, then it seemed to me she was quite prepared to lie about everything else as well. Including poor Herr Klingerhoefer. I picked up the dollars and went over to his table.

Frau Klingerhoefer seemed to have overcome all her previous reservations about the price of dinner in the Walterspiel and was working on a leg of lamb like a mechanic going after a set of rusty spark plugs with a wrench and a rubber hammer. She didn't stop eating for a moment. Not even when I bowed and said hello. She probably wouldn't have stopped if the lamb had let out a bleat and inquired where Mary was. Her son, Felix, was partnered with the veal, cutting neat little triangles off it like one of those newspaper cartoons we were always seeing of Stalin carving slices from a map of Europe.

"Herr Klingerhoefer," I said. "I believe we owe you an apology. This is not the first time this kind of thing has happened. You see, the lady is much too vain to wear glasses. It's quite possible that you have indeed met before, but I'm afraid she was much too short-sighted to recognize you from wherever it was that you might have met. On a plane, I think you said?"

Klingerhoefer stood up politely. "Yes," he said. "On a plane from Vienna. My business often takes me there. That's where she lives, isn't it? Vienna?"

"Is that what she told you?"

"Yes," he said, obviously disarmed by my question. "Is she in any kind of trouble? My mother told me you're a detective."

"That's right, I am. No, she's not in any kind of trouble. I look after her personal security. Like a kind of bodyguard." I smiled. "She flies. I go by train."

"Such a good-looking woman," said Frau Klingerhoefer, gouging the marrow out of the lamb bone with the tip of her knife.

"Yes, isn't she?" I said. "Frau Warzok's divorcing her husband," I added. "As far as I'm aware, she's undecided whether she's going to stay on in Vienna. Or live here in Munich. Which is why I was a little surprised to hear that she mentioned living in Vienna to you."

Klingerhoefer was looking thoughtful and shaking his head. "Warzok? No, I'm sure that wasn't the name she used," he said.

"I expect she was using her maiden name," I suggested.

"No, it was definitely Frau something-else," he insisted. "And not Fräulein. I mean, a good-looking woman like that. It's the first thing you listen out for. If she's married or not. Especially when you're a bachelor who's as keen to get married as I am."

"You'll find someone," said his mother, licking the marrow off her knife. "You just have to be patient, that's all."

"Was it Schmidt?" I asked. That was the name she had used when first she had contacted Herr Krumper, my late wife's lawyer.

"No, it wasn't Schmidt," he said. "I'd have remembered that, too."

"My maiden name was Schmidt," his mother explained, helpfully.

I hovered for a second in the hope that he might remember the name she had used. But he didn't. And after a while, I apologized once again and made for the door.

The maître d' rushed to my side, his elbows held high and pumping him forward like a dancer. "Was everything all right, sir?" he asked.

"Yes," I said, handing over her dollars. "Tell me something. Have you ever seen that lady before?"

"No, sir," he said. "I'd have remembered that lady anywhere."

"I just got the impression that maybe you had met her before," I said. I fished in my pocket and took out a five-mark note. "Or maybe this was the lady you recognized?"

The maître d' smiled and almost looked bashful. "Yes, sir," he said. "I'm afraid it was."

"Nothing to be afraid of," I said. "She won't bite. Not this lady. But if you ever see that other lady again, I'd like to hear about it." I tucked the note and my card into the breast pocket of his cutaway.

"Yes, sir. Of course, sir."

I went out onto Marstallstrasse in the vague hope that I might catch a glimpse of Britta Warzok getting into a car, but she was gone. The street was empty. I said to hell with her and started to walk back to where I had left my car.

All clients are liars.

## SIXTEEN

Walking down Marstallstrasse onto Maximilianstrasse, I was already thinking of how I was going to spend the next day. It was going to be a day without Nazi war criminals and Red Jackets and crooked Croatian priests and mysterious rich widows. I was going to spend the morning with my wife, apologizing for all my earlier neglect of her. I was finally going to call Herr Gartner, the undertaker, and provide him with the words I wanted on Kirsten's memorial tablet. And I was going to speak to Krumper and tell him to drop the price on the hotel. Again. Maybe the weather at the cemetery would be fine. I didn't think Kirsten would mind if, while I was in the garden of remembrance where her ashes were scattered, I got a little sun on my face. Then, in the afternoon, maybe I'd head back to that art gallery—the one next to the Red Cross building—and see if I could sign up for a crash course in art appreciation. The kind where a slim but attractive younger woman takes you by the nose and escorts you around a few museums and tells you what's what and what's not, and how to tell when a chimpanzee painted one picture and a fellow wearing a little black beret painted another. And if that didn't pan out, I would head to the Hofbrauhaus with my English dictionary and a packet of cigarettes and spend the evening with a nice brunette. Several brunettes probably—the silent kind, with nice creamy heads and not a hard-luck story between them, all lined up along a bartop. Whatever I ended up doing I was going to forget all about the things that were now bothering me about Britta Warzok.

I had left my car parked a few blocks east of the Vier Jahreszeiten, pointed west toward Ramersdorf, in case I fancied the idea of checking out that address she'd given me. I didn't fancy it much. Not on top of two Gibsons. Britta Warzok had been right about that much, at least. The Vier Jahreszeiten did serve an excellent cocktail. Near the car, Maximilianstrasse widens into an elongated square called the Forum. I guess someone must have thought the square reminded them of ancient Rome, probably because there are four statues there that look vaguely classical. I daresay it looks more like the ancient Roman Forum than it once did, because the Ethnographic Museum, which is on the right side of the square as you go toward the river, is a bombed-out ruin. And it was from this direction that the first of them came. Built like a watchtower and wearing a badly creased, beige linen suit, he walked meanderingly toward me with his arms spread wide, like a shepherd trying to intercept escaping sheep.

Having no wish to be intercepted by anyone, let alone someone as large as this fellow, I turned immediately north, in the direction of St. Anna's and found a second man coming my way down Seitzstrasse. He wore a leather coat, a bowler hat, and carried a walkingstick. There was something in his face I didn't like. Mostly it was just his face. His eyes were the color of concrete and the smile on his cracked lips reminded me of a length of barbed wire. The two men broke into a run as I turned quickly on my heel and sprinted back up Maximilianstrasse and straight into the path of a third man advancing on me from the corner of Herzog-Rudolf-Strasse. He didn't look like he was collecting for charity either.

I reached for the gun in my pocket about five seconds too late. I hadn't taken Stuber's advice and left one in the barrel, and I would have had to work the slide to put one up the spout and make it ready to fire. It probably wouldn't have made any difference anyway. No sooner was it in my fist than the man with the stick caught up with me and hit my wrist with it. For a moment I thought he'd broken my arm. The little gun clattered harmlessly onto the road and I almost went down with it, such was the pain in my forearm. Fortunately I have two arms, and the other drove my elbow back into his stomach. It was a hard, solid blow and sufficiently well delivered to knock some of my bowler-hatted attacker's breath from his body. I smelled it whistle past my ear, but there wasn't nearly enough of it to put him down on the ground.

The other two were on me by now. I lifted my paws, squared up to them, jabbed hard into the face of one and connected a decent right hook with the chin of the other. I felt his head shift against my knuckles like a balloon on a stick and ducked a fist the size of a small Alp. But it was no use. The walking stick hit me hard across the shoulders, and my hands dropped like a drummer's arms. One hauled my jacket down over my shoulders so that my arms were pinned by my sides, and then another delivered a punch to my stomach that scraped against my backbone and left me on my knees, throwing up the remains of my cocktail-onion dinner onto the little Beretta.

"Aw, look at his little gun," said one of my new friends, and he kicked it away, just in case I felt stupid enough to try to pick it up. I didn't.

"Get him on his feet," said the one with the bowler.

The biggest one grabbed me by my coat collar and hauled me up to a position that only vaguely resembled standing. I hung from his grip for a moment, like a man who had dropped his change, my hat slipping slowly off the top of my head. A big car drew up in a squeal of tires. Someone thoughtfully caught my hat as, finally, it tipped off my head. Then the one holding my collar tucked his fingers under my belt and shifted me toward the curbside. There seemed little point in struggling. They knew what they were doing. They'd done it many times before, you could tell. They were a neat little triangle around me now. One of them opening the car door and throwing my hat onto the backseat, one of them handling me like a sack of potatoes, and one of them with the stick in his hand, in case I changed my mind about going to the picnic with them all. Up close they looked and smelled like something out of a painting by Hieronymus Bosch—my own pale, compliant, sweating face surrounded with a triad of stupidity, bestiality, and hate. Broken noses. Gap teeth. Leering eyes. Five-o'clock shadows. Beery breath. Nicotine fingers. Belligerent chins. And yet more beery breath. They'd had quite a few before keeping their appointment with me. It was like being kidnapped by a Bavarian brewers' guild.

"Better cuff him," said the bowler hat. "Just in case he tries anything."

"If he does, I'll tap him with this," said one, producing a blackjack.

"Cuff him all the same," said the bowler hat.

The big one holding me by the belt and collar let go for a moment. That was the moment I ordered myself to escape. The only trouble was, my legs were not obeying orders. They felt like they belonged to someone who hadn't walked in several weeks. Besides, I would just have been sapped. I've been sapped before and my head didn't care for it. So, politely, I let the big one gather my hands in his mitts and snap some iron around my wrists. Then he lifted me up a bit, grabbed my belt again, and launched me like a human cannonball.

My hat and the car seat broke my fall. As the big one got into the car behind me, the door on the other side opened in front of my face and the ape with the blackjack put his tire-size hip beside my head and barged me into the middle. It wasn't the kind of sandwich I liked. The one with the bowler got into the front seat and then we were off.

"Where are we going?" I heard myself croak.

"Never mind," said the one holding the blackjack, and crushed my hat on top of my face. I let it stay there, preferring the sweet, hair-oil smell of my hat to their brewery breath and the stink of something fried that hung on their clothes. I liked the smell on my hatband. And for the first time I got to understand why a small child carries a little blanket around, and why it's called a comforter. The smell in my hat reminded me of the normal man I'd been a few minutes before and whom I hoped to be again when these thugs were finished with me. It wasn't exactly Proust's madeleine, but maybe something close.

We drove southeast. I knew that because the car had been pointing east, up Maximilianstrasse, when I was pushed into it. And soon after we drove off, we crossed the Maximilian Bridge, and turned right. The journey was over a little sooner than I had expected. We drove into a garage or a warehouse. A shutter that came up in front of us came down behind us. I didn't need my eyes to know approximately where we were. The sweet-and-sour smell of mashed hops coming from three of Munich's largest breweries was as much of a city landmark as the Bavaria statue in the Theresa Meadow. Even through the felt of my hat it was as strong and pungent as a walk across a newly fertilized field.

Car doors opened. My hat was swept off my face and I was half pushed, half pulled out of the car. The three from the Forum had become four in the car and there were another two waiting for us in a semi-derelict warehouse that was littered with broken pallets, beer barrels, and crates of empty bottles. In one corner was a motorcycle and sidecar. A truck was parked in front of the car. Above my head was a glass roof, only most of the glass was under my feet. It cracked like ice on a frozen lake as I was frog-marched toward a man, neater than the others, with smaller hands, smaller feet, and a small mustache. I just hoped his brain was large enough to know when I was telling the truth. My stomach still felt like it was sticking to my backbone.

The smaller man was wearing a gray Trachten jacket with hunter green lapels and matching oak-leaf-shaped pockets, cuffs, and elbows. His trousers were gray flannel, his shoes were brown, and he looked like the Führer ready to make a night of it at Berchtesgaden. His voice was soft and civilized, which might have made a pleasant change but for the fact that experience has taught me how it's usually the quiet ones who are the worst sadists of all—especially in Germany. Landsberg Prison was full of quiet-spoken, civilized types like the man wearing the Trachten jacket. "You're a lucky man, Herr Gunther," he said.

"That's how I feel about it, too," I said.

"You really were in the SS, weren't you?"

"I try not to brag about it," I said.

He stood perfectly still, almost to attention, his arms by his side, as if he had been addressing a parade. He had a senior SS officer's manner and bearing and a senior SS officer's eyes and way of speaking. A tyrant, like Heydrich, or Himmler—one of those borderline psychopaths who used to command police battalions in the far-flung corners of the greater German Reich. Not the kind of man to be flippant with, I told myself. A real Nazi. The kind of man I hated, especially now that we were supposed to be rid of them.

"Yes, we checked you out," he said. "Against our battalion lists. We have lists of former SS men, you know, and you are on it. Which is why I say that you are very fortunate."

"I could tell," I said. "I've been getting a strong feeling of belonging ever since you boys picked me up."

All those years I had kept my mouth shut and said nothing, like everyone else. Perhaps it was the strong smell of beer and their Nazi manners, but suddenly I remembered some SA men coming into a bar and beating up a Jew and me going outside and leaving them to it. It must have been 1934. I should have said something then. And now that I knew they weren't going to kill me, suddenly I wanted to make up for that. I wanted to tell this little Nazi martinet what I really thought of him and his kind.

"I wouldn't make light of it, Herr Gunther," he said gently. "The only reason you're alive now is that you're on that list."

"I'm very glad to hear it, Herr General."

He flinched. "You know me?"

"No, but I know your manners," I said. "The quiet way you expect to be obeyed. That absolute sense of chosen race superiority. I suppose that's not so very surprising given the caliber of men you have working for you. But that was always the way with the SS general staff, wasn't it?" I looked with distaste at the men who had brought me there. "Find some feeble-minded sadists to carry out the dirty work, or better still, someone from a different race altogether. A Latvian, a Ukrainian, a Romanian, even a Frenchman."

"We're all Germans here, Herr Gunther," said the little general. "All of us. All old comrades. Even you. Which makes your recent behavior all the more inexcusable."

"What did I do? Forget to polish my knuckle-duster?"

"You should know better than to go around asking questions about the Web and the Comradeship. Not all of us have so little to hide as you, Herr Gunther. There are some of us who could be facing death sentences."

"In the present company, I find that all too easy to believe."

"Your impertinence does you and our organization no credit," he said, almost sadly. "'My honor is my loyalty.' Doesn't that mean anything to you?"

"As far as I'm concerned, General, those were just some words on a belt buckle. Another Nazi lie, like 'Strength Through Joy.'" Another reason I said what I said to the little general, of course, was that I never had the brains to make general myself. Maybe they weren't going to kill me. But perhaps I ought to have borne in mind the fact that they could still hurt me. Perhaps. Part of me always knew they were going to hurt me. I think I knew that was always what was on the cards. And under those circumstances I think I figured I had nothing to lose by speaking my mind. "Or the best lie of all. My own favorite. The one the SS dreamed up to make people feel better about their situation. 'Work makes you free.'"

"I can see we will have to reeducate you, Herr Gunther," he said. "For your own good, of course. So as to avoid any more unpleasantness in the future."

"You can dress it up how you like, General. But you people always did prefer hitting people to—"

I didn't finish my sentence. The general nodded to one of his men—the one with the blackjack—and it was like letting a dog off his lead. Immediately, without a second's hesitation, the man took a step forward and let me have it hard on both arms, and then on both shoulders. I felt my whole body arch in an involuntary spasm as, still handcuffed, I tried to lower my head between my shoulder blades.

Enjoying his work he chuckled softly as the pain put me down on my knees and, coming around behind me, he hit near the top of my spine—a crippling blow that left my mouth tasting of Gibson mixed with blood. They were expert blows, I could tell, and they were meant to cause me the maximum amount of pain.

I collapsed onto my side and lay on the ground at his feet. But if I thought he would have been too lazy to bend down and keep hitting me, I was mistaken. He took his jacket off and handed it to the man with the bowler hat. Then he started to hit me again. He hit me on the knees, on the ankles, on the ribs, on the buttocks, and on the shins. Each time he hit me the blackjack sounded like someone beating a rug with a broom handle. Even as I prayed for the beating to stop someone started swearing, as if the ferocity of the blows to my body seemed remarkable, and it took several more agonizing seconds for me to realize that the curses were uttered by me. I had been beaten before, but never quite so thoroughly. And probably the only reason I felt it lasted as long as it did was that he avoided hitting me about the face and head, which might have rendered me mercifully unconscious. Most agonizing of all was when he started to repeat the blows, hitting where he had hit me already and there was now just a painful bruise. That was when I started to scream, as if angry with myself that I could not lose consciousness and escape from the pain.

"That's enough for the moment," the general said, finally.

The man wielding the blackjack stood back, breathing hard, and wiped his brow with his forearm.

Then the man with the bowler laughed and, handing him his jacket, said, "Hardest work you've done all week, Albert."

I lay still. My body felt as if I had been stoned for adultery without the pleasure of the memory of the adultery. Every part of me was in pain. And all for ten red ladies. I'd had a thousand marks and I told myself there would be another thousand red marks when I looked at myself in the morning. Assuming I still had the stomach to look at myself ever again. But they were not yet finished with me.

"Pick him up," said the general. "And bring him over here."

Cracking jokes and cursing my weight, they dragged me over to where he was now standing, beside a beer barrel. On top of this lay a hammer and a chisel. I didn't like the look of the hammer and the chisel. And I liked them even less when the big man picked them up with the look of someone who is about to start work on a piece of sculpture. I had the horrible feeling that I was this ugly Michelangelo's chosen piece of marble. They backed me up to the barrel and flattened one of my handcuffed hands on the wooden lid. I started to struggle with what remained of my strength and they laughed.

"Game, isn't he?" said the big one.

"A real fighter," agreed the man with the blackjack.

"Shut up, all of you," said the general. Then he took hold of my ear and twisted it painfully against my head. "Listen to me, Gunther," he said. "Listen to me." His voice was almost gentle. "You have been sticking your fat fingers in things that shouldn't concern you. Just like that stupid little Dutch boy who stuck his finger into the hole in the dike. Do you know something? They never tell the whole story of what happened to him. And more importantly of what happened to his finger. Do you know what happened to his finger, Herr Gunther?"

I yelled out loud as someone took hold of my hand and pressed it down flat against the lid of the barrel. Then they separated my little finger from the others with what felt like the neck of a beer bottle. Then I felt the sharp edge of the chisel pressed against the joint and, for a moment, I forgot about the pain in the rest of my body. The big greasy paws holding me tightened with excitement. I spat blood from my mouth, and answered the general. "I get the message, all right?" I said. "I'm warned off, permanently."

"I'm not sure that you are," said the general. "You see, a cautionary tale only works as such if the caution is reinforced by a taste of what consequences might follow. Some sort of sharp reminder of the sort of thing that might befall you should you stick your fingers into our affairs again. Show him what I'm talking about, gentlemen."

Something shiny flashed through the air—the hammer, I presumed—and then descended on the handle of the chisel. For a second there was an indescribable amount of pain and then a thick fog rolling in from the Alps enveloped me. I let go of my breath and closed my eyes.

## SEVENTEEN

I ought not to have smelled so bad. I knew I had wet myself. But it ought not to have smelled so bad. Not as quickly as this. I smelled worse than the filthiest tramp. That cloying, sickly-sweet ammonia smell you get off people who haven't bathed or changed their clothes in months. I tried to wrestle my head away from it, but it stayed with me. I was lying on the floor. Someone was holding me by the hair. I blinked my eyes open and found there was a small brown bottle of smelling salts being held beneath my nose. The general stood up, screwed the cap on the bottle of salts, and dropped it into the pocket of his jacket.

"Give him some cognac," he said.

Greasy fingers took hold of my chin and pushed a glass between my lips. It was the best brandy I ever tasted. I let it fill my mouth and then tried to swallow but without much success. Then I tried again and this time some of it trickled down. It felt like something radioactive traveling through my body. By now someone had taken away the handcuffs and I saw that there was a large and bloody handkerchief wrapped around my left hand. My own.

"Put him on his feet," said the general.

Once more I was hauled up. The pain of standing made me feel faint so that I wanted to sit down again. Someone put the glass of brandy in my right hand. I put it to my mouth. The glass clattered against my teeth. My hand was trembling like an old man's. That was no surprise. I felt like I was a hundred years old. I swallowed the rest of the brandy, which was quite a lot, and then dropped the glass onto the floor. I felt myself sway as if I had been standing on the deck of a ship.

The general stood in front of me. He was close enough for me to see his Aryan blue eyes. They were cold and unfeeling and as hard as sapphires. A little smile was playing on the corner of his mouth, as if there was something funny he wanted to tell me. There was. But I didn't yet get the joke. He held something small and pink in front of my nose. At first I thought it was an undercooked prawn. Raw and bloody at one end. Dirty at the other. Hardly appetizing at all. Then I realized it wasn't anything to eat. It was my own little finger. He took hold of my nose and then pushed the upper half of my little finger all the way into one of my nostrils. The smile became more pronounced.

"This is what comes of sticking your fingers into things that ought not to concern you," he said, in that quiet, civilized, Mozart-loving voice of his. The Nazi gentleman. "And you can think your-self lucky we decided it wasn't your nose that got you into trouble. Otherwise, we might have cut that off instead. Do I make myself clear, Herr Gunther?"

I grunted feebly. I was all out of impertinence. I felt my finger start to slip out of my nostril. But he caught it just in time and then tucked it into my breast pocket, like a pen he had borrowed. "Sou-venir," he said. Turning away, he said to the man in the bowler hat, "Take Herr Gunther to wherever he wants to go."

They dragged me back to the car and pushed me into the back-seat. I closed my eyes. I just wanted to sleep for a thousand years. Just like Hitler and the rest.

Car doors closed. The engine started. One of my comrades el-bowed me properly awake. "Where do you want to go, Gunther?" he asked.

"The police," said someone. To my surprise it was me. "I want to report an assault."

There was laughter in the front seat. "We *are* the police," said a voice.

Maybe that was true, and maybe it wasn't. I hardly cared. Not anymore. The car started to move and quickly gathered speed.

"So where are we taking him?" someone said after a minute or two. I glanced out of the window with half an eye. We seemed to be heading north. The river was on our left.

"How about a piano store?" I whispered.

They thought that was very funny. I almost laughed myself except that it hurt when I tried to breathe.

"This guy is very tough," said the big man. "I like him." He lit a cigarette and, leaning over me, put it in my mouth.

"Is that why you cut my finger off?"

"'S right," he said. "Lucky for you, I like you, huh?"

"Friends like you, Golem, who needs enemies?"

"What did he call you?"

"Golem."

"It's a soap word," said the bowler hat. "But don't ask me what it means."

"Soap?" I was still whispering but they could hear me all right. "What's that?"

"Jew," said the big man. And then he jabbed me painfully in the side. "Is it a soap word? Like he said?"

"Yes," I said. I didn't want to provoke him anymore. Not with nine fingers still on my paws. I liked my fingers and, more importantly, so did my girlfriends, back in the days when I had had any girlfriends. So I backed off telling him that the Golem was a big, stupid, only vaguely human monster that was as ugly as it was evil. He wasn't ready for that level of honesty. And neither was I. So I said, "Means big guy. Very tough guy."

"That's him, all right," said the driver. "They don't come much bigger. And they sure don't come any tougher."

"I think I'm going to be sick," I said.

At this the big guy grabbed the cigarette out of my mouth,

opened the window and threw it out, then pushed me toward the cool night air rushing past the car. "You need some fresh air is all," he said. "You'll be all right in a minute."

"Is he all right?" The driver glanced around nervously. "I don't want him throwing up in this car."

"He's all right," said the big man. He unscrewed a hip flask and poured some more brandy into my mouth. "Aren't you, tough guy?"

"Doesn't matter now," said the bowler hat. "We're here."

The car stopped. "Where's here?" I asked.

They got me out of the car and dragged me into a well-lit doorway where they propped me up against a pile of bricks. "This is the state hospital," said the big man. "At Bogenhausen. You rest easy awhile. Someone will find you in a minute, I expect. Get you fixed up. You'll be all right, Gunther."

"Very thoughtful," I said, and tried to collect my thoughts, enough to focus on the registration number of the car. But I was seeing double and then, for a moment, nothing at all. When I opened my eyes again the car was gone and a man with a white coat was kneeling in front of me.

"You've been hitting it rather hard, haven't you, mister?" he said.

"Not me," I said. "Someone else. And the 'it' was me, Doc. Like I was Max Schmeling's favorite punch bag."

"You sure about that?" he asked. "You do stink of brandy."

"They gave me a drink," I said. "To make me feel better about cutting off my finger." I waved my bloody fist in his face by way of an affidavit.

"Mm-hmm." He sounded like he had yet to be convinced. "We get a lot of drunks who injure themselves and come here," he said. "Who think we're just here to clean up their mess."

"Look, Mr. Schweitzer," I whispered. "I've been beaten to a pulp. If you laid me flat on the ground you could print tomorrow's newspaper on me. Now, are you going to help me or not?"

"Maybe. What's your name and address? And just so I won't feel like an idiot when I find the bottle in your pocket, what's the name of the new chancellor?"

I told him my name and address. "But I have no idea what the name of our new chancellor is," I said. "I'm still trying to forget the last one."

"Can you walk?"

"Maybe as far as a wheelchair, if you can point one out."

He fetched one from the other side of the double doors and helped me sit in it.

"In case the ward matron asks," he said, wheeling me inside. "The new German chancellor is Konrad Adenauer. If she gets a sniff of you before we've had a chance to remove your clothes, she's liable to ask. She doesn't like drunks."

"I don't like chancellors."

"Adenauer was the mayor of Cologne," said the man in the white coat. "Until the British dismissed him for incompetence."

"He should do nicely then."

Upstairs he found a nurse to help me strip. She was a nice-looking girl, and even in a hospital, there must have been more pleasant things for her to look at than my white body. There were so many blue stripes on it I looked like the flag of Bavaria.

"Jesus Christ," exclaimed the doctor when he returned to examine me. As it happened, I now had a better idea of what he had felt like, after the Romans had finished with him. "What happened to you?"

"I told you," I said. "I got myself beaten up."

"But by whom? And why?"

"They said they were policemen," I said. "But it could be they just wanted me to remember them kindly. Always thinking the worst of people. That's a character defect of mine. Along with not minding my own business and my smart mouth. Reading between the bruises, I'd say that's what they were trying to tell me."

"That's quite a sense of humor you have there," observed the doctor. "I've a feeling you're going to need it in the morning. These bruises are pretty bad."

"I know."

"Right now, we're going to get you X-rayed. See if there's anything broken. Then we'll fill you full of painkillers and take another look at that finger of yours."

"Since you ask, it's in the pocket of my jacket."

"I guess I mean the stump." I let him unwrap the handkerchief and examine the remains of my little finger. "This is going to need some stitches," he said. "And some antiseptic. Having said all that, it's a nice neat job, for a trauma injury. The two upper joints are gone. How did they do it? I mean, how did they cut it off?"

"Hammer and chisel," I said.

Both doctor and nurse winced in sympathy. But I was shivering. The nurse put a blanket around my shoulders. I kept on shivering. I was sweating, too. And very thirsty. When I started to yawn, the doctor pinched my earlobe.

"Don't tell me," I said, through clenched teeth. "You think I'm cute."

"You're in shock," he said, lifting my legs onto the bed and helping me to lie down. They both heaped some more blankets on top of me. "Lucky for you you're here."

"Everyone thinks I'm lucky tonight," I said. I was starting to feel pale and gray about the gills. Agitated, too. Even anxious. Like a trout trying to swim on a glass coffee table. "Tell me, Doc. Can people really catch the flu and die in summer?" I took a deep breath and let out a mouthful of air, almost as if I'd been running. Actually I was dying for a cigarette.

"Flu?" he said. "What are you talking about? You haven't got the flu."

"That's odd. I feel like I have."

"And you're not going to die."

"Forty-four million died of flu in 1918," I said. "How can you be so sure? People die of flu all the time, Doc. My wife, for one. And my wife for another. I don't know why. But there was something about it I didn't like. And I don't mean her. Although I didn't. Not lately. In the beginning I did. I liked her a lot. But not since the end of the war. And certainly not since we got to Munich. Which is probably why I deserved the hiding I took tonight. You understand? I deserved it, Doc. Whatever they did, I had it coming."

"Nonsense." The doctor said something else. He asked me a question, I think. I didn't understand it. I didn't understand anything. The fog was back. It rolled in like steam from a sausage kitchen on a cold winter's day. Berlin air. Quite unmistakable. Like going home. But just the smallest part of me knew that none of it was true and that for the second time that evening I had only passed out. Which is a little like being dead. Only better. Anything is better than being dead. Maybe I was luckier than I thought. Just as long as I could tell the one from the other everything was more or less all right.

## EIGHTEEN

It was day. Sunshine was streaming through the windows. Dust motes floated in brilliant beams of light like tiny characters from some celestial movie projector. Perhaps they were just angels sent to conduct me to someone's idea of heaven. Or little threads of my soul, impatient for glory, intrepidly scouting out the way to the stars ahead of the rest of me, trying to beat the rush. Then the sunbeam moved, almost imperceptibly, like the hands of a giant clock, until it touched the bottom of the bed and, even through the sheet and the blankets covering them, warmed my toes, as if reminding me that my worldly tasks were not yet done.

The ceiling was pink. A great glass bowl was hanging from it on a brass chain. At the foot of the bowl lay four dead flies, like a whole squadron of downed fighters in some terrible insect war. After I was done staring at the ceiling, I stared at the walls. They were the same shade of pink. Against one of the walls was a medical cabinet full of bottles and dressings. Beside it was a desk with a lamp where the nurses sometimes sat. On the opposite wall was a large photograph of Neuschwanstein Castle, the most famous of the three royal palaces built for Ludwig II of Bavaria. He was sometimes referred to as Mad King Ludwig, but since entering that hospital, I found I had a better understanding of him than most people. Not least because for a week or more I had been raving myself. On several occasions I had found myself locked in the topmost tower of that castle—the one with the weather vane and the eagle's-eye view of fairyland. I'd even had visits from the Seven Dwarfs and an elephant with big ears. A pink one, of course.

None of this was at all surprising. Or so the nurses told me. I had pneumonia. I had pneumonia because my resistance to infection had been low on account of the beating I had taken and because I was a heavy smoker. It came on like a bad dose of flu and, for a while, that was what they thought I had. I remembered this because it seemed very ironic. Then it got worse. For around eight or nine days I had a temperature of 104, which must have been when I went to stay at Neuschwanstein. Since then my temperature had returned to near normal. I say near normal, but in view of what happened next I must have been anything but normal. That's my excuse, anyway.

Another week passed, a long weekend in Kassel, with nothing at all happening and nothing to look at. Not even my nurses were diverting. They were solid, German housewives with husbands and children and double chins and powerful forearms and skin like orange peel and chests like pillows. In their stiff, white pinafores and caps they looked and behaved like they were armor-plated. Not that it would have made any difference if they'd been better-looking. I was as weak as a newborn. And it puts a brake on a man's libido when the object of his attention is the one who fetches and carries and, presumably, empties his bedpan. Besides, all of my mental energy was reserved for thoughts that had nothing to do with love. Revenge was my abiding preoccupation. The only question was, revenge on whom?

Apart from the certainty that the men who beat me to a pulp had been put up to it by Father Gotovina, I knew nothing at all about them. Except that they were ex–SS men like myself, and possibly policemen. The priest was my only real lead and, gradually, I resolved to be revenged on the person of Father Gotovina himself.

I did not, however, underestimate the gravity and difficulty of such a task. He was a big, powerful man and, in my much weakened state, I knew I was not equal to the task of taking him on. A five-year-old girl with a roll of sweets in her fist and a good right hook would have wiped the kindergarten floor with me. But even if I had been strong enough to tackle him, he would certainly have recognized me and then told his SS friends to kill me. He didn't strike me as being the kind of priest who would be squeamish about such a thing. So whatever I did to the priest was obviously going to require a firearm and, as soon as I understood this, I also realized that I was going to have to kill him. There seemed no alternative. Once I pointed a gun at him there would be no room for half measures. I would kill him or he would surely kill me.

Killing a man because he had counseled other men to hurt me may look disproportionate, and perhaps it was. The balance of my mind could have been disturbed by all that had happened to me. But perhaps there was also another reason. After all I had seen and done in Russia, I had less respect for human life than of old. My own included. Not that I would ever have made much of a Quaker. In peacetime I had killed several men. I'd taken no pleasure in it. But when you have killed once it becomes easier to kill again. Even a priest.

Once I had resolved who, the questions turned into when and how. And these questions led me to the realization that if I did manage to kill Father Gotovina, it might be a good idea to leave Munich for a while. Perhaps permanently. Just in case some of his finger-chopping friends in the Comradeship put two and two together and made me. It was my doctor—Dr. Henkell—who offered me a solution to the problem of where I would go if I did leave Munich.

Henkell was as tall as a lamppost, with Wehrmacht-gray hair and a nose like a French general's epaulette. His eyes were a milky shade of blue with irises the size of pencil points. They looked like two lumps of caviar on Meissen saucers. On his forehead was a frown line as deep as a railway cutting; a dimple made his chin look like the badge on a Volkswagen. It was a grand, commanding sort of face that belonged properly on some fifteenth-century bronze duke, astride a horse cast from melted cannons and set in front of a palazzo with hot-and-cold-running torture chambers. He wore a pair of steel-framed glasses that were mostly on his forehead and rarely on his nose and, around his neck, a single Evva key that was for the medicine cabinet in my room and several others like it elsewhere in the hospital. Drugs were often being stolen in the state hospital. He was tanned and fit-looking, which wasn't surprising given that he had a chalet near Garmisch-Partenkirchen and went there nearly every weekend—hill-walking and climbing in summer, and skiing in winter.

"Why don't you go and stay there?" he said while he was telling me about the place. "It would be just the thing for someone recuperating from an illness like yours. Some fresh mountain air, good food, peace, and quiet. You would be back to normal in no time."

"You're kind of caring, aren't you?" I remarked. "For a doctor, I mean."

"Maybe I like you."

"I know. I'm real easy to like. I sleep all day and half the night. You've really seen me at my best, Doc."

He straightened my pillow and looked me in the eye.

"It could be I've seen more of Bernie Gunther than he thinks," he said.

"Aw, you've found my hidden quality," I said. "And after all the trouble I took to hide it."

"It's not so well hidden," he said. "Provided one knows what to look for."

"You're starting to worry me, Doc. After all, you've seen me naked. I'm not even wearing makeup. And my hair must be a mess."

"It's lucky for you you're flat on your back and weak as a kitten," he said, wagging a finger at me. "Any more remarks like that and my bedside manner is liable to turn into a ringside manner. I'll have you know that at university I was considered to be a very promising boxer. Believe me, Gunther, I can open a cut just as quickly as I can stitch one."

"Wouldn't that be against the Hippocratic Oath, or whatever you pill pushers call it when you're taking yourselves too seriously? Something Greek anyway."

"Maybe I'll make an exception in your case and strangle you with my stethoscope."

"Then I wouldn't get to hear about why you like me," I said. "You know, if you really liked me you'd find me a cigarette."

"With your lungs? Forget it. If you take my advice you'll never smoke again. The pneumonia's very likely left a scar on your lung." He paused for a moment and then added: "A scar as pronounced as the one under your arm."

Outside my room someone started drilling. They were repairing the hospital, just like the women's hospital where Kirsten had died. Sometimes it seemed like there wasn't anywhere in Munich that wasn't having some building work done. I knew Dr. Henkell was right. A chalet in Garmisch-Partenkirchen would be a lot more peaceful and quiet than the builder's yard I was in now. Just what the doctor ordered. Even if it was a doctor who was beginning to sound suspiciously like an old comrade.

"Maybe I never got around to telling you about the men who put their paws on me," I said. "They had hidden qualities, too. You know, like honor and loyalty. And they used to wear black hats with funny little signs on them because they wanted to look like pirates and frighten children."

"As a matter of fact, you told me that they were cops," he said. "The ones who beat you up."

"Cops, detectives, lawyers, and doctors," I said. "There's no end to what old comrades can turn their hands to."

Dr. Henkell did not contradict me.

I closed my eyes. I was tired. Talking made me tired. Everything seemed to make me feel tired. Blinking and breathing at the same time made me feel tired. Sleeping made me feel tired. But nothing made me feel quite so tired as the old comrades.

"What were you?" I asked. "Inspector of concentration camps? Or just another guy who was obeying orders?"

"I was in the Tenth SS Panzer Division Frundsberg," he said.

"How the hell does a doctor end up in a tank?" I asked.

"Honestly? I thought it would be safer inside a tank. And, for the most part, it was. We were in the Ukraine from 1943 until June

1944, when we were ordered to France. Then we were at Arnhem and Nimegen. Then Berlin. Then Spremberg. I was one of the lucky ones. I managed to surrender to the Amis, at Tangermünde." He shrugged. "I don't regret joining the SS. Those men who survived with me will be my friends for the rest of my life. I'd do anything for them. Anything."

Henkell did not question me about my own service with the SS. He knew better than to ask. It was something you either talked about or you didn't talk about. I never wanted to talk about it again. I could see that he was curious. But that just made me all the more determined not to say anything about it. He could think what he liked. I really didn't care.

"As a matter of fact," he said, "you would be doing me a huge favor. If you went to Mönch. That's the name of my house in Sonnenbichl. A friend of mine is living there at the moment. You could keep him company. He's been in a wheelchair since the war and he gets rather depressed. You could help him to keep his spirits up. It would be good for you both, you see. There's a nurse and a woman who comes in to cook. You'd be very comfortable."

"This friend of yours—"

"Eric."

"He wouldn't be an old comrade, too, would he?"

"He was in the Ninth SS Panzer Division," said Henkell. "Hohenstaufen. He was also at Arnhem. His tank got hit by a Tommy armor-piercing seventeen-pounder in September 1944." Henkell paused. "But he's no Nazi, if that's what you're worried about. Neither of us was ever a Party member."

I smiled. "For what it's worth," I said, "neither was I. But let me give you some free advice. Don't ever tell people that you were never a Party member. They'll think you've got something to hide. It beats me where all those Nazis disappeared to. I guess the Ivans must have them."

"I never thought of it like that," he said.

"I'll just pretend I didn't hear what you said and then I won't be too disappointed when he turns out to be Himmler's smarter brother, Gebhard."

"You'll like him," said Henkell.

"Sure I will. We'll sit by the fire and sing each other the Horst Wessel Song before we turn in at night. I'll read him some chapters of *Mein Kampf* and he'll delight me with *Thirty War Articles for the German Volk* by Dr. Goebbels. How does that sound?"

"Like I made a mistake," Henkell said grimly. "Forget I ever mentioned it, Gunther. I just changed my mind. I don't think you'd be good for him, after all. You're even more bitter than he is."

"Take your foot off the Panzer's gas pedal, Doc," I said. "I'll go. Anywhere would be better than this place. I'll need a hearing aid if I stay here any longer."

## NINETEEN

One of the nurses was from Berlin. Her name was Nadine. We got along just fine. She'd lived on Güntzelstrasse, in Wilmersdorf, which was very close to where I had once lived, on Trautenaustrasse. We had been practically neighbors. She had worked at the Charité Hospital, which is where she had been raped by twenty-two Ivans in the summer of 1945. After that she lost her enthusiasm for the city and moved to Munich. She had a rather refined, almost noble face, a high-set neck, big shoulders, and a long, strong back and correctly formed legs. She was built like an Oldenburg mare. She was calm, with a pleasant temper, and, for some reason, she liked me. After a while I liked her, too. It was Nadine who got a message to little Faxon Stuber, the export cabdriver, asking him to visit me in hospital.

"My God, Gunther," he said. "You look like last week's sauerkraut."

"I know. I should be in hospital. But what can you do? A man has to earn a living, right?"

"I couldn't agree more. And that's why I'm here, I hope."

Without further ado I directed him to the closet where my clothes were hanging and the wallet in the inside pocket and the ten red ladies that were waiting there.

"Find them?"

"Red ladies. My favorite kind of gal."

"There are ten of them and they're yours."

"I don't kill people," he said.

"I've seen the way you drive and it's only a matter of time, my boy."

"But assume you've got my attention."

I told him what I wanted to do. He had to sit close to my bed to hear what I was saying because my voice was sometimes very faint. I sounded like a frog in the Flying Dutchman's throat.

"Let me get this straight," he said. "As well as the other, I wheel you out, drive you to where you want to go, and drive you back here. Right?"

"It'll be visiting time so no one will even know that I'm gone," I told him. "Plus, we'll be wearing builder's overalls. I'll just slip them over my pajamas. Builders are invisible in this city. What's the matter? You look like a cat creeping around the milk."

"If it tastes funny it's because I don't see you going out of here in anything other than a wooden box, Gunther. You're a sick man. I've seen stronger-looking crane-flies. You wouldn't make it as far as the car park."

"I already thought of that," I said and showed him a little bottle of red liquid I had been hiding under the bedclothes. "Methamphetamine. I stole it."

"And you think this will put you back on your feet?"

"Long enough to do what I need to do," I said. "They used to give it to Luftwaffe pilots during the war. When they were exhausted. They were flying and they didn't even need a plane."

"All right," he said, folding away the red ladies. "But if you wander off or tip over don't expect me to handle the porterage. Sick or not you're still a big man, Gunther. Josef Manger couldn't pick you up. Not if his Olympic gold medal depended on it. And another thing. From what I've heard, that ox-blood is apt to make a man gabby. But I don't want to know, see? Whatever it is that you're hatching, I don't want to know. And the minute you tell me, I'll feel free to brush you off. Clear?"

"As clear as a half bottle of Otto," I said.

Stuber grinned. "It's all right," he said. "I didn't forget." He took a half liter of Fürst Bismarck out of his pocket and slipped it under my pillow. "Just don't drink too much of that stuff. Grain schnapps and an armful of ox-blood might not mix too well. I don't want you throwing up in my taxi like some stinking Popov."

"You don't have to worry about me, Faxon."

"I'm not worried about you. If I look like I'm worried about you it's because I'm worried about me. It doesn't look like it, but there's a big difference, see?"

"Sure, I understand. It's what the shrinks call a gestalt."

"Yeah, well, you'd know more about that than me, Gunther. From what I've heard so far, you probably want your head examined."

"We all do, Faxon, my boy. We all do. Haven't you heard of collective guilt? You're as bad as Joseph Goebbels, and me, I'm just as bad as Reinhard Heydrich."

"Reinhard who?"

I smiled. It was true, Heydrich had been dead for more than seven years. But it was just a little disconcerting to discover Stuber had never heard of him. Maybe he was younger than I had supposed.

Either that or I was a lot older than I felt. Which hardly seemed possible.

# TWENTY

The ox-blood in my veins left me feeling like it was my twenty-first birthday. It was plain to see why they'd given the stuff to Luftwaffe pilots. With enough of that whiz-juice in your blood you wouldn't have thought twice about landing a Messerschmitt on the roof of the Reichstag. I felt better than I looked, of course. And I knew I wasn't nearly as vigorous as the dope told me I was. I walked like someone learning to walk again. My legs and hands felt as if I had borrowed them from one of Geppetto's rejected puppets. With my pale face, dirty ill-fitting black overalls, sweaty hair, and unaccountably heavy shoes, I told myself I lacked only a bolt through my neck to make the final casting in a Frankenstein movie. It was worse when I spoke. My voice made the monster sound like Marlene Dietrich.

I walked as far as the elevator and then sat in a wheelchair. The hospital was full of visitors and no one paid me or Stuber any attention, least of all the doctors and nurses who commonly took advantage of visiting time to have a break or catch up with some paperwork. All of them were overworked and underpaid.

Stuber wheeled me quickly to his Volkswagen taxi. I got into the passenger seat and, conserving my energy, let him close the door. He ran around the front, jumped inside, and was already revving the garden-mower engine before I had told him where we were going. He lit two cigarettes, fed one between my lips, let out the clutch, and then drove quickly onto the Maximilianstrasse roundabout, from where we could have gone in any direction. "So where to?" he asked, holding the steering wheel hard to the left so that we kept on going round and round.

"Across the bridge," I said. "West along Maximilianstrasse and then down Hildegard Strasse, onto Hochbruchen."

"Just tell me where we're going," he growled. "I'm a taxi driver, remember? That little license you see there from the Municipal Transport Office means I know this city like I know your wife's pussy."

My ox-blood let that one go. Besides, I preferred him like this. An apology or embarrassment might have slowed him down. Speed and efficiency were what was required, before the whizz-juice and my malice gave out. "The Holy Ghost Church, on Tal," I said.

"A church?" he exclaimed. "What do you want to go to a church for?" He thought about that for a moment as we raced across the bridge. "Or are you having second thoughts about this? Is that it? Because if you are, then Saint Anna's is nearer."

"So much for your knowledge of gynecology," I said. "Saint Anna's is still closed." As we came through the Forum, I caught sight of the street corner where the comrades had given me an early taste of the blackjack before bundling me into their car. "And I'm not having second thoughts. Besides, didn't you tell me I wasn't to get gabby? What do you care what I want in a church? It's none of your business. You don't want to know. That's what you said."

He shrugged. "I just thought you was having second thoughts about this. That's all."

"When I have second thoughts, you'll be the first to know," I said. "Now, where's the rattle?"

"Down there." He nodded at my feet. There was a leather tool bag on the floor. I was so ragged up I hadn't noticed it. "In the bag. There are some spanners and screwdrivers in there to give it some respectable company. Just in case anyone gets nosy."

I leaned slowly forward and lifted the bag into my lap. On the side of the bag was the city coat of arms and "Post Office Motorbus Services, Luisenstrasse."

"It belonged to a bus mechanic, I figure," he said. "Someone left it in the cab."

"Since when did bus mechanics start taking export taxis?" I asked.

"Since they started screwing American nurses," he said. "She was a real peach, too. I'm not surprised he forgot his tools. They couldn't keep their faces off each other." He shook his head. "I was watching them in the rearview mirror. It was like her tongue was looking for her door key inside his flap."

"You paint a very romantic picture," I said and opened the bag. Among all the tools was a U.S. government–issue Colt automatic. A nice pre–Great War .45. The sound suppressor attached to the muzzle was homemade but most of them were. And the Colt was the ideal gun for a silencer. The only trouble was its length. Wearing the pipe the whole thing was almost eighteen inches long. It was as well Stuber had thought to supply a tool bag. A rig like that might sound quiet but to look at was about as inconspicuous in your hand as Excalibur.

"That gun is as cold as Christmas," he said. "I got it off a shit-skin sergeant who does guard duty at the American Officers' Club in the Art House. He swears on his black momma's life that the gun and the pipe were last used by a U.S. Army Ranger to assassinate an SS general."

"So it's a lucky gun, then," I said.

Stuber gave me a sideways look. "You're a strange one, Gunther," he said.

"I doubt it."

We drove down Hochbruchen in sight of the Hofbrauhaus, which, unusually for that time of day, was doing brisk business. A man wearing lederhosen staggered drunkenly along the pavement and narrowly avoided colliding with a pretzel cart. The smell of beer was in the air—more so than seemed normal, even for Munich. A posse of American soldiers ambled along Brauhstrasse with a proprietorial swagger, turning the air blue with their sweet Virginia tobacco. They looked too large for their uniforms, and their boozy laughter echoed down the street like small-arms fire. One of them started to dance a buck-and-wing as, somewhere, a brass band began to play "The Old Comrades March." The tune seemed appropriate for what I had in mind. "What's all the fuss about?" I growled.

"It's the first day of Oktoberfest," said Stuber. "Lots of Amis wanting taxis and here I am driving you around."

"You've been paid very handsomely for the privilege."

"I'm not complaining," he said. "It just sounded that way. Me using the wrong tense to tell you what I was thinking. The present progressive, I think."

"When I want you to tell me what you're thinking, sonny, I'll twist your ear. Future conditional." We reached the church. "Turn left toward Viktualienmarkt and pull up at the side door. Then you can help me get out of this walnut shell. I feel like a pea in a street game of three-card monte."

"That's the sucker move you're describing, Gunther," he said. "Where I get the pea out and nobody notices me doing it."

"Shut up and get the door, beetle jockey."

Stuber stopped the car, jumped out, ran around the front, and threw open the door. It exhausted me just watching him.

"Thanks."

I sniffed the air like a hungry dog. Down on the market square they were roasting almonds and warming pretzels. Another brass band was launching into "The Clarinet Polka." If I'd had one leg I couldn't have felt less like dancing a polka. Listening to it made me want to sit down and take a breather. Over at the festival meadow on Theresienwiese, the revels would be in full swing. Big-breasted girls in dirndls would be demonstrating the Charles Atlas course by lifting four beer steins in each hand. Brewers would be parading with their usual mix of bombast and vulgarity. Small children would be eating their way through gingerbread hearts. Fat stomachs would be filling up with beer as people tried to forget all about the war and others tried, sentimentally, to remember it.

I remembered the war only too well. That was why I was here. Mostly, I remembered that awful summer of 1941. I remembered Operation Barbarossa, when three million German soldiers, myself included, and more than three thousand tanks had crossed into the Soviet Union. I remembered with an all-too-painful clarity the city of Minsk. I remembered Lutsk. I remembered everything that had happened there. Despite all my best efforts, it seemed I wasn't ever likely to forget it.

*The speed of the advance took everyone by surprise—ourselves as much as the Popovs. That's what we called the Ivans in those days. On June 21, 1941, we had grouped on the Soviet border, full of trepidation for what was to follow. Five days later we had traveled an astonishing two hundred miles and were in Minsk. Bombarded by a massive artillery barrage and hammered by the Luftwaffe, the Red Army had taken a severe mauling and many of us thought the war was more or less over at that point. But the Reds fought on where others—the French, for example—would certainly have surrendered. Their tenacity was at least in part because NKVD security detachments had checked a wholesale panic with the threat of summary executions. Doubtless the Reds knew that this was no idle threat, for they were certainly aware of the fate that had befallen thousands of Ukrainian and Polish political prisoners in Minsk,*

*Lvov, Zolochiv, Rivne, Dubno, and Lutsk. So swift had been the progress of the Wehrmacht in the Ukraine that the retreating Soviets had no time to evacuate the prisoners held in the NKVD jails. And they hardly wanted to let them fall into our hands, where they could become SS auxiliaries, or German partisans. So before abandoning these cities to their fate, the NKVD set the prisons on fire—with all the prisoners still locked up inside. No, that's not true. They took the Germans with them. I suppose they intended to swap them for Reds later on. But it didn't turn out that way. We found them later, in a clover field on the road to Smolensk. They'd been stripped and machine-gunned to death.*

*I was with a reserve police battalion attached to the 49th Army. It was our job to find NKVD murder squads and put an end to their activities. We had intelligence that a death squad from Lvov and Dubno had gone north to Lutsk and, in our light panzer wagons and Puma armored cars, we tried to get there ahead of them. Lutsk was a small town on the Styr River with a population of seventeen thousand. It was the seat of a Roman Catholic bishop, which was hardly likely to endear it to the communists. When we arrived there we found almost the entire population gathered around the NKVD prison and in great distress about the fate of relatives incarcerated there. One wing of the prison was well ablaze, but using our armored cars we managed to break down a wall and save the lives of more than a thousand men and women. But we were too late for almost three thousand others. Many had been shot in the back of the head. Others had been killed by grenades tossed in the windows of cells. But most had just been burned to death. I will never forget the smell of burnt human flesh as long as I live.*

*The local townspeople told us which way the death squad had gone and so we gave chase, which was easy enough in the panzer wagons. The dirt roads were hard as concrete. We caught up with them only a few miles north in a place called Goloby. A firefight ensued. Thanks to the cannon mounted on our car, we won it easily. Thirty of them were captured. They hadn't even had time to throw away their distinctive red identification documents, which, inconveniently for them, contained photographs. One of them even had the keys to Lutsk Prison still in his pocket as well as numerous files relating to some of the murdered prisoners. There were twenty-eight men and two women. None of them was older than twenty-five or -six. The youngest, a woman, was nineteen and good-looking in that high-cheekboned, Slavic way. It was hard to connect her with the murders of so many people. One of the prisoners spoke German and I asked him why they had murdered so many of their own people. He told me the order had come straight from Stalin and that their party commissars would have had them shot if they had failed to carry out his order. Several of my men were for taking them with us so they could be hanged in Minsk. But I did not care for this extra baggage. And so we shot them all, in four groups of seven, and headed north again, toward Minsk.*

*I had joined the 316th Battalion straight from Berlin, at a place called Zamosc, in Poland. Prior to this, the 316th and the 322nd, with whom we operated, had been in Kraków. At that time, so far as I was aware, no mass murders had been carried out by either of these two police battalions. I knew that many of my colleagues were anti-Semitic, but just as many were not, and I didn't see any of this as a problem until we got to Minsk, where I made my report. I also handed over the two dozen sets of identification papers we had confiscated before executing their murderous bearers. It was July 7.*

*My superior, an SS colonel called Mundt, congratulated me on our successful action while at the same time issuing a reprimand for not bringing back the two women so they could be hanged. It seemed Berlin had issued a new order: all NKVD women and female partisans were to be hanged, in public, as an example to the population of Minsk.*

*Mundt spoke better Russian than I did at the time, and he could also read the language. Prior to his attachment to Special Action Group B in Minsk he had been with the Jewish Office of the RSHA. And it was he who noticed something about the NKVD prisoners we had executed. But even when he read aloud their names I still didn't understand.*

*"Kagan," he had said. "Geller, Zalmonowitz, Polonski. Don't you get it, Obersturmführer Gunther? They're all Jews. That was a Jewish NKVD death squad you executed. It just goes to show you, doesn't it? That the Führer is right about Bolshevism and Judaism being one and the same poison."*

*Even then it didn't seem to matter that much. Even then I told myself that I hadn't known they were all Jews when we shot them. I told myself that it probably wouldn't have made any difference—they had murdered thousands of people in cold blood and they deserved to die. But that was on the morning of July 7. By the afternoon I had started to look upon the police action I'd led somewhat differently. By the afternoon I had heard about the "registration," as a result of which two thousand Jews had been identified and shot. Then, the following day, I had happened upon an SS firing squad, commanded by a young police officer I had known back in Berlin. Six men and women were shot and their bodies fell into a mass grave in which perhaps a hundred bodies already lay. That was the moment when I realized the real purpose of the police battalions. That was the moment when my life changed, forever.*

*It was fortunate for me that the general commanding Special Action Group B, Arthur Nebe, was an old friend of mine. Before the war he had been the chief of Berlin's criminal police, a career detective like myself. So I went to him and asked for a transfer to the*

*Wehrmacht for front-line duties. He asked me my reason. I told him that if I stayed it would only be a matter of time before I was shot for disobeying an order. I told him that it was one thing to shoot a man because he had been a member of an NKVD death squad, but that it was quite another to shoot him just because he was a Jew. Nebe had thought that was funny.*

*"But Obersturmbannführer Mundt tells me the people you shot* were *Jews," he said.*

*"Yes, but that's not why I shot them, sir," I said.*

*"The NKVD is full of Jews," he said. "You know that, don't you? Chances are you catch some more of these death squads, they'll be Jews. What then?"*

*I stayed silent. I didn't know what then. "All I know is that I'm not going to spend this war murdering people."*

*"War is war," he said, impatiently. "And frankly, we may have bitten off rather more than we can chew in Russia. We have to win in this theater as quickly as possible if we're to secure ourselves for the winter. That means there's no room for sentiment. Frankly, we'll have a job looking after our own army let alone Red Army prisoners and the local population. It's difficult work we have ahead of us, make no mistake. Not everyone is suited to it. I don't particularly care for it myself, Bernie. Do I make myself clear?"*

*"Clear enough," I said. "But I'd rather shoot at people who were shooting back. I'm peculiar like that."*

*"You're too old for front-line duty," he said. "You won't last five minutes."*

*"I'll take my chances, sir."*

*He looked at me for a moment longer and then stroked his long, crafty nose. His was a cop's face. Shrewd, tough, good-humored. Until then I hadn't really thought of him as a Nazi at all. I knew for a fact that only three years before he had been part of an army plot to depose Hitler as soon as the British declared war on Germany following the annexation of the Sudetenland. Of course, the British never declared war. Not in 1938. As for Nebe, he was a survivor. And anyway, in 1940, after Hitler defeated the French in just six weeks, a lot of his opponents in the army had changed their opinion of him. That victory had seemed like a kind of miracle to many Germans, even those who disliked Hitler and all that he stood for. I supposed Nebe was one of these.*

*He could have had me shot, although I never heard of anyone who was shot for disobeying the so-called Commissar Order, which became little more than a license to murder Russian civilians. He could have had me sent to a punishment battalion. Those did exist. Instead, Nebe sent me to join Gehlen's Foreign Armies East Intelligence Section, where I spent several weeks organizing captured NKVD records. And subsequently I was transferred back to Berlin, to the War Crimes Bureau of the German High Command. I figured that was Arthur Nebe's idea of a joke. He always did have a strange sense of humor.*

I thought of all the excuses for what had happened in Lutsk. That I wasn't to know they were Jews. That they were murderers. That they had killed nearly three thousand people—probably more. That they certainly would have killed many more political prisoners if we hadn't shot them.

But it always came up the same way.

I had executed thirty Jews. That they had killed all those prisoners simply to stop them from collaborating with the Nazi invaders—as almost certainly they would have. That Stalin had recruited large numbers of Jews to the NKVD because he knew they had more to fight for. That I had played a part in the greatest crime in recorded history.

I hated myself for that. But I hated the SS more. I hated the way I had become complicit in their genocide. No one knew better than me what had been done in the name of Germany. And that was the real reason I was walking into that church with murder on my mind. It wasn't just about a severe beating and the loss of my little finger. It was about something far more important. If anything, the beating had brought me to my senses about who these people were and what they had done, not just to millions of Jews, but to millions of Germans like me. *To me.* That was something worth killing for.

## TWENTY-ONE

I sat in the fifteenth-century aisle of the Holy Ghost Church, close to the confessional, and waited for it to become free. I was more or less certain that Gotovina was in there because the two other priests I'd seen on my earlier visit were visible to me. One of them, a real understanding sort with a suffer-the-little-children smile, was having a quiet talk with a largish, market-ready woman just inside the front door. The other, dainty-looking with dark hair and a pimp mustache, and holding a walking stick with a silver top, was limping toward the high altar like an insect with only three legs, as if someone had swatted him hard and he was on his way to pray for them.

The place smelled strongly of incense, new-cut timber, and building mortar. A man with an eye patch was tuning a grand piano in a way that left you thinking he was probably wasting his time. About six or seven rows in front of me, a woman knelt in prayer. There was plenty of light coming through the tall arched windows and, above them, the smaller round windows. The ceiling looked like the lid on a very fancy biscuit tin. Someone moved a chair and, in the cavernous church interior, it sounded like a donkey braying a strong note of dissent. Now that I saw it again, the high altar, made of black marble and gold, reminded me of a Venetian undertaker's fanciest gondola. It was the kind of church where you almost expected to find a bellboy to help you carry your hymnal.

The ox-blood was wearing off a little. I wanted to lie down. The polished wooden bench I was sitting on began to look very comfortable and inviting. Then the green curtain in the confessional twitched and was drawn back, and a good-looking woman of about thirty stepped out. She was holding a rosary, crossing herself more for form's sake than anything else. She was wearing a tight red dress and it was easy to see why she had spent such a long time in the confessional. From the look of her, none of the venial sins would have detained her. She was built for just the one kind of sin, the mortal kind that cried aloud to heaven when you managed to touch her in the right places. She closed her eyes for a moment and took a deep breath that drop-kicked my libido to the top of the rococo pillars and down again. The scarlet gloves matched the handbag that matched the shoes that matched the lipstick that matched the veil on the little hat that was doing what it was supposed to do. Scarlet was her color all right. She looked like the word made flesh, just as long as the word was "sex." A kind of epiphany. The heavyweight champion of all scarlet women. When you saw her, you told yourself that the Book of Revelation was probably well named. It was Britta Warzok.

She did not see me. She made no act of contrition or penance. She just turned on her high heel and walked quickly up the aisle and out of the church. For a moment I was too surprised to move. If I had been less surprised I might have made it to the confessional in time to blow Father Gotovina's brains out. But by the time I had gathered myself together, the priest was out of the confessional and walking toward the altar. He spoke to the dainty-looking priest for a moment and then disappeared through a door at the back of the church.

He had not seen me. For a moment I considered pursuing the Croatian priest into the sacristy—if that was where he had gone—and killing him in there. Except that there were now questions he needed to answer. Questions for which I did not yet have the strength. Questions about Britta Warzok. Questions that would have to wait until I was feeling stronger. Questions that required a little more thinking before I asked them.

I picked up my tool bag and shuffled slowly out of the church and onto Viktualienmarkt, where the cooler air revived me a little. The bell in the church clock tower was ringing the half hour. I took a few steps and then leaned on the Nivea girl who was adorning a poster pillar. I could have used a whole tin of Nivea on my soul. Better still, a whole of tin of her.

Stuber's beetle came quickly toward me. For a minute I thought he was going to run me down. But he came to an abrupt halt, leaned across the passenger seat, and threw open the door. I wondered why he was in such a hurry. Then I remembered he was probably working under the assumption that I had shot and killed someone in the church. I took hold of the car door.

"It's all right," I said. "There's no hurry. I didn't go through with it."

He pulled on the brake and got out, calmer now, helping me into the car as if I had been his old mother, and lighting me another cigarette when finally I was stowed away. Back in the driver's seat, he revved the car hard, waited for a small troop of cyclists to pedal past, and then fired us on our way.

"So what changed your mind?" he asked.

"A woman."

"That's what they're for, I suppose," he said. "Sounds to me like she was sent by God."

"Not this one," I said. I sucked on the cigarette and winced as the heat of it hit my most recent scar. "I don't know who the hell sent her. But I'm going to find out."

"A woman of mystery, huh?" he said. "You know, I got a theory: Love is just a temporary form of mental illness. Once you know that, you can deal with it. Deal with it. Medicate for it."

Stuber started going on about some girlfriend he'd had who had treated him badly and I stopped listening for a while. I was thinking about Britta Warzok.

A small part of my brain was telling me that maybe she was a better Roman Catholic than I had given her credit for. In which case, her meeting with Father Gotovina might just have been a coincidence. That maybe hers had been a genuine confession and that she could have been on the level all along. I paid attention to this part of my brain for a minute or two and then blew it off. After all, this was the part of my brain that still believed in the perfectibility of man. Thanks to Adolf Hitler we all know what that's worth.

## TWENTY-TWO

Days passed. I got a little better. The weekend came along and Dr. Henkell said I was fit to travel. He had a newish, maroon-colored Mercedes four-door sedan that he had gone all the way to the factory in Sindelfingen to collect, and of which he was very proud. He let me sit in the back so I would be more comfortable on the fifty-eight-mile journey to Garmisch-Partenkirchen. We left Munich on Autobahn Number 2, a very well-engineered highway that took us through Starnberg, where I told Henkell about the eponymous baron and the fabulous house where he lived and the Maybach Zeppelin he was using to run down to the shops. And, because he liked cars a lot, I also told him about the baron's daughter, Helene Elisabeth, and the Porsche 356 she drove.

"That's a nice car," he said. "But I like Mercedes." And he proceeded to tell me about some of the other cars that were stored in his Ramersdorf garage. These now included my own Hansa, which Henkell had kindly driven away from the place where I had left it on the night I had been picked up by the comrades.

"Cars are a bit of a hobby of mine," he confessed as we drove on to Traubing and into the Alpine foothills. "So is climbing. I've climbed all of the big peaks in the Ammergau Alps."

"Including the Zugspitze?" The Zugspitze, Germany's highest mountain, was why most people went to Garmisch-Partenkirchen in the first place.

"That's not a climb," he said. "That's a walk. You'll be walking up it yourself, in a couple of weeks." He shook his head. "But my real interest is tropical medicine. There's a small laboratory in Partenkirchen that the Amis let me use. I'm rather friendly with one of their senior officers. He comes to play chess with Eric once or twice a week. You'll like him. He speaks perfect German and he's a damned good chess player."

"How did you meet?"

Henkell laughed. "I was his prisoner. There used to be a POW camp in Partenkirchen. I ran the hospital for him. The lab was part of the hospital. The Amis have their own doctor, of course. Nice fellow, but he's not much more than a pill pusher. Anything surgical, they usually ask me."

"Isn't it a bit unusual researching tropical medicine in the Alps?" I said.

"On the contrary," said Henkell. "You see, the air is very dry and very pure. So is the water. Which makes it an ideal place to avoid specimen contamination."

"You're a man of many parts," I told him.

He seemed to like that.

Just after Murnau, our road crossed the Murnauer marshes. Beyond Farchant, the basin of Garmisch-Partenkirchen opened out and we had our first view of the Zugspitze and the other Wetterstein Mountains. Coming from Berlin, I rather disliked mountains, especially the Alps. They always looked sort of melted, as if someone had carelessly left them out in the sun too long. Two or three miles farther on, the road divided, my ears popped, and we were in Sonnenbichl, just a short way north of Garmisch.

"The real action is down in Garmisch," he explained. "All the Olympic facilities, of course, from 'thirty-six. There are some hotels—most of them requisitioned by the Amis—a couple of bowling alleys, the officers' club, one or two bars and restaurants, the Alpine Theater, and the cable car stations for the Wank and the Zugspitze. Pretty much everything else comes under the control of the Southeastern Command of the U.S. Third Army. There's even a hotel named after General Patton. In fact, there are two, now that I think of it. The Amis like it here. They come here from all over Germany for what they call R-and-R. Rest and recreation. They play tennis, they play golf, they shoot skeets, and in winter they ski and go ice-skating. The ice rink at the Wintergarten is something to see. The local girls are friendly, and they even show American movies at two of the four movie theaters. So, what's not to like? A lot of them are from towns in the U.S. that are not so different from Garmisch-Partenkirchen."

"With one crucial difference," I said. "Those towns don't have an army of occupation."

Henkell shrugged. "They're not so bad when you get to know them."

"So are some Alsatian dogs," I said, sourly. "But I wouldn't want one around the house all day."

"Here we are at last," he said, turning off the road. He drove onto a gravel driveway that led between two clumps of lofty pines and across an empty green field at the end of which stood a three-story wooden house with a roof as steep as Garmisch's famous ninety-meter ski jump. The first thing you noticed about the place was that one wall was covered with a large heraldic coat of arms. This was a gold shield with black spots, and three main devices: a decrescent moon, a cannon with some cannonballs, and a raven. It all meant that the suit of armor from whom Henkell was probably descended had enjoyed shooting ravens, by the light of the silvery moon, with a piece of artillery. Beneath all this decorative nonsense was an inscription. It read "*Sero sed serio,*" which was Latin for "We're richer than you are." The house itself was nicely positioned on the edge of another field that descended steeply into the valley, affording the occupants a superb view. Views were what counted in this part of the world and this particular house enjoyed the sort of view normally obtained only from an eagle's nest. Nothing interrupted it, except a cloud or two. And perhaps the odd rainbow.

"I guess your family have never suffered from acrophobia," I said. Or poverty, I felt like adding.

"It's quite a sight, isn't it?" he said, pulling up outside the front door. "I never get tired of looking at that view."

Neat piles of logs framed the front door like so many cigarettes. Above the door was a smaller version of the coat of arms on the exterior wall. The door was the robust kind that looked as if it had been borrowed from Odin's castle. It opened to reveal a man in a wheelchair with a rug on his lap and a uniformed nurse at his shoulder. The nurse looked warmer than the rug and I knew instinctively which one of them I'd have preferred to have had on my lap. I was getting better.

The man in the chair was heavyset with longish, fair hair and a beard you might have picked for an important chat with Moses. The mustaches were waxed and left his face like the quillions on a broadsword. He wore a blue suede Schliersee jacket with staghorn buttons, a *Landhaus*-style shirt, and an edelweiss collar-chain made of bits of horn, pewter, and pearl. On his feet were black Miesbacher shoes with a high heel and a fold-over tongue. They were the kind of shoes you wear when you want to slap someone wearing leather shorts. He was smoking a briar pipe that smelled strongly of vanilla and reminded me of burnt ice cream. He looked like Heidi's Uncle Alp.

If Heidi had grown up she might have looked something like the nurse of the man in the wheelchair. She wore a pink knee-length dirndl, a white low-cut blouse with short puffy sleeves, a white cotton apron, lacy kneesocks, and the same sort of sensible shoes as her bearded charge. I knew she was supposed to be a nurse, because she had a little upside-down watch pinned to her blouse and a white cap on her head. She was blond, but not the sunny kind of blond, or the gilded kind, but the enigmatic, wistful kind you might find lost in some sylvan glade. Her mouth was slightly sulky and her eyes were a sort of lavender color. I tried not to notice her bosom. And then I tried again, only it kept on singing to me like it was perched on a rock in the Rhine River and I was some poor, dumb sailor with an ear for music. All women are nurses at bottom. It's in their nature to nurture. Some look more like nurses than others. And some women manage to make being a nurse look like Delilah's last stratagem. The nurse at Henkell's house was the second kind. With a face and figure like hers she would have made my old army great-coat look like a silk dressing gown.

Henkell caught me licking my lips and grinned as he helped me out of the Mercedes. "I told you you would like it here," he said.

"I love it when you're right like this," I said.

We went into the house, where Henkell introduced me. The man in the wheelchair was Eric Gruen. The nurse's name was Engelbertina Zehner. Engelbertina means "bright angel." Somehow it suited her. They both seemed quite excited to see me. Then again the house wasn't exactly the kind of place you would just drop in unannounced. Not unless you were wearing a parachute. They were probably glad of new company, even if the company was wrapped up in himself. We all shook hands. Gruen's hand was soft and a little moist, as if he was nervous about something. Engelbertina's hand was as hard and rough as a sheet of sandpaper, which shocked me a little and made me think that private nursing had its tough side. I sat down on a big, comfortable sofa and let out a big, comfortable sigh.

"That's quite a walk," I said, glancing back at the enormous drawing room. Engelbertina was already stuffing a cushion behind my back. That was when I noticed the tattoo on the top of her left forearm. Which went a long way to explaining how it was her hands were so tough. The rest of her must have been pretty tough, too. But for now I put it out of my mind. I was trying to get away from things like that. Besides, something good was cooking in the kitchen and, for the first time in weeks, I felt hungry. Another woman appeared in the doorway. She was attractive, too, in the same older, larger, slightly worn way that I was attractive myself. Her name was Raina, and she was the cook.

"Herr Gunther is a private detective," said Henkell.

"That must be interesting," said Gruen.

"When it gets interesting, that's usually the time to reach for a gun," I said.

"How does one get into that line of work?" asked Gruen, relighting his pipe. Engelbertina didn't seem to like the smoke and waved it away from her face with the flat of her hand. Gruen ignored her and I made a mental note not to, and to smoke outside for a while.

"I used to be a cop in Berlin," I said. "A detective with KRIPO. Before the war."

"Did you ever catch a murderer?" she asked.

Normally I'd flick a question like that off my lapel. But I wanted to impress her. "Once," I said. "A long time ago. A strangler called Gormann."

"I remember that case," said Gruen. "That was a famous case."

I shrugged. "Like I said. It was a long time ago."

"We shall have to watch our step, Engelbertina," said Gruen. "Otherwise Herr Gunther will know all our nastiest little secrets. I expect he's already started sizing us up."

"Relax," I told them. "Truth is, I never was much of a cop. I have a problem with authority."

"That's hardly very German of you, old boy," said Gruen.

"That's why I was in the hospital," I said. "I got warned off a case I was working on. And the warning didn't take."

"I suppose you have to be very observant," said Engelbertina.

"If I was, maybe I wouldn't have got myself beaten up."

"Good point," agreed Gruen.

For a minute he and Engelbertina discussed a favorite detective story, which was my cue to switch off, briefly. I hate detective stories. I glanced at my surroundings. At the red-and-white-checked curtains, the green shutters, the hand-painted cabinets, the thick fur rugs, the two-hundred-year-old oak beams, the four-poster fireplace, the paintings of vines and flowers, and—no Alpine home was complete without one—an old ox harness. The room was big but I still felt as cozy as a slice of bread in an electric toaster.

Lunch was served. I ate it. More than I had expected to eat. Then I had a sleep in an armchair. When I woke up I found myself alone with Gruen. He seemed to have been there for a while. He was looking at me in a curious sort of way that I felt deserved some kind of explanation.

"Was there something you wanted, Herr Gruen?"

"No, no," he said. "And please, call me Eric." He wheeled his chair back a little. "It's just that I had the feeling we'd met somewhere before, you and I. Your face seems very familiar to me."

I shrugged. "I guess I must have that kind of face," I said, remembering the American back at my hotel in Dachau. I recalled him making a similar remark. "I guess it's lucky I became a cop," I added. "Otherwise my photograph might get me pinched for something I hadn't done."

"Were you ever in Vienna?" he asked. "Or Bremen?"

"Vienna, yes," I said. "But not Bremen."

"Bremen. It's not an interesting town," he said. "Not like Berlin."

"It seems that these days, there's nowhere quite as interesting as Berlin," I said. "That's why I don't live there. Too dangerous. If ever there's another war, Berlin is where it will start."

"But it could hardly be more dangerous than Munich," said Gruen. "For you, I mean. According to Heinrich, the men who beat you up almost killed you."

"Almost," I said. "By the way, where is Dr. Henkell?"

"Gone down to the laboratory, in Partenkirchen. We won't see him again until dinner. Maybe not even then. Not now that you're here, Herr Gunther."

"Bernie, please."

He bowed his head politely. "What I mean is, he won't feel obliged to have dinner with me, as he usually does." He leaned across, took hold of my hand, and squeezed it companionably. "I'm very glad to have you here. It gets pretty lonely here, sometimes."

"You have Raina," I said. "And Engelbertina. Don't ask me to feel sorry for you."

"Oh, they're both very nice, of course. Don't get me wrong. I wouldn't know what to do without Engelbertina to look after me. But a man needs another man to talk to. Raina stays in the kitchen and keeps to herself. And Engelbertina isn't much of a conversationalist. I daresay that's not so very surprising. She's had a hard life. I expect she'll tell you all about it in due course. When she's ready."

I nodded, remembering the number tattooed on Engelbertina's

forearm. With the possible exception of Erich Kaufmann, the Jewish lawyer who had given me my first case in Munich, I hadn't ever met a Jew from one of the Nazi death camps. Most of them were dead, of course. The rest were in Israel or America. And the only reason I knew about the number was because I had read a magazine article about Jewish prisoners being tattooed and, at the time, it had struck me that at least a Jew could wear such a tattoo with a certain amount of pride. My own SS number, tattooed under my arm, had been removed, rather painfully, with the aid of a cigarette lighter. "Is she Jewish?" I asked. I didn't know if Zehner was a Jewish name. But I could see no other explanation for the blue numbers on her arm.

Gruen nodded. "She was in Auschwitz-Birkenau. That was one of the worst camps. It's near Kraków, in Poland."

I felt the eyebrows lift on my forehead. "Does she know? About you and Heinrich? And about me? That we were all in the SS?"

"What do you think?"

"I think if she knew she would be on the first train to the DP camp at Landsberg," I said. "And then on the next ship for Israel. Why on earth would she stay?" I shook my head. "I don't think I'm going to like it here after all."

"Well, you're in for a surprise," Gruen said, almost proudly. "She does know. About me and Heinrich, anyway. What's more, she doesn't care."

"Good God, why? I don't understand that at all."

"It's because after the war," said Gruen, "she became a Roman Catholic. She believes in forgiveness and she believes in the work being done at the laboratory." He frowned. "Oh, don't look so surprised, Bernie. Her conversion is not without precedent. Jews were the first Christians, you know." He shook his head in wonder. "For how she's dealt with what happened to her, I really admire her."

"Hard not to, I suppose. When you look at her."

"Besides, all that insanity is behind us."

"So I was led to believe."

"Forgive and forget. That's what Engelbertina says."

"Funny thing about forgiveness," I said. "Someone has to look and act like they're sorry for there to be any chance of real forgiveness."

"Everyone in Germany is sorry for what happened," said Gruen. "You believe that, don't you?"

"Sure we're sorry," I said. "We're sorry we got beat. We're sorry our cities got bombed to rubble. We're sorry our country is occupied by the armies of four other countries. We're sorry our soldiers are accused of war crimes and imprisoned in Landsberg. We're sorry we lost, Eric. But not for much else. I just don't see the evidence."

Gruen let out a sigh. "Maybe you're right," he said.

I shrugged back at him. "What the hell do I know? I'm just a detective."

"Come now," he said with a smile. "Aren't you supposed to know who did it? Who committed the crime? You have to be right about that, don't you?"

"People don't want cops to be right," I said. "They want a priest to be right. Or a government. Even a lawyer, on occasion. But never a cop. It's only in books that people want cops to be right. Most of the time they much prefer us to be wrong about nearly everything. That makes them feel superior, I suppose. Besides, Germany's all through with people who were always right. What we need now are a few honest mistakes."

Gruen was looking miserable. I smiled at him and said: "Hell, Eric, you said you wanted to have some real conversation. It looks like you got it."

## TWENTY-THREE

We got along pretty well, Gruen and I. After a while I even liked him. Quite a few years had passed since I'd had any kind of a friend. That was one of the things I missed most about Kirsten. For a while she had been my best friend as well as my wife and lover. I didn't appreciate how much I missed having a friend until I started talking to Gruen. There was something about the man that got to me, in a good way. Maybe it was the fact that he was in a wheelchair and yet somehow managed to be cheerful. More cheerful than me, anyway, which wasn't saying much. Maybe it was the fact that he stayed in good spirits even though his general health was not good—some days he was too ill to get out of bed, which left me alone with Engelbertina. Occasionally, when he was feeling well enough, he went with Henkell to the laboratory in Partenkirchen. Before the war he had also been a doctor and he enjoyed helping Henkell with some of the lab work. That also left me alone with Engelbertina.

When I started to feel a little better myself I would take Gruen outside for a walk, which is to say I rolled him up and down the garden for a while. Henkell had been right. Mönch was a great place for improving your health. The air was as fresh as morning dew on gentian, and there is always something about a view of a mountain or a valley that eventually penetrates the hard membrane of one's own view of things in general. Life looks better in an Alpine meadow, especially when the accommodation is Pullman class.

One day I was wheeling Gruen along a path cut into the mountain side, when I noticed him staring at my hand on the handle of his wheelchair.

"I've only just noticed," he said.

"Noticed what?" I asked.

"Your little finger. You don't have one."

"Actually, I do," I said. "But there was a time when I had two. One on each hand."

"And you a detective, too," he scolded, and held up his own left hand to reveal that half of his little finger was missing. Just like mine. "So much for your powers of observation. Actually, I'm beginning to doubt you were ever a detective at all, my friend. And if you were, you can't have been a very good one. What is it that Sherlock Holmes says to Dr. Watson? You see but you do not observe." He grinned and twisted the end of one of his mustaches, apparently enjoying my surprise and momentary discomfiture.

"That's crap and you know it," I said. "The whole idea of my coming here was so that I could switch off for a while. And that's what I've been trying to do."

"You're making excuses, Gunther. Next thing you'll be saying is that you've been ill, or some nonsense like that. That you didn't notice my missing finger because the beating detached your retina. Which is also why you haven't noticed that Engelbertina is a little in love with you."

"What?" I stopped the wheelchair, kicked on the brake, and came around the front.

"Yes, really, it's quite noticeable." He smiled. "And you call yourself a detective."

"What do you mean, a little in love with me?"

"I don't say that she's madly in love with you," he said. "I say a little bit." He got out his pipe and started to fill it. "Oh, she hasn't said as much. But after all, I happen to know her quite well. Well enough to know that being a little in love is all she's probably capable of, the poor lamb." He patted his pockets. "I seem to have left my matches back at the house. Do you have a strike?"

"What's your evidence?" I tossed him a box of matches.

"It's too late to sound like a proper detective now," he said. "The damage is already done." He used two matches to get his smoke going and then threw the box back. "Evidence? Oh, I don't know. The way she looks at you. The girl's a proper Rembrandt where you're concerned, old boy. Her eyes follow you all the way around the room. The way she touches her hair all the time when she's speaking to you. The way she bites her lip when you leave the room, as if she was already missing you. Take it from me, Bernie. I know the signs. There are two things in life that I have a feel for. Rubber tires and romance. Believe it or not, I used to be quite a ladies' man. I may be in a wheelchair, but I haven't lost my understanding of women." He puffed his pipe and grinned at me. "Yes, she's a little in love with you. Astounding, isn't it? Matter of fact, I'm a little surprised myself. Surprised and a little jealous, I don't mind confessing. Still, it's a common enough mistake, I suppose, to assume that just because a girl is very good-looking she also has good taste in her choice of men."

I laughed. "She might have fallen for you if you didn't have all that wire wool on your face," I said.

He touched his beard self-consciously. "You think I should get rid of it?"

"If I were you I'd drop it in a sack with a couple of heavy stones and then look for a nice deep river. You would only be putting the poor creature out of its misery."

"But I like this beard," he said. "It took a long time to grow."

"So does a prize pumpkin. But you wouldn't want to take one to bed with you."

"I expect you're right," he said, good-humored as always. "Although I can think of better reasons than a beard for her not being interested in me. It wasn't just the use of my legs I lost in the war, you know."

"How did it happen?"

"Really, there's not much to tell. You might just as well explain how an armor-piercing round works. A solid manganese round encased in a strong steel shell. There's no explosive charge. The manganese round depends on kinetic energy to penetrate the tank armor, and then just bounces around inside the tank like a rubber ball, killing and maiming everything it hits until it runs out of steam. Simple but very effective. I was the only one inside my tank to survive. Although not so as you would have noticed at the time. It was Heinrich who saved my life. If he hadn't been a doctor, then I wouldn't be here now."

"How did you two meet?"

"We know each other from before the war," he said. "We met at medical school, in Frankfurt. In 1928. I would have studied in Vienna, where I was born, but for the fact that I had to leave in rather a hurry. There was a girl I left in a bit of a clamp. You know the kind of thing. Rather an inglorious moment, I'm afraid. Still, these things happen, eh? After med school I got a job at a hospital in West Africa for a while. Then Bremen. When the war started neither Heinrich nor I was much interested in saving lives, I'm afraid. So we joined the Waffen-SS. Heinrich was interested in tanks—the way he's interested in nearly everything with an engine. I went along for the ride, so to speak. My parents were not very pleased with my choice of military service. They didn't like Hitler or the Nazis. My father is dead now, but my mother hasn't spoken to me since the war. Anyway, things went all right for us until the last weeks of the war. Then I got hit. That's it. That's my story. No medals. No glory. And definitely no pity, if you don't mind. Frankly, I had it coming. I did something wrong, once. And I don't mean that poor girl I left bumped up. I mean in the SS. The way we went through France and Holland just killing people whenever the idea took us."

"We all did things we're not proud of," I said.

"Perhaps," he said. "Sometimes I find it very hard to believe that any of it happened at all."

"It's the difference between war and peace, that's all," I told him. "War makes killing seem feasible and matter-of-fact. In peacetime, it isn't. Not in the same way. In peacetime everyone just worries that if you kill someone it will leave a dreadful mess on the carpet. Worrying about the mess on the carpet and whether it matters is the only real difference between war and peace." I took a hit on my cigarette. "It's not Tolstoy, but I'm working on it."

"No, I like it," he said. "For one thing it's a lot shorter than Tolstoy. These days I fall asleep when I read anything longer than a bus ticket. I like you, Bernie. Enough to give you some good advice about Engelbertina."

"I like you, too, Eric. But there's no need to tell me to lay off her because you think of her like a sister. Believe it or not, I'm not the kind to take advantage."

"That's just it," he said. "You couldn't take advantage of Engelbertina if your middle name was Svengali and she wanted to sing at the Regina Palace Hotel. No, if anyone takes advantage it will be her. Believe me. It's you who needs to be careful. She'll play you like a Steinway if you let her onto your piano stool. Sometimes it's fun to be played. But only if you know it and you don't mind it. I'm just telling you so that you don't fall all the way for her. Specifically this: She isn't the marrying kind." He removed the pipe from his mouth and studied the bowl judiciously. I tossed him the matches again. "The plain fact of the matter is, she's married already."

"I get it," I said. "The husband disappeared in a camp."

"No. Not at all. He's an American soldier who was stationed over at Oberammergau. She married him and then he disappeared. Most likely deserted. Her and the army. It would be a shame if you let her sucker you into taking her on as client, to look for the guy. He's no good, and it would be best if he stayed disappeared."

"That's kind of up to her, isn't it? She's a big girl."

"Yes, I saw you noticing that," he said. "Have it your own way, shamus. Just don't say I didn't warn you."

I flicked my cigarette away and then kicked off the brake on his chair. "Keep your seat," I told him. "I'm all through with blondes and missing husbands. It was looking for a missing husband that cost me my damned finger. I'm real easy to educate that way. Like Pavlov's dog. Some housewife so much as hints that her old man is late back from a card game and could I maybe go look for him, and I'm going to be looking for a pair of concrete gardening gloves. That or a suit of armor." I shook my head. "I'm getting old, Eric. I don't bounce as high as I used to when I take a beating."

I wheeled Gruen back to the house. He was feeling tired, so he went to lie down, and I went to my room. After a moment or two there was a knock at the door. It was Engelbertina. She had a gun in her hand. A Mauser. It was made for shooting bigger things than mice. Fortunately it wasn't pointed at me.

"I wonder if I might ask you to look after this for me," she said.

"Don't tell me you've killed someone."

"No, but I'm afraid Eric might kill himself with it. You see, it's his gun. And, well, sometimes he gets depressed. Depressed enough to use this on himself. I thought that it might be best if it was somewhere safe."

"He's a big boy," I said, taking the gun from her and checking that it was safe. It wasn't. I thumbed on the safety. "He ought to be able to look after his own gun. Besides, he doesn't strike me as the type to kill himself."

"It's all an act," she said. "His cheerfulness. He's not really like that. Inside he's very low. Look, I was going to throw it away, but then I thought that wasn't a good idea. Someone might find it and have an accident. And then I thought, you being a detective, you would know what to do with a gun." She grasped my hand urgently. "Please. If he has to ask you for it, then he won't be able to do anything without talking to someone first."

"All right," I said. After she had gone, I hid the gun behind the hot-water tank in the bathroom.

As usual, something delicious was happening in the kitchen. I wondered what was for dinner. And I wondered if what Gruen had said about Engelbertina could really be true. I didn't have long to wait before any doubts I had on that score were removed.

## TWENTY-FOUR

From time to time, Engelbertina would take my temperature, dose me with penicillin, and inspect the scarred stump of my little finger with the same amount of loving concern a child might have displayed for a sick rabbit. When she took to kissing it I knew that her bedside manner implied a little more bed than was usual. I had never asked her the story of her life. I decided that if she ever wanted to talk about what had happened to her, she would. And one day, while examining my finger in the flirtatious manner already described, she did:

"I'm Austrian," she said. "Did I tell you that before? No, perhaps not. Sometimes I say I'm from Canada. Not because I'm from Canada, but because Canada saved my life. Not the country. I don't mean the country. Canada was what they called one of the sorting areas at Auschwitz where we girls—there were about five hundred of us—had to look through the belongings of all the arriving prisoners for valuables, before they were gassed." She spoke without emotion, as if she had been describing any kind of routine factory work. "At Canada we got better food, nicer clothes, enough sleep. We were even allowed to grow our hair again.

"I went to Auschwitz in 1942. First I worked in the fields. That was very hard. I would have died if I'd continued doing that, I think. And the work ruined my hands. I went to Canada in 1943. Of course it wasn't a holiday camp. Things still happened. Bad things. I was raped three times by SS men while I was there." She shrugged it off. "The first time was the worst. He beat me afterward. Out of guilt I suppose. But he could just as easily have killed me, which sometimes happened out of fear that the girl would tell someone. The second and third time I didn't resist, so I don't know that you could call it rape, really. I didn't want it. But I didn't want to get hurt, either. The third time I even tried to enjoy it, which was a mistake. Because when they opened the camp brothel later that year, someone remembered that and I was transferred to work there, as a prostitute.

"No one called it a brothel, mind. And we certainly didn't think of ourselves as prostitutes, at the time. We were just doing our job, which was to stay alive. It was just Block Twenty-four and we were treated comparatively well. We had clean clothes, showers, exercise, and access to medical attention. We even had perfume. I can't tell you what that was like. To smell nice again. After smelling of sweat, and worse, for a whole year. The men we had sex with weren't SS. They weren't allowed. Some of them risked it. But most restricted themselves to looking through the spy holes in the doors while we were doing it. I made a regular friend in the Auschwitz fire brigade. A Czech man, who treated me very kindly. One hot day, he even sneaked me into the fire-brigade swimming pool. I didn't wear a costume. I remember how nice it felt to feel the sun on my naked body. And how kind all the men were. How they treated me like an object of veneration and worship. It seemed like the happiest day of my life. He was a Catholic and we went through a sort of secret marriage ceremony that was conducted by a priest.

"Things were okay for us until October 1944, when there was a mutiny in the camp. My friend was involved and he was hanged. Then, with the Red Army just a few miles away, they marched us out. That march was the worst thing. Worse than anything I had experienced before. People dropped in the snow and were shot where they fell. Eventually we were herded onto trains and went to Bergen-Belsen, which was much worse than Auschwitz and more terrible than I describe. For a start, there was no food. Nothing. I starved for two months. If I hadn't been so well fed in Block Twenty-four, I would certainly have died at Belsen. When the British liberated the camp in April 1945, I weighed just seventy-five pounds. But I was alive. That was the main thing. Nothing else matters besides that, does it?"

"Nothing at all," I said.

She shrugged. "It happened. I had sex four hundred and sixteen times at Auschwitz. I counted every one of them so that I knew exactly what my survival cost me. I'm proud of my survival. And I'm telling you because of that, and because I want people to know what was done to Jews and communists and Gypsies and homosexuals in the name of National Socialism. I'm also telling you because I like you, Bernie, and because if you should happen to want to go to bed with me, then it's best you know all the facts. After the war I married an Ami. He ran away when he found out what kind of woman I was. Eric thinks that it bothers me, but it doesn't really. It doesn't bother me at all. And why should it matter how many men I slept with? I never killed anyone. To me that would seem like a much worse thing to bear. Like Eric. He shot some French partisans in retaliation for the killing of some men in a German army ambulance. Well, I wouldn't want his conscience. I think to have murder on your conscience would be something much worse than the memory of what I have to live with. Don't you agree?"

"Yes," I said. "I do."

I touched her face with my fingertips. There were no scars on her cheek, but I couldn't help think of the scars she had inside. At least four hundred of them, probably. What she had been through made my own experience seem ordinary, though I knew it wasn't. I had seen some service during the Great War, so I was probably better prepared for it than she had been. Some men might be repelled by what she had told me—like her Ami. I wasn't. Perhaps it would have been better for me if I had been. But what she said made me think we had something in common.

Engelbertina finished smearing ointment on the stump of my finger and then covered it with a piece of gauze and sticking plaster. She said, "Anyway, now you know all of that, you'll know how it is I come to have a whore's manner. And that it's not something I can help. When I like a man, I go to bed with him. It's as simple as that. And I like you, Bernie. I like you a lot."

I'd had more straightforward and matter-of-fact propositions, but only in my dreams. If I'm being honest, I might have judged her more harshly if she'd looked like Lotte Lenya or Fanny Blankers-Koen. But since she looked like the Three Graces rolled into one Hellenistic erotic show, I was more than happy to let myself be played. Like a Steinway, if she felt so inclined. Besides, it had been a while since a woman had looked at me with anything more than puzzlement or curiosity. So, later that night, while Gruen was asleep and Henkell back at the state hospital in Munich, she came to my room to administer a different kind of healing. And over the next ten days, my recovery proceeded to our mutual satisfaction. Mine, anyway.

It's funny the way you feel when you've made love after a long furlough. Like you joined the human race again. As things turned out I hadn't done either of those two things. I didn't know that then. But I was used to not knowing what was what. Being in the dark is an occupational hazard for a detective. Even when a case is closed, it's remarkable how much you still don't know. How much remains hidden. With Britta Warzok I wasn't at all sure if she represented a closed case or not. It was true I had been paid, and handsomely. But there was so much that remained unexplained. One day I managed finally to remember her telephone number and resolved to ring her up and ask her some straight questions about what still puzzled me. Like how it was she knew Father Gotovina. Also, I thought it was time she became aware of just how hard her thousand marks had been earned. And so, while Engelbertina was helping Gruen in the bathroom, I picked up the telephone and dialed the number I had remembered.

I recognized the maid's voice from before. Wallace Beery in a black dress. When I asked to speak to her mistress the already guarded voice grew scornful, as if I had suggested that we might meet for a romantic dinner before going back to my place. "My what?" she growled.

"Your mistress," I said. "Frau Warzok."

"Frau Warzok?" Scorn turned to derision. "She is not my mistress."

"All right, then, who is?"

"That's really none of your business," she said.

"Look here," I said, a little desperate now. "I'm a detective. I could make it my business."

"A detective? Really?" The derision continued unabated. "You're not much of a detective if you don't know who lives here."

She had a point. I felt it keenly, as if the point was one that had been made by Vlad the Impaler.

"I spoke to you one night a few weeks ago. I gave you my name and my telephone number and asked you to ask Frau Warzok to call me. And since she did I presume that you and she are at least on speaking terms. And here's another thing. It's an offense to obstruct a policeman in the execution of his duty," I said. I hadn't actually said I was a cop. That was an offense, too.

"Just a minute, please." She put the phone down somewhere. It sounded like someone hitting the bass key on a xylophone. I heard muffled voices, and there was a longish pause before the receiver was gathered up again and someone else came on the line. The well-spoken voice was a man's. I half-recognized it. But from where?

"Who is this, please?" asked the voice.

"My name is Bernhard Gunther," I said. "I'm a detective. Frau Warzok is my client. She gave me this number to get in touch with her."

"Frau Warzok does not live here," said the man. He was cool but polite. "She never did live here. For a while we collected messages for her. When she was in Munich. But I believe she has gone home now."

"Oh? And where's that?"

"Vienna," he said.

"Do you have a telephone number where I can reach her?"

"No, but I have an address," he said. "Would you like me to give it to you?"

"Yes. Please."

There was another longish pause while, I presumed, whoever it was looked up the address. "Horlgasse forty-two," he said, finally. "Apartment three, Ninth District."

"Thanks, Herr . . . ? Look, whoever are you? The butler? The maid's sparring partner? What? How do I know that address isn't a phony? Just to get rid of me."

"I've told you all that I can," he said. "Really."

"Listen, chum, there's money involved. A lot of money. Frau Warzok hired me to track down a legacy. And there's a substantial recovery fee. I can't collect if I don't get a message to her. I'll give you ten percent of what I'm on if you help me out here with some information. Like—"

"Good-bye," said the voice. "And please don't call again."

The phone went dead. So I called again. What else could I do? But this time there was no reply. And the next time the operator told me that the number was out of order. Which left me sitting in the ink and without a change of trousers.

I was still pondering the possibility that Britta Warzok had kicked some sand in my eyes and was now a perfect stranger to me when another stranger came out of the bathroom. He was sitting in Gruen's wheelchair, which was being pushed, as usual, by Engelbertina but, already confounded by my telephone conversation with Wallace Beery and friend, it was a few seconds before I realized the stranger was Eric Gruen.

"What do you think?" he said, stroking his now smoothly shaven face.

"You've shaved off your beard," I said, like an idiot.

"Engelbertina did it," he said. "What do you think?"

"You look much better without it," she said.

"I know what you think," he said. "I was asking Bernie."

I shrugged. "You look much better without it," I said.

"Younger," she added. "Younger and better-looking."

"You're just saying that," he said.

"No, it's true," she said. "Isn't it, Bernie?"

I nodded, studying the face more carefully now. There was something familiar in its features. The broken nose, the pugnacious chin, the tight mouth, and the smooth forehead. "Younger? Yes, I believe so. But there's something else I can't quite put my finger on." I shook my head. "I don't know. Maybe you were right, Eric. When you said that you thought we'd met before. Now that you've got rid of the face guard, there's something about you that does strike me as familiar."

"Really?" He sounded vague now. As if he wasn't quite sure himself.

Engelbertina uttered a loud tut of exasperation. "Can't you see it?" she said. "You pair of idiots. Isn't it obvious? You look like brothers. Yes, that's it. Brothers."

Gruen and I looked at each other and straightaway we knew that she was right. We did look quite alike. But she still fetched a hand mirror and obliged us to bow our heads together and view our reflection. "That's who each of you is reminded of when you look at the other," she announced, almost triumphantly. "Yourself, of course."

"I always did want an older brother," said Gruen.

"What's with the older?" I asked.

"Well, it's true," he insisted, and started to fill his pipe. "You look like an older version of me. A little more gray and worn-looking. Harder-bitten, certainly. Perhaps even a little coarser, on the edges. And I think you look less intelligent than me. Or maybe just a little puzzled. Like you can't remember where it was you left your hat."

"You forgot to mention taller," I said. "By about two and half feet."

He looked at me squarely, grinned, and lit his pipe. "No, on second thought, I do mean less intelligent. Perhaps even a little stupid. The stupid detective."

I thought of Britta Warzok and how it didn't make any sense her retaining me if she had any idea that Father Gotovina was part of the Comradeship. Unless she did know all along and I was just too stupid to see through what she had been up to. Which of course I didn't. The stupid detective. It had a nice ring to it. Like it might just have been true.

# TWENTY-FIVE

The next day Heinrich Henkell turned up for the weekend and declared he was going straight on to his laboratory. Gruen wasn't feeling very well and had stayed in bed, so Henkell offered to take me with him.

"Besides," he added, by way of an extra reason for me to accompany him. "You've not really seen anything of Garmisch-Partenkirchen, have you, Bernie?"

"No, not yet."

"Well then, you must come along and have a look. It would do you good to get out of here for a while."

We drove slowly down the mountain, which was just as well, since, around a bend, we encountered a small herd of cattle crossing the road that ran parallel to the railway track. A little farther on, Henkell explained just how significant the railway track was in Garmisch-Partenkirchen.

"The railway line provides the clearest division between the two old towns," he said. "Garmisch, on our left and to the east of the track, is a little more modern. Not least because that's where the Olympic ski stadium is. Partenkirchen, to the west of the track, feels a lot older. It's also where most of the Amis are based."

As we drove onto Bahnhofstrasse and along Zugspitzstrasse, he pointed out the façades of houses that were decorated with what were called "air paintings," some of them resembling the façades on some of Munich's elaborate rococo churches. Garmisch-Partenkirchen could not have seemed more Catholic if the pope had owned a ski chalet there. But the town also looked prosperous, and it was easy to see why. There were Americans everywhere, as if the war had only just ended. Most of the vehicles on the roads were Jeeps and U.S. Army trucks and, on every second building, was hanging the Stars and Stripes. It was hard to believe we were in Germany at all.

"My God, look at it," I exclaimed. "Next thing, they'll be painting frescoes of Mickey Mouse on the buildings they've requisitioned."

"Oh, it's not that bad," said Henkell. "And you know, they mean well."

"So did the Holy Inquisition," I said. "Pull up at that tobacconist's. I need to get some Luckies."

"Didn't I warn you about smoking?" he said, but he pulled up anyway.

"With all this fresh air around?" I said. "Where's the harm?"

I stepped out of the car and went into the tobacconist's. I bought some cigarettes and then walked several times around the shop, enjoying the sensation of behaving like a normal person again. The shopkeeper eyed me suspiciously.

"Was there something else?" he asked, pointing at me with the stem of his meerschaum.

"No, I was just looking," I said.

He pushed the pipe back in his smug little face and rocked on a pair of shoes that were decorated with edelweiss, oak leaves, and Bavarian blue-and-white ribbons. They lacked only a Blue Max or an Iron Cross to be the most German-looking shoes I had ever seen. He said, "This is a shop, not a museum."

"Not so as you'd notice," I said, and went out quickly, the shop bell ringing in my ear.

"I bet this place is real cozy in winter," I said to Henkell when I was back in the car. "The locals are about as affable as a cold pitchfork."

"They're really quite friendly when you get to know them," he said.

"Funny. That's the same thing people say after their dog has bitten you."

We drove on toward the southwest of Partenkirchen, toward the foot of the Zugspitze, past the Post Hotel, the American Officers' Club, the General Patton Hotel, the headquarters of the U.S. Army Southeastern Area Command, and the Green Arrow Ski Lodge. I might as well have been in Denver, Colorado. I had never been in Denver, Colorado, but I imagined it probably looked a lot like Partenkirchen. Patriotic, affected, overornamented, unfriendly in a friendly kind of way, and, ultimately, more than a little absurd.

Henkell drove down a street of typical old Alpine houses and pulled into the driveway of a two-story white stucco villa with a wraparound wooden balcony and an overhanging roof that was as big as the deck on an aircraft carrier. On the wall was a fresco of a German Olympic skier. I knew he was German because his right arm appeared to be reaching for something, but just what this might be there was no way of telling, as someone had painted over his hand and wrist. And perhaps only a German would now have realized what the skier's right hand had really been up to. Everything in Garmisch-Partenkirchen looked so committed to Uncle Sam and his welfare that it was hard to believe Uncle Adolf had ever been here.

I stepped out of the Mercedes and glanced up at the Zugspitze that hung over the houses like a petrified wave of gray seawater. It was a hell of a lot of geology.

Hearing gunshots I flinched, probably even ducked a bit, and then looked behind me. Henkell laughed. "The Amis have a skeet range on the other side of the river," he said, walking toward the front door. "Everything you see around here was requisitioned by the Amis. They let me use this place for my work. But before the war it was the science lab for the local hospital, on Maximilianstrasse."

"Doesn't the hospital need a lab anymore?"

"After the war the hospital became the prison hospice," he said, searching for his door key. "For incurably sick German POWs."

"What was wrong with them?"

"Psychiatric cases, most of them, poor fellows," he said. "Shell shock, that kind of thing. Not my line really. Most of them died following an outbreak of viral meningitis. The rest they transferred to a hospital in Munich, about six months ago. The hospital is now being turned into a rest and recreation area for American service personnel."

He opened the door and went inside. But I stayed where I was, staring at a car parked across the street. It was a car I had seen before. A nice, two-door Buick Roadmaster. Shiny green, with whitewall tires, a rear end as big as an Alpine hillside, and a front grille like a dentist's star patient.

I followed Henkell through the door and into a narrow hallway that was noticeably warm. On the walls were several photographs of winter Olympians—Maxi Herber, Ernst Baier, Willy Bognor taking the Olympic oath, and a couple of ski jumpers who must have been thinking they could make it all the way to Valhalla. The air in the house had a chemical edge to it, as well as something decayed and botanical, like a pair of wet gardening gloves.

"Shut the door behind you," yelled Henkell. "We have to keep it warm in here."

As I turned to close the door I heard voices and when I turned back, I found the corridor blocked by someone I recognized. It was the American who had persuaded me to dig up my back garden in Dachau.

"Well, if it isn't the kraut with principles," he said.

"Coming from you, that's not much of a compliment," I said. "Stolen any Jewish gold lately?"

He grinned. "Not lately. There's not so much of it about these days. And you? How's the hotel business?" He didn't wait for my answer and, without taking his eyes off me, inclined his head back across his shoulder and shouted, "Hey, Heinrich. Where did you find this kraut? And why the hell is he here?"

"I told you." Henkell stepped back into the corridor. "This is the man I met at the hospital."

"You mean *he's* the detective you were talking about?"

"Yes," said Henkell. "Have you two met before?"

The American was wearing a different sports coat. This one was gray and cashmere. He wore a gray shirt, a gray woolen tie, gray flannels, and a pair of black wingtips. His glasses were different, too. These were tortoiseshell. But he still looked like the cleverest boy in the class.

"Only in my previous life," I said. "When I was a hotelkeeper."

"You had a hotel?"

Henkell looked as if he found the idea of that absurd. Which it was, of course.

"And guess where it was?" said the American, with amused contempt. "Dachau. About a mile from the old camp." He laughed out loud. "Jesus, that's like opening a health spa in a funeral parlor."

"It was good enough for you and your friend," I remarked. "The amateur dentist."

Henkell laughed. "Does he mean Wolfram Romberg?" he asked the American.

"He means Wolfram Romberg," said the American.

Henkell came along the corridor and put a hand on my shoulder. "Major Jacobs works for the Central Intelligence Agency," he explained, guiding me into the next room.

"Somehow I didn't figure him for an army chaplain," I said.

"He's been a good friend to me and Eric. A very good friend. The CIA provides this building and some money for our research."

"But somehow it never seems to be quite enough," Jacobs said pointedly.

"Medical research can be expensive," said Henkell.

We went into an office with a neat, professional, medical look. A large filing cabinet on the floor. A Biedermeier bookcase with dozens of medical texts inside, and a human skull on top. A first-aid cabinet on the wall next to a photograph of President Truman. An Art Deco drinks tray with a large selection of liquor bottles and mixers. A rococo walnut writing desk that was buried under several feet of papers and notebooks, with another human skull being used as a paperweight. Four or five cherry-wood chairs. And a bronze of a man's head with a little plaque that said the likeness was of Alexander Fleming. Henkell pointed through two sets of sliding glass doors at a very well equipped laboratory.

"Microscopes, centrifuges, spectrometers, vacuum equipment," he said. "It all costs money. The major here has sometimes had to find several unauthorized streams of revenue in order to keep us going. Including Oberscharführer Romberg and his Dachau nest egg."

"Right," growled Jacobs. He drew aside the net curtain and stared suspiciously out of the office window into the back garden of the villa. A couple of birds had begun a noisy fight. There is a lot to be said for the way Nature handles itself. I wouldn't have minded taking a sock at Jacobs myself.

I smiled. "It's certainly none of my business what the major did with all those poor people's stolen valuables."

"You got that right," said Jacobs. "Kraut."

"What exactly are you working on, Heinrich?" I asked.

Jacobs looked at Henkell. "For Christ's sake, don't tell him," he said.

"Why not?" asked Henkell.

"You don't know anything about the guy," he said. "And have you forgotten that you and Eric are working for the American government? I would use the word 'secret,' only I don't think you guys know how to spell it."

"He's staying in my house," said Henkell. "I trust Bernie."

"I'm still trying to figure out why that is," said Jacobs. "Or is it just an SS thing? Old comrades. What?"

I was still wondering a little about that myself.

"I told you why," said Henkell. "Eric gets a bit lonely, sometimes. Possibly even suicidal."

"Jesus, I wish I was as lonely as Eric is," snorted Jacobs. "That broad who looks after him, Engelbertina, or whatever her name is. How anyone could be lonely with her around sure beats me."

"He does have a point," I said.

"You see? Even the kraut agrees with me," said Jacobs.

"I wish you wouldn't use that word," said Henkell.

"'Kraut'? What's wrong with it?"

"It's like me calling you a kike," said Henkell. "Or a yid."

"Yeah, well, get used to it, buddy," said Jacobs. "The yids are in charge now. And you krauts will have to do what you're told."

Henkell looked at me and, quite deliberately, as if to irritate the major, said, "We're working on finding a cure for malaria."

Jacobs sighed loudly.

"I thought there *was* a cure for that," I said.

"No," said Henkell. "There are several treatments. Some of them are more effective than others. Quinine. Chloroquine. Atebrin. Proguanil. Some of them have rather unpleasant side effects. And of course, in time, the disease will become resistant to these drugs. No, when I say a cure, I mean something more than that."

"Give him the keys to the safe, why don't you?" said Jacobs.

Henkell continued, hardly deterred by the Ami's obvious displeasure. "We're working on a vaccine. Now that really would be something worthwhile, wouldn't you say so, Bernie?"

"I guess so."

"Come and have a look." Henkell ushered me through the first set of glass doors. Jacobs followed.

"We have two sets of glass doors to keep things extra warm in the lab. You may find you have to remove your jacket." He closed the first set of glass doors before opening the second set. "If I'm in here for any length of time, I usually wear just a tropical shirt. It really is quite tropical in here. Like a hothouse."

As soon as the second set of doors was open, the heat hit me. Henkell had not exaggerated. It was like walking into a South American jungle. Jacobs had already started to sweat. I removed my jacket and rolled up my sleeves.

"Every year almost a million people die of malaria, Bernie," said Henkell. "A million." He nodded at Jacobs. "He just wants a vaccine to give to American soldiers before they go to whichever part of the world they intend to occupy next. Southeast Asia, possibly. Central America, for sure."

"Why don't you write an article for the newspapers?" said Jacobs. "Tell the whole goddamn world what we're up to here."

"But Eric and I want to save lives," said Henkell, ignoring Jacobs. "This is his work as much as it is mine." He took off his jacket and unbuttoned his shirt collar. "Think of it, Bernie. The idea that Germans could do something that would save a million lives a year. That might go a long way to balancing the books for what Germany did during the war. Wouldn't you say so?"

"It might at that," I admitted.

"A million lives saved every year," said Henkell. "Why, in six years, even the Jews might have forgiven us. And in twenty, perhaps the Russians, too."

"He wants to give it to the Russians," murmured Jacobs. "Beautiful."

"That's what drives us forward, Bernie."

"To say nothing of all the money they'll make if they do manage to synthesize a vaccine," said Jacobs. "Millions of dollars."

Henkell shook his head. "He doesn't have the first idea of what really drives us," he said. "He's a bit of a cynic. Aren't you, Jonathan?"

"If you say so, kraut."

I glanced around the hothouse laboratory. There were two work benches, one on either side of the room. One was home to a variety of scientific equipment, including several microscopes. On the other were ranged a dozen or so heated glass cases. Under a window looking out onto another part of the neat garden were three sinks. But it was the glass cases that drew my attention. Two of them were teeming with insect life. Even through the glass you could hear the whining sound of the many mosquitoes, like tiny opera singers trying to sustain a high note. It made my flesh creep just to look at them.

"Those are our VIPs," said Henkell. "The *Culex pipen.* The stagnant-water variety of mosquito and therefore the most dangerous, as it carries the disease. We try to breed our own in the lab. But from time to time we have to get new specimens sent all the way from Florida. The eggs and larvae are surprisingly resilient to the low temperatures of long-distance air travel. Fascinating, aren't they? That something so small can be so lethal. Which malaria is, of course. For most people, anyway. Studies I've seen show that it's nearly always fatal in children. But women are more resistant than men. Nobody knows why."

I shuddered and stepped away from the glass case.

"He doesn't care for your little friends, Heinrich," said Jacobs. "And I can't say that I blame him. I hate the little bastards. I have nightmares that one of them will get out and bite me."

"I'm sure they have more taste than that," I said.

"Which is why we need more money. For better isolation chambers and handling facilities. An electron microscope. Specimen holders. New slide staining systems." All of this was directed at Major Jacobs. "To prevent just such an accident from happening."

"We're working on it," Jacobs said and yawned ostentatiously, as if he had heard all of this many times before. He took out a cigarette case and then seemed to think better of it under Henkell's disapproving eye. "No smoking in the laboratory," he murmured, slipping the cigarette case back into his pocket. "Right."

"You remembered," said Henkell, smiling. "We're making progress."

"I hope so," said Jacobs. "I just wish you'd remember to keep a lid on all of this." He had one eye on me when he said this. "Like we agreed. This project is supposed to be a secret." And he and Henkell began to argue again.

I turned my back on them and leaned over an old copy of *Life* magazine that was lying on the bench, next to a microscope. I flipped the pages, giving my English a little exercise. Americans looked so wholesome. Like another master race. I started to read an article titled "The Battered Face of Germany." There was a series of aerial pictures of what German towns and cities looked like after the RAF and U.S. 8th Air Force had finished. Mainz looked like a mud-brick village in Abyssinia. Julich, like someone had experimented with an early atomic bomb. It was enough to remind me of just how total had been our annihilation.

"It wouldn't matter so much," Jacobs was saying, "if you didn't leave papers and documents lying around. Things that are sensitive and secret." And so saying he removed the magazine from my eyes and went through the double glass doors back into the office.

I followed him, full of curiosity. So did Henkell.

Standing in front of the desk, Jacobs fished a key chain out of his trouser pocket, unlocked a briefcase, and tossed the magazine inside. Then he locked it again. I wondered what was in that magazine. Nothing secret, surely. Every week *Life* magazine was sold all over the world, with a circulation in the millions. Unless they were using *Life* as a codebook. I'd heard that was the way things like that were done these days.

Henkell closed the glass doors carefully behind him and uttered a laugh. "Now he just thinks you're crazy," he said. "Me, too, probably."

"I don't give a damn what he thinks," said Jacobs.

"Gentlemen," I said. "It's been interesting. But I think I ought to be going. It's a nice day and I could use some exercise. So if you don't mind, Heinrich, I'm going to try to walk back to the house."

"It's four miles, Bernie," said Henkell. "Are you sure you're up to it?"

"I think so. And I'd like to try."

"Why don't you take my car? Major Jacobs can drive me back when he and I have finished up here."

"No, really," I said. "I'll be fine."

"I'm sorry he was so rude," said Henkell.

"Don't get sore," Jacobs told him. "It's nothing personal. He surprised me, turning up again like this, that's all. In my business, I don't like surprises. Next time we'll meet at the house. We'll have a drink. It'll be more relaxed that way. All right, Gunther?"

"Sure," I said. "We'll have a drink and then go and dig in the garden. Just like old times."

"A German with a sense of humor," said Jacobs. "I like that."

## TWENTY-SIX

When they first make you a cop they put you on a beat. They make you walk so you have enough time to notice things. No one ever notices much from the inside of a stripe wagon traveling at thirty miles an hour. "Flatfoot" and "gumshoe" are words that come at you when you wear hobnailed boots. If I had left Henkell's laboratory in the Mercedes, I would never have glanced in the window of Major Jacob's Buick and I would never have seen that he had left it unlocked. Nor would I have looked back at the villa and remembered that it was impossible to see the road and the car from the office window. I didn't like Major Jacobs, in spite of his approximate apology. That was no reason to search his car, of course. But then, "snooper" is another word for what I do and what I am. I am a professional sniffer, an oven-peeper, a nosey parker, and I was feeling very nosy about a man who had dug up my back garden in search of Jewish gold and who was sufficiently secretive—not to say paranoid—to lock away an old copy of *Life* magazine in order to stop me from looking at it.

I liked his Buick. The front seat was as big as the bunk in a Pullman sleeping car, with a steering wheel the size of a bicycle tire and a car radio that looked like it had been borrowed from a café jukebox. The speedometer said it went up to one hundred twenty miles per hour, and with its straight eight and Dynaflow transmission, I figured it was good for at least a hundred of that. About a yard away from the speedometer, on the sunny side of the dash, was a matching clock, so you'd know when it was time to go and buy more gas. Below the clock was a glove box for a man with bigger hands than Jacobs had. Actually it looked like a glove box for the goddess Kali with room for a couple of garlands of skulls as well.

I leaned across the seat, thumbed it open, and raked around for a moment. There was a snub-nosed thirty-eight-caliber Smith & Wesson—a J-frame with a nice rubberized grip. The one he had pointed at me in Dachau. A Michelin road map of Germany. A commemorative postcard to celebrate Goethe's two hundredth anniversary. An American edition of *The Goebbels Diaries*. A Blue Guide to northern Italy. Inside the Blue Guide, at the pages for Milan, was a receipt from a jeweler's shop. The jeweler's name was Primo Ottolenghi, and the receipt was for ten thousand dollars. It seemed reasonable to assume that Milan had been where Jacobs had sold the box of Jewish valuables dug up in my back garden, especially since the receipt was dated a week or so after his stay with us. There was a letter from the Rochester Strong Memorial Hospital, in the State of New York, itemizing some medical equipment delivered to Garmisch-Partenkirchen, via the Rhein-Main Air Base.

There was a notepad. The first page was blank, but I could just make out the indentation of what had been written on the previous page. I tore off the first few pages in the hope that later on I might shade up whatever Jacobs had written down.

I returned everything else to the glove box, closed it, and then glanced over my shoulder at the backseat. There were copies of the Paris edition of the *Herald* and the *Süddeutsche Zeitung,* and a rolled-up umbrella. Nothing else. It wasn't much, but I knew a little more about Jacobs than before. I knew he was serious about guns. I knew where he was likely to hawk the family heirlooms. And I knew he was interested in Joey the Crip. Maybe that kraut Goethe, too, on a good day. Sometimes knowing only a little is a preface to knowing a lot.

I got out of the car, shut the door quietly, and, keeping the River Loisach on my right, walked northeast, in the direction of Sonnenbichl, taking a shortcut through the grounds of what had once been the hospital and was now being turned into an R&R center for American servicemen.

I started to think about returning to Munich to pick up the threads of my business. I decided that, in the absence of any new clients, I might see if I could find any trace of the last one. Perhaps I would go back to the Holy Ghost Church and hope that she turned up there. Or speak to poor Felix Klingerhoefer at American Overseas Airlines. Perhaps he could remember something about Britta Warzok other than that she had come from Vienna.

The walk back to Mönch took longer than I had bargained for. I had forgotten that a lot of the walk, most of it in fact, was uphill, and even without a knapsack on my back I was something less than the happy wanderer by the time I crept into the house, crawled onto my bed, unlaced my shoes, and closed my eyes. It was several minutes before Engelbertina realized I had returned and came to find me. Her face told me immediately that something was wrong.

"Eric had a telegram," she explained. "From Vienna. His mother is dead. He's rather upset about it."

"Really? I thought they hated each other."

"They did," she said. "I think that's part of the problem. He realizes he won't ever be able to make it up with her now. Not ever." She showed me the telegram.

"I don't think I should be reading his telegram," I said, reading his telegram all the same. "Where is he now?"

"In his room. He said he just wanted to be left alone."

"I can understand that," I said. "Your mother dies, it's not like losing a cat. Not unless you're a cat."

Engelbertina smiled sadly and took my hand. "Do you have a mother?"

"Naturally I used to have one," I said. "A father, too, if memory serves. Only somewhere along the way I seem to have lost them both. Careless of me."

"Me, too," she said. "That's something else we have in common, isn't it?"

"Yes," I said, without much enthusiasm. As far as I was concerned, there was only one thing we seemed to have in common, and that was what went on in her bedroom, or mine. I looked at Gruen's telegram again. "This suggests that he has come into a considerable fortune," I said.

"Yes, but only if he goes to Vienna to see the lawyers in person and claims it," she said. "And somehow I can't see that happening. Not in his present condition. Can you?"

"Just how sick is he, anyway?" I asked her.

"If it was just the use of his legs he had lost, he wouldn't be so bad," she said. "But he lost his spleen as well."

"I didn't know that," I said. "Is that serious?"

"Losing your spleen increases your risk of infection," she said. "The spleen is a kind of blood filter and reserve supply. That's why he runs out of energy so easily." She shook her head. "I really don't think he could make it to Vienna. Even in Heinrich's car. Vienna's almost three hundred miles away, isn't it?"

"I don't know," I said. "It's a long time since I was in Vienna. What's more, when you do get there it seems even farther away than you had bargained for. If you know what I mean. There's something about the Viennese I don't like. They turn out a very Austrian sort of German."

"You mean like Hitler?"

"No, Hitler was a very German sort of Austrian. There's a difference." I thought for a moment. "How much money is involved, do you think? With Eric's family, I mean."

"I'm not exactly sure," she said. "But the Gruen family owned one of the largest sugar factories in Central Europe." She shrugged. "So it could be quite a lot. Everyone has a sweet tooth, don't they?"

"They do in Austria," I said. "But that's as sweet as they ever get."

"Aren't you forgetting something?" she said. "I'm Austrian."

"And I bet that makes you really proud," I said. "When the Nazis annexed Austria, in 1938, I was living in Berlin. I remember Austrian Jews coming to live in Berlin because they thought Berliners would be more tolerant than the Viennese."

"And were they?"

"For a while. The Nazis never really liked Berlin, you know. It took them a long time to bring the city to heel. A long time and a lot of blood. Berlin was just the showcase for what happened. But the real heart of Nazism was Munich. Still is, I shouldn't wonder." I lit a cigarette. "You know, I envy you, Engelbertina. At least you have a choice between calling yourself an Austrian and calling yourself a Jew. I'm a German and there's nothing I can do about that. Right now it feels like the mark of Cain."

Engelbertina squeezed the hand she was still holding. "Cain had a brother," she said. "And in a way, so do you, Bernie. Or at least someone who looks a lot like your brother. Maybe you can help him. That's your job, isn't it? Helping people?"

"You make it sound like a very noble calling," I said. "Parsifal and the Holy Grail and five hours of Wagner. That's not me at all, Engelbertina. I'm more your beer mug kind of knight with three minutes of Gerhard Winkler and his Regent Classic Orchestra."

"Then make it something noble," she said. "Do something better. Something selfless and unmercenary. I'm sure you can think of a noble thing you could do. For Eric, perhaps."

"I don't know. Where's the profit in doing something selfless and unmercenary?"

"Oh, I can tell you," she said. "If you've got the time and patience to listen. And the willingness to make a change in your life."

I knew she was talking about religion. It wasn't one of my favorite topics of conversation, especially with her. "No, but maybe there is something I could do," I said, quickly changing the subject. "Something sort of noble. At least, it's as noble an idea as I'm capable of thinking up without a couple of drinks inside me."

"Then let's hear it," she said. "I'm in the mood to be impressed by you."

"My dear girl, you are always in the mood to be impressed by me," I said. "Which I am unable to account for. You look at me and you seem to think I can do no wrong. I can and I do." I paused for a moment and then added: "Tell me, do you really think I look a lot like Eric?"

She nodded. "You know you do, Bernie."

"And there was just his mother, right?"

"Yes. Just his mother."

"And she didn't know he was in a wheelchair?"

"She knew he'd been badly injured," she said. "But that's all. Nothing more specific."

"Then answer me this," I said. "Do you think I could pass for him? In Vienna. With his family lawyers."

She looked me square in the face and thought about that for a moment and then started to nod. "That's a great idea," she said. "As far as I know, he hasn't been back to Vienna in twenty years. People can change a lot in twenty years."

"Especially the last twenty years," I said, wiggling my fingers. "I used to be the church organist. Where's his passport?"

"It's a brilliant idea," she said enthusiastically.

"It's not very noble," I said.

"But it's practical. And maybe in this particular situation, practical is better than noble. I'd never have thought of something like that."

Engelbertina stood up and opened a bureau from which she removed a manila envelope. She handed me the envelope.

I opened it and took out a passport. I checked the date and the photograph. The passport was still valid. I studied the photograph critically. Then I handed it to her. She looked at the picture and then ran her fingers through my hair as if checking out the amount of gray there and wondering if perhaps it was too much. "Of course, we'd have to change your hairstyle," she said. "You're older than Eric. The funny thing is, though, you don't look much older. But, yes, you could pass for him." She bounced a little on the edge of my bed. "Why don't we ask him what he thinks?"

"No," I said. "Let's wait awhile. Let's wait until this evening. Right now he's probably too upset to think clearly about anything very much."

## TWENTY-SEVEN

"It's a crazy idea," said Eric Gruen, when I had finished describing my suggestion to him. "The craziest idea I ever heard of."

"Why?" I asked. "You say you've never met the family lawyer. He doesn't know you're in a wheelchair. I show him your passport, and he sees an older, thicker version of the person in the photograph. I sign the papers. You get your estate. What could be simpler? Just as long as there's no one who really remembers you."

"My mother was a very difficult woman," said Gruen. "With very few friends. It wasn't just me with whom she had a problem. Even my father couldn't stand her. She didn't even go to his funeral. No, there's just the lawyer. But look here, they know I'm a doctor. Suppose they ask you a medical question?"

"I'm collecting an inheritance," I said. "Not applying for a job at a hospital."

"True." Gruen inspected the contents of his pipe. "All the same, there's something about it that I don't like. It feels dishonest."

Engelbertina adjusted the rug over his legs. "Bernie's right, Eric. What could be simpler?"

Gruen looked up at Henkell and handed him his passport. Henkell had yet to offer an opinion on my scheme. "What do you think, Heinrich?"

Henkell studied the photograph for a long moment. "I don't think there's any doubt that Bernie could easily pass for an older version of you, Eric," he said. "And there's no doubt that the money would be useful for our research. Major Jacobs is being difficult about buying that electron microscope we asked him for. He says we'll have to wait until the spring of next year, when his department will get some new budgets."

"I'd forgotten that," said Gruen. "You're right. The money would be very useful, wouldn't it? My mother's money could easily underwrite our work." He laughed bitterly. "My God, she'd hate that."

"I have spent quite a bit of my own money, Eric," Henkell said. "Not that I mind a bit. You know that. I'll do whatever it takes to isolate this vaccine. But Jacobs is becoming a nuisance. If we had access to some new funds, we could afford to get rid of him and the Amis. It would make this an exclusively German scientific effort. Just like it was before."

"If Bernie did go in my place it really would solve a lot of problems, wouldn't it?" he said. "I'm really not up to going myself. You were right about that."

"The question is," said Henkell, "whether you're up to doing this yourself, Bernie. You're only just back to full health. And you say you find yourself tiring very easily."

"I'm all right," I said, dusting off his concern. "I'll be fine."

In many ways staying at Henkell's house had suited me very well. I was putting on some weight. Even my chess game had improved thanks to Gruen's helpful hints. On the face of it, I couldn't have been more comfortable if I had been a bug in the mane of the Emperor Caligula's favorite horse. But I was keen to go to Vienna. One reason was that I had gone over the blank sheets of paper I had taken from Major Jacob's pad and found the outline of an address in Vienna. Horlgasse, 42. Apartment 3. Ninth District. Curiously, this was the same address I had been given for Britta Warzok. But another reason was Engelbertina.

"Then I agree," said Gruen, puffing some life back into his pipe. "I agree, but I have one or two conditions. And these cannot be set aside. The first condition, Bernie, is that you should be paid. My family is rich and I will be forever in your debt, so it ought to be a decent amount. I think twenty thousand Austrian schillings would be a suitable sum for performing such a valuable service."

I started to protest that it was too much, but Gruen shook his head. "I won't hear any objections. If you won't agree to my fee, then I won't agree to your going."

I shrugged. "If you insist," I said.

"And not just your fee but all your expenses," he added. "You ought to stay in the kind of hotel I'd stay in myself, now that I'm rich."

I nodded, hardly inclined to argue with such largesse.

"My third condition is more delicate," he said. "I think you probably remember me telling you that I left a girl in trouble, in Vienna. It's a bit late, I know, but I should like to make amends. Her child. My child, must be twenty-one years old by now. I'd like to give them both some money. Only I'd rather they didn't know it was from me. So I'd like you to go and see them as if you were a private detective retained by a client who prefers to remain anonymous. Something like that, anyway. I'm sure you know the form, Bernie."

"Suppose they're dead," I said.

"If they're dead, they're dead. I have an address. You could check it out for me."

"I'll get Jacobs to help with the relevant papers," Henkell said. "You'll need an Allied Forces Permit to pass through the British, French, and American zones. And a Gray Pass to go through the Russian zone of occupation. How will you get there?"

"I prefer to go by train," I said. "I'll attract less attention that way."

"There's a travel agency I use at the main station in Munich," said Henkell. "I'll get them to buy you a ticket. When will you go?"

"How soon can Jacobs get those travel documents?"

"Not long, I should think," said Henkell. "He's pretty well connected."

"So I gathered."

"Twenty-four hours?" said Henkell.

"Then I'll go the day after tomorrow."

"But in whose name should I book it?" asked Henkell. "Yours or Eric's? We have to think this through carefully. Suppose you were searched and they found you had another passport. They'd assume one was false and that you were an illegal refugee from the Russian Zone. You'd be handed over to them and tossed into a labor camp." He frowned. "It's quite a risk, Bernie. Are you really sure you want to do this?"

"It would look odd if my travel warrant was in one name and my hotel registration in another," I said. "That's something your family lawyer might easily discover. No, for continuity's sake, everything—tickets, travel warrants, hotel bookings—ought to be done in the name of Eric Gruen. And I'll leave my own passport at my apartment in Munich." I shrugged. "As it happens, I'd rather not use my own passport in Vienna. The Ivans might have flagged my name. The last time I was in Vienna, I had a run-in with an MVD colonel named Poroshin."

"What about the funeral?" asked Gruen.

"Might be risky to go," said Henkell.

"It would look odd if I didn't," I said.

"I agree," said Gruen. "I'll telegraph the lawyers to let them know I'm coming. I'll have them open a drawing account at my mother's bank. So you'll have your money as soon as you get there. And your expenses, of course. Not to mention the money for Vera and her daughter." He smiled sheepishly. "Vera Messmann. That's her name. The one I left in the lurch, in Vienna."

"I wish I could go to Vienna," said Engelbertina, pouting girlishly.

I smiled, trying to seem indulgent, but the plain fact of the matter was that the other reason I was keen to go to Vienna was to get away from Engelbertina. For a while anyway. And I was beginning to understand just why her second husband, the Ami, had fled to

Hamburg. I've known women who have slept with a lot of men. My wife for one, although maybe not four hundred of them. And when I was a cop, back in Berlin, there were always snappers who were in and out of the Alex. I'd been fond of one or two of them, too. It wasn't Engelbertina's promiscuous history that made me feel uncomfortable with her so much as the many other strange little things I had noticed about her.

For one thing, I noticed that she always stood up whenever Gruen or Henkell came into a room. I found it a little strange the way she exhibited a deference to them both that verged on the slavish. I also noticed that she never once met their eyes. Whenever either man glanced in her direction she would look at the floor, and sometimes even bow her head. Well, perhaps this wasn't so unusual in a German employer-employee relationship. Especially given that they were doctors and she was a nurse. German doctors can be martinets, some of them, and quite intimidating, as I myself had discovered when Kirsten was dying.

Some of the other strange things I had noticed about Engelbertina I also found irritating, like lines of spider's thread that I kept pulling off my face as our relationship went along. Such as her tendency to infantilism. Her room was full of soft toys that Henkell and Gruen had bought for her. Teddy bears mostly. There must have been three or four dozen of them. Shoulder to shoulder, their eyes beady and thoughtful, their mouths thin and tightly stitched, they looked as if they were planning a putsch to take over her room. And naturally I suspected that I would have been the first victim of the ursine purge that would have followed their takeover. The teddy bears and I did not see eye to eye. Except on one thing, perhaps. Very probably the second victim of the purge would have been her Philco tabletop radio phonograph, which had been a wedding present from her missing Ami. And if not the phonograph itself, then certainly the one record she seemed to own. This was a rather melancholy ballad—"Auf Wiedersehen," from Sigmund Romberg's musical *Blue Paradise,* and sung on her record by Lale Andersen. Engelbertina played it over and over again, and pretty soon it had me climbing the walls.

Then there was Engelbertina's devotion to God. Every night, including the nights when she had been making love with me, she would get out of bed and, kneeling beside it, her hands clasped as tightly as her eyes were closed, she would pray out loud, as if she had been throwing herself on the mercy of a Prussian magistrate. And while she prayed, sometimes—on the nights when I felt too tired to get up and leave her room—I listened and was shocked to discover that Engelbertina's hopes and aspirations for herself and the world were so banal, they would have left a stuffed panda stupefied with boredom. After praying, she would invariably open her Bible and literally riffle through the pages in search of her God's answer. More often than not her random choice of chapter and verse allowed her to form the unlikely conclusion that she had indeed been given one.

But the strangest and most irritating thing about Engelbertina was her conceit that she possessed the gift of healing hands. Despite her medical training, which was genuine, she would sometimes place a tea towel on her head—quite unself-consciously—and her hands on her victim/patient and proceed to enter some kind of trance that left her breathing loudly through her nose and shaking violently like someone in an electric chair. She did it once with me, placing her hands on my chest and going into her Madame Blavatsky routine, managing to convince me only that she was a complete spinner.

These days the only time I enjoyed her company was when she was kneeling in front of me, with both hands clutching the sheet as if she hoped that very soon it would all be over. And usually it was. I wanted to get away from Engelbertina in the same way a cat wants to escape from the sticky clutches of a clumsily affectionate child. And as quickly as possible.

## TWENTY-EIGHT

I glanced up at the pewter Austrian sky from which snow was now descending onto the roof of the International Patrol vehicle, drifting there like a layer of whipped cream. Of the four elephants inside the truck, probably only the Russian corporal felt homesick when he saw the snow. The other three just looked cold and sick. Even the diamonds in an adjacent jewelry shop were looking a little chilly. I turned up my coat collar, pulled my hat over my ears, and walked quickly along the Graben, past the baroque monument that had been erected to the memory of the hundred thousand Viennese who had died in the plague of 1679. In spite of the snow, or perhaps even because of it, the Graben Café was doing a brisk business. Well-dressed, well-built women were hurrying through the revolving doors with their shopping. With half an hour to kill before my meeting with the Gruen family lawyers, I hurried after them.

In the back room there was a stage set for a small orchestra, and a few tables where some dead fish masquerading as men were playing dominoes, nursing empty coffee cups, reading the newspapers. Finding an empty table near the door, I sat down, unbuttoned my coat, eyed a handsome brunette, and then ordered a one-horse cab—black coffee in a tall glass with only one inch of cream on top. I also ordered a large cognac, because of the cold. That's what I tried to persuade myself, anyway. But I knew it had more to do with meeting Gruen's lawyers for the first time. Lawyers make me uncomfortable. Like the idea of catching syphilis. I drank the cognac but only half the coffee. I had my health to consider. Then I went outside again.

Situated at the top of the Graben, Kohlmarkt was a typical Viennese street, with an art gallery at one end and an expensive confectioner at the other. Kampfner and Partners occupied three floors at number fifty-six, between a shop selling leather goods and another selling antique religious reliquaries. As I went through the door I was almost tempted to buy myself a couple of rosaries. For luck.

Behind the first-floor reception desk sat a redhead with all the trimmings. I told her I was there to see Dr. Bekemeier. She asked me to take a seat in the waiting room. I walked over to a chair, ignored it, and stared out the window at the snow, the way you do when you're wondering if you're shoes are up to it. There was a fine pair of boots in Bretschneider's that I and my expenses were thinking of getting acquainted with. Provided things worked out with the lawyer. I watched the snow as far as the window of the embroidery shop opposite, where Fanny Skolmann—according to the name painted on the window—and her several employees were stitching petit point in light that promised to make them blind in no time at all.

A throat cleared discreetly behind me and I turned to face a man wearing a neat, gray suit with a wing collar that looked as if it had been tailored by Pythagoras. Under white spats, his black shoes shone like the metalwork on a new bicycle. Or perhaps it was just more cream on top of yet more black coffee. He was a small man, and the smaller the man, the more carefully he seems to dress. This one was straight out of a shop window. He looked sharp. He couldn't have been more than five feet tall and yet he had the look of a creature that killed weasels with his teeth. It was as if his mother had prayed for a baby terrier and changed her mind at the last minute.

"Dr. Gruen?" he asked.

For a moment I had to remind myself it was me he was talking to. I nodded. He bowed in a courtly kind of way.

"I am Dr. Bekemeier," he said. He motioned me into the office behind him and continued speaking in a voice that creaked like the door on a Transylvanian castle. "Please, Herr Doktor. Step this way."

I went into his office where a well-behaved fire was burning quietly, as fires in lawyers' offices always do, for fear of being put out.

"May I take your coat?" he said.

I shrugged it off and watched him hang it on a mahogany hat stand. Then we sat down on opposite sides of a partner's desk—I on a leather button-backed chair that was the little brother of the one he sat on.

"Before we proceed," he said, "you will forgive me if I trouble you to confirm your identity, Herr Doktor. I am afraid that the sheer size of your late mother's estate requires an extra amount of caution. Given these unusual circumstances I am sure you understand that it behooves me to be quite sure of your bona fides. May I look at your passport, please?"

I was already reaching for Gruen's passport. Lawyers, underneath their library-pale skins, are all the same. They cast no shadows and they sleep in coffins. I handed it over without a word.

He opened the passport and scrutinized it, turning every page before coming back to the photograph and the description of the bearer. I let him roll his eyes across my face and then the photograph without comment. To have said anything at all might have invited suspicion. People always get gabby when they're pulling a stroke and start to lose their nerve. I held my breath, enjoyed feeling the fumes of the cognac still inside my tubes, and waited. Eventually he nodded, and handed the passport back to me.

"Is that it?" I asked. "Formal identification of the body and all that?"

"Not quite." He opened a file on his desktop, consulted something typewritten on the top sheet of paper and then closed the file again. "According to my information, Eric Gruen suffered an accident to his left hand, in 1938. He lost the two upper joints of his little finger. May I please see your left hand, Herr Doktor?"

I leaned forward and laid my left hand on his blotter. There was a smile on my face where, perhaps, there ought to have been a frown, for it now struck me as odd that the injury to Gruen's hand should have occurred so long ago, and that he hadn't made more of it in connection with the whole procedure of my identification as him. Somehow I had formed the now apparently incorrect impression that he had lost his little finger during the war, at the same time he had lost his spleen and the use of his legs. There was also the fact that the lawyer, Dr. Bekemeier, had been so very precise about the injury to Gruen's little finger. And it occurred to me now that but for this detail there could have been no positive identification of myself as Eric Gruen. In other words, my finger, or lack of it, had been much more important than I could have known.

"Everything seems to be in order," he said, smiling at last. Which was the first time I noticed that he had no eyebrows. And that the hair on his head appeared to be a wig. "There are of course some papers for you to sign, as the next of kin, Herr Gruen. And also so that you can establish the line of credit with the bank until the will has been administered. Not that I expect there will be any problems. I drew the will up myself. As you may know, your mother banked with Spaengler's all her life, and naturally they will be expecting you to come in and attend to the withdrawals you specified in your telegram. You'll find the manager, Herr Trenner, to be most helpful."

"I'm sure I will," I said.

"Am I correct in thinking that you're staying at the Erzherzog Rainer, Herr Doktor?"

"Yes. Suite three twenty-five."

"A wise choice, if you don't mind my saying so. The manager, Herr Bentheim, is a friend of mine. You must keep us both informed if there's anything we can do to make your stay in Vienna more agreeable."

"Thank you."

"The funeral service will be held at eleven o'clock tomorrow, at Karlskirche. It's just a few blocks northeast of your hotel. At the opposite end of Gusshausstrasse. And the interment immediately afterward in the family vault at the Central Cemetery. That's in the French sector."

"I know where the Central Cemetery is, Dr. Bekemeier," I said. "And while I remember, thank you for making all the arrangements. As you know, Mother and I didn't exactly get on."

"It was my honor and privilege to do so," he said. "I was your mother's lawyer for twenty years."

"I imagine she had alienated everyone else," I said, coolly.

"She was an old woman," he said, as if this was all the explanation that was required for what had happened between Eric Gruen and his mother. "Even so, her death was still somewhat unexpected. I had thought she would be alive for several years yet."

"So she didn't suffer at all," I said.

"Not at all. Indeed, I saw her the day before she died. At the Vienna General Hospital, on Garnisongasse. She seemed fit enough. Bedridden, but quite cheerful, really. Most curious."

"What is?"

"The way death comes, sometimes. When we are not expecting it. Will you be attending, Dr. Gruen? The funeral?"

"Of course," I said.

"Really?" He sounded a little surprised.

"Let bygones be bygones, that's what I say."

"Yes, well, that's an admirable sentiment," he said, as if he didn't quite believe it himself.

I took out a pipe and began to fill it. I had started smoking the pipe in an effort to look and feel more like Eric Gruen. I didn't much like pipes, or all the paraphernalia that went with them, but I couldn't think of a better way of convincing myself I was Eric Gruen, short of buying a wheelchair. "Is there anyone else coming to the funeral I might know?" I asked, innocently

"There are one or two old servants coming," he said. "I'm not sure if you would know them or not. There will be others, of course. The Gruen family name still resonates here in Vienna. As might be expected. I assume you won't wish to lead the mourners yourself, Herr Dr. Gruen."

"No, that would be too much," I said. "I shall remain very much in the background throughout the proceedings."

"Yes, yes, that would probably be best," he said. "All things considered." He leaned back in his chair and, with his elbows on the armrests, brought the ends of his fingers together like the poles of a tent. "In your telegram you said that it was your intention to liquidate your holdings in Gruen Sugar."

"Yes."

"Might I suggest that the announcement be delayed until perhaps you have left the city?" he said carefully. "It's just that such a sale will attract a certain amount of attention. And with you being as private a man as you are, some of that attention may, perforce, be unwelcome. Vienna is a small city. People talk. The very fact of your being here at all will occasion a certain amount of comment perhaps. Perhaps even, dare I say, some notoriety."

"All right," I said. "I don't mind delaying the announcement for a few days. As you said."

He tapped his fingers together nervously as if my presence in his office unsettled him. "Might I also inquire if it is your intention to remain in Vienna for very long?"

"Not very long," I said. "I have a private matter to attend to. Nothing that need concern you. After that I shall probably go back to Garmisch."

He smiled in a way that left me thinking of a small stone Buddha. "Ah, Garmisch," he said. "Such a lovely old town. My wife and I went there for the Winter Olympics, in 'thirty-six."

"Did you see Hitler?" I asked, managing at last to light my pipe.

"Hitler?"

"You remember him, surely? The opening ceremony?"

The smile persisted but he let out a sigh, as if he had adjusted a small valve on his spats. "We were never very political, my wife and I," he said. "But I think we did see him, albeit from a great distance away."

"Safer that way," I said.

"It all seems such a long time ago, now," he said. "Like another life."

"Dr. Jekyll and Mr. Hyde," I said. "Yes, I know exactly what you mean."

A silence ensued and finally Bekemeier's smile evaporated like a smudge on a windowpane.

"Well," I said. "I had better sign these papers, hadn't I?"

"Yes, yes, of course. Thank you for reminding me. With all of this pleasant reminiscence I'm afraid I had almost forgotten our main business."

I doubted that. I couldn't envisage Bekemeier forgetting anything, except perhaps Christmas, or his infant daughter's birthday, always assuming that a creature with just one pair of chromosomes could reproduce anything more than a gelatinous specimen of legal pond life.

He opened a drawer and took out a pen case, from which he removed a gold Pelikan and handed it to me with both hands, as if he had been presenting me with a field marshal's baton. About two or three dozen documents followed, which I signed with a perfect facsimile of Eric Gruen's signature. I had practiced it in Garmisch, so that I might match the signature on the passport. Which, incidentally, Bekemeier remembered to check. Then I returned the pen and, our business apparently concluded, stood up and fetched my coat from his hat stand.

"It's been a pleasure, Dr. Gruen," he said, bowing again. "I shall always endeavor to serve your family's interests. You may depend on that, sir. As you may also depend on my absolute discretion regarding your place of residence. Doubtless there will be inquiries as to how you may be contacted. Rest assured that I shall resist them with all my usual vigor, sir." He shook his head with distaste. "These Viennese. They inhabit two worlds. One is the world of fact. The other is the world of rumor and gossip. The greater the wealth, the greater the attending rumor, I suppose. But what can you do, Herr Doktor?"

"I'm grateful for everything," I said. "And I'll see you tomorrow. At the funeral."

"You'll be there, then?"

"I said so, didn't I?"

"Yes, you did. I'm sorry. I tell you frankly, sir, my memory is not what it was. It's a terrible thing for a lawyer to admit to his client, but there it is. Things were hard for us here in Vienna, after the war. We all of us had to deal on the black market, just to stay alive. Sometimes it seems I've forgotten so much. And sometimes I think it's best that way. Especially with me being a lawyer. I have to be careful. My reputation. The standing of this firm. I live in the Russian sector, you know. I'm sure you understand."

I walked back to my hotel understanding only that there had been something I had not understood about Dr. Bekemeier. I felt like a man who had been trying to handle an eel. Every time I thought I had grasped it, the thing slipped away from me again. I decided to mention our curious conversation to Eric Gruen when I telephoned him with the good news that the meeting with the lawyer had gone without a hitch, and that his inheritance was as good as in the bank.

"How's the weather in Vienna?" he asked. Gruen sounded like a man who wasn't much interested in money. "It snowed a lot here last night. Heinrich is already waxing his skis."

"It's snowing here, too," I reported.

"What's your hotel like?"

I glanced around my suite. Gruen had done me proud. "I'm still waiting for the search party to come back from the bathroom and tell me what it's like," I said. "And apart from the echo everything is just fine."

"Engelbertina's right here," he said. "And she says that she sends her love. And that she's missing you."

I bit some skin off the inside of my lip. "I miss her, too," I lied. "Listen, Eric, this call is costing you a fortune, so I'd better come to the point. As I said, I met with Bekemeier, and everything went fine. Which is to say he seems quite convinced that I am you."

"Good, good."

"But there was something strange about him. Something he wasn't telling me. Something he kept on creeping around. I couldn't make out what it might be. Do you have any idea?"

"Yes, I think I might." He laughed derisively and then his voice became awkward, like a man who has borrowed your car without telling you. "There was a time, years ago, when it was thought that old Bekemeier and my mother were, you know, lovers. If he seemed awkward to you, then that's probably the reason. I guess he might have thought you knew about it. And was embarrassed. It was stupid of me not to have mentioned it."

"Well," I said, "that makes sense, I suppose. I'm going to see your old girlfriend this afternoon. The one you left with a bump in her road."

"Remember what I said, Bernie. She mustn't know the money comes from me. Otherwise she might not take it."

"You told me. An anonymous benefactor."

"Thanks, Bernie. I really appreciate it."

"Forget it," I said. And I dropped the phone back into its cradle.

After a while, I went out again and rode a number 1 bus clockwise around the Ring as far as the Hotel de France, for a spot of lunch. It was open to all, even though it was still under requisition by the French army of occupation. That was one thing against it. On the other hand, the food, according to the concierge at my own hotel, was the best in the city. Besides, it was just around the corner from my next port of call.

## TWENTY-NINE

I got to Liechtensteinstrasse, in the heart of the Ninth District, as the light began to fade, which is always the best time of day in Vienna. The bomb damage, which isn't much when compared with Munich, and nothing at all compared with Berlin, stops being noticeable and it becomes easy to imagine the city as the grand imperial capital it used to be. The sky had turned a purple shade of gray and it had finally stopped snowing, although this did nothing to deter the enthusiasm of those people buying ski boots in Moritz, which was next door to the apartment building where Vera Messmann lived.

I went into the building and started up the steps, which would have been easy enough if I hadn't been recovering from pneumonia and hadn't had such an excellent lunch. Her apartment was on the top floor and, several times, I had to stop and catch my breath, or at least watch it billow out of my mouth in the plummeting temperatures. The metal handrail was sticky with cold. By the time I reached the top, it had started to snow again and the flakes were hitting the stairwell window like soft icy bullets from the rifle of some heavenly sniper. I leaned against the wall and waited for my breathing to slow down enough to allow me the power of speech. Then I knocked on Fräulein Messman's door.

"My name's Gunther, Bernie Gunther," I said, removing my hat politely and presenting her with one of my Munich business cards. "It's all right, I'm not selling anything."

"That's good," she said. "Because I'm not buying anything."

"Are you Vera Messmann?"

She flicked her eyes on my card and then at me. "That all depends," she said.

"On what, for instance?"

"On whether you think I did it, or not."

"Did what?" I didn't mind her playing with me. It's one of the perks of the job when an attractive brunette teases you.

"Oh, you know. Murdered Roger Ackroyd."

"Never heard of him."

"Agatha Christie," she said.

"Never heard of her, either."

"Don't you read books, Herr—" She read the card again, teasing me some more. "Gunther."

"Never," I said. "It's terribly bad for business to sound like I know more than my clients tell me. Mostly they want someone who is not a cop to behave like a cop. They don't want someone who can quote Schiller."

"Well, at least you've heard of *him*," she said.

"Schiller? Sure. He's the guy who said that truth lives on in the midst of deception. We keep that quotation over the office door. He's the patron saint of detectives everywhere."

"You'd better come in, Herr Gunther," she said, standing aside. "After all, he that is overcautious will accomplish little. That's Schiller, too, in case you didn't know. As well as private detectives, he's also the patron saint of single women."

"You learn something new every day," I said. I went into the apartment, enjoying her perfume as I moved past her body.

"No, not every day," she said, closing the door behind me. "Not even every week. Not in Vienna. Not lately, anyway."

"Maybe you should buy a newspaper," I said.

"I got out of the habit," she said. "During the war."

I took another look at her. I liked the glasses. They made her look as if she had probably read all the books on the shelves that lined the entrance to her apartment. If there's one thing I like, it's a woman who starts off looking plain but gets better-looking the more you look at her. Vera Messmann was that kind of woman. After a while I formed the impression that she was a rather beautiful woman. A beautiful woman who happened to wear glasses. Not that she herself was in much doubt about any of that. There was a quiet confidence about the way she carried herself and the way she spoke. If there had been a beauty pageant for lady librarians, Vera Messmann would have won it hands down. She wouldn't even have had to take off her glasses and unpin her brown hair.

We remained, a little awkwardly, in the entrance hall. I had yet to make her day, although from what she was saying, my just being there represented a welcome novelty.

"Since I haven't murdered anyone," she said, "or committed adultery—not since last summer, anyway—I'm intrigued as to what a private detective could want with me."

"I don't do many murders," I said. "Not since I stopped being a bull. Mostly I get asked to look for missing persons."

"Then you should have plenty of work to keep you busy."

"It comes as rather a pleasant change to be the bearer of good news," I said. "My client, who wants to remain anonymous, wishes you to have some money. You don't have to do anything for it. Nothing at all except turn up at Spaengler's Bank tomorrow afternoon at three o'clock and sign a receipt for cash. And that's pretty much all that I'm allowed to tell you except the amount. It's twenty-five thousand schillings."

"Twenty-five thousand schillings?" She took off her glasses, which let me see how right I had been. She was a peach. "Are you sure there's not been some kind of mistake?"

"Not if you're Vera Messmann," I said. "You'll need some form of identity to prove who you are at the bank of course. Bankers are rather less trusting than detectives." I smiled. "Especially banks like Spaengler's. It's in Dorotheengasse. In the International Zone."

"Look, Herr Gunther, if this is a joke," she said, "it's not a very funny one. Twenty-five thousand to someone like me. To anyone. That's serious money."

"I can leave now, if you'd prefer," I said. "You won't ever see me again." I shrugged. "Listen, I can understand you being nervous about me coming here like this. Maybe I'd be nervous if I were you. So perhaps I should go, anyway. But just promise me you'll come to the bank at three. After all, what have you got to lose? Nothing."

I turned and reached for the door handle.

"No, please don't leave yet." She turned on her heel and walked into the living room. "Take off your hat and coat and come on through."

I did what I was told. I like doing what I'm told when there's a half-decent woman involved. There was a baby grand with the lid up and a piece by Schubert on the music stand. In front of the French window was a pair of silver gilt dolphin side chairs with blue tufted upholstery. Against one of the walls was a gilt-trimmed floral-design settee with roll arms. There were a couple of blackamoor pedestals that didn't seem to feel the cold, and a big carved cabinet with cupid heads on the door. There were plenty of old pictures and an expensive-looking Murano wall mirror that showed me up looking about as out of place as a wild boar in a toy shop. There was a French marble clock with a bronze fop reading a book. I guessed it wasn't a book by Agatha Christie. It was the kind of room where books were discussed more often than football, and women sat with their knees together and listened to plangent zither music on the radio. It told me that Vera Messmann didn't need the money as much as she needed the glasses. She put them on again and faced a neat little drinks table underneath the mirror.

"Drink?" she said. "I have schnapps, cognac, and whiskey."

"Schnapps," I said. "Thanks."

"Please smoke if you want. I don't smoke myself but I enjoy the smell of it." She handed me my drink and steered us to the blue chairs.

I sat down, took out my pipe, looked at it for a moment, and then slipped it back into my pocket. I was Bernie Gunther now, not Eric Gruen, and Bernie Gunther smoked cigarettes. I found some Reemtsmas and began a roll-up with the pipe tobacco.

"I love to watch a man make one of those," she said, leaning forward on her chair.

"If my fingers weren't so cold," I said, "I might make a better job of it."

"You're doing fine," she said. "I might have a puff of that when you're finished." I finished with the makings, lit the cigarette, puffed it, and then handed it to her. She smoked it with genuine pleasure, as if it had been the choicest delicacy. Then she handed it back again. Without so much as a cough.

"Of course, I know who it is," she said. "My anonymous benefactor. It's Eric, isn't it?" She shook her head. "It's all right. You don't have to say anything. But I know. It so happened that I did see a newspaper, a few days ago. There was something in it about his mother's death. You don't have to be Hercule Poirot to work out that particular chain of causation. He's got his hands on her money and now he wants to make amends. Always supposing that such a thing is possible after the dreadful thing he did. I'm not at all surprised that he sent you instead of coming here in person. I expect he doesn't dare show his face for fear of, whatever it is that someone like him is in fear of." She shrugged and sipped some of her drink. "Just for the record? When he ran out on me, in 1928, I was just eighteen years old. He wasn't much older, I suppose. I gave birth to a daughter. Magda."

"Yes, I was going to ask about your daughter," I said. "I'm to give her the same sum as I've given you."

"Well, you can't," she said. "Magda is dead. She was killed during an air raid, in 1944. A bomb hit her school."

"I'm sorry," I said.

Vera Messmann kicked off her shoes and folded her stockinged feet underneath her nicely curved behind. "For what it's worth, I don't hold any of that against him. Compared with what happened during the war, it's not much of a crime, is it? To leave a girl with a bump in her road?"

"No, I suppose not," I said.

"But I'm glad he sent you," she said. "I wouldn't want to see him again. Especially now Madga's dead. That would be too unpleasant. Also, I should be much more reluctant to take his money if it was him in person. But twenty-five thousand schillings . . . I can't say that wouldn't come in handy. Despite what you see here, I've not got much saved. All of this furniture is quite valuable, but it was my mother's, and this apartment is all that I've got to remind me of her. This apartment was hers. She had excellent taste."

"Yes," I said, glancing around, politely. "She did indeed."

"There's no point in selling any of it, though," she said. "Not right now. There's no money for this kind of stuff. Not even the Amis want it. Not yet. I'm waiting for the market to come back. But now"—she toasted me, silently—"now, maybe, I won't have to wait for the market at all." She drank some more. "And all I have to do is turn up at this bank and sign a receipt?"

"That's all. You won't even have to mention his name."

"That's a relief," she said.

"Just walk in the door and I'll be waiting for you. We'll go to a private room and I'll hand you the cash. Or a banker's draft, as you prefer. Simple as that."

"It would be nice to think so," she said. "But nothing involving money is ever simple."

"Don't look a gift horse in the mouth," I said. "That's my advice."

"It's bad advice, Herr Gunther," she said. "Think about it. All those veterinary bills if the nag is no good. And let's not forget what happened to those poor dumb Trojans. Maybe if they had listened to Cassandra instead of Sinon they might have done just that. If they'd looked the Greek gift horse in the mouth they would have seen Odysseus and all his Greek friends huddled inside." She smiled. "Benefits of a classical education."

"You have a point," I said. "But it's difficult to see how you could do it in this particular case."

"That's because you're just a cop who's not a cop," she said. "Oh, I don't mean to be rude, but maybe if you had a little more imagination you could think of a way for me to get a closer look at the pony you walked in here."

She removed the roll-up from my fingers and took another short puff on it before extinguishing it in an ashtray. Then she snatched off her glasses and leaned toward me until her mouth was just an inch or two away from mine.

"Open wide," she said, and opening her lips and teeth, she pressed her luscious mouth against mine.

We were there for quite a while. When she pulled herself back, there was honey in her eyes.

"So what did you discover?" I asked. "Any sign of a Greek hero?"

"I haven't finished looking," she said. "Yet." And standing up she took me by the hand and tugged me up onto my feet.

"Where are we going now?" I asked.

"Helen is taking you into her palace boudoir," she said.

"Are you sure about this?" I stayed put for a moment, curling my toes to get a better grip on the carpet. "Maybe it's my turn to play Cassandra. Maybe if I had a little more imagination I might think I was just handsome enough to rate this kind of hospitality. But we both know I'm not. Maybe we should delay this until after you've had your twenty-five thousand."

"I appreciate what you said," she said, still holding my hand. "But I'm not exactly in the first flush of youth myself, Herr Gunther. Let me tell you about myself. I'm a corset maker. A good one. I own a shop on Wasagasse. All of my clients are women, it goes without saying. Most of the men I once knew are dead, or maimed. You're the first able-bodied, reasonable-looking man I've spoken to in six months. The last man I exchanged more than two dozen words with was my dentist, and I'm long overdue for a checkup. He's sixty-seven and has a clubfoot, which is probably the only reason he's still alive. I'm thirty-nine years old in two weeks, and I'm already taking evening classes in spinsterhood. I even have a cat. He's out of course. Having a better life than I have. Today is early closing at the shop. But most evenings I come home, cook a meal, read a detective story, have a bath, read some more, and then go to bed, alone. Once a week I go to Maria am Gestade, and every so often I seek absolution for what I jokingly refer to as my sins. You get the picture?" She smiled, a little bitterly it seemed to me. "Your business card says you're from Munich, which implies that when your business is concluded in Vienna, you'll be going back there. That gives us maybe three or four days at most. What I said about Schiller? And not being overcautious. I was perfectly serious."

"You're right about my going back to Munich," I told her. "I think you'd probably make quite a good private detective."

"I'm afraid I don't think you'd make much of a corset maker."

"You'd be surprised what I know about women's corsets," I said.

"Oh, I do hope so," she said. "Either way I intend to find out. Do I make myself clear?"

"Very." I kissed her again. "Are you wearing a corset?"

"Not for much longer," she said, and looked at her watch. "In about five minutes, you're going to take it off. You know how to take a woman's corset off, don't you? You just pull all the little hooks out of all the little eyelets until your mouth goes dry and you start to hear me breathing. You could try and tear it off, of course. But my corsets are well-made. They don't tear off that easily."

I followed her into her bedroom. "That classical education of yours," I said.

"What about it?"

"What happened to Cassandra, anyway?"

"The Greeks dragged her out of the Temple of Athena and raped her," she said, kicking the door shut behind her. "Me, I'm perfectly willing."

"Perfectly willing sounds perfectly good to me," I said.

She stepped out of her dress and I stood back to get a better look at her. Call it professional courtesy, if you like. She had a fine, well-proportioned figure. I felt like Kepler admiring his Golden Section. Except I knew I was going to have more fun than he ever did. He'd probably never looked at a woman wearing a well-tailored corset. If he had, then I might have been a better mathematician when I was at school.

# THIRTY

I stayed the night, which was just as well, since, just after midnight, Vera's apartment had an intruder.

After our early-evening performance she was trying to coax me into a putting on a late show, when she froze on top of me for a moment. "Listen," she whispered. "Did you hear that?" And then, when I failed to hear anything other than the sound of my own heavy breathing, she added: "There's someone in the sitting room." She lay down beside me, pulled the bedclothes up to her chin and waited for me to agree with her.

I lay still, long enough to hear footsteps on the parquet floor, and then sprang out of bed. "Are you expecting anyone?" I asked, hauling on my trousers, and thumbing my braces over my naked shoulders.

"Of course not," she hissed. "It's midnight."

"Do you have any kind of a weapon?"

"You're the detective. Don't you have a gun?"

"Sometimes," I said. "But not when I have to travel through the Russian Zone. Carrying a gun would get me sent to a labor camp. Or worse."

I grabbed a hockey stick and threw open the door. "Who's there?" I said, loudly, and groped for a light switch.

Something moved in the dark. I heard someone go into the hall and through the front door. I caught a vague scent of beer and tobacco and men's cologne, and then the sound of footsteps down the stairwell. I sprinted after him and got as far as the first-floor landing before my bare feet slipped and I fell. I picked myself up, limped down the last flight of stairs, and ran out into the street just in time to see a man disappear around the corner of Turkenstrasse. If I had been wearing shoes I might have gone after him, but in bare feet, in an inch of snow and ice, there was nothing I could do but go back upstairs.

Vera's neighbor was standing outside her front door when I arrived on the top floor. She eyed me with suspicious, shrewish eyes, which was a bit of a nerve given she looked like the kind of bride Frankenstein's monster would have left standing at the altar. She had the same Nefertiti hairstyle, reptilian clawlike hands, and long shroud of a white nightgown, but even a scientist as mad as a March hare would have known better than to try to pass off a midget creature with a mustache as a plausible-looking woman.

"Fräulein Messmann," I said, limply. "There was an intruder in her apartment."

Saying nothing, the hideous, sharp-boned creature gave a little jerk, like a frightened bird, and then darted inside her own apartment, slamming the door behind her so that the whole icy stairwell echoed like a forgotten tomb.

Back in Vera Messmann's apartment, I found her wearing a dressing gown and a worried look on her face.

"He got away," I said, shivering.

She took off the dressing gown and put it around my shoulders and, unashamedly naked, went into the kitchen. "I'll make some coffee," she said.

"Is anything missing?" I asked, following her.

"Not as far as I can see," she said. "My handbag was in the bedroom."

"Anything in particular he might have been after?"

She filled a drip coffeemaker and placed it on the stove. "Nothing that's easy to carry," she said.

"Ever have a break-in before?"

"Never," she said. "Not even a Russian. This is a very safe area."

I watched her naked body absently as it moved around the kitchen and, for a moment, my mind turned to Cassandra's fate. I decided not to mention the possibility that the intruder had had something other than theft on his mind.

"Strange it should have happened while you were here," she said.

"It was you who persuaded me to stay," I said. "Remember?"

"Sorry."

"Don't mention it." I went back into the hallway with the intention of examining the lock on the door. It was an Evva. An excellent lock. But there would have been no need to have picked, raked, or forced it. It was immediately clear to me how the intruder had gained entry to her apartment. The front door key was hanging on a length of cord, below the letterbox. "He didn't break in," I announced. "He didn't need to. Look."

She stepped into the corridor and watched me tug away the cord from her door. "Not exactly the most sensible thing to do with your key when you're a woman living on her own," I said.

"No," she said, sheepishly. "Normally I bolt the door when I go to bed. But I must have had something else on my mind tonight."

I bolted the door. "I can see I'm going to have to teach you a lesson about crime prevention," I said, leading her back into the bedroom.

## THIRTY-ONE

Following a thinly attended service at Karlskirche on Karlsplatz, the funeral cortege attending Elizabeth Gruen's casket drove slowly along Simmeringer Hauptstrasse, to Vienna's Central Cemetery. I traveled to and from the baroque church, with its landmark green copper dome, in a Cadillac Fleetwood driven by an off-duty American soldier who was running a chauffeur business on the side out of a PX garage in Roetzergasse. Everyone in Vienna had something on the side. Except perhaps the dead. All the same, if you are dead, then Vienna is probably the best place in the world to be. The Central Cemetery, in the Eleventh District, is, at five hundred acres and with two million residents, like a city within a city, a necropolis of trees and flowers, elegant avenues, handsome statuary, and distinguished architecture. Provided that you have the money and you are dead, of course, you may spend eternity here inhabiting the sort of monumental grandeur normally afforded only to self-aggrandizing emperors, dynastic monarchs, and tyrannous satraps.

The Gruen family vault comprised a bunker of black marble about the size of a gun turret on the Bismarck. Carved into the main body of the mausoleum, in modest gold letters, were the words "Familie Gruen" and, near the base of the edifice, the names of several individual Gruens who were interred inside it, including Eric's father, Friedrich. The stepped façade featured a bronze of a somewhat scantily clad female figure who was supposed to be prostrate with grief, only, somehow, she managed to look more like a chocolady who had enjoyed a hard night of it at the Oriental Club. The temptation to find her a warm coat and a cup of strong, black coffee was almost overwhelming.

The vault was modest by the standard of an Egyptian pharaoh. But with its four matching sphinxes—one on each corner—I was sure a whole litter of Ptolemies would have felt perfectly at home in its three-for-the-price-of-one interior. And when I emerged from inside, having paid my formal respects to Eric's mother, I half expected the sexton to frisk me for gold scarabs and shards of lapis lazuli. As it was, I had so many strange looks and suspicious, even hostile stares you would have thought I was Mozart looking for his unmarked grave. Even the priest conducting the burial service—who, in his purple cape, resembled a French cake in Demel's window—gave me the evil eye.

I had hoped that by remaining at a distance from the other mourners and wearing a pair of dark glasses—it was a very cold but bright sunny day—I would remain relatively anonymous. Dr. Bekemeier knew who he thought I was and, in the circumstances, this was all that really mattered. But I hadn't bargained on a hostile reception from one of Elizabeth Gruen's servants, who let me know what she thought of Eric Gruen being there at all.

She was a red-faced, bony, ill-dressed creature, like a rib of beef in a sack, and when she spoke her plate shifted on her upper jaw as if the result of a small earthquake in her head. "You've got a nerve, showing your face here like this," said the crone, with evident distaste. "After all these years. After what you did. Your mother was ashamed of you, that's what she was. Ashamed and disgusted that a Gruen should behave in such a way. Disgrace. That's what you brought to your family name. Disgrace. Your father would have horsewhipped you."

I murmured some bromide about this all being a very long time ago and then walked swiftly back to the main gate where I had left the American with the car. Despite the icy weather, the cemetery was busy. Other funerals were in progress and there were several people heading the same way as me. I paid them little or no regard. Not even to the IP Jeep that was parked a short way away from the Cadillac. I jumped in and the American driver took off at speed, like a wanted criminal.

"What the hell's going on?" I shouted once I had picked myself off the floor. "I've been attending a funeral not robbing a bank."

The driver, who wasn't much more than a kid, with hedgehog hair and ears like two trophy handles, nodded at his rearview mirror. "International Patrol," he said, in reasonable German.

I turned to look through the rear window. Sure enough the Jeep was on our tail. "What do they want?" I yelled as, gunning the engine loudly, he veered the car off Simmeringer and down a narrow side street.

"Either they're after you for something, buddy," he said, "or they're after me."

"You? What have you done?"

"The gasoline in this car is PX," shouted my driver. "Occupation personnel only. So is the car. And so are the cigarettes and booze and nylons in the trunk."

"Great," I said. "Thanks a lot. I really want to be in trouble with the police on the day of my mother's funeral." It was just something to say to make him feel bad.

"Don't worry," he said, with a big, well-brushed grin. "They gotta catch us first. And this car has the edge on a Jeep with four elephants in it. So long as they don't radio in for an intercept car we'll probably lose them. Besides, an American has to drive that IPV. That's the rule. Our vehicle, our driver. And American drivers aren't usually crazy. Now, if it was the Ivan driving, we might have a problem. Those Ivans are the craziest drivers you ever saw."

Having been driven before by a Russian, I knew he wasn't exaggerating.

We hurtled through the eastern approaches to the city center. The Jeep kept us in sight as far as the railway line before we lost them.

"Here," I said, tossing some banknotes onto the backseat as we skidded around Modena Park. "Let me out on the corner. I'll walk the rest of the way. My nerves can't stand it."

I jumped out, slammed the door shut, and watched the Cadillac sprint away with a loud squeal of tires along Zaunergasse. I walked after it, onto Stalin Platz, and then down Gusshausstrasse, back to my hotel. It felt like it had been quite a morning. But my day had hardly started.

I had a light lunch and then went back up to my room for a rest before going to meet Vera Messmann at the bank. I hadn't been lying on my bed for long when there was a light knock at the door, and thinking it was the maid, I got up and opened it. I recognized the man standing there from the funeral. For a moment I thought I was going to receive another earful of abuse about how I had brought disgrace on the Gruen family name. Instead the man snatched off his hat respectfully and stood holding the brim tightly in front of him like the reins on a small pony and cart.

"Yes?" I said. "What do you want?"

"Sir, I was your mother's butler, sir," he said, in what I suppose was a Hungarian accent. "Tibor, sir. Tibor Medgyessy, sir. May I speak with you a moment, please, sir?" He glanced nervously along the hotel corridor. "In private, sir? Just a few minutes, sir. If you'd be so kind."

He was tall and well-built for a man his age, which I estimated was around sixty-five. Possibly older. He had a full head of white, curly hair that looked as if it had been shorn from the back of a sheep. His teeth looked like they were made of wood. He wore thick, metal-framed glasses, and a dark suit and tie. His bearing was almost military and I guessed the Gruens preferred it that way.

"All right, come in." I watched him limp into my room. It was a limp that made you think there was something wrong with his hip rather than his knee or his ankle. I closed the door. "Well? What is it? What do you want?"

Medgyessy glanced around the suite with obvious appreciation. "Very nice, sir," he said. "Very nice, indeed. I don't blame you for staying here rather than your mother's house, sir. Especially not after what happened at the funeral this morning. Most regrettable that was. And quite uncalled for. I've reprimanded her already, sir. Fifteen years I was your mother's butler, sir, and that was the first time I ever heard Klara speak out of turn."

"Klara, was it, you say?"

"Yes, sir. My wife."

I shrugged. "Look, forget about it," I said. "Less said the better, eh? I appreciate you coming here like this, to apologize, but really it doesn't matter."

"Oh, I didn't come here to apologize, sir," he said.

"You didn't?" I shook my head. "Then why did you come here?"

The butler smiled a curious little smile. It was like looking at a heavily weathered picket fence. "It's like this, sir," he said. "Your mother left us some money in her will. But she made it quite a while ago, and I daresay the sum she left for us would have done us very nicely if recently we hadn't had that change in the value of the Austrian schilling. Of course, she meant to change it, but her dying so suddenly, well, she didn't have time to do it. So we're a bit stuck, now, the wife and I. What she left us isn't enough to retire on, and at our time of life, we're too old to look for another position. We were wondering if you'd care to help us, sir. You being a wealthy man, now. We're not greedy people. We wouldn't ask at all, if your mother hadn't meant to change her will. You can ask Dr. Bekemeier, if you don't believe me, sir."

"I see," I said. "If you don't mind me saying so, Herr Medgyessy, your wife, Klara, didn't sound like she wanted my help. Anything but."

The butler shifted on his legs and came to the at-ease position.

"She was just a bit shook up, that's all, sir. On account of the suddenness of your mother's death in the hospital, sir. And also because, since she died, the International Patrol have been there, asking questions about you, sir. Wanting to know if you were coming back to Vienna for the funeral. That kind of thing."

"Now, why would the Allied police be at all interested in me?" Even as I spoke I was recalling my getaway drive from the Central Cemetery. It was beginning to look as if my American driver might have made an error. As if it had been Eric Gruen the International Patrol had been pursuing, not a black marketeer.

Medgyessy smiled his sylvan smile. "There's no need for that, sir," he said. "We're not stupid people, the wife and I. Just because we never talk about it, doesn't mean we don't know about it."

It was clear there was more here than just a girl left with a bump in her road. A lot more.

"So please don't speak to me like I'm an idiot, sir. That won't help either of us. All we're asking is that we continue to serve your family, sir. In the only way we can now, since I can't imagine you'll be staying on in Vienna, sir. Not officially, anyway."

"How exactly do you think you can serve me?" I asked him, patiently.

"With our silence, sir. I knew most of your mother's affairs. Very trusting, she was. And very careless, too, if you know what I mean."

"You're trying to blackmail me, aren't you?" I said. "So why don't you just tell me how much?"

Medgyessy shook his head, irritably. "No, sir. It's not blackmail. I wish you wouldn't look at it that way. All we want is to serve the Gruen family, sir. That's all. A proper reward for loyalty. That's what this is all about. Maybe what you did was right, sir. That's hardly for me to say. But it's only fair that you should recognize your debt to us, sir. For not telling the police where you live, for instance. Garmisch, is it? Very nice. I've not been there myself, but I've heard it's very beautiful."

"How much?"

"Twenty-five thousand schillings, sir. That's not much, considering. Not when you think about it, sir."

I hardly knew what to say. It was now obvious that Eric Gruen had not been honest with me, and that there was something in his past that made his being in Vienna of interest to the Allies. Or had he been honest after all? Could it have been the execution of those prisoners of war, in France, that Engelbertina had mentioned? Why not? After all, the Allies already had dozens of SS men imprisoned in Landsberg for the Malmedy massacre. Why not another massacre involving Eric Gruen? Whatever the reason, one thing was clear: I needed to stall Medgyessy long enough to speak to Gruen himself. I had little choice but to go along with the butler's blackmail, for now. With all the documentation I possessed being in the name of Eric Gruen, I could hardly go back to being Bernie Gunther.

"All right," I said. "But I'll need some time to get the money together. The will hasn't yet been proved."

His face grew harder. "Don't play me for a fool, sir," he said. "*I'd* never betray you. But the wife is a very different story. As you probably gathered at the funeral. Shall we say twenty-four hours? This time tomorrow." He glanced at his pocket watch. "Two o'clock. That'll give you plenty of time to get to Spaengler's and make all the necessary arrangements."

"Very well," I said. "Until two o'clock tomorrow." I opened the door for him and he limped out, like a man waltzing by himself. I had to hand it to him. He and his wife had handled it very nicely. Good cop, bad cop. And all of that guff about loyalty. It was an effective pitch. Especially the way he had dropped the name of Spaengler's Bank and Garmisch.

I closed the door, picked up the phone, and asked the hotel operator to connect me with Henkell's house in Sonnenbichl. After a few minutes the operator called me back and said there was no reply, so I put on my coat and hat and took a taxi to Dorotheengasse.

Most of the buildings in this narrow, cobbled street had been repaired. At one end was a yellow stucco church with a spire like a V-2 rocket, and at the other end, an ornate fountain with a lady who had picked the wrong day for going topless in Vienna. In its massive baroque portal, the green door of Spaengler's Bank looked like Hitler's train stuck in a railway tunnel. I approached the top-hatted doorman, informed him of the name of the person I had come to see, and was directed into what could have passed for the Hall of the Mountain King. And with footsteps echoing against the ceiling like the tintinnabulation of a broken bell, I walked up a staircase as wide as an autobahn.

The Gruen family's bank manager, Herr Trenner, was waiting for me at the top of the stairs. He was younger than me but looked as if he had been born with gray hair and wearing glasses and a morning coat. He was as obsequious as a Japanese ivy plant. Wringing his hands as if he hoped to squeeze the milk of human kindness from his fingernails, he showed me to an upstairs room furnished with a table and two chairs. On top of the table was twenty-five thousand schillings and, as arranged, a smaller pile of cash, to cover my immediate expenses. On the floor beside the table was a plain leather holdall in which to carry the money. Trenner handed me a key to the door of the room, informed me that he would be at my service so long as I remained in the building, bowed gravely, and then left me alone. I pocketed the smaller pile of cash, locked the door, and went back downstairs to wait by the front door for Vera Messmann. It was ten minutes to three.

## THIRTY-TWO

I waited until almost half past three, by which time I had concluded that Vera Messmann had had second thoughts about accepting Gruen's money and wasn't coming. So I went back upstairs, transferred the money to the holdall, and set off to find her.

It was a twenty-minute walk through the city center to Liechtensteinstrasse. I rang Vera's doorbell and knocked at the door. I even shouted through the letterbox, but there was no one at home. Of course there's no one at home, I told myself. It's only four o'clock. She's at her shop. Around the corner, on Wasagasse. She was at home yesterday afternoon only because it was early closing. But today is a normal working day. You're some detective, Bernie Gunther.

So I went around the corner. I suppose I assumed she would change her mind about the money when she saw it in the bag. There's something about the sight of hard cash that always makes people think in a different way. That has always been my own experience, anyway. And naturally I assumed Vera would be no different. That she would change her mind because she would see the money and listen to me and let herself be persuaded. And if that failed I would be stern with her and tell her she had to take Gruen's money. How could she fail to do what she was told when, in the bedroom, she had been so willingly submissive?

The shop faced the back of Vienna University's Institute of Chemistry. The sign above the window read "Vera Messmann. Salon for Made-to-Measure Corselettes, Bodices, Girdles, and Brassieres." The window contained a female tailor's dummy wearing a pink silk corset and matching brassiere. Beside it was a show-card featuring a line drawing of a girl wearing a different ensemble. She had a bow in her hair and, but for her lack of glasses, she reminded me a little of Vera. A little bell tinkled above my head as I opened the door. There was a simple, glass-topped counter no bigger than a card table and, next to this, another anonymous girdled female trunk. In the back, a ceiling light was burning dimly near a heavily draped changing cubicle. In front of this sanctum sanctorum stood a French chair, as if someone might sit there and, with seignorial satisfaction, watch his lover or mistress appear from behind the curtain wearing some well-engineered undergarment. Who said I didn't have a vivid imagination?

"Vera?" I called. "Vera, it's me, Bernie. Why didn't you show up at the bank?"

Idly, I drew open a narrow drawer to reveal a dozen or so black brassieres pressed together like slaves on a ship bound for the plantations in the West Indies. I picked one up and felt the wires in it hard underneath my fingers, thinking that it looked and felt like the harness for early and ill-advised attempt at human flight.

"Vera? I waited at the bank for half an hour. Did you forget, or did you just change your mind?"

The thing was, I hardly wanted to go blundering into the back of the shop and find some well-fed Vienna housewife wearing just her knickers. I tugged open another drawer and picked out an item of vaguely aqueductian shape that, eventually, I identified as being a garter belt. Another minute passed. A woman peered in the window and looked taken aback to see me standing there with something lacy suspended from my fingers, like a cat's cradle. I put the undergarment down and advanced, boldly, into the back of the shop, thinking perhaps Vera was upstairs, if an upstairs there was.

"Vera?"

Then I saw it and my heart missed a beat. Protruding from under the drawn curtain of the changing cubicle was a woman's stockinged foot. It was without a shoe. I took hold of the curtain, paused for a moment, bracing myself for what I knew I was about to find. And then I drew it aside. It was Vera and she was dead. The nylon stocking that had killed her was still wrapped tight around her neck like a near-invisible snake. I let out a long sigh and closed my eyes for a moment. After a minute or two I stopped behaving like a normal human being and started to think like a detective. I went back to the door and locked it, just in case. The last thing I wanted now was for one of Vera's customers to walk in on me while I examined her dead body. Then I returned to the changing cubicle, drew the curtain behind me and knelt beside her corpse to make sure she really was dead. But her skin was quite cold and my fingers felt nothing when I pushed them underneath the twist in the stocking and against her jugular vein. She had been dead for several hours. There was dried blood in her nostrils and in her gums, and on the side of her face. And lots of scratches and finger marks around her chin and near the tie in the stocking. Her eyes were closed. I'd seen drunks look worse who were still alive. Her hair was a mess and her glasses lay broken on the floor. The changing cubicle chair had been knocked over and the mirror on the wall had a large crack in it. It was obvious that she had put up quite a struggle before yielding her life. It was a conclusion that I underlined when I lifted her hands and saw the bruises on her knuckles. It looked as if she had managed to punch her attacker. Perhaps several times.

I stood up, glanced around the floor, saw a cigarette end and picked it up. It was a Lucky, which wasn't at all Lucky for me. There was an ashtray full of them back in my hotel room. I put the cigarette end in my pocket. There was enough circumstantial evidence against me already without giving the police a present of more. She and I had had sex the night before. I hadn't been wearing a condom. Vera had said it was safe, which was another reason she had been keen to go to bed with me. A postmortem would find my blood type.

I looked around for Vera's handbag, hoping to find her door key so that I might let myself into her apartment and reclaim my business card. But her bag was gone. I wondered if the murderer had taken it. Probably the same man who had let himself into her apartment the previous night. I cursed myself for having taken the key off the cord. But for that I could have let myself in. Doubtless the police would find my card. And doubtless the neighbor who had seen me returning to her apartment wearing just my trousers and carrying a hockey stick would be able to give the police a good description. That would tally with the description from the woman who had seen me through Vera's shop window just a few minutes earlier. There was no doubt about it. I was in a tight spot.

I switched the light out and went around the shop polishing everything I had touched with a pair of knickers. My fingerprints would be all over her apartment of course, but I saw no sense in leaving them at the scene of the crime. I opened the front door, cleaned the door handle, closed it, locked up again, and then drew down the blinds on the door and the display window. With any luck it might be a day or two before her body was found.

A back door led into a courtyard. I turned up the collar of my coat, pulled the brim of my hat about my eyes, picked up the holdall containing Vera's money, and stepped quietly outside. It was getting dark now and I kept to the center of the courtyard, away from lighted windows and an early patch of moonlight. At the opposite end of the courtyard I passed down an alley and opened a door that led onto the street that intersected with Wasagasse. This was Horlgasse and, for some reason, this seemed to mean something to me. Horlgasse. Horlgasse.

I walked southwest, onto Roosevelt Platz. A church stood in the middle of the square. The Votive Church. It had been built in gratitude to God for the preservation of the young Emperor Franz Josef's life following an assassination attempt. I had half an idea that Roosevelt Platz had once been Göring Platz. It had been a while since I had thought of Göring. Briefly, back in 1936, he had been a client of mine. But Horlgasse hadn't finished jostling with my brain cells. *Horlgasse. Horlgasse.* And then I remembered. Horlgasse. That was the address I had been given for Britta Warzok. The same address I had found indented on the notepad in Major Jacobs's Buick. I took out my notebook and checked the street number. I had been planning to visit Britta Warzok's given address as soon as Gruen's business was concluded, but now seemed as good a time as any. Not least because I was asking myself if the contiguity of these two addresses—Britta Warzok and Vera Messmann—was simply a coincidence? Or more than simple coincidence? A *meaningful* coincidence, perhaps. Jung had a fancy word for this, which I might have remembered had not the circumstances of the coincidence pushed everything else from my mind. I might also have remembered that not every meaningful coincidence is a positive one.

I turned around and walked east along Horlgasse. It took me just two minutes to find number forty-two. It was situated just before the tram line, where Horlgasse merged with Turkenstrasse, and overlooking Schlick Platz. The Vienna Police Academy was only fifty yards away. I found myself facing yet another baroque portal. A couple of Atlantes were standing in for columns to support an entablature garlanded with boughs of ivy. A small door cut into the main door stood open. I went inside and stood opposite some letterboxes. There were only three apartments in the building, one on each floor. Appearing on the box belonging to the top apartment was the name "Warzok." It was bulging with post that hadn't been collected in several days, but I went up anyway.

I climbed the stairs. The door was open. I pushed it wide and poked my head into the unlit hallway. The place felt cold. Too cold for the comfort of anyone living there.

"Frau Warzok?" I called out. "Are you there?"

It was a big apartment with triple-height ceilings and double-height windows. One of these was open. Something unpleasant pricked my nostrils and the back of my throat. Something stale and rotten. I took out a handkerchief to cover my nose and mouth and discovered that I was holding the knickers I'd used to wipe my fingerprints from Vera Messmann's shop. But it hardly seemed to matter. I advanced into the apartment telling myself first that no one could be about, that no one could have stood the cold or that smell for very long. Then I told myself that someone must have opened the window, and recently, too. I walked over to the open window and looked out onto Schlick Platz as a tram went by, clanging like a fire alarm. I took a deep breath of fresh air and headed back into the shadows, to where the smell seemed to get worse. Then the lights went on and I spun around on my heel to find myself facing two men. They were both holding guns. And the guns were both pointed at me.

## THIRTY-THREE

Neither man was very big, and, but for their guns, I might easily have pushed them aside like a pair of small swing doors. They looked a little more intelligent than the average gun-toting thug, although unremarkably so. Theirs were the kind of faces that resisted immediate description, like a field of grass or a gravel path. You had to look at them hard to fix them in your mind. I was looking hard. I look hard at anyone who points a gun at me. But this didn't stop me from putting my hands up. That's just good manners when a firearm comes into the room.

"What's your name, Fritz? And what are you doing here?"

The one who spoke first had tried to affect a stern tone, like he was trying to forget some education and breeding for the sake of the effect it might have on me. He had gray-white hair and a beard and mustache that were arranged in a perfect heptagon around his mouth, and which lent his soft-skinned face some much-needed masculinity. Behind his light-framed glasses his eyes were wide, with too much white around his yellow-brown irises, as if he was uncertain of what he was doing. He wore a dark suit, a short leather coat, and a little trilby that made him look as if he were planning to balance a tray of bread on his head.

"Dr. Eric Gruen," I said. Whatever the crime Eric Gruen had committed, with only Eric Gruen's passport in my pocket I had no other choice but to say I was him. Besides, from what Medgyessy had told me, it was the Allied police who were after Gruen, not the Austrian police. And these were Austrian policemen, I was certain of that. They were both carrying the same gun—a shiny new Mauser automatic, the kind they gave to all the cops on Vienna's denazified police force.

"Papers," said the second cop.

Slowly, I put my hand in my pocket. The two cops didn't look like they had much more policing experience between them than a scoutmaster. And I didn't want to get shot because some new bug cop was nervous. I handed over Gruen's passport carefully, and put my hands up again.

"I'm a friend of Frau Warzok's," I said, and sniffed the air. It wasn't just the room that smelled. It was the whole situation. If the cops were there then something bad had happened. "Look here, is she all right? Where is she?"

The second cop was still looking at the passport. I wasn't worried that he would think it wasn't me so much as that he would be abreast of whatever it was that Gruen was supposed to have done.

"It says here that you're from Vienna," he said. "You don't sound like you're from Vienna." He was wearing the same outfit as his colleague, only without the baker's hat. A smile was stapled to the opposite cheek from the way his nose was angled. He probably thought it made him look wry or even skeptical, but it just came off oblique and distorted. All of his recessive genes seemed to have concentrated where his chin ought to have been. And the hairline on his high forehead matched the line of a long S-shaped scar. He handed the passport back to me as he spoke.

"Before the war, I lived in Berlin for ten years," I said.

"A doctor, huh?"

They were starting to relax.

"Yes."

"Her doctor?"

"No. Look here, who are you? And where's Frau Warzok?"

"Police," said the one with the hat, flashing a warrant disk at me. "Deutschmeister Platz."

This seemed reasonable enough. The Kommissariat on Deutschmeister Platz was less than a hundred yards away from where we were standing.

"She's in there," said the cop with the scar.

The two cops put away their guns and led me into a tiled bathroom. It had been built at a time when a bathroom was not a bathroom unless a football team could bathe in it. As it happened, there was only one woman in the bath. Except for the one nylon stocking she was wearing, she was naked. The nylon stocking was knotted around her neck. It wasn't the kind of knot that would have detained Alexander the Great for very long, but it was effective enough. The woman was dead. She had been strangled. Beyond the fact that I had never seen her before it was impossible to say more because the smell didn't encourage delay. Both the body and the water it was lying in were a slimy shade of poisonous green. And there were flies. Curious the way there are always flies on bodies, even when it's very cold.

"Good grief," I said, reeling from the bathroom like a man who hadn't seen a cadaver since medical school, instead of less than half an hour earlier. And it was my hand I put up to my nose this time. For the moment the kickers were safely in my pocket. The effect the smell had on me was real enough. I went straight back to the open window and leaned into some fresh air. But it was just as well the stench left me gagging for a moment or two. Otherwise I might have said something stupid about how the body in the bathroom wasn't Britta Warzok. And that would have spoiled everything, in view of what the cop in the hat now said:

"Sorry to let you have it like that," he said, following me to the window. It was now plain to see that it had been the two cops who had opened it. "It was a bit of a shock for me, too. Frau Warzok used to give me piano lessons, when I was a kid." He pointed to a piano behind the door. "We'd only just found her ourselves when you came in. The neighbor downstairs reported the smell and the mail stacked up in her box."

"How do you know her?" asked the other cop. He was eyeing the holdall I had arrived with, and was probably wondering what was in it.

I was inventing my story even as I told it to him, trying to fix a plausible chain of causation in my head. The body in the bath had the look of a body that had been in the water for not quite a week. That would be my approximate start point.

"I knew her husband," I said. "Friedrich. Before the war. Before he—" I shrugged. "About a week ago I received a letter from her. At my home in Garmisch. It said that she was in trouble. It took me a while to get away from my medical practice. And I arrived in Vienna just a short while ago. I came straight here."

"Do you still have the letter?" asked the cop with the scar.

"No, I'm afraid I left it in Garmisch."

"What kind of trouble?" he asked. "Did she say?"

"No, but Britta isn't—*wasn't* the kind of person to say that kind of thing lightly. The letter was really short. It just asked me to come to Vienna as soon as I could. Well then. I telephoned before I left Garmisch. But there was no reply. So I came anyway."

I started to wander across the parquet wooden floor like some ordinary Fritz, distracted with grief. Which in part I was, of course. Vera Messmann's dead body was all too vivid in my memory. There were some nice rugs, a few elegant chairs and tables. Some good Nymphenburger porcelain. A vase of flowers that looked as if they had been dead for about as long as the woman in the bath. There were lots of framed photographs on a sideboard. I went to take a closer look at them. Many of them featured the woman in the bath. In one of them she was getting married to a face I recognized. It was Friedrich Warzok. I was quite sure it was him because he was wearing his SS uniform. I shook my head as if I was upset. But not in the way they imagined I was upset. I was upset because I had a very bad feeling about everything that had happened to me since a woman calling herself Britta Warzok had walked into my office.

"Who would have done such a thing?" I asked the two cops. "Unless."

"Yes."

"It's no secret that Friedrich, her husband, is wanted for war crimes," I said. "And of course, one hears things. About Jewish revenge gangs. Perhaps they came looking for her husband and killed her instead."

The cop with the hat was shaking his head. "It's a nice idea," he said. "But it so happens we think we know who killed her."

"Already? That's amazing."

"Did you ever hear her mention a man called Bernhard Gunther?"

I tried to contain my surprise and look thoughtful for a moment. "Gunther, Gunther," I said, as if raking through the bottom drawer of my memory. If I was going to pump them for information I would have to give them something first.

"Yes, yes, I think I have heard that name before. But it wasn't in connection with Britta Warzok. A few months ago, a man turned up at my house in Garmisch. I think his name might have been Gunther. He said he was a private detective and that he was looking for a witness who might assist in the appeal of another old comrade I used to know. A fellow named von Starnberg. He's currently serving a sentence for war crimes in Landsberg Prison. What does your Bernhard Gunther look like?"

"We don't know," admitted the cop with the scar. "But from

what you've told us, he's the man we're looking for all right. A private detective, based in Munich."

"Can you tell us anything about him?" asked the other.

"Yes, but look here, do you mind if I sit down? I've had a bit of a shock."

"Please."

They followed me to a big leather sofa where I sat down. I took out the pipe and started to fill it, then hesitated. "Do you mind if I smoke?"

"Go ahead," said the hat. "It will help get rid of the smell."

"He wasn't very tall," I said. "Well dressed. A bit too fastidious, you might say. Brown hair. Brown eyes. Not from Munich, I'd say. Somewhere else, probably. Hamburg maybe. Berlin, possibly."

"He's from Berlin," said the scar. "He used to be a policeman."

"A policeman? Yes, well, he did strike me a bit that way. You know. Full of himself. A bit officious." I hesitated. "No offense, gentlemen. What I mean is, he was very correct. I must say he didn't strike me as the type to murder anyone at all. If you don't mind my saying so. I've met a few psychopathic personalities during my years as a doctor, but your Herr Gunther wasn't one of those." I settled back on the sofa and puffed at my pipe. "What makes you think it was he who killed her?"

"We found his business card on the mantelpiece," said the hat. "There was blood on it. We also found an initialed handkerchief with blood on it. His initials."

I remembered using my own handkerchief to staunch the flow of blood from the stump of my little finger. "Gentlemen, she was strangled," I said, carefully. "I don't see that a bit of blood proves anything."

"The handkerchief was on the bathroom floor," said the scar. "We figure that she might have hit him before she died. Anyway, we phoned the murder in to the IP on Kärntnerstrasse. It seems the Amis have a file on this Gunther. There's an Ami on his way here now. From the Stiftskaserne. Matter of fact, we thought you might be him until we heard you call out for Frau Warzok. And saw the bag."

I felt my ears prick up at the mention of the Stiftskaserne. This was where the headquarters of the U.S. Military Police in Vienna was located, on Mariahilferstrasse. But it was also the home of the American intelligence community in Vienna. I'd been there before. Back in the days when the CIA had been called the OSS.

"My clothes," I said. "I was expecting to be here for a couple of days."

There was something about what these cops were telling me that just didn't add up. But there was no time now to quiz them further. If the Americans had a file on me, then it was equally possible they had a photograph, too. I had to get out of there, and fast. But how? If there's one thing cops like to hang on to it's a witness. Then again, if there's one thing they hate it's a forensic amateur—a member of the public who thinks he might be able to offer some advice.

"The Stiftskaserne," I said. "That's the 796th U.S. Military Police, isn't it? And the CIA. Not the IP. So this must be an intelligence matter, as well as a murder. I wonder what Britta could have got herself mixed up in that might involve the CIA."

One cop looked at the other. "Did we mention the CIA?"

"No, but it's obvious that they're involved from what you've already told me," I said.

"Is it?"

"Of course," I said. "I was in the Abwehr during the war. So I know quite a bit about this kind of thing. Perhaps I can be of assistance when the Ami turns up. After all, I've met this Bernie Gunther. And I did know Britta Warzok. So if there's anything I can do to help catch her murderer, then obviously I'd like to help. As well as being a doctor, I also speak English. That might come in handy, too. It goes without saying that I can be discreet if this involves something top secret between the CIA and the Austrian police."

The two cops were already looking like they wanted me gone from there, and as quickly as possible. "Perhaps later on you could be of assistance, Doctor," said the hat. "When we've had a chance to examine the crime scene in further detail." He picked up my bag and carried it to the door for me.

"We'll be in touch," said the other cop, taking me by the arm, and encouraging me onto my feet.

"But you don't know where I'm staying," I said. "And I don't know your names."

"Call us at Deutschmeister Platz and let us know later," said the hat. "I'm Inspector Strauss. He's Kriminalassistent Wagner."

I stood up, affecting a show of reluctance to be gone from the apartment, and allowed myself to be steered to the door. "I'm at the Hotel de France," I lied. "It's not far from here. Do you know it?"

"We know where it is," said the hat patiently. He handed me my bag.

"All right," I said. "I'll call you later. Wait. What's your telephone number?"

The hat handed me his business card. "Yes, please call us later," he said, trying not to grimace too obviously.

I felt his hand in the small of my back and then I was out on the landing, with the door closing behind me. Pleased with my own performance I went quickly down the stairs and stopped outside the apartment beneath Britta Warzok's from where, allegedly, the phone call about the smell and the mail had originated. None of that felt plausible now. For one thing there was no smell detectable on this floor. And for another there was no nosey-parker neighbor peering out of the door to see what the police were up to. As there ought to have been if the story I had been told had been a true one.

I was about to continue with my swift exit when I h... in the hallway below and, glancing out of the second-... I saw a black Mercury sedan parked on the street belo... that it might be wise to avoid crossing the American... knocked quickly at the door of the apartment.

After several agonizing seconds, the door opened to reveal a man wearing trousers and a vest. He was a hairy man. A very hairy man. Even his hair seemed to have smaller hairs growing on it. He made Esau look as smooth as sheet of window glass. I handed him the cop's business card and glanced nervously behind me as the mounting footsteps grew nearer. "Sorry to disturb you, sir," I said. "I wonder if I might come in and have a word with you for a moment."

## THIRTY-FOUR

Esau looked at Inspector Strauss's business card for what seemed like an eternity before inviting me inside. I went in past him and smelled dinner. It didn't smell good. Someone had been using some old, worn-out fat in cooking whatever it was. He closed the door at just about the moment the Ami would have rounded the corner on the stairs and seen the second-floor apartment's door. I breathed a small sigh of relief.

The entrance to the apartment, like the one on the floor above, was as big as a bus station. There was a silver tray for mail by the front door and an umbrella stand made out of an elephant's foot. But it might just as easily have belonged to the large woman standing in the kitchen doorway. She was wearing a pinafore and was supporting herself on a pair of crutches, having only one leg. "Who is it, Heini?" she asked.

"It's the police, dear," he said.

"The police?" She sounded surprised. "What do they want?"

I had been right after all. Clearly these people hadn't reported anything to the police at Deutschmeister Platz, or anywhere else for that matter.

"I'm very sorry to disturb you," I said. "But there's been an incident in the apartment upstairs."

"An incident? What kind of incident?"

"I'm afraid I can't tell you too much at this stage," I said. "However, I was wondering when you last saw Frau Warzok. And when you did, if she was with anyone. Or if you heard anything unusual from upstairs, perhaps."

"We haven't seen her in over a week," said Heini, absently combing the hairs on his arms with his fingers. "And then just for a minute or two. I thought she was away. Her mail's still there."

The woman on crutches had maneuvered herself toward me. "We don't really have much to do with her," she said. "We say hello and good morning. A quiet woman."

"When she's around we never hear very much," said Heini. "Just her piano, and then only when the window is open in summer. She plays beautifully. Used to give concerts before the war. When people still had money for that kind of thing."

"It's mostly children and their mothers who come to see her now," said Heini's wife. "She gives piano lessons."

"Anyone else?"

They were quiet for a moment.

"There was someone, about a week ago," said Heini. "An Ami."

"In uniform?"

"No," he said. "But you can tell, can't you? The way they walk. Their shoes. Their haircuts. Everything."

"What did this Ami look like?"

"Well dressed. Nice sports jacket. Well-pressed trousers. Not tall. Not short. Average height, really. Glasses. Gold watch. Quite tanned, too. Oh yes, and another reason I knew he was an American. His car was parked outside. An American car. A green one with white tires."

"Thank you," I said, retrieving the inspector's business card. "You've been most helpful."

"But what's happened?" asked Heini's wife.

"If anyone asks, I didn't tell you," I said. "I shouldn't be saying anything at all. Not yet. But you're respectable people, I can see that. Not the kind of people to go around spreading idle talk about something like this. Frau Warzok is dead. Murdered, probably."

"Murdered! Here?" She sounded shocked. "In this building? In this district?"

"I've already said more than I should," I told them. "Look, one of my senior officers will speak to you in more detail later on. You'd best pretend that it's news to you when he does, all right? Or it might be my job."

I opened the door a crack. I could hear no steps in the building. "And you'd best lock the door behind me," I said, and went out.

By now it was dark and it had started to snow again. I walked quickly out of the building and down onto the Ring, to a taxi stand where I took a cab back to my hotel. There was no question of staying there, of course. Not now that I knew that Eric Gruen was as interesting to the International Patrol as Bernie Gunther. I would collect my things, check out of the hotel, and then go to a bar and try to figure out what to do.

The cab turned onto Wiedner Hauptstrasse, and as it neared the hotel entrance, I saw the IP vehicle parked outside. My already queasy stomach turned over, as if someone had stirred it with a long wooden spoon. I told the driver to pull up on the corner. I paid and then meandered innocently to the back of a small crowd of nosey-parkers that had gathered beside the doorway, apparently eager to watch someone get arrested. Two military policemen were stopping people from going in or coming out of the Erzherzog Rainer.

"What's all the excitement?" I asked one of the nosey-parkers.

An old man, as thin as a pipe cleaner, wearing pince-nez and a black homburg, supplied an answer. "They're arresting someone," he said. "Don't know who, though."

I nodded vaguely and then edged away, certain that it was me they were probably after. After the scene at the cemetery there could be little doubt about it. I saw no point in looking for another hotel, either. If they were looking for Eric Gruen, the other hotels and pensions would be the first places they would check. Then the railway stations, the bus stations, and the airport. A wind was getting up. The snow in my face felt like a case of frozen chicken pox. Hurrying through the darkened streets, hunted and with no place to go, I felt like Peter Lorre in *M*. As if I really had murdered two women. Friendless, harried, desperate, and cold. But at least I had money. I had plenty of money. With money the situation might yet be rescued.

I walked across Karlsplatz and the Ring. On Schwarzenberg Strasse I stepped into a Hungarian bar called Czardasfurstin to figure out my next move. There was a band with a zither. I ordered coffee and cake and tried to think through the sentimental, melancholy music. I realized I needed to find somewhere I could stay the night, no questions asked. And I told myself there was only one place I knew where a bed could be had as easily as coffee and cake. A place where money was all that mattered. I was taking a bit of a risk going back there after only a couple of years. But I hadn't much choice. For me, risk was now something unavoidable, like old age—if I was lucky—and death, if I wasn't. I went to the Oriental, on Petersplatz.

With its dimly lighted booths, scantily clad girls, sarcastic orchestra, pimps, and prostitutes, the Oriental was strongly reminiscent of some of the old clubs I'd known in Berlin during the decadent dog days of the Weimar Republic. It was said that the Oriental had been a great favorite with Vienna's Nazi Bonzen—the bigwigs who ran the city. Now it was a favorite with black-marketeers and Vienna's burgeoning intelligence community. As well as the Egyptian Night Cabaret—an excuse for a lot of girls to dress like slave girls, which is to say they wore very little at all—there was a casino. Where there is a casino there is always plenty of easy money. And where there is easy money there are snappers. When I had last been there the girls had been amateurs—widows and orphans doing it for cigarettes and chocolate, or just to make ends meet. I'd had a thing with a girl there. I couldn't remember her name. Things had changed a lot since 1947. The girls in the Oriental were hard-faced professionals who were interested only in one thing: cash. To that extent, only the atmosphere seemed authentically oriental.

I stepped down a curving stairway into the club, where the orchestra was playing some American tunes, such as "Time Out for Tears" and "I Want to Cry." They must have heard I was coming. American servicemen were not allowed in the Oriental, but, of course, out of uniform and with plenty of money in their pockets, it was hard to keep them out. Which was why, from time to time, the place got raided by the IP. But usually not until much later on, by which time I hoped I would be gone. I sat down in a booth, ordered a bottle of cognac, some eggs, and a packet of Luckies and, confident that very soon I would find a bed for the night, I tried to make some sense of everything that had occurred that day. Of everything that had happened to me since my arrival in Vienna. And even earlier than that.

It wasn't easy. But as far as I was able to determine, I had been set up as the prime suspect in two murders, most probably by the CIA. The American with the green car described by Frau Warzok's neighbor could only have been Major Jacobs. But as to the true identity of the woman who had come to see me in my offices in Munich, purporting to be Frau Warzok, I had no idea. The real Frau Warzok was dead, murdered by Jacobs, or some other agent of the CIA. Very likely I had been given her address in order that I could be implicated in her murder. The same reason I had been given Vera Messmann's address by Eric Gruen. Which meant that he and Henkell and Jacobs were all in it together. Whatever *it* was.

The cognac arrived with my cigarettes. I poured myself a glass and lit a cigarette. Already there were several girls gathered at the bar who were looking my way. I wondered if there was a pecking order, or if, as at a taxi stand, it would be whoever was next in line. I felt like a piece of fish in an alley full of cats. The band struck up with "Be a Clown," which also seemed appropriate. I wasn't much of a detective, that was certain at least. Detectives were supposed to notice things. Clowns, on the other hand, were supposed to be easily tricked, and to take the fall for the laughs. I had that part down pat. Back at the bar, two of the snappers were arguing. I supposed it was about which of them would have the dubious honor of picking me up. I hoped it would be the redhead. She looked like she had some life in her, and life was something I badly needed to be around. Because the more I thought about my situation, the more I wanted to blow my brains out. If I had owned a gun I might have considered it more seriously. Instead, I did some more thinking about the spot I was in, and how I had got there.

If the fake Britta Warzok had been involved with Henkell, Gruen, and Jacobs from the very beginning, then there was a strong possibility that it had been them who had arranged for me to lose a finger and end up in hospital under Henkell's care. The men who'd beaten me up had driven me to his hospital, hadn't they? And Henkell himself had found me in the doorway. The handkerchief I had used to stanch the blood had ended up at the scene of the real Britta Warzok's murder. Along with my business card. That was neat. And losing half my finger had been important. I could see that now. Without that I could hardly have passed as Eric Gruen. Of course, I hadn't seen the physical similarity between myself and Gruen until after he had shaved off his beard. But they must have known. Probably as early as the day Jacobs had turned up at my hotel in Dachau. Hadn't he said something then about me reminding him of someone? Was that when the idea had come to him? The idea of passing me off as Eric Gruen? So that the real Eric Gruen could go and be someone else? It was an idea that stood a better chance of success, of course, if someone called Eric Gruen was under arrest for war crimes. Whatever these war crimes were. A massacre of prisoners of war? Or something even worse. Something medical perhaps. Something sufficiently heinous that Jacobs would have known that war crimes investigators of every political shade and religious creed would not have rested until they had Dr. Eric Gruen in custody. No wonder people like Bekemeier and Elizabeth Gruen's servants had been surprised to see me back in Vienna again. And to think I had actually volunteered for it all. That was really the clever part, the way they had let me make all the running. With a little help from Engelbertina, of course. No wonder I hadn't realized what was happening with her there to kick sand in my eyes. To distract me with that fabulous body of hers. If I hadn't thought of the idea of impersonating Eric Gruen, she would probably have suggested it herself. And yet they could hardly have predicted the death of Gruen's mother. Unless someone had helped the old woman on her way. Was it possible Gruen had counseled the death of his own mother? Why not? There was no love lost between mother and son. Both Bekemeier and Medgyessy had mentioned the suddenness of the old woman's death. Jacobs must have killed her, too. Or had someone kill her. Someone from the CIA or the ODESSA perhaps. But I still didn't quite see why Vera Messmann and the real Britta Warzok had been killed.

One thing was quite clear at any rate. I had been a damn fool. But what a lot of trouble they had taken. I felt like a very small picture by an old master, surrounded by an enormous and ornate gilt frame—the kind of frame that is supposed to accentuate the importance of the picture. Framed. The word seemed hardly adequate for the Byzantine conspiracy that had enveloped me. I didn't feel like a stooge so much as all three at once, rolled into one pitiful idiot whose face deserved to have been slapped and slapped again. I was the paw of the stupidest cat that ever sat beside a fire and a monkey and a handful of hot chestnuts.

"May I sit down?"

I looked up and realized that the redhead had won. She looked a little flushed, as if the competition for the pleasure of my company had been keen. Half standing, which was the way I was feeling, I smiled and then indicated the seat on the opposite side of my table. "Please," I said. "Be my guest."

"That's what I'm here for," she said, bending sinuously into the booth. Hers was a better sinuous bend than anything that was happening on the Oriental's pagodalike stage. "My name is Lilly. What's yours?"

I almost laughed. My own Lilly Marlene. It was typical of a snapper to give herself a fancy name. There were times when I thought the only reason girls went walking a line was so they could give themselves a new Johanna. "Eric," I said. "Would you like a drink, Lilly?" I beckoned the waiter toward me. He had Hindenburg's mustache, Hitler's blue eyes, and Adenauer's personality. It was like being served by fifty years of German history. Lilly looked at the man with disdain.

"He's already got a bottle, right?" The waiter nodded. "Then just bring another glass. And a brown bowl. Yes, a brown bowl." The waiter nodded and went away without a word.

"You're drinking coffee?" I said.

"I might have a small glass of cognac, but so long as you've ordered a bottle, I can drink what I like," she said. "That's the rule."

She smiled. "You don't mind, do you? Saves you a little money. Nothing wrong with that, eh?"

"Nothing wrong with that at all," I said.

"Besides, it's been a long day. During the day I work in a shoe shop."

"Which one?"

"I couldn't tell you that," she said. "You might come along and drop me in it."

"I'd have to drop myself in it at the same time," I said.

"True," she said. "But it's best you don't know. Imagine the shock if you saw the real me, fetching shoes and measuring feet."

She helped herself to one of my cigarettes, and while I put a match to it, I got a better look at her. Her face had just a few freckles around the nose, which was, perhaps, just a little too pointed. It made her seem sharp and speculating, which, of course, she probably was. Her eyes were a green shade of avarice. The teeth were small and very white with the bottom jaw just a little too prominent. With just the one expression so far, she looked like one of those Sonneberg dolls with the porcelain face and the kind of underwear that's played with every day.

My eggs arrived with her coffee—a bowl of half coffee, half milk. While I ate, she talked about herself and smoked, and sipped her coffee, and had a little cognac. "I haven't seen you here before," she observed.

"It's been a while," I said. "I've been living in Munich."

"I'd like to live in Munich," she said. "Somewhere farther west than Vienna, anyway. Somewhere there aren't any Ivans around."

"You think the Amis are any better?"

"Don't you?"

I let that one go. She didn't want to hear my opinions of the Americans. "What do you say we go back to your place?"

"Hey, quit stealing my lines," she said. "I'm supposed to make the running, not you?"

"Sorry."

"What's your hurry, anyway?"

"I've been on my shoes all day," I said. "You should know what that's like."

She tapped the cognac bottle with a fingernail as big as a paper knife. "This isn't herbal tea you're drinking here, Eric," she said, sternly. "This is more of a put-you-down than a pick-me-up."

"I know, but it takes the edge off the ax I've been grinding for the last few hours."

"Oh? Against who?"

"Me."

"Like that, huh?"

I pushed my hand across the table and lifted it a little to let her see the hundred-schilling note that was under my palm. "I need a bit of looking after, that's all. Nothing weird. Fact is, that'll be the easiest hundred you ever put in your brassiere."

She regarded the hundred as she might have regarded a cannibal's offer of a free lunch. "You need a hotel, mister," she said. "Not a girl."

"I don't like hotels," I said. "Hotels are full of lonely strangers. People sitting alone in their rooms waiting until it's time to go home. I don't want that. I just need somewhere to stay until tomorrow morning."

She covered my hand with hers. "What the hell?" she said. "I could use an early night."

## THIRTY-FIVE

Lilly's apartment was across the Danube in the Second District, close to the Diana Baths, on Upper Danube Strasse. It was small but comfortable, and I enjoyed a relatively peaceful night's sleep with Lilly that was broken only by the sound of a barge blowing its horn as it went south along the canal, toward the river. In the morning she seemed both surprised and pleased that she hadn't had to satisfy anything other than my appetite for breakfast.

"Well, that's a first," she said, making us some coffee. "I must be losing my touch. Either that, mister, or you're keeping it nice and warm for the boys."

"Neither," I said. "And how would you like to make another hundred?"

A little less obdurate by day than by night, she agreed with alacrity. She wasn't a bad sort of girl. Not really. Her parents had been killed in 1944, when she was just fifteen years old, and everything she had she'd worked for herself. It was a common enough story, including her being raped by a couple of Ivans. A good-looking girl, she knew she had been lucky it had been just two Ivans. There were women I knew in Berlin who had been raped as many as fifty or sixty times during the first months of the occupation. I liked her. I liked the way she didn't complain. And I liked the way she didn't ask too many questions. She was bright enough to know I was probably hiding from the police, and bright enough not to ask why.

On her way to work—the shoe shop was Fortschritt, on Kärntnerstrasse—she showed me a barber's shop where I could get a shave, as I had been obliged to leave my razor and everything that came with it back at the hotel. I took the holdall with me. I liked Lilly.

But I didn't trust her not to steal twenty-five thousand Austrian schillings. I had a shave and a haircut. And, at a men's store inside the Ring, I bought a clean shirt, some underwear, some socks, and a pair of boots. It was important for me to look respectable. I was going to the Russian Kommandatura, in what used to be the city's Board of Education, with the aim of examining their files on wanted war criminals. As someone who had been in the SS, who had escaped from a Russian POW transport, and killed a Russian soldier—not to mention more than two dozen NKVD—I was taking a considerable risk entering the Kommandatura at all. But it was a risk I calculated was slightly less than the risk of carrying out a similar inquiry at the IP headquarters. Besides, I spoke fluent Russian, knew the name of an important colonel of MVD, and was still possessed of Inspector Strauss's business card. And if all else failed, I would try bribery. In my experience, all Russians in Vienna and, in Berlin for that matter, were open to bribery.

The Palace of Justice, on Schmerlingplatz, in the Eighth District, was the meeting place for Vienna's Inter-Allied Command, and the headquarters of the International Patrol. The flags of all four nations flew in front of this imposing building, with the flag of the nation that had temporary police control of the city—in this instance, the French—flying on top. Opposite the Palace of Justice stood the Russian Kommandatura, easily identifiable by the communist slogans and a large illuminated red star that lent the snow in front of the building a wet, pinkish hue. I walked into a grand entrance hall and asked one of the Red Army guards for the office responsible for the investigation of war crimes. Under his forage cap was a scar on his forehead that went down right to the skull, as if his head had once been scratched by something more lethal than a fingernail. Surprised to be spoken to in Russian and so politely, too, he directed me to a room at the top of the building and, with my heart in my mouth, I mounted the huge stone steps.

Like all public buildings in Vienna, the Board of Education had been built at a time when the Emperor Franz Josef had ruled an empire comprising 51 million souls and 675,000 square kilometers. There were just over 6 million people living in Austria in 1949, and the greatest European empire was long gone, but you wouldn't have known that walking up the stairs of this imposing building. At the top was a wooden fingerpost sign, crudely painted with department names in Cyrillic. I followed the sign around the balustrade to the other side of the building, where I found the office I was looking for. The sign on a little wooden stand beside the door was in German, and it read: "SOVIET WAR CRIMES COMMISSION, AUSTRIA. For the investigation and examination of the misdeeds of the German fascist invaders and their accomplices in the monstrous atrocities and crimes of the German government." Which seemed to describe it pretty well, all things considered.

I knocked on the door and went into a small outer office. Through a glass wall I could see a large room with several freestanding bookcases and about a dozen filing cabinets. On the wall of the office was a large picture of Stalin, and a smaller one of a plump-looking man in glasses who might have been Beria, the head of the Soviet secret police. A threadbare Soviet flag hung limply from a scout-size flagpole. Arranged along the wall behind the door was a montage of photographs featuring Hitler, a Nazi rally at Nuremberg, liberated concentration camps, piles of dead Jewish bodies, the Nuremberg war trial, and several convicted war criminals actually standing on the trap door of the gallows. It looked as clear a piece of inductive reasoning as you could have found outside a textbook on the general principles of logic. In the outer office, a thin, severe-looking woman wearing a uniform looked up from what she was typing and prepared to treat me like the fascist invader I had of course been. She had sad, hollow eyes, a spectacularly broken nose, a fringe of red hair, a sulky mouth, and cheekbones as high as the zygomatic bones on a Jolly Roger. The shoulder boards on her uniform were blue, which meant she was MVD. I wondered what she would have made of the Federal Republic's Amnesty Law. Politely, in quite good German, she asked me my business. I handed her Inspector Strauss's business card and, as if I had been auditioning for a part in a play by Chekhov, spoke to her in my best *velikorruskij*.

"I apologize for disturbing you, Comrade," I said. "This is not a formal inquiry. I'm not here on duty." All of that was to preempt any requests to see my nonexistent warrant disk. "Does the name Poroshin, of the MVD, mean anything to you?"

"I know a General Poroshin," she said, adjusting her manner very slightly. "In Berlin."

"Perhaps he has already telephoned you," I continued. "To explain my being here."

She shook her head. "I'm afraid not," she said.

"No matter," I said. "I have an inquiry relating to a fascist war criminal here in Austria. The general recommended that I come to this office. That the legal officer in this office was one of the most efficient in the Special State Commission. And that if anyone could help me to track down the Nazi swine I'm looking for, it would be her."

"The general said that?"

"Those were his exact words, Comrade," I said. "He mentioned your name, but I'm afraid that I have forgotten it. I do apologize."

"First Legal Officer Khristotonovna," she said.

"Yes, indeed. That was it. Once again, my apologies for having forgotten it. My inquiry relates to two SS men. One of them was born here in Vienna. His name is Gruen. Eric Gruen. G-R-U-E-N. The other is Heinrich Henkell. That's Henkell as in the champagne. I'm afraid I'm not sure where he was born."

The lieutenant moved quickly out of her chair. The mention of Poroshin's name had seen to that. I wasn't surprised. He had scared me when I had known him, first in Vienna and then in Berlin two years later. She opened the glass door and led me to a table, where she invited me to sit down. Then she turned to face a large wooden card index, drew out a drawer as long as her arm, and riffled through several hundred cards. She was taller than I had supposed. Her blouse, buttoned up to the neck, was dun-colored, her longish skirt was black, and her army boots, like the belt around her waist, were as black and shiny as a village pond. On the right arm of her blouse was a stripe indicating that she had been wounded in combat, and on the left two medals. Russians wore actual medals rather than just the ribbons, like the Amis, as if they were too proud to take them off.

With two cards in her hand, Khristotonovna went over to a filing cabinet and started to search there. Then she excused herself from the room and went out a door in the back. I wondered if she was going off to check my story with the Austrian police, or even Poroshin in Berlin, if she would be coming back to the room with a Tokarev in her hand or even a couple of guards. I bit my lip and stayed where I was, diverting myself by thinking of yet more ways in which Gruen and Henkell and Jacobs had played me for a fool.

The way they had taken me into their confidence. The way Jacobs had pretended to be so surprised to see me again. The way he had pretended to distrust me. The way "Britta Warzok" had sent me on a wild-goose chase for no other purpose than to make me believe that an assault occasioning the loss of my finger had been the direct result of asking awkward questions about the Comradeship.

Khristotonovna was gone for about ten minutes, and when she returned she was carrying two files. She laid them on the table in front of me. She had even brought me a notebook and a pencil. "Do you read Russian?" she asked.

"Yes."

"Where did you learn?" she asked. "Your Russian is very good."

"I was an intelligence officer, on the Russian front," I said.

"So was I," she said. "That is where I learned German. But your Russian is better than my German, I think."

"Thank you for saying so," I said.

"Perhaps . . ." But then she seemed to think better of whatever it was she had been about to say. So I said it for her.

"Yes. Perhaps we were adversaries once. But now we are on the same side, I hope. The side of justice." A bit corny, perhaps. It's odd, but Russian is a language that always brings out the sentimental in me.

"The files are in German and Russian," she said. "One more thing. The rules state that when you have finished I shall have to ask you to sign a document stating that you have examined them. This document must remain on the file. Do you agree, Inspector?"

"Of course."

"Very well." Khristotonovna tried a smile. Her teeth were going bad. She needed a dentist like I needed a new passport. "Can I bring you some Russian tea?" she asked.

"Thank you, yes. If it's no trouble. That would be very kind of you."

"It's no trouble." She went away, her underskirt rustling like dried leaves, leaving me regretting my earlier unkind thought about her. She was much friendlier than I could ever have supposed.

I opened Gruen's file and began to read.

There was everything and more. Gruen's SS record. His Nazi Party record—he had joined the party in 1934. His officer's commission. His SS record—"exemplary." The first revelation was that Gruen had never been with the SS Panzer Corps at all. He had never served in France, nor on the Russian front. In fact, he had seen no front-line service at all. According to his medical records, which were sufficiently detailed to mention his missing little finger, he had never even been wounded. Gruen's most recent medical examination had been in March 1944. Nothing had been overlooked. Not even a slight case of eczema. No mention there of a missing spleen, or any spinal injury. I felt my ears start to burn as I read this. Was it really possible that he had faked his illness? That he wasn't confined to a wheelchair at all? That he hadn't lost his spleen? If so, they really had played me like a piano. Nor was Gruen the junior officer he had claimed to be. The file contained copies of his promotion certificates. The last one, dated January 1945, revealed that Eric Gruen had ended the war as an SS Oberführer—a senior colonel—in the Waffen-SS. But it was what I read next that disturbed me most of all, although I was half expecting it after the revelation that he had never been in the SS Panzer Corps.

Born to a rich Viennese family, Eric Gruen had been considered a brilliant young doctor. After graduating medical school he had spent some time in Cameroon and Togo, where he had produced two influential papers on tropical diseases that had been published in the *German Medical Journal*. Upon his return in 1935, he had joined the SS and been a member of the Interior Health Department, where it was suspected he had been involved in experiments on mentally handicapped children. After the outbreak of war, he had been a doctor at Lemberg-Janowska, at Majdanek, and finally at Dachau. At Majdanek, it was known that he had infected eight hundred Soviet POWs with typhus and malaria and conducted studies of the progress of the disease. At Dachau, he had assisted Gerhard Rose, a brigadier general in the medical service of the Luftwaffe. There was some cross-referencing to Rose. A professor at the Robert Koch Institute of Tropical Medicine in Berlin, Rose had performed lethal experiments on concentration camp inmates at Dachau in pursuit of vaccines for malaria and typhus. More than twelve hundred prisoners at Dachau, including many children, had been deliberately given malaria by infected mosquitoes or injections of malaria-infected blood.

The details of the experimentation made extremely uncomfortable reading. In the Dachau doctors' trial of October 1946, a Roman Catholic priest, one Father Koch, had testified that he had been sent to the malaria station at Dachau, where, every afternoon, a box of mosquitoes had been placed between his legs for half an hour. After seventeen days he left the station, and it was another eight months before he succumbed to a malaria attack. Other priests, children, Russian and Polish prisoners, and, of course, many Jews, had not been so lucky, and several hundred had died in the three years that these malaria experiments had continued.

For their crimes, seven of the so-called Nazi doctors had been hanged at Landsberg in June 1948. Rose had been one of five sentenced to life in prison. Another four doctors had been sentenced to terms of imprisonment ranging from ten to twenty years. Seven had been acquitted. At his trial, Gerhard Rose had justified his actions, arguing that it was reasonable to sacrifice "a few hundred" in pursuit of a prophylactic vaccine capable of saving tens of thousands of lives.

Rose had been assisted by a number of other doctors including Eric Gruen and Heinrich Henkell, and a nurse-kapo called Albertine Zehner.

Albertine Zehner. That was a real shock. But it had to be the same girl. And it seemed to explain a great deal that had been a mystery to me. Engelbertina Zehner had been a Jewish prisoner turned kapo and nursing assistant in the medical block at Majdanek and Dachau. She had never worked in a camp brothel at all. She had been a nurse-kapo.

Gruen's file described him as being still at large, a wanted war criminal. An early investigation into Gruen's case by the legal officer of the 1st Ukrainian Front and two legal officers from the Soviet Special State Commission had come to nothing. Statements from inmates at all three camps, and F. F. Bryshin, a forensic medical expert from the Red Army, were provided.

The last page in the file was the record of file protocol, and this, too, provided a surprise for me, for here I found the following note: *This file examined by American occupation authorities in Vienna, October 1946, in the person of Major J. Jacobs, United States Army.*

Khristotonovna returned with a glass of hot Russian tea on a little tin tray. There was a long spoon and little bowl of sugar lumps. I thanked her and turned my attention to Heinrich Henkell's file. This was less detailed than Gruen's. Before the war he had been involved in Aktion T4, the Nazi Euthanasia Program, at a psychiatric clinic in Hadamar. During the war, as a Sturmbannführer in the Waffen-SS, he had been deputy director of the German Institute of Military Scientific Research and had seen service at Auschwitz, Majdanek, Buchenwald, and Dachau. At Majdanek, he had assisted Gruen in his typhus experiments, and later, at Dachau, his malaria experiments. In the course of his medical research he had amassed a large collection of human skulls of different racial types. Henkell was believed to have been executed by American soldiers at Dachau, following the camp's liberation.

I sat back heavily in my chair. My loud sigh brought Lieutenant Khristotonovna back to my side. And she mistook the lump in my throat for something other than feeling sorry for myself.

"Tough going?"

I nodded, too choked to say anything for a moment. So I finished my tea, signed the protocol, thanked her for her help, and went outside. It felt good to be breathing clean, fresh air. At least until I saw four military policemen come out of the Ministry of Justice and climb into a truck, ready to patrol the city. Four more elephants followed. And then another four. I stayed in the doorway, watching from a safe distance and smoking a cigarette until they had all gone.

I had heard about the Nazi doctors trial, of course. I remembered the surprise I had felt that the Allies should have seen fit to hang the president of the German Red Cross—at least that is until I read about how he had conducted sterilization experiments, and forced Jews to drink seawater. A lot of people—most people, including Kirsten—had refused to believe any of the evidence presented at the trial. Kirsten had said that the photographs and documents presented during the four-month-long trial had been faked in a grand sham to humiliate Germany even more. That the witnesses and victims who had survived had all been lying. I myself had found it all hard to comprehend—that we, perhaps the most civilized nation on earth, could have done such appalling things in the name of medical science. Hard to comprehend, yes. But not so hard to believe. After my own experiences on the Russian front, I came to believe human beings were capable of an unlimited degree of inhumanity. Perhaps that—our very inhumanity—is what makes us human most of all. I was beginning to understand what was going on. I still had one question about what Gruen and Jacobs and Henkell were up to. But it was the kind of question to which I had a good idea where to find the answer.

When the last IP vehicle had set off from outside the Justice building, I walked onto Heldenplatz, the great square of green that faced onto the Ring. Ahead of me was the New Palace, also occupied by the Russian army, and decorated with a large picture of Uncle Joe. I passed through an arcaded walk and onto a cobbled square that was home to the empty Spanish Riding School—the horses were all safe from Russian appetites—and the National Library. I went inside the library. A man was polishing a wooden floor as big as a football field. The library itself was chilly and, for the most part, unused. I approached the main desk and awaited the attention of the librarian, who was busy writing a catalogue card. The sign on her desk said "Inquiries." But it might just as easily have said *"Cave canem."* A couple of minutes passed before, with her glasses flashing the Morse code for "Go away," she finally condescended to acknowledge my presence by looking at me.

"Yes?"

There was a blue rinse in her gray hair and her mouth was as severe as a geometry box. She wore a white blouse and a double-breasted navy blue jacket. She reminded me a little of Admiral Dönitz. There was a hearing aid attached to her pocket. I bent toward it and pointed at one of the marble statues.

"Actually, I think he's been waiting rather longer than I have," I said.

Just for that she showed me her teeth. They were better than the Russian woman's. Strong-looking, too. Someone had been feeding her meat.

"Sir," she said crisply. "This is the National Library of Vienna. If it's laughs you want, I suggest you find a cabaret. If it's a book, then maybe I can help you."

"Actually, I'm looking for a magazine," I told her.

"A magazine?" She uttered the word as if it were something venereal.

"Yes. An American magazine. Do you keep American magazines here?"

"Sadly, yes, we do. Which magazine was it that you were looking for?"

"*Life* magazine," I said. "The issue for June 4, 1945."

"Follow me, please," she said, getting up from behind her wood-paneled redoubt.

"I'd be delighted to."

"Most of what we have here is from the collection of Eugene of Savoy," she said. "However, for the benefit of our American visitors, we do keep copies of *Life* magazine. Frankly, it's the only thing they ever ask for."

"Then I guess it's my lucky day," I said.

"Isn't it just?"

Five minutes later I was seated at a refectory table staring at the magazine Major Jacobs had not wanted me to see. And on the face of it, it was hard to see why. On the front was an open letter written by the U.S. Joint Chiefs of Staff to the American people. And when I turned the pages it was full of patriotic war effort and wholesome American smiles, as well as advertisements for General Electric, Iodent, and Westinghouse. There was a nice picture of Humphrey Bogart getting married to Lauren Bacall, and an even nicer one of Himmler taken minutes after he had poisoned himself. I liked it better than the one of Bogart. I turned some more pages. Pictures of an English seaside resort. And then, on page forty-three, what I presumed I was looking for. A short article about how eight hundred convicts in three American penitentiaries had volunteered to be infected with malaria so that medical men could study the disease. It was easy to see why Jacobs might have been sensitive about such an article. What the American Office of Scientific Research and Development had done in prisons in Georgia, Illinois, and New Jersey looked very much like what SS doctors had done in Dachau. Clearly, the Americans had hanged men for what they themselves had done in their own prisons. It was true that all of these convicts were volunteers, but then Gruen and Henkell might easily have argued the same excuse. Engelbertina, or Albertine, was probably the proof of that. Reading this story in *Life* and seeing the photographs gave me an itch. Not the kind of itch you get from seeing men with bottles containing infected mosquitoes pressed to their abdomens—a curiously medieval-looking picture, like some ancient bee-sting remedy. But another kind of itch. The kind of itch you get when you start to suspect something unpleasant has been going on. The kind of itch that won't be satisfied until you have scratched it.

I found a copy of Lange's medical dictionary and, looking up the symptoms of malaria and those of viral meningitis, discovered that the two illnesses produced several symptoms that were more or less identical. In the Bavarian Alps, where mosquitoes are not exactly common, it would have been all too easy to have passed off several dozen men dying of malaria as an outbreak of viral meningitis. Who would have suspected it? All those German POWs had been used for medical experiments. Just like eight hundred American convicts. Not to mention all those people at Dachau and Majdanek. It seemed hard to believe, but experiments on human beings, for which seven Nazi doctors had been hanged at Landsberg, were obviously still going on, and under the protection of the CIA. The hypocrisy of it was staggering.

## THIRTY-SIX

There was an Overseas Telephone and Telegraph Office on the ground floor of the Alliance Building in Alserstrasse, in the Ninth District. I approached an operator. He had a nose like a windsock and hair that was a sort of badger-color—gray on the outside and darker underneath. I gave him the Garmisch number, bought a kilogram of coins, and went to the telephone booth he had indicated. I didn't expect to get through, but I figured it was worth a try. While I waited for my connection I thought about what I was going to say and hoped I could restrain myself from just using a lot of the words we used to use on the Russian front. I sat in the booth for about ten minutes before the telephone rang and the operator told me that the other phone was ringing. After a moment or two it was picked up and I heard a distant voice. Garmisch was only three hundred miles, but I imagined the call had to go through the telephone exchange in Linz, which was in the Russian zone of occupation, before being rerouted via Salzburg (in the American zone) and Innsbrück (in the French). The French were considered the least efficient of the four powers and the poor quality of the line was very likely their fault. But recognizing Eric Gruen's voice, I started to pump a fistful of ten-groschen coins into the telephone, and after fifteen or twenty seconds we were speaking. Gruen seemed genuinely pleased to hear from me.

"Bernie," he said. "I was hoping you would call. So that I might have a chance to tell you how sorry I am for landing you in a tight spot. Really, I am."

"A tight spot," I said. "Is that what you call it when you try to put another man's head in a noose that's meant for you?"

"I'm afraid it has to be that way, Bernie," he said. "You see, I can't begin my new life in America until Eric Gruen is officially dead, or in prison for his so-called war crimes. You can blame Jacobs for that. He says the CIA won't have it any other way. If it ever got out that they had allowed a Nazi doctor into the country there would be hell to pay. It's really as simple as that."

"That much I understand," I said. "But why have two innocent women killed if all you wanted was for me to take your rap? You, or Jacobs, or whichever Ami does your dirty work here in Vienna, could have just arranged for my arrest at the hotel."

"And if we'd done what you say? Think about it, Bernie. You would have told them you were Bernie Gunther. Even without a passport the Allied authorities would probably check out your story, find out who you really are. No, we had to make sure that Bernie Gunther had nowhere to go. And I mean nowhere. When you're planning your next move, you might think about this, Bernie. The penalty for murder, especially the despicable murders you have committed, is death. They'll hang Bernie Gunther if they catch him. But depending on who catches Eric Gruen, you might get away with life imprisonment. And the way things are going in the Federal

Republic right now, you'll probably be out in less than ten years. It could even be just five. You can do my time and then come out to some money in the bank. If you stop to think about it, Bernie, you'll agree that I've been remarkably generous. I mean, you've got the money, haven't you? Twenty-five thousand schillings is not a bad sum to have waiting for you when you come out of Landsberg. Really, Bernie, I could have left you without a groschen to your name."

"You've been very generous," I said, biting my lip and hoping that he might let something slip. Some crumb of information that might be useful to me in working my escape from Vienna.

"You know, if I were you, I'd give myself up. As Eric Gruen, of course. And you'd best do it before they catch Bernie Gunther and hang him."

I shoved some more coins into the telephone and laughed. "I don't see how things could be any worse than they already are," I said. "You've made quite sure of that."

"Oh, but they could," he said. "Believe me. Vienna's a closed city, Bernie. It's not so easy to get out of it. And under those circumstances I don't think it would take one of those squads of Israeli avengers very long to track you down. What do they call themselves? The Nakam? Or is it the Brichah? Some soap name, anyway. Did you know that they are based in Austria? No, probably not. In fact, Linz and Vienna are their center of operations. Major Jacobs knows some of these soaps quite well. For one thing, he's a soap himself, of course. And for another, there are several of those soaps working for the Nakam who are also working for the CIA. As a matter of fact, it was a CIA soap who killed the real Frau Warzok. Hardly surprising after what she did at Lemberg-Janowska. Really terrible things. I know, I was there. She was a real beast, that woman. Killing Jews for sport, that kind of thing."

"Whereas you only killed them to further the cause of medical science," I said.

"Now you're just being sarcastic, Bernie," he said. "And I don't blame you. But what you say is quite true. I never killed anyone for the pleasure of it. I'm a doctor. None of us did, as a matter of fact."

"And Vera? What's your justification for killing her?"

"I can't say that I approved of that," said Gruen. "But Jacobs thought it would help to put you on your toes."

"Maybe I will give myself up as Bernie Gunther after all," I said. "Just to spoil your plans."

"You could do that, yes," he said. "But Jacobs has some powerful friends in Vienna. Somehow I think they'll make it stick that you're Eric Gruen. Even you will get to see the sense of it when you're in police custody."

"Whose idea was this, anyway?"

"Oh, Jacobs. He's a very devious sort of person, our Major Jacobs. He got the idea when he and Wolfram Romberg came to dig up your garden in Dachau. He noticed the similarity between us as soon as he met you, Bernie. Originally he was going to come back to Dachau and get things started to frame you there. But then, of course, you moved to Munich and returned to your former trade. And that's when we hatched the scheme to have you go looking for Friedrich Warzok. Just to make you think you'd stepped on the toes of some old comrades. Enough to earn yourself a good beating, so we might effect some important alterations to the tailor-made suit we were making for you. Such as losing that all-important finger. Those old SS files are irritatingly precise in the way they describe all of one's distinguishing characteristics. That was rather clever of him, don't you think? It's the first thing any Allied War Crimes investigator or Jewish avenger squad would look for. That missing finger of mine."

"And the woman who hired me?"

"My wife. The first time she came to look for you was in Dachau, and of course you'd gone. Then she came to your offices to take a good look at you, to see if Jacobs was right about there being a resemblance. And she agreed, there was. Which is when we sat down with the major and helped him to cook up the whole plot. Which I have to say was the fun part. It was kind of like writing our own play, inventing our own parts. And making sure our stories all worked out. Then all we had to do was get you down here to Garmisch so that you and I could get to know each other better."

"But you could hardly know that your mother was going to die," I said. "Or could you?"

"She'd been ill for some time," he said. "She could have died at any time. But as it happens, when the time was right, we did help to ease her passing. It's not so difficult to kill people in a hospital. Especially when they're in a private room. You know something? It was a real kindness to her."

"You had her murdered," I said, pushing yet more coins into the telephone. "Your own mother."

"Not murdered," insisted Gruen. "No. This was euthanasia. Preemptive triage. That's the way most German doctors still look on that kind of mercy killing. It still goes on. More often than you might suppose. You can't change the whole medical system, just like that. Euthanasia has been part of the normal hospital routine in Germany and Austria since 1939."

"You killed your own mother to save your skin."

"On the contrary, Bernie. I did it for the work. The ends do justify the means in this particular situation. I thought Heinrich explained all this. The importance of the work. A malaria vaccine really is something that's worth everything that has been done in its name. I thought you understood that. What are a few hundred lives, maybe a couple of thousand, beside the millions that a vaccine will save? My conscience is clear, Bernie."

"I know. That's what makes this so tragic."

"But for our work to proceed to the next stage, we simply have to have access to American medical research facilities. Laboratories. Equipment. Money."

"New prisoners for experimentation," I added. "Like those German POWs in Garmisch-Partenkirchen. Who would have suspected that they had died of malaria in the Alps? I have to hand it to you, Eric. That was clever. So where will you go? Atlanta? New Jersey? Illinois? Or Rochester?"

For a moment, Gruen hesitated. "What makes you think I'll go to any of those places?" he asked, carefully.

"Maybe I'm just a better detective than you think I am."

"Don't try to look for me, Bernie. For one thing, who's going to believe you? You, a war criminal, against the word of someone like me. Someone who's trusted by the CIA, no less. Believe me, Jacobs has done his homework on you, old friend. He found some very interesting photographs of you with Reichsführer Himmler, General Heydrich, and Arthur Nebe. There's even a picture of you with Hermann Göring. I had no idea you were so well connected. The soaps will like that. It'll make them think you're the real thing. That Eric Gruen was much more important to the Reich than he really was."

"Eric, I'm going to find you," I said. "All of you. And I'm going to kill you. You, Henkell, Jacobs, and Albertine."

"Ah, so you know about her as well, do you? You've been busy, Bernie. I congratulate you. What a pity that your powers as a detective didn't kick in earlier. Well, what am I to say to such an idle threat?"

"It's no idle threat."

"Only what I said before. My new friends are very powerful. If you try to come after me, it won't just be the soaps who are after you. It'll be the CIA as well."

"You forgot to mention the ODESSA," I said. "Let's not leave them out."

He laughed. "What do you think you know about the ODESSA?"

"Enough to know that they helped set me up. Them and your friend, Father Gotovina."

"Then you don't know as much as you think you do. As a matter of fact, Father Gotovina had nothing to do with what happened to you. He's not part of the ODESSA at all. Or this. I wouldn't like you to harm him. Really. His hands are clean."

"No? Then why did your wife go and see him at the Holy Ghost Church, in Munich?"

"Well, I wouldn't be at all surprised if the Father was involved with the Old Comradeship." Gruen laughed again. "Not a bit. But he's not part of the ODESSA, or connected with the CIA in any way. And my wife visiting him? That was quite innocent, I can assure you. You see, Father Gotovina goes to Landsberg Prison a great deal. He's chaplain to all of the Roman Catholics at Landsberg. And occasionally I have him take a message to a friend of mine. Someone who's serving a life sentence for so-called war crimes. He brings him medical journals. That kind of thing. For old time's sake."

"Gerhard Rose," I said. "Your friend, I suppose."

"Yes. You have been busy. I underestimated you—in that respect at least. That's another thing my mother's money is going to come in handy for, Bernie. Paying for a legal appeal against that man's sentence. He'll be out in five years. You mark my words. And you ought to. It's in your interests, too."

"Eric?" I said. "I've got to go now. I've run out of coins. But I will find you."

"No, Bernie. We won't see each other again. Not in this life."

"In hell then."

"Yes. In hell, perhaps. Good-bye, Bernie."

"*Auf Wiedersehen*, my friend. *Auf Wiedersehen*."

I put the phone down and stared at my new boots, reflecting on what I had just learned. I almost breathed a sigh of relief. It was the ODESSA and not the Comradeship that was behind everything that had happened to me. I wasn't exactly out of the Vienna woods. Not yet. Not by a long shot. But if, as Fritz Gebauer had told me when I had visited him in his prison cell in Landsberg, the ODESSA and the Comradeship were not connected, then it was only the CIA and the ODESSA I had to fear. It meant there was nothing at all to stop me from seeking help from the Comradeship myself. I would ask my old comrades in the SS for their help in getting out of Vienna. I would go to the Web. Like any other common or garden Nazi rat.

## THIRTY-SEVEN

It seemed somehow appropriate that Ruprechtskirche on Ruprechtsplatz should be the contact point in Vienna for old comrades who were on the run from Allied justice. Ruprechtsplatz lies just south of the canal and Morzinplatz, which was where the Gestapo had had its headquarters in Vienna. Perhaps that was why the church had been chosen. There was very little else to recommend it. The church was the oldest in Vienna and somewhat dilapidated. Unusually this was not, according to a sign inside the door, the result of Allied bombing, but because of the negligent demolition of a neighboring building. Inside, it was as cold as a Polish cowshed and almost as plain. Even the Madonna looked like a milkmaid. But there is a surprise in store for anyone visiting the church. Under a side altar, preserved in a glass casket, lies the blackened skeleton of Saint Vitalis. It's as if Snow White had waited much too long for her prince to come and rescue her from a deathlike slumber with love's first kiss.

Father Lajolo—the Italian priest named by Father Gotovina as someone who was connected to the Comradeship—was almost as thin as Saint Vitalis, and not much better preserved. As thin as a coat hanger, he had hair like wire wool and a face like a billhook. He was quite tanned and as gap-toothed as a Ming dynasty lion. Wearing a long black cassock, he looked very Italian to me, like a face in a crowd scene in a canvas by some Florentine old master. I followed him into a side apse and, in front of an altar, I handed him a railway ticket for Pressbaum. As in Munich, with Father Gotovina, I had crossed out all of the letters on the ticket, except the *ss*.

"I was wondering if you could recommend a good Catholic church in Pressbaum, Father," I said.

Seeing my ticket and hearing my carefully worded question, Father Lajolo winced a little, as if pained by this meeting and, for a moment, I thought he would answer that he knew nothing at all about Pressbaum. "It's possible I can help, yes," he said, in a thick Italian accent. It was almost as thick as the smell of coffee and cigarettes with which it was coated. "I don't know. That all depends. Come with me."

He led me into the sacristy, which was warmer than the church. Here there were a holy-water font, a freestanding gas fire, a closet for various vestments in all the latest liturgical colors, a wooden crucifix on the wall, and through an open door, a lavatory. He closed the door through which we had come and locked it. Then he went over to a small table with a kettle, some cups and saucers, and a simple gas-ring.

"Coffee?" he asked.

"Please, Father."

"Sit down, my friend." He pointed to one of a pair of threadbare armchairs. I sat down and took out my cigarettes.

"Do you mind?" I asked, offering him a Lucky.

He chuckled. "No, I don't mind." Taking a cigarette, he added. "I think most of the disciples would have been smokers, don't you? After all, they were fishermen. My father was a fisherman, from Genoa. All Italian fishermen smoke." He lit the gas and then my cigarette and his own. "When Christ went aboard the fishing boat and there was a storm, they would have smoked then, especially. Smoking is the one thing you can do when you are afraid that doesn't make you look like you're afraid. But if you're in a bad storm at sea and you start praying or singing hymns, well, that's hardly something to inspire courage, is it?"

"I think that would depend on the hymn, don't you? I asked, guessing that this was my cue.

"Perhaps," he said. "Tell me, what's your own favorite hymn?"

"'How Great Thou Art,'" I answered, without hesitation. "I like the tune."

"Yes, you're right," he said, sitting down on the chair opposite. "That's a good one. Personally I prefer 'Il Canto degli Arditi,' or 'Giovinezza.' That's an Italian marching song. For a while we did have something to march about, you know. But that hymn of yours is a good one." He chuckled. "I have heard a rumor that the tune is very like the Horst Wessel Song." He took a little puff on his cigarette. "It has been such a long while since I heard that song, I've almost forgotten the words. Perhaps you could remind me."

"You don't want me to sing it, surely," I said.

"Yes," he said. "If you don't mind. Humor me, please."

I had always detested the Horst Wessel Song. And yet I knew the words well enough. There had been a time in Berlin when, just walking around the city, you would have heard it several times a day, and I could easily remember when it was almost impossible to go to the pictures without hearing it on the newsreels. I remembered Christmas 1935, and some people had started singing it in church, during a carol service. But I myself had sung the song only when not to have done so would have been to have risked a beating at the murderous hands of the SA. I cleared my throat and began singing the words in my almost tuneless baritone:

"Flag high, ranks closed,
The SA marches with solid silent steps.
Comrades shot by the Red Front and Reaction
March in spirit with us in our ranks.

"The street free for the brown battalions,
The street free for the Storm Troopers.
Millions, full of hope, look up at the swastika,
The day breaks for freedom and for bread."

He nodded and then handed me a small cup of black coffee. I wrapped my hands around it gratefully and inhaled the bittersweet aroma. "Do you want the other two verses as well?" I asked him.

"No, no." He smiled. "There's no need. It's just one of the things I ask people to do. Just to help make sure who I am dealing with, you understand." He fixed the cigarette in the corner of his mouth, screwed up his eye against the smoke, and took out a notebook and a pencil. "One has to be careful, you know. It's an elementary precaution."

"I'm not sure what the Horst Wessel Song could tell you," I said. "By the time Hitler came to power, the Reds probably knew the words as well as we did. Some of them were even forced to learn it in concentration camps."

He sipped his coffee loudly, ignoring my objections. "Now, then," he said. "A few details. Your name."

"Eric Gruen," I said.

"Your Nazi Party number, your SS number, your rank, your place and date of birth, please."

"Here," I said. "I've written it down for you already." I handed him the page of notes I had made while studying Gruen's file in the Russian Kommandatura.

"Thank you." He glanced over the paper and nodded while he read it. "Do you have any means of identification with you?"

I handed over Eric Gruen's passport. He studied that carefully and then slipped it and the sheet of paper into the back of his notebook.

"I'm afraid I shall have to hang on to this for now," he said. "Now, then. You had better tell me what prompted you to come and ask for my help."

"It was my own stupidity, really, Father," I said, affecting ruefulness. "My mother died, more than a week ago. The funeral was yesterday. At the Central Cemetery. I knew it was a risk coming back here to Vienna, but, well, you've only got one mother, haven't you? Anyway, I thought I might be safe, if I stayed in the background. If I tried to keep a low profile. I wasn't even sure the Allies were actually looking for me."

"And you came under your real name?"

"Yes." I shrugged. "After all, it's been more than five years, and one reads things in the newspapers about the possibility of there being an amnesty for . . . for old comrades."

"I'm afraid not," he said. "Not yet, anyway."

"Well, it turns out they were looking for me. After the funeral I was recognized. By one of my mother's servants. He told me that unless I gave him some ludicrously large sum of money, he would tell the authorities where to find me. I thought I'd stalled him. I went back to my hotel, intending to check out and go home immediately, only to find that the International Patrol was waiting there for me already. Since then I've been walking around Vienna. Staying in bars and cafés. For fear that I couldn't go and stay in another hotel or pension. Last night I went to the Oriental and allowed myself to be picked up by a girl, and spent the night with her. Not that anything happened, mind. But I couldn't think of anywhere else to go."

He shrugged, almost as if he agreed with me. "Where have you been living until now? I mean outside Vienna."

"Garmisch-Partenkirchen," I said. "It's a quiet little place. No one pays me any attention there."

"Can you go back there?"

"No," I said. "Not now. The person who told me to get out of Vienna also knew where I'd been living. I doubt he'll hesitate to inform the Allied authorities in Germany."

"And this girl you stayed with last night," he said. "Can she be trusted?"

"As long as I keep paying her, yes, I think so."

"Does she know anything about you? Anything at all."

"No. Nothing."

"Keep it that way, please. And she doesn't know that you've come here today?"

"No, of course not, Father," I said. "No one does."

"Can you stay with her for one more night?"

"Yes. As a matter of fact I've already arranged it."

"Good," he said. "Because I'm going to need at least twenty-four hours to make some arrangements to get you out of Vienna, to a safe house. Is that all your luggage?"

"It is now. The rest is in the hotel. I don't dare go back for it."

"No, of course not," he said, picking the cigarette out of his mouth. "That would be foolish. Meet me back here tomorrow afternoon at around four o'clock. And be ready to leave. Wear warm clothes. Buy some if you don't have them. Also, between now and tomorrow I want you to have your photograph taken." He scribbled an address on his pad, tore off a sheet of paper, and handed to me. "There's a shop on Elisabeth Strasse, opposite the Opera House. Ask for Herr Weyer. Siegfried Weyer. He's a friend and can be trusted absolutely. Tell him I sent you. He'll know what needs to be done. I've put his phone number down there in case something happens to delay you. B26425. Keep away from the stations, telegraph offices, and the post offices. Go to the cinema. Or the theater. Somewhere dark, with lots of people. Have you much money?"

"Enough to get by, for now," I said.

"Good. A weapon?"

I hesitated, slightly surprised to be asked such a thing by a man of God. "No."

"It would be a shame for you to get captured now," said Father Lajolo. "Especially now that we're putting all the wheels in motion for you to get out of Vienna." He opened the closet for vestments and removed the padlock from a little footlocker. Inside were several pistols. He took one out—a nice-looking Mauser—eased out the magazine with his clubby, nicotine-stained fingers, and checked that it was loaded before handing it over. "Here," he said. "Take this one. Don't use it unless you absolutely have to."

"Thank you, Father," I said.

He went to the back door of the sacristy, opened it, and stepped into a small alleyway that led down the side of the church, underneath some scaffolding. "When you come back tomorrow," he said, "don't go through the main church. Come down this alleyway, and then use this door. It won't be locked. Just come inside, sit down, and wait."

"Yes, Father."

"Until tomorrow, then."

# THIRTY-EIGHT

The next day I left Vienna. My driver was a German named Walter Timmermann. He was from Vienna but lived in Pfungstadt, near Darmstadt. He drove a truck for the U.S. Army delivering copies of *The Stars and Stripes,* the American army newspaper, from its printing presses in Griesheim, to Salzburg and Vienna. The truck was a Dodge three-ton cargo truck with canvas sides and U.S. Army livery, which meant that it was never searched by the military police of any of the four powers. On the way back to Germany, the truck carried unsold copies of the previous edition so that these could be pulped and used again. And it was among these that I hid when we were crossing from one zone of occupation into another. The rest of the time I sat in the cab with Timmermann and listened as he talked, which, he said, he liked to do because most of the time he was driving he was usually on his own, and it could get a bit lonely on the road at times. That suited me just fine as I had little or nothing to say to anyone. He had served in the Luftwaffe during the war, at Griesheim, which was how he had come to be there when the war ended. And how he had come to start driving for the Amis some two years earlier.

"They're not so bad to work for," he said. "Once you get to know them. Most of them just want to get home. Of the four powers, they're the best people to work for. But probably the worst soldiers. Seriously. They don't give a damn about anything. If the Russians ever attack they'll walk right on through Germany. The security on the bases is nonexistent. Which is how I get away with so much. All those Amis have some kind of racket going. Booze, cigarettes, dirty books, medicines, women's hosiery, you name it, I've hauled it for them. Believe me, you're not the only illicit cargo this truck is moving."

He didn't say what the truck's illicit cargo was on this occasion, and I didn't ask. But I did ask him about Father Lajolo.

"I'm a Roman Catholic, see?" he said. "And the father, he married me and my wife when he was at a different parish, during the war. Saint Ulrich's, in the Seventh District. My wife, Giovanna, she's half Italian, too, see? Half Austrian, half Italian. Her brother was in the SS, and Father Lajolo helped get him out of Austria after the war. He's living in Scotland now. Can you believe it? Scotland. Plays golf all the time, he says. The Comradeship got him a new name, a home, a job. He's a mining engineer in Edinburgh. No one will ever think of looking for him in Edinburgh. So, ever since then, I've helped the father out when he wanted to move an old comrade somewhere those Reds can't get their bloody hands on him. You ask me, Vienna's finished. It'll go the same way as Berlin. You mark my words. One day, they'll just roll their tanks in and nobody will do a thing to stop them. The Amis think it won't ever happen. Either that or they just don't care. None of this would have happened if they'd made a peace with Hitler. If they hadn't forced that unconditional surrender on us. We'd still have a Europe that looked like Europe, not next week's Soviet republic."

It was a long journey. On the road from Vienna to Salzburg there was a speed limit of only forty miles an hour. But in the villages and small towns it was as low as ten miles an hour. By the time I had endured several hours of listening to Timmermann's opinions of the Reds and the Amis, I was ready to ram a copy of *The Stars and Stripes* down his throat.

At Salzburg we got on the Munich autobahn and our speed increased. Soon we were across the German border. We drove north and then west, through Munich. There seemed little point in getting out of the truck in Munich. I didn't doubt that Jacobs would make sure the police were waiting for me there. And until the Comradeship was able to provide me with a new identity and passport, my best course of action seemed to be to stay where I was being taken. We drove on through Landsberg before turning south to Kempten, which nestles in the foothills of the Alps, in the Allgäu region of southwest Bavaria. My journey finally ended at an old Benedictine monastery in the hills outside Kempten. This was temptingly close to Garmisch-Partenkirchen, which, Timmermann told me, was just sixty-five miles to the west of Kempten, and I knew it would not be long before I was tempted.

The monastery was a fine Gothic building with pink brick walls and two high pagoda-like bell towers that dominated the snow-covered landscape for miles around. But it was only when you drove through the main gate that you perceived the true size of the place and, as a corollary, the wealth and power of the Roman Catholic Church. That there should be such a huge Catholic monastery in such a small and out-of-the-way place like Kempten made me aware of just what resources and manpower were at the command of the Vatican and, by extension, the Comradeship. And I wondered what was in it for the Church, providing a ratline for old Nazis and escaping war criminals like myself.

The truck stopped and I got out. I was in an inner court that was as big as a military parade ground. Timmermann led me into a doorway, through a basilica the size of an aircraft hangar, with an altar that only a Holy Roman Emperor might have thought modest. I thought it looked as gaudy as a Polish Christmas cake. Someone was playing the organ and a choir of local boys was singing sweetly. But for an overpowering smell of beer that filled the air, the atmosphere seemed predictably holy. I followed Timmermann into a small office, where we were met by a monk. He had the look of someone who enjoyed a glass of beer. Father Bandolini was a big man with a large stomach and the hands of a good butcher. His hair was short and silver-colored, which seemed to match the gray in his eyes. He had a face as strong as anything I had seen carved on a totem pole. He met us with bread, cheese, cold meats, pickles, a glass of the beer brewed in the monastery, and some warm words of welcome. Shooing me closer to the fire, he asked if our journey had been difficult.

"No problems at all, Father," said Timmermann, who soon excused himself as he wanted to get back to Griesheim that night.

"Father Lajolo tells me that you're a doctor," said Father Bandolini, after Timmermann had left. "Is that right?"

"Yes," I said, dreading the possibility that I might be asked to perform some medical procedure that would reveal me as a fraud. "But I haven't practiced medicine since before the war."

"But you are a Roman Catholic," he said.

"Of course," I said, thinking it best that I seemed to agree with the creed of the people who were helping me. "Although not a very good one."

Father Bandolini shrugged. "Whatever that is," he said.

I shrugged back. "Somehow I always imagined that monks were probably good Catholics," I said.

"It's easy to be a good Catholic when you live in a monastery," he said. "That's why most of us do it. There's not much temptation in a place like this."

"I don't know," I said. "The beer is excellent."

"Isn't it?" He grinned. "It's been brewed here to the same recipe for hundreds of years. Perhaps that's why many of us stay."

His voice was quiet and he was well-spoken, which made me think I might have misheard him when, after I finished eating, he explained that the monastery—and, in particular, the St. Raphael Community that was based there—had been helping German Catholic émigrés since 1871, and that many of these had been non-Aryan Catholics.

"Did you say 'non-Aryan Catholics'?"

He nodded.

"Is that just a fancy Church term for an Italian?" I asked.

"No, no. That's what we used to call the Jews we helped. Many of them became Catholics, of course. But some others we just called Catholics in order to persuade countries like Brazil and Argentina to take them."

"Wasn't that rather dangerous?" I said.

"Oh yes. Very. The Gestapo in Kempten had us under surveillance for almost a decade. One of our brethren even died in a concentration camp for helping Jews."

I wondered if the irony of his helping Eric Gruen, the vilest of war criminals, was apparent to him. I soon learned that it was.

"It is the will of God that the Saint Raphael Community should help those who once organized its persecution," he said. "Besides, it's a different enemy now, but one no less dangerous. An enemy that regards religion as an opiate poisoning the minds of people."

But none of this was as surprising as what was to follow.

I was to be accommodated not in the cloister, with the rest of the monks, but in the infirmary, where, Father Bandolini assured me, I would be much more comfortable. "For one thing," he said, leading me across the huge quadrangle, "it's a lot warmer there. Fires are permitted in the rooms. There are comfortable armchairs and the bathroom facilities are superior to anything in the cloister. Your meals will be brought to you, but you're free to join us for Mass in the basilica. And let me know if you seek absolution. I'll send a priest to you." He opened a heavy wooden door and led me through a chapter house into the infirmary. "You won't be on your own," he added. "We have two other guests staying with us at the moment. Gentlemen like yourself. They'll probably show you the ropes. Both of them are waiting to emigrate to South America. I'll introduce you. But don't worry. We don't encourage the use of old names here, for obvious reasons. If you don't mind I'll use your new name. The name that will be in your passport when eventually it arrives from Vienna."

"How long does that usually take?" I asked him.

"It might take several weeks," he said. "After that you'll need a visa. Probably it will be Argentina you're going to. Right now everyone's going there, I believe. The government there is very sympathetic to German emigration. Then of course you'll need passage on a ship. The Comradeship will organize that, too." He smiled encouragingly. "I think you should reconcile yourself to being with us with for a month or two at least."

"My father lives near here," I said. "In Garmisch-Partenkirchen. I should like to see him before I leave the country. It'll be my last chance I think."

"You're right, Garmisch is not all that far away. As the crow flies, fifty or sixty miles. We deliver our beer to the American army base down there. They've a real taste for beer, those Amis. Perhaps you could go with the beer truck on our next delivery. I'll see what I can do."

"Thank you, Father, I appreciate it."

Of course, as soon as I had my new identity and passport I was going to head for Hamburg. I'd always liked Hamburg. And it was as far away as I could get from Munich and Garmisch and whatever I was going to do in Garmisch, without actually leaving Germany. There was no way on earth that I was going to end up on a slow boat to a banana republic like the old comrades to whom I was about to be introduced.

Father Bandolini knocked quietly on a door and then opened it to reveal a cozy little sitting room, and two men taking it easy in armchairs with the newspapers. There was a bottle of Three Feathers on the table and an open packet of Regents. A good sign, I thought. On the wall was a crucifix and a picture of Pope Pius XII wearing what looked like a beehive on his head. Maybe it was the little rimless glasses and the ascetic face, but there was always something about the pope that reminded me of Himmler. The pope's face was also quite like the face of one of the two men who were in the room. The last time I had seen him was January 1939, and he'd been standing between Himmler and Heydrich. I remembered thinking him to be a relatively simple, intellectually uninteresting sort of man, and even now, I found it hard to believe that he could be the most wanted man in Europe. To look at he was quite ordinary. He was sharp-faced, narrow-eyed, with somewhat prominent ears, and, above a small Himmler-like mustache—always a mistake—a longish nose on which sat a pair of black-framed glasses. He looked like a Jewish tailor, which, I knew, was a description he'd have hated because the man was Adolf Eichmann.

"Gentlemen," said Father Bandolini, addressing the two men seated in the monastery's guest sitting room. "I'd like to introduce you to someone who will be staying with us for a while. This is Herr Doktor Hausner. Carlos Hausner."

That was my new name. Father Lajolo had explained that when giving a man a new identity suitable for Argentina, the Comradeship recommended a name that implied dual South American and German nationality. Which is how I ended up being called Carlos. I had no intention of winding up in Argentina, but with two sets of police on my tail, I was hardly in a position to argue about a name.

"Herr Doktor Hausner." Father Bandolini raised his hand in Eichmann's direction. "This is Herr Ricardo Klement." He turned toward the second man. "And this is Pedro Geller."

Eichmann made no sign that he recognized me. He bowed his head curtly and then shook my outstretched hand. He looked older than he ought to have done. I estimated he was around forty-two, but with most of his hair gone, the glasses, and behind them a tired, hunted look like an animal that hears the hounds on its tail, he looked much older. He wore a thick tweed suit, a striped shirt, and a small bow tie that made him seem very clerkish. But there was nothing clerkish about the handshake. I'd shaken hands with Eichmann before, when his hands had been soft, almost delicate. But now his hands were the hands of a laborer, as if, since the war, he had been obliged to earn a living in some physically arduous way. "Pleased to meet you, Herr Doktor," he said.

The other man was much younger, better-looking, and better turned out than his infamous companion. He wore an expensive-looking watch and gold cuff links. His hair was fair, his eyes were blue and clear, and his teeth looked as if he'd borrowed them from an American film star. Next to Eichmann, he was as tall as a flagpole and bore himself like a rare species of crane. I shook his hand and found that, by contrast with Eichmann's, it was well-manicured and as soft as a schoolboy's. Looking at Pedro Geller more closely, I supposed he couldn't have been more than twenty-five, which made it hard to imagine what war crime he could have committed as an eighteen- or nineteen-year-old that now necessitated him changing his name and escaping to South America.

Geller was carrying a Spanish–German dictionary under his arm, and another lay open on the table in front of the chair where Eichmann—Ricardo Klement—had been sitting. The younger man smiled. "We were just testing each other's Spanish vocabulary," he explained. "Ricardo is much better at languages than I am."

"Really?" I said. I might have mentioned Ricardo's knowledge of Yiddish, but thought better of it. I glanced around the sitting room noting the chessboard, the Monopoly set, the library full of books, the newspapers and magazines, the new General Electric radio, the kettle and the coffee cups, the full ashtray, and the blankets—one of these had been over Eichmann's legs. It was plain to see that these two men spent a lot of time sitting in that room. Holed up. Hiding. Waiting for something. A new passport, or passage on a ship to South America.

"We're very lucky that there's a priest from Buenos Aires here in the monastery," said the Father. "Father Santamaría has been teaching Spanish to our two friends, and telling them all about Argentina. It makes a real difference going somewhere when you can already speak the language."

"Did you have a good journey?" asked Eichmann. If he was nervous at seeing me again he did not show it. "Where have you come from?"

"Vienna," I said. And then shrugged. "The journey was tolerable. Do you know Vienna, Herr Klement?" I offered my cigarettes around.

"No, not really," he said, with a flicker of an eyelid. I had to hand it to him. He was good. "I don't know Austria at all. I'm from Breslau." He took one of my cigarettes and let me light him. "Of course it's now called Wrocław, or something, in Poland. Can you imagine it? Are you from Vienna, Herr—?"

"Dr. Hausner," I said.

"A doctor, eh?" Eichmann smiled. His teeth hadn't improved any, I noticed. No doubt it amused him to know that I wasn't a doctor. "It'll be interesting to have a medical man around, won't it, Geller?"

"Yes, indeed," said Geller, smoking one of my Luckies. "I always wanted to be a doctor. Before the war, that is." He smiled sadly. "I don't suppose I shall ever be a doctor, now."

"You're a young man," I said. "Anything is possible when you're young. Take my word for it. I was young once myself."

But Eichmann was shaking his head. "That was true before the war," he said. "In Germany anything was possible. Yes. We proved that, to the world. But not now. I'm afraid it's no longer true. Not now that half of Germany is ruled by godless barbarians, eh,

Father? Shall I tell you the true meaning of the Federal Republic of Germany, gentlemen? We are simply a slit trench in the front line of a new war. A war waged by the—"

Eichmann checked himself. And then he smiled. The old Eichmann smile. As if he objected to my tie.

"But what am I saying? None of it matters now. Not anymore. Today has no meaning. For us, today does not exist any more than yesterday. For us, there is only tomorrow. Tomorrow is all that's left." For a moment his smile grew slightly less bitter. "Just like the old song says. Tomorrow belongs to me. Tomorrow belongs to me."

## THIRTY-NINE

The monastery beer was excellent. It was what they called a Trappist beer, which meant it was made under strictly controlled conditions and only by Benedictine monks. The beer they produced, which was called Schluckerarmer, was copper-colored, with a head like an ice cream. It had a sweet, almost chocolaty taste and a strength that belied its flavor and origins. And it was a lot easier to imagine it being drunk by American soldiers than austere and God-fearing monks. Besides, I had tasted American beer. Only a country that had once prohibited alcohol could have produced a beer that tasted like fortified mineral water. Only a country like Germany could have produced a beer strong enough to make a monk risk the wrath of the Roman Catholic Church by nailing ninety-five theses to a church door in Wittenberg. That was what Father Bandolini told me, anyway. Which was just one reason why he preferred wine.

"If you ask me, the whole Reformation can be blamed on strong beer," he opined. "Wine is a perfect Catholic drink. It makes people sleepy and complicit. Beer just makes them argumentative. And look at the countries that drink a lot of beer. They're mainly Protestant. And the countries where they drink a lot of wine? Roman Catholic."

"What about the Russians?" I asked. "They drink vodka."

"That's a drink to help you find oblivion," said Father Bandolini. "Nothing to do with God at all."

But none of this was as interesting as what he told me next. Which was that the monastery's beer truck was leaving for Garmisch-Partenkirchen later that same morning. And that I was welcome to accompany it.

I fetched my coat and my gun, but I left the bag with my money in my room. It would have looked odd to have taken it with me. Besides, I had a key to the door. And I was coming back for my new passport. Then I followed the Father to the brewery where the truck was already being loaded with beer crates.

There were two monks manning the truck, which was an old two-cylinder Framo. Each man was a testament to the mesomorphic, manly qualities of the beer. Father Stoiber, bearded and quite obviously bibulous, had a belly like a millstone. Father Seehofer was as burly as a kiln-dried barrel. There was room for the three of us in the cab of the truck, but only when we exhaled. By the time we reached Garmisch-Partenkirchen, I felt as thin as the sausage in a Saxon pastor's sandwich. But it wasn't just a tight squeeze. The Framo's small, 490cc engine delivered only fifteen-brake horsepower and, with my extra weight, we struggled a bit on some of the icy mountain roads. And it was just as well that Stoiber, who had seen action in the Ukraine through the worst of a Russian winter, was an excellent driver.

We drove into town, not from the north through Sonnenbichl, but up from the southwest, along Griesemer Strasse and in the cold shadow of the Zugspitze, to that part of Partenkirchen where most of the Americans were based. The two monks told me they had deliveries for the Elbsee Hotel, the Crystal Springs Hotel, the Officers' Club, the Patton Hotel, and the Green Arrow Ski Lodge. They dropped me at the junction of Zugspitzstrasse and Bahnhofstrasse, and looked slightly relieved when I told them I would try to make my own way back to the monastery.

I found the street of old Alpine-style villas where Gruen and Henkell had performed some of their more recent experiments. I couldn't remember the number, but the villa, with its Olympic skier fresco, was easy enough to find. In the distance I heard the muffled gunshots from the skeet range, just like before. The only difference was that there was a lot more snow on the ground. It was heaped on top of and around the gingerbread houses like powdered icing sugar. There was no sign of Jacobs's Buick Roadmaster, just a pile of horse dung on the street where it had been parked. I had seen several sleighs around town and I was banking on getting one to take me up to Mönch, at Sonnenbichl, when I'd finished snooping around the villa.

I wasn't exactly sure of what I thought I might find. From the tenor of my last conversation with Eric Gruen, it was hard for me to know if he and the others had already left the area. But the possibility that they hadn't was strong, since they could hardly have expected me to effect an escape from Vienna so quickly. Vienna was a closed city and not easy to get in or out of. Gruen had been right about that. All the same, he would surely have been aware that the money he had given me, by way of compensation, made my return to Garmisch, at the very least, reasonably possible. And if they were still in the area they would certainly have taken some precautions with their security. I tightened my hand on the gun in my pocket and went around to the back of the house to look in the window of the laboratory. With the snow in the garden up to my knees, it was just as well I had bought boots and gaiters in Vienna. The snow around Mönch would be even deeper.

There were no lights on in the villa. And there was no one in the lab. I pressed my nose closer to the window, close enough to see through the double glass doors into the office beyond. That was deserted, too. I selected a handy-looking log from a neat pile of firewood underneath the balcony and glanced around for a window to knock in. The piles of snow behind me muffled the noise of breaking glass nicely. Deep snow is a burglar's best friend. Carefully I chipped out a few jagged edges that had stayed in the frame and then put my hand in, lifted the catch, opened the window, and climbed inside. Glass crunched under my feet as I jumped down to the laboratory floor. Everything was just as it had been before. Nothing had been moved. All was hot and still. Except the mosquitoes, of course. These became more agitated as I laid the palm of my hand on the glass side of their habitat to check how warm it was. It felt just right, which is to say even warmer than the room, which was saying something, of course. They were all doing just fine. But I could fix that. And reaching behind each tank I switched off the heaters that kept these deadly little bugs alive. With a broken window letting freezing cold air into the lab, I figured they would all be dead in a few hours.

I opened and closed both sets of glass doors and went into the office. Straightaway I understood that I had not come too late. Far from it. On the blotter in the center of Gruen's desk were four new American passports. I picked one up and opened it. The woman I had known as Frau Warzok, Gruen's wife, was now Mrs. Ingrid Hoffman. I looked at the others. Heinrich Henkell was now Mr. Gus Braun. Engelbertina was Mrs. Bertha Braun. And Eric Gruen was now Eduard Hoffman. I started to write down the new names. Then I just pocketed all four passports. They could hardly go anywhere without them. Nor without their air tickets, which were also on the blotter. These were U.S. military tickets. I checked the date, the time, and the destination. Mr. and Mrs. Braun and Mr. and Mrs.

Hoffman were leaving Germany that night. They were all booked on a midnight flight to Langley Air Force Base in Virginia. All I had to do was sit down and wait. Someone—Jacobs, probably—would surely be along quite soon to collect these tickets and the passports. And when he came, I would make him drive me up to Mönch, where, with three fugitives from Allied Justice cornered, I would take my chances and call the police in Munich. Let them sort it out.

I sat down, took out my gun—the one given to me in Vienna by Father Lajolo—worked the slide to put one up the spout, thumbed off the safety, and laid the weapon on the desk in front of me. I was looking forward to seeing my old friends again. I thought about smoking a cigarette and then decided against it. I didn't want Major Jacobs smelling the smoke as he came through the front door.

Half an hour passed and, becoming a little bored, I decided to poke around the filing cabinet; when, eventually, I spoke to the police, it might look better if I had some documentary evidence to support what I was going to tell them. Not that Gruen and Henkell had experimented on Jews at Dachau. But that they had continued their medical experiments on local German POWs. They wouldn't like that any more than I did. If, by some chance, a court wasn't inclined to indict Gruen, Henkell, and Zehner for what they had done during the war, no German court could have ignored the murders of German servicemen.

The manila files were quite meticulous, being neatly arranged in alphabetical order. There were no records of what had happened before 1945, but for every person who had been infected with malaria since then, there was a detailed set of case notes. The first one I examined from the top drawer of the cabinet was for a Lieutenant Fritz Ansbach, who had been a German POW receiving treatment for nervous hysteria in the Partenkirchen hospital. He had been injected with malaria in the last days of November 1947.

Within twenty-one days he had developed the full-blown disease, at which point the test vaccine, Sporovax, had been injected into his bloodstream. Ansbach was dead seventeen days later. Cause of death: malaria. Official cause of death: viral meningitis. I read several other files from that drawer. They were all the same. I left them out on the desk, ready to take with me when I went to Mönch. I had all that I needed. And I almost didn't open the middle drawer in that evil filing cabinet at all. In which case I would never have come across the file labeled "Handlöser."

I read the file slowly. And then I read it again. It used a lot of medical words that I didn't understand and one or two that I did. There were lots of graphs showing the "subject's" temperature and heart rate before and after they had put her arms inside a box containing up to a hundred infected mosquitoes. I remembered how I had thought she had been bitten by fleas or bed lice. And all that time, Henkell had been turning up at the Max Planck psychiatric hospital with his little box of death. They had given her the test vaccine, Sporovax IV, but it hadn't worked. The way it hadn't worked for any of the others. And so Kirsten had died. It was easily done. And very easily explained. Malaria could be written off as influenza just as easily as viral meningitis, especially in Germany, in a hospital where facilities were few. My wife had been murdered. I felt my stomach collapse in upon itself like an imploding balloon. The bastards had murdered my wife, just as surely as if they'd put a gun to her head and blown out her brains.

I looked again at her case notes. Mistakenly booked into the hospital as a single woman, and wrongly described as mentally retarded, it had been assumed that no one would really miss her. There was no mention of me. Only that she had been transferred to the General Hospital, where she had "succumbed" to the disease. "Succumbed." They made it sound like she had just gotten tired and gone to sleep, instead of having died. As if they didn't know the one from the other any more than they knew that I had been this poor woman's husband. Otherwise they would surely have recorded my name in their damned file.

I closed my eyes. Not fleas or bed lice at all. But *mosquito bites.* And the insect that had bitten me during one visit to the Max Planck? A single escaped mosquito, perhaps? Perhaps that explained the so-called pneumonia I had caught following my beating at the hands of Jacobs's friends in the ODESSA. Perhaps it had not been pneumonia at all. Perhaps it had been a mild dose of malaria. Henkell wouldn't have been able to tell the one from the other. There was no reason at all for him to have suspected that my own fever had an "entomological vector," as they called it, any more than there was reason for him to have known that Kirsten Handlöser was my wife. Not under those circumstances. Which was probably just as well. They might have given me Sporovax.

This put a very different complexion on things. Involving the police looked much too unpredictable now. I needed to know that these men would be properly punished for their crimes. And to know that for sure I would have to punish them myself. Suddenly it had become much easier to understand those Jewish avenger squads. The Nakam. What kind of punishment was a few years in prison for men who had committed such disgusting crimes? Men like Dr. Franz Six from the Jewish Department at the SD. The man who, back in September 1937, had sent me to Palestine. Or Israel, as we now had to call it. I had no idea what had happened to Paul Begelmann, the Jew whose money Six coveted. But I remembered seeing Six again, in Smolensk, where he had commanded a Special Action Group that had massacred seventeen thousand people. And for this he had received a sentence of just twenty years. If the new federal government of Germany had its way, he would be out on parole before he'd served even a quarter of that sentence. Five years for murdering seventeen thousand Jews. No wonder the Israelis felt obliged to murder these men.

Hearing a sound above me I opened my eyes and recognized much too late that the sound had been the hammer on a snub-nosed thirty-eight-caliber Smith & Wesson being thumbed back. The nice thirty-eight with the J-frame and rubberized grip I had seen in the glove box of Jacobs's Buick. Only now it was in his hand. I never forget a gun. Especially when it's pointed at my face.

"Lean back from the desk," he said quietly. "And put your hands on your head. Do it slowly. This thirty-eight has a very light action and might easily go off if your hand goes within three feet of that Mauser. I saw your footprints in the snow. Just like Good King Wenceslas. You should have been more careful."

I sat back in the chair and placed my hands on my head, watching the black hole of the two-inch barrel as it got closer. We both knew I was a dead man if he pulled the trigger. A thirty-eight provides a human skull with a lot of surplus ventilation.

"If I had more time," he said, "I might be real curious as to how you got yourself out of Vienna as quickly as you did. Impressive. Then again, I told Eric not to let you have the money. You used it to get out of the city, right?" He leaned forward, carefully, and picked up my gun.

"As a matter of fact, I still have the money," I said.

"Oh? Where is it?" He eased the hammer off my automatic and tucked it under his trouser belt.

"About forty miles from here," I said. "We could go and get it, if you like."

"And I could pistol-whip it out of you, Gunther. Luckily for you, I'm rather pressed for time."

"Catching a plane?"

"That's right. Now hand over those passports."

"What passports?"

"If I have to ask a second time, you'll lose the ear. And don't delude yourself that anyone will hear the shot and give a shit. Not with that skeet range around the corner."

"Good point," I said. "Can I use my hand to get them? They're in my coat pocket. Or would you prefer I tried for them with my teeth?"

"Forefinger and thumb only." He took a step back, grabbing hold of his wrist, and extended the hand holding the gun at my head. Like he was getting ready to fire. At the same time his keen eyes glanced down at the open file I had been reading. I said nothing about the file. There was no point in putting him on guard any more than he already was. I lifted the passports out of my pocket and tossed them on top of the file.

"What's that you're reading?" He took the passports and then the tickets and pocketed them in his own short leather coat.

"Just the case notes on one of your protégé's patients," I said, closing the file.

"Hands on top of your head again," he said.

"As doctors, I think they're lousy," I said. "All of their patients have a nasty habit of dying." I was trying hard to control my anger, but my ears were burning. I hoped he would put the color in them down to the cold. I wanted to beat his face to a pulp but I could only do that if I avoided getting shot.

"That's a price worth paying," he said.

"Easy to say when you're not the one paying it."

"Nazi POWs?" He sneered. "I don't think anyone is going to miss a few sick krauts."

"And the guy who you brought to Dachau?" I asked. "Was he one of those Nazi POWs, too?"

"Wolfram? He was expendable. We picked you for the same reason, Gunther. You're expendable, too."

"But when the local supply of sick Nazi POWs dried up? They

started using incurable patients in Munich's mental hospitals. Just like the old days. They were also expendable, huh?"

"That was stupid," said Jacobs. "A risk they didn't need to take."

"You know, I can understand them doing it," I said. "They're criminals. Fanatics. But not you, Jacobs. I know you know what they did, during the war. I saw the file in the Russian Kommandatura, in Vienna. Experiments on concentration camp prisoners? A lot of them were Jews, just like you. Doesn't that bother you just a little?"

"That was then," he said. "This is now. And more importantly, there's tomorrow."

"You sound like someone I know," I said. "A die-hard Nazi."

"It might take another year or two," he continued, leaning back against the wall, relaxing just enough to make me think I stood half a chance. Maybe he hoped I would go for him, so he had the excuse to shoot me. Assuming he needed an excuse. "But a malaria vaccine is something much more important than some misplaced sense of justice and retribution. Have you any idea what a malaria vaccine might be worth?"

"There's nothing more important than retribution," I said. "Not in my book."

"It's lucky you feel that way, Gunther," he said. "Because you're going to play the starring role in a little court of retributive justice, right here in Garmisch. I don't think you Germans have a word for it. We call it a kangaroo court. Don't ask me why. But it means an unauthorized court that disregards all normal legal procedures. The Israelis call them Nakam courts. Nakam meaning 'vengeance.' You know? Where the verdict and the sentence come within a minute or two of each other." He jerked his gun up in the air. "On your feet, Gunther."

I stood up.

"Now come around the desk, into the corridor, and go ahead of me."

He backed out of the doorway as I came toward him. I was praying for some kind of external distraction that might make him take his eyes off me for half a second. But he knew that, of course. And would be ready for it, if or when it came.

"I'm going to lock you up somewhere nice and warm," he said, herding me along the corridor. "Open that door and go downstairs."

I continued to do exactly what I was told. I could feel the aim of that thirty-eight squarely between my shoulder blades. From three or four feet, the bullet of a thirty-eight would have gone straight through me, leaving a hole the size of an Austrian two-shilling piece.

"And when you're locked up," he said, coming downstairs behind me and switching on the light as we went, "I'm going to telephone some people I know in Linz. Some friends of mine. One of them used to be CIA. But now he's Israeli intelligence. That's how they like to think of themselves anyway. Assassins. That's what I call them. And that's how I use them."

"I suppose they're the ones who killed the real Frau Warzok," I said.

"I wouldn't shed any tears for her, Gunther," he said. "After what she did? She had it coming."

"And Gruen's old girlfriend, Vera Messmann?" I asked. "Did they kill her, too?"

"Sure."

"But she wasn't a criminal," I said. "What did you tell them about her?"

"I told them she'd been a guard at Ravensbrück," he said. "That was a training base for female SS supervisors. Did you know that? The British hanged quite a few of the women from Ravensbrück—Irma Grese was just twenty-one years old—but some of them got away. I told the Nakam that Vera Messmann used to set her wolfhounds on Jews to tear them to pieces. Stuff like that. Mostly the information I give them is good. But now and then I slip someone onto the list who's not a real Nazi. Someone like Vera Messmann. And now you, Gunther. They'll be really pleased to get you. They've been after Eric Gruen for a long time. Which is why they'll have all the relevant documents proving you're Gruen. Just in case you thought you could argue your way out if it. An Allied public trial in Germany would have been more clear-cut. But really it's not the German government who are making great efforts to track down war criminals. It's not even the Allies. We've got other fish to fry. Like the Reds. No, the only people who are really keen to track down and execute wanted war criminals these days are the Israelis. And once they figure they've killed Eric Gruen, we'll close the file on him. And so will the Russians. And the real Eric Gruen will be in the clear. That's where you come in, Gunther. You're going to take the fall for him." I reached the bottom of the stairs. "Open the door in front of you and go inside."

I stopped.

"Or, if you prefer, I can shoot you in the calf, and we'll just have to hope that you don't bleed to death in the three or four hours it takes for them to get here from Linz. Your choice."

I opened the cellar door and walked inside. Before the war I might have tackled him. But I was quicker then. Quicker and younger.

"Now sit down and put your hands on your head."

Once again I obeyed. I heard the door close behind me and, for a moment, I was plunged into darkness. A key turned in the lock, and then the light was switched on from the outside.

"Here is something to think about," Jacobs said through the door. "By the time they get here, we'll be well on our way to the airport. At midnight tonight, Gruen, Henkell, and their two lady friends will be on their way to a new life in America. And you'll be lying facedown in a shallow grave somewhere."

I said nothing. There seemed nothing left to say. To him at least. I hoped the Israelis coming from Linz could speak good German.

## FORTY

I heard Jacobs moving around upstairs for a while and then everything went quiet. I stood up and kicked at the door, which helped get some of the anger and frustration out of me but did nothing to aid my escape. The cellar door was made of oak. I could have kicked it all day and not even scratched it. I looked around for some sort of tool.

The cellar had no windows and no other doors. There was a central-heating radiator the size of a coiled anaconda and as hot as a lightbulb. The floor was concrete, with walls to match. Some old kitchen appliances were heaped in one corner, and I supposed that part of the laboratory upstairs had once been the villa's kitchen. There were several pairs of skis, boots, and poles; an old toboggan; some ice skates; and a bicycle with no tires. I practiced using one of the skis as a sort of pikestaff and decided that it might serve as a useful weapon if the Israelis coming to see were armed only with the strength of the Lord. If they had guns, I was in trouble. I abandoned a similar plan to use the blade of an ice skate for the same reason.

As well as an assortment of junk there was a small wine rack containing some dusty-looking bottles of Riesling. I smashed the neck off one and drank the contents without much pleasure. There's nothing worse than warm Riesling. By now I was feeling warm myself. I removed my coat and my jacket, smoked a cigarette and turned my attention to several largish packages that were ranged on either side of the radiator. All of them were addressed to Major Jacobs and labeled "U.S. Government. Urgent Laboratory Specimens." Another label read: "Extreme caution advised. Handle with care. Store in a warm place only. Danger of infectious disease. Contains live insectary. Should only be opened by trained entomologist."

I had my doubts that an Israeli avenger squad would be deterred from killing me by a couple of squadrons of mosquitoes, but I tore the packaging off the first box and removed the lid all the same. Inside the box was a lot of straw and, in the middle of the straw, a handy little travel habitat for the friends of Henkell and Gruen. A couple of sheets of paper described an inventory of what was inside the box. It had been prepared by someone from the Committee on Medical Sciences in the Department of Defense at the Pentagon, in Washington, D.C. It read as follows: "Insectary contains live and preserved anopheles and culex eggs, larvae, pupae, and adult specimens, both male and female. Adults and live eggs are in mosquito cages. Insectary also contains sucking tubes, to pick up mosquitoes from the cage and several blood meals to sustain insect life for up to thirty days."

Two of the other packages contained similar live insectaries. A fourth package contained "dissecting and compound microscopes, forceps, slides, cover slips, droppers, petri dishes, pyrethrin solution, pipettes, bioassay units, insecticide-free nets, and chloroform." This last item set me wondering if I might be able to chloroform one of the Israelis. But once again I came up against the realization that it's not so easy to attack a man when he's holding a gun on you.

A couple of hours passed. I drank some more warm wine and lay down on the floor. There seemed to be nothing else to do except sleep. And in that respect at least, the Riesling was almost as helpful as the chloroform.

Footsteps on the floor above woke me a short while later. I sat up feeling a little sick. It wasn't the wine so much as a strong sense of anxiety as to what was about to happen to me. Unless I managed somehow to convince these men that I was not Eric Gruen, I had no doubt that I was going to be murdered, and in the way Jacobs had described.

Nothing happened for almost thirty minutes. I heard furniture being moved around and smelled cigarettes being smoked. I even heard laughter. Then there were heavy footsteps on the stairs, followed by the sound of the key in the lock. I stood up and moved back into the cellar and tried to put out of my mind the idea of what would very probably be in their minds: the huge satisfaction of having apprehended one of the most loathsome war criminals ever. Finally the door swung open and two men stood in front of me, their faces filled with quiet distaste and their hands filled with bright, shiny forty-five automatics. They were light on their toes. As if they had just stepped out of the boxing ring and were hoping I might resist a bit, so that they could spar with me for a while.

Both wore roll-neck sweaters and ski pants. One was younger than the other. His brown hair was stiff-looking, as if he had just stepped out of a barbershop, with something on it, like hair oil or cream, or maybe a handful of laundry starch. He had eyebrows that looked like a monkey's fingers and big brown eyes that belonged properly to some kind of big dog, as indeed did the rest of his face. His partner was taller, uglier, with ears like a baby elephant and a nose like the lid of a grand piano. His sports jacket fit him like a lampshade.

They walked me upstairs, as if I was carrying an unexploded bomb, and back into the office. They had moved the desk so that it now faced the glass doors of the laboratory. There was a man behind it, and a single chair in front of it, like the chair in a witness box. Politely the man behind the desk invited me to sit down. He sounded American. As I did so, he leaned forward with the air of an examining magistrate, his fingers clasped as if he were planning to say a prayer before questioning me. He was in shirtsleeves, which were rolled up as if he meant business. But it could just as easily have been the heat in the room. It was still very warm. He had thick, gray hair that fell in his eyes, and he was as thin as the trail of shit from a neglected goldfish. His nose was smaller than the noses of the other two men, but only just. Not that you paid much attention to the size of his nose. It was the color that distracted you. There were so many burst capillaries on that nose it looked more like a species of orchid or poisonous mushroom. He picked up a pen and prepared to write in a nice new notebook.

"What is your name?"

"Bernhard Gunther."

"What were you called before?"

"My name has always been Bernhard Gunther."

"How tall are you?"

"One meter eighty-seven."

"What size shoes do you wear?"

"Forty-four."

"What size jacket?"

"Fifty-four."

"What was your membership number in the NSDAP?"

"I was never a member of the Nazi Party."

"What was your number in the SS?"

"85 437."

"What is your date of birth?"

"July 7, 1896."

"Place of birth?"

"Berlin."

"Under what name were you born?"

"Bernhard Gunther."

My interrogator sighed and put down his pen. Almost reluctantly he opened a drawer and took out a file, which he opened. He handed me a German passport in the name of Eric Gruen. I opened it. He said: "Is this your passport?"

I shrugged. "It's my picture," I said. "But I've never seen this passport before."

He handed me another document. "A copy of an SS file in the name of Eric Gruen," he said. "That is also your photograph, is it not?"

"That's my photograph," I said. "But this is not my SS file."

"An application for the SS, completed and signed by Eric Gruen, with a medical report. Height one meter eighty-eight, hair blond, eyes blue, distinguishing characteristic, subject is missing the little finger of his left hand." He handed the document over. I took it with my left hand, without thinking. "You are missing the little finger on your left hand. You can hardly deny that."

"It's a long story," I said. "But I'm not Eric Grüen."

"More photographs," said my interrogator. "A picture of you shaking hands with Reich Marshal Hermann Göring, taken in August 1936. Another of you with SS Obergruppenführer Heydrich, taken at Wewelsburg Castle, Paderborn, November 1938."

"You'll notice I'm not wearing a uniform," I said.

"And a picture of you standing next to Reichsführer Heinrich Himmler, believed taken October 1938. He's not wearing a uniform either." He smiled. "What did you discuss? Euthanasia, perhaps. Aktion T-four?"

"I met him, yes," I said. "It doesn't mean we sent each other Christmas cards."

"A photograph of you with SS Gruppenführer Arthur Nebe. Taken Minsk, 1941. You are wearing a uniform in this picture. Are you not? Nebe commanded a Special Action Group that killed—how many Jews was it, Aaron?"

"Ninety thousand Jews, sir." Aaron sounded more English than American.

"Ninety thousand. Yes."

"I'm not who you think I am."

"Three days ago you were in Vienna, were you not?"

"Yes."

"Now we're getting somewhere. Exhibit Eight. The sworn testimony of Tibor Medgyessy, formerly employed as the Gruen family butler, in Vienna. Shown your photograph, the one from your own SS file, he positively identified you as Eric Gruen. Also the statement of the desk clerk at the Hotel Erzherzog Rainer. You stayed there following the death of your mother, Elisabeth. He also identified you as Eric Gruen. It was foolish of you to go to the funeral, Gruen. Foolish, but understandable."

"Look, I've been framed," I said. "Very handsomely by Major Jacobs. The real Eric Gruen is leaving the country tonight. Aboard a plane from an American military airfield. He is going to work for the CIA and Jacobs and the American government, to produce a malaria vaccine."

"Major Jacobs is a man of the very highest integrity," said my interrogator. "A man who has put the interests of the State of Israel ahead of those of his own country, and at no small peril to himself." He leaned back in his chair and lit a cigarette. "Look, why don't you admit who you are? Admit the crimes you committed at Majdanek and Dachau. Admit what you've done and it will go easier for you, I promise."

"Easier for you, you mean. My name is Bernhard Gunther."

"How did you come by that name?"

"It's my name," I insisted.

"The real Bernhard Gunther is dead," said the interrogator and handed me yet another piece of paper. "This is a copy of his death certificate. He was murdered by the ODESSA or some other old comrades organization in Munich, two months ago. Presumably so that you could assume his identity." He paused. "With this expertly forged passport." And he handed me my own passport. The one I left at Mönch before traveling to Vienna.

"That's not forged," I said. "That's a real passport. It's the other one that's a fake." I sighed and shook my head. "But if I'm dead, then does it matter what I say? You'll be killing the wrong person. But then of course that wouldn't be the first time you've killed the wrong person. Vera Messmann wasn't the war criminal Jacobs told she was. As it happens, I can prove who I say I am. Twelve years ago, in Palestine . . ."

"You bastard," yelled the big man with the elephant ears. "You murdering bastard." He came toward me quickly and hit me hard with something in his fist. I think the younger man might have tried to restrain him, but it didn't work. He wasn't the type to be restrained by anything much except perhaps a heavy machine gun. The blow when it came knocked me off the chair. I felt as if I had been hit by fifty thousand volts. My whole body was left tingling, with the exception of my head, which felt as if someone had wrapped it in a thick, damp towel so I couldn't hear anything, or see anything. My own voice sounded muffled. Then another towel got wrapped around my head and there was just silence and darkness and nothing at all except a magic carpet that picked me up and floated me away to a place that didn't exist. And that was a place where Bernie Gunther—the real Bernie Gunther—felt very much at home.

# FORTY-ONE

Everything was white. Excluded from the beatific vision, but purified from sin, I lay in a temporary place awaiting some sort of a decision about what to do with me. I hoped they would hurry up and decide because it was cold. Cold and wet. There was no sound, which is as it should have been. Death is not noisy. But it ought to have been warmer. Curiously, one side of my face seemed much colder than the other and, for a dreadful moment, I thought the decision about me had already been made and I was in hell. A small cloud kept visiting my head as if anxious to communicate something to me, and it was another moment or two before I realized that it was my own breath. My earthly torment was not yet over. Slowly I lifted my head from the snow and saw a man digging in the ground, just a few feet from my head. It seemed a curious thing to be doing in a forest in the middle of winter. I wondered what he was digging for.

"Why's it me who has to dig?" he moaned. This one sounded like the only real German of the three.

"Because you're the one who hit him, Shlomo," said a voice. "If you hadn't hit him we could have made him dig that grave."

The man digging threw down his spade. "That'll have to do," he said. "The ground is frozen solid. It'll snow soon enough and the snow will cover it up, and that will be the end of him until the spring."

And then my head throbbed painfully. Most likely it was the explanation of why the man was digging striking a few brain cells. I pushed my arm underneath my forehead and let out a groan.

"He's coming around," said the voice.

The man who had been digging stepped out of the grave and hauled me to my feet. The big man. The man who had hit me. Shlomo. The German Jew.

"For God's sake," said the voice, "don't hit him again."

Weakly I glanced around me. Gruen's laboratory was nowhere to be seen. Instead I was standing on the edge of the tree line on the mountainside just above Mönch. I recognized the coat of arms painted on the wall of the house. I put my hand on my head. There was a lump the size of a golf ball. One that had just been driven in excess of a hundred yards. Shlomo's handiwork.

"Hold the prisoner straight." It was my interrogator speaking.

His nose was not faring well in the cold. It looked like something from a song that was always on the radio these days. "Rudolph the Red-Nosed Reindeer."

Shlomo and Aaron—the younger one—each grabbed an arm and straightened me up. Their fingers felt like pincers. They were enjoying this. I started to speak. "Silence," growled Shlomo. "You'll get your turn, you Nazi bastard."

"The prisoner will strip," said the interrogator.

I didn't move. Not much anyway. I was still swaying a bit from the blow on my head.

"Strip him," he said.

Shlomo and Aaron went at it roughly, like they were looking for my wallet, flinging my clothes into the shallow grave in front of me. Shivering I folded my arms around my torso like a fur wrap. A fur wrap would have been better. The sun had dipped behind the mountain. And a wind was getting up.

Now that I was naked the interrogator spoke again.

"Eric Gruen. For crimes against humanity you are sentenced to death. Sentence to be carried out immediately. Do you wish to say anything?"

"Yes." My voice sounded like it belonged to someone else. As far as these Jews were concerned, it did of course. They thought it belonged to Eric Gruen. No doubt they expected I would say something defiant like "Long live Germany" or "Heil Hitler." But Nazi Germany and Hitler could not have been farther from my mind. I was thinking of Palestine. Perhaps Shlomo had hit me for not calling it Israel. Either way I had very little time left if I was going to talk my way out of a bullet in the back of the head. Shlomo was already checking the magazine of his big Colt automatic.

"Please listen to me," I said through chattering teeth. "I'm not Eric Gruen. There's been a mistake. My real name is Bernie Gunther. I'm a private detective. Twelve years ago, in 1937, I did a job in

Israel for Haganah. I spied on Adolf Eichmann for Fievel Polkes and Eliahu Golomb. We met in a café in Tel Aviv called Kaplinsky's. Kaplinsky, or Kapulsky, I really don't remember. It was near a cinema on Lilienblum Strasse. If you telephone Golomb he'll remember me. He'll vouch for me. I'm sure of it. He'll remember that I borrowed Fievel's gun. And what I advised him to do."

"Eliahu Golomb died in 1946," said my interrogator.

"Fievel Polkes, then. Ask him."

"I'm afraid I've no idea where he is."

"He gave me an address to write to, if ever I had some information for Haganah, and I couldn't contact Polkes," I said. "Polkes was Haganah's man in Berlin. I was to write to an address in Jerusalem. To a Mr. Mendelssohn. I think it was Bezalel Workshops. I don't remember the street. But I do remember that I was to place an order for a brass object damascened in silver, and a photograph of the Sixty-five Hospital. I've no idea what it means. But he said it would be a signal for someone in Haganah to get in contact with me."

"Maybe he did meet with Eliahu Golomb." Shlomo spoke angrily to my interrogator. "We know he had contact with senior people in the SD. Including Eichmann. So what? You've seen the photographs, Zvi. We know he was chummy with the likes of Heydrich and Himmler. Anyone that shook that bastard Göring's hand deserves a bullet in the head."

"Did you shoot Eliahu Golomb?" I asked. "Because he shook hands with Eichmann?"

"Eliahu Golomb is a hero of the State of Israel," Zvi said stiffly.

"I'm very glad to hear it," I said, shivering violently now. "But ask yourself this, Zvi. Why would he have trusted me with a name and address if he hadn't trusted me? And while you're thinking about it, here's something else to consider. If you kill me, you'll never find out where Eichmann is hiding."

"Now I'm sure he's lying," said Shlomo, and pushed me into the grave. "Eichmann is dead." He spat into the grave beside me and worked the slide on his automatic. "I know because we killed him ourselves."

The grave was only a couple of feet deep and the fall didn't hurt. Or at least I didn't feel any pain. I was too cold. And I was talking for my life. Shouting for it.

"Then you killed the wrong man," I said. "I know, because yesterday I spoke to Eichmann. I can take you to him. I know where he's hiding."

Shlomo leveled the gun at my head. "You lying Nazi bastard," he said. "You'd say anything to save your own skin."

"Put the gun down, Shlomo," commanded Zvi.

"You don't really buy that crap, do you, boss?" protested Shlomo. "He'll say anything to stop us shooting him."

"I don't doubt that for a moment," said Zvi. "But as the intelligence officer of this cell, it's my job to evaluate any information that comes our way." He shivered. "And I refuse to do that on a mountainside in the middle of winter. We'll take him in the house and question him some more. Then we'll decide what to do with him."

They frog-marched me to the house, which was deserted, of course. I guessed it must have been rented. Either that or Henkell did not care what happened to it. For all I knew, the documents I had signed in Vienna, at Bekemeier's office, had transferred all of Gruen's wealth to the United States. In which case the two of them would be set up nicely for a good long while.

Aaron made some coffee, which all of us drank gratefully. Zvi threw a blanket over my shoulders. It was the one that had been on Gruen's legs while he had sat in his wheelchair, pretending to be a cripple.

"All right," said Zvi. "Let's talk about Eichmann."

"Just humor me a minute," I said. "And let me ask the questions."

"All right." Zvi looked at his watch. "You have exactly one minute."

"The man you shot," I said. "How did you identify him?"

"We had a tip-off it was him," said Zvi. "And he wasn't surprised to see us. Nor did he deny that he was Eichmann. I think he would have denied it if he'd been someone else. Don't you?"

"Maybe. Maybe not. Did you check his teeth? Eichmann has two gold plates, from before the war. They would certainly have appeared on his SS medical record."

"There was no time," admitted Zvi. "And it was dark."

"Do you remember where you left the body?"

"Of course. There's a maze of underground tunnels the SS planned to use for the secret murder of thirty thousand Jews from the Ebensee concentration camp. He's under a pile of rocks in one of those tunnels."

"Did you say Ebensee?"

"Yes."

"And the tip-off was from Jacobs, right?"

"How did you know?"

"Have you ever heard of Friedrich Warzok?"

"Yes," said Zvi. "He was the deputy commander of the Janowska Concentration Camp."

"Look, I'm pretty sure the man you shot wasn't Eichmann but Warzok," I said. "But it ought to be easy enough to check. All you have to do is go back to Ebensee and examine the body. Then you'll know for sure that I'm telling the truth and that Eichmann is still alive."

"Why didn't Warzok deny that he was Eichmann?" asked Zvi.

"What would be the point?" I said. "To deny being Eichmann he would have had to have proved he was Warzok. And you'd have shot him anyway."

"True. But why would Jacobs sell us a dummy?"

"I don't know. All I know is that Eichmann is about sixty miles from here. Right now. He's in hiding. I know where. I can take you to him."

"He's lying," said Shlomo.

"Anyone would think you don't want to find Eichmann, Shlomo," I said.

"Eichmann is dead," said Shlomo. "I shot him."

"Can you really risk being wrong about something like that?" I asked.

"We would probably be walking into some kind of trap," said Shlomo. "There's only three of us. And supposing we did find Eichmann. What would we do with him?"

"I'm glad you mentioned that Shlomo," I said. "You let me go. That's what you do. If you ask him nicely, Eichmann will even tell you my real name. He'll also confirm part of my story. About being in Palestine before the war. Letting an innocent man go in return for helping you to find Eichmann seems like a very small price to pay."

Aaron said, "And what about those photographs? You were in the SS. You knew Heydrich and Himmler. And Nebe. Do you deny that?"

"No, I don't. But it's not how it looks, that's all. Look, it would take a long time to explain. Before the war I was a cop. Nebe was the boss of the criminal police. I was a detective. That's all."

"Give me five minutes with him, Zvi," said Shlomo. "I'll find out if he's telling the truth or not."

"So you do admit that it's a possibility?"

"Why did you say that the body in the tunnels must be Friedrich Warzok's?" asked Zvi.

"A priest I know, who works for the Comradeship, told me that Warzok disappeared from a safe house near Ebensee. He was supposed to go to Lisbon and get on a boat bound for South America. The same place that Eichmann is headed. They figure you killed Warzok the same way you killed Willy Hintze."

"Well, that's true, at any rate," agreed Zvi. "I was working for the CIA then. Or the OSS as we called it. And Aaron, he was British Army Intelligence. We did kill Willy Hintze. In the wood near Thalgau. A few months after Eichmann. The man we thought was Eichmann, anyway. Eichmann's brother used to go to a small village in the Ebensee hills. His wife used to go to the same place. We went there in the dark. Kept the place under surveillance. There were four men staying in a chalet in the woods near the village. The man we killed matched the description we had of Eichmann."

"You know what I think?" I said. "I think Eichmann's family were drawing you off, so that he could be somewhere else."

"Yes," said Zvi. "That's been done."

I'd said my piece. I was exhausted. I asked for a cigarette. Zvi gave me one. I asked for more coffee. Aaron poured me a cup. I was getting somewhere.

"What are we going to do, boss?" Aaron asked Zvi.

Zvi sighed irritably. "Lock him up somewhere while I think," he said.

"Where?" Aaron looked at Shlomo.

"The bathroom," said Shlomo. "There's no window and there's a key in the door."

I felt my heart leap in my chest. The bathroom was where I had hidden the gun that Engelbertina had given me. The one she claimed she wanted me to have in case Eric Gruen had used it on himself. But would it still be there?

The two Jews escorted me to the bathroom. I waited until I heard the key removed from the lock on the other side of the door before opening the airing cupboard and reaching behind the hot-water tank. For a moment, the gun eluded me. The next second it was in my hand.

The magazine in a Mauser is not much bigger than a cigarette lighter. I turned the gun upside down and, with frozen, nervous fingers, slid it up and out of the grip. Eight-millimeter ammunition is about the same size as the nib on a decent fountain pen. And it doesn't look much more deadly. But there was an old saying in KRIPO: It's not what you hit them with, it's where you hit them. There were seven rounds in the magazine and one in the breech. I hoped I wouldn't have to use any of them. But if I did I knew I would have the element of surprise. No one expects a naked man with just a blanket wrapped around him to be armed with a pistol. I pushed the magazine back into the grip and thumbed back the hammer. With the safety off, the gun was now ready to fire. There seemed little point in worrying about an accidental shot. These men were professional killers. If it came down to a gunfight I knew I would be lucky to get just one of them. I drank some water, used the lavatory, and then held the gun under the spot where my other hand held the blanket around my neck. At least I wouldn't die like a dog. I had seen enough men shot on the edge of a ditch to know that I would shoot myself before I'd even allow that to happen. About half an hour passed, during which time I thought a lot about Kirsten and the men who had murdered her. If I managed ever to escape from these Israelis, I told myself, I was going to go after them. Even if it meant pursuing them all the way to America. At the very least I was going to follow them to the airbase. But which one? There were American airbases all over Germany. Then I remembered the letter I had found in Jacobs's glove box. The letter from the Rochester Strong Memorial Hospital itemizing some medical equipment delivered to Garmisch-Partenkirchen, via the Rhein-Main Air Base. It seemed a safe bet that Rhein-Main would be where they were headed. I glanced at my wristwatch. It was almost six o'clock. The plane to Virginia was leaving at midnight. Finally I heard the sound of the key in the lock of the bathroom door. Even if he hadn't been pointing a gun at me, Zvi's face would have told me the worst.

"No go, huh?"

"I'm sorry," he said. "But what you say is just too fantastic. Even if you're not who we think you are, you're still SS. That much you have admitted. And then there are those photographs of you with Himmler and Heydrich. They were the sworn enemies of my people."

"In the wrong place at the wrong time," I said. "Story of my life, I guess."

He stood back from the door and waved his gun at the corridor leading toward the door. "Come on," he said grimly. "Let's get this over with."

Gripping the gun tightly under my blanket, I came out of the bathroom and walked ahead of him. Aaron was waiting by the front door. Shlomo was outside. But so far only Zvi had a gun in his hand. Which meant I would certainly have to shoot him first. We came out of the house in darkness. Thoughtfully Shlomo switched on the outside light so that they could see what they were doing. We trudged up the slope toward the tree line and the open grave that awaited me. I had figured out when I would make my move.

"I suppose this is your idea of poetic justice," I said. "This kind of degrading execution." My voice sounded brave but my stomach was in knots. "To my mind this makes you as bad as one of those Special Action Groups." I was hoping that at least one of them, Aaron perhaps, would start to feel a little disgusted with himself, and look away. I would shoot Zvi first, and then Shlomo. Shlomo was the only one of the three I really wanted to kill. The side of my head still ached miserably. At the edge of my grave I stopped and glanced around. All three of them were less than six feet away from me, within easy range of even a bad shot. It had been a while since I had killed a man. But there would be no hesitation. If necessary I would kill all three.

## FORTY-TWO

It was bitterly cold. A wind whipped my blanket around my head for a moment. My clothes lay in the grave below me, dusted with a light covering of snow. But I was glad of the snow. The snow would show the blood if I hit a man. I'm a good shot—better with a pistol than with a rifle, that's for sure—but with an eight-mill in the open air, it's easy to think you've missed. Unlike a forty-five. If Zvi or Shlomo got one off I'd stay hit and look that way until I bled to death.

"Any chance of a last cigarette?" I asked. Give a man something to think about before you take him on. That's what they had taught us in the police academy.

"A cigarette?" said Zvi.

"You must be joking," said Shlomo. "In this weather?"

But Zvi was already reaching for his own packet when I dropped my blanket, turned, and fired. The shot hit Zvi on the cheek, just next to his left ear. I fired again and took the end of his nose off. Blood spattered onto Shlomo's neck and shirt collar like a careless sneeze. At the same time the big man grappled, oxlike, for the gun under his armpit. And I shot him in the throat, dumping him on his backside in the snow like a heavy backpack. With one hand pressed to his Adam's apple, and gurgling like a coffee machine, he found the handle of his gun and fumbled it out of his holster, pulling the trigger involuntarily as it appeared in front of his astonished-looking face, this shot killing Zvi stone dead. I pulled the trigger again and shot Shlomo between the eyes even as I stepped quickly toward Aaron and kicked him hard between the legs with a frozen foot. Despite the pain, he held onto my foot at least until I jabbed the gun into his eye. He yelled with pain and let go of my foot. I slipped on the snow and fell and then watched as Aaron staggered back for another second, tripped over Shlomo's motionless body and fell down beside him. Scrambling up onto my knees I leveled my pistol at his head and yelled at him not to reach for his gun. Aaron didn't hear me, or perhaps he chose to ignore me, but either way he pulled the Colt out of his holster and tried to make it ready to fire. But his fingers were cold. As cold as mine, probably, except that my finger was already on the trigger. And I had more than enough time on my side and feeling in my hand to adjust my aim and shoot the young Jew in the calf muscle. He yelped like a beaten dog, dropped his gun, and clutched his leg in agony. I thought I had fired five or six, perhaps more, I couldn't remember for sure. So I picked up Zvi's gun, and threw my own into the trees. Then I collected Aaron's gun, and Shlomo's, and quickly threw those after it. With Aaron effectively incapacitated, I went to the shallow grave, retrieved my half-frozen clothes and started to dress. And while I got dressed again, I spoke to Aaron:

"I'm not going to kill you," I panted. "I'm not going to kill you, because I want you to listen. My name is not and never has been Eric Gruen. At some stage in the future, if it's humanly possible, I'm going to kill that man. My name is and always has been Bernhard Gunther. I want you to remember that name. I want you to tell that name to whichever fanatic is in charge of Haganah these days. So that you'll remember it was Bernhard Gunther who told you that Adolf Eichmann is still alive. And that you owe me a favor. Only the next time you look for Eichmann, it had better be in Argentina, because that's where we're both headed. Him for obvious reasons. And me because Eric Gruen—the real Eric Gruen—has framed me to look like him. Him and your friend Jacobs. And now I can't afford to take the risk of staying here Germany anymore. Not now that this has happened. Understand?"

He bit his lip and nodded.

I finished dressing. I helped myself to Shlomo's shoulder holster and buttoned the Colt into it. Then I searched the big man's pockets, taking money, cigarettes, and a lighter. "Where are the car keys?" I asked.

Aaron put his hand into his pocket and tossed them to me, covered in blood. "It's parked all the way down the drive," he said.

"I'm taking your car and I'm taking your boss's gun. So don't try to follow me. I'm pretty handy with this thing. Next time I see you I'm liable to finish the job." I lit two cigarettes, put one in Aaron's mouth and one in my own, and started down the hill toward the house.

"Gunther," he said. I turned. He was sitting up, but looking very pale. "For what it's worth," he said, "I believe you."

"Thanks." I stayed put for a moment. There was more blood coming from his leg than I had imagined there would be. If he stayed there he would bleed or freeze to death.

"Can you walk?"

"I don't think so."

I got him onto his feet and helped him back down to the house. There I found some sheets and started fixing a tourniquet around his leg. "I'm sorry about your two friends," I said. "I didn't want to kill them. But I had no choice. It was them or me, I'm afraid."

"Zvi was okay," he said. "But Shlomo was a bit of a head case. It was Shlomo who strangled those two women. He wanted to kill every Nazi that ever existed, I think."

"Can't say as I blame him, really," I said, finishing off the bandage. "There are too many Nazis still walking around as free as air. Only I'm not one of them, see? Gruen and Henkell murdered my wife."

"Who is Henkell?"

"Another Nazi doctor. But it would take too long to explain. I have to get after them. You see, Aaron, I'm going to do your job for you, if I can. I'm probably too late. I'll probably end up getting killed myself. But I've got to try. Because that's what you do when someone murders your wife in cold blood. Even though it was finished between us, she was still my wife and that has to count for something. Doesn't it?" I wiped my face with the remainder of the sheet and went to the door, pausing only to check the phone. It was dead.

"The phone isn't working," I said. "I'll try to call an ambulance for you when I get a chance. All right?"

"Thanks," he said. "And good luck, Gunther. I hope you find them."

I went outside, walked down the drive, and found the car. There was a warm-looking leather coat in the back. I put it on and sat in the driver's seat. The car was a black Mercury sedan. The fuel tank was almost full. With its five-liter engine it was a good, fast car with a top speed of over a hundred kilometers an hour. Which was approximately the speed I was going to have to do if I was going to make Rhein-Main before midnight.

I drove back via the lab in Garmisch-Partenkirchen. Jacobs had cleared out the filing cabinets. But I wasn't interested in the files. Instead I went back down to the cellar to collect a couple of the packages and paperwork that were—I hoped—going to gain my entry to the U.S. airbase. It wasn't much of a plan. But I remembered something Timmermann, the *Stars and Stripes* driver who had taken me from Vienna to the monastery at Kempten, had told me about American security being almost nonexistent. That's what I was relying on. That and an urgent package for Major Jacobs.

After telephoning to get an ambulance for Aaron, I drove west and north toward Frankfurt. It was a city I knew little about except that it was five hundred kilometers away and full of Amis. The Amis seemed to like Frankfurt even more than they liked Garmisch. And Frankfurt liked the Amis. Who could blame them? The Amis had brought jobs and money, and the city—once seen to be of little importance—now had the reputation of being one of the most affluent places in the Federal Republic. Rhein-Main Air Base, just a few miles south of Frankfurt, was America's principal European air transport terminal. It was from Rhein-Main that the city of Berlin had been kept supplied during the famous "Operation Vittles" airlift from June 1948 to September 1949. Without the airlift, Berlin would have become just another city in the Russian Zone. Because of Rhein-Main's strategic importance, all roads to and from Frankfurt had been very quickly repaired after the war, and were the best in Germany. And I made good progress as far as Stuttgart, when the fog came down, a real sea of mist that had me cursing at the top of my voice like a human foghorn, until I remembered that planes couldn't fly in fog. Then I almost cheered. With fog like that there were was still half a chance that I could make it in time. But what was I going to do when I got there? I had the forty-five automatic of course, but my appetite for shooting people had diminished a little after what had happened at Mönch. Besides, shooting four, possibly five people in cold blood had only limited appeal. And even before I had reached the airbase just after midnight, I had already concluded I could not shoot the two women. For the others I would just have to hope they wanted to make a fight of it. I tried to banish all such considerations from my mind as I pulled the car up outside the main gatehouse to the airport. I switched off the engine, collected my paperwork, straightened my tie, and walked toward the security guard. I hoped that my English would be equal to the lie I had been rehearsing during the course of my six-hour journey.

The guard looked too warm and well fed to be alert. He wore a green gabardine coat, a beret, a muffler, and thick green woolen gloves. He was blond and blue-eyed and about six feet tall. The name plate on his coat read "Schwarz," and for a moment, I thought he was in the wrong army. He looked more German than I did. But his spoken German was about as good as my spoken English.

"I have some urgent package for a Major Jonathan Jacobs," I said. "He was scheduled to fly out to the States at midnight tonight. To Langley Air Force Base, in Virginia. The major is stationed in Garmisch-Partenkirchen and the packages arrived for him after he had already left to catch his plane."

"You've driven all the way from Garmisch?" The guard looked surprised. And he was looking closely at my face. I remembered the hammer blow I had received from Shlomo. "In this fog?"

I nodded. "That's right. I ran off the road a while ago. Which is how I got this bruise on my head. Lucky it wasn't worse, really."

"That's one hell of a drive."

"Sure," I said modestly. "But take a look at this paperwork. And these packages. It's all really urgent stuff. Medical supplies. And I promised the major that if they arrived after he had left, then at least I would make an attempt to make sure they caught up with him." I smiled nervously. "Perhaps you could check if that flight has taken off yet?"

"Don't need to. Nothing's flying tonight," said Schwarz. "Even the birds are grounded. On account of this damned fog. Been like this since late this afternoon. You're in luck. You've got plenty of time to catch your major. Nothing's going out of here until the morning." But he carried on checking through his paperwork anyway. Then he said, "Looks like there are only four supernumeraries on that Langley flight."

"Supernumeraries?"

"Nonmilitary passengers."

"Dr. Braun and his wife, and Dr. Hoffmann and his wife," I said. "Right?"

"That's right," said the guard. "Your Major Jacobs escorted them through here about five or six hours ago."

"If they're not flying tonight," I asked, "where would they be now?"

Schwarz pointed across the airfield. "You can't see it now because of the fog. But if you drive down there and bear left you'll see a five-story airport building. With the words 'Rhein-Main' down one side. Behind is a small hotel attached to the main air force barracks. Which is probably where you'll find your major right now. Happens a lot with that midnight flight to Langley. On account of the fog. Yes, sir, I expect they're all tucked up for the night. As snug as a bug in a rug."

"As snug as a bug in a rug." I repeated the phrase with a kind of fascination for the dexterity of the English language. And then a grim fascination with an idea that suddenly came to me. "Yes, I see. Well, I'd better not disturb him, had I? He might be asleep. Perhaps you could direct me to the cargo bay for that flight. I'll leave the package there."

"Next to the barracks. Can't miss it. All the lights are on."

"Thanks," I said, heading back to my car. "Oh, and by the way. I'm from Berlin originally. Thanks for what you did there. The airlift? As a matter of fact, that's half the reason I bothered to drive all the way here tonight. Because of Berlin."

Schwarz grinned back at me. "No problem," he said.

I got back into the car and drove into the airbase, hoping that this small show of sentiment would forestall any suspicions the Ami might possibly entertain about me after I had gone. It was something I had learned as an intelligence officer during the war: The essence of deception is not the lie that's told but the truths that are told to support it. I meant what I'd said about the airlift.

The Rhein-Main airport building was a white, Bauhaus-style edifice of the kind the Nazis hated, which was probably the only reason to like it. To me it was just big windows, blank walls, and a lot of egalitarian hot air. Looking at it you sort of imagined that Walter Gropius would have an apartment on the top floor with a lavatory wall expertly doodled on by Paul Klee. I parked my car and my cultural Philistinism and maneuvered one of the packages out of the backseat. Then I saw it. Jacobs's green Buick Roadmaster, with the white-wall tires, parked just a few places away from where I'd left the Mercury. I was in the right place all right. I tucked the package under my arm and walked toward the building. Behind me, on the edge of the fog, stood several C-47 airplanes and a Lockheed Constellation. All of them looked bedded down for the night.

I went through a side door and found myself in a cargo area that was the size of a large factory. A roller conveyer ran the length of its sixty or seventy yards and there were multiple sets of folding doors that gave onto the runways. Several forklift trucks were parked where they had stopped, and dozens of luggage carts and cargo cages containing kitbags and suitcases, army backpacks, duffel bags and footlockers, parcels and packages, stood around like an airlift that was waiting to happen. There were consignments for almost everywhere in the United States—from Bolling AFB in Washington to Vandenberg in California. A radio was playing quietly somewhere. In the doorway of a small office an American serviceman with a Clark Gable mustache, a set of greasy overalls, and a hat like a tea cozy sat on a box marked "Fragile" smoking a cigarette. He looked tired and bored. "Can I help you?" he said.

"I have some late cargo for the Langley flight," I said.

"There ain't nobody around, 'cept me. Not this time of night. 'Sides, that flight ain't going out till morning now. 'Cause of the fog. Hell, no wonder you guys didn't win the war. Getting planes in and out of this place is a bitch."

"I would like that explanation better if it didn't let that useless fat bastard Hermann Göring off the hook," I said, ingratiatingly. "Blaming it all on the weather, like that."

"Good point," said the man. He pointed at the package under my arm. "That it?"

"Yes."

"You got any paperwork for it?"

I showed him the paperwork I had brought from Garmisch. And repeated the explanation I had made at the gatehouse. He looked at it for a while, scrawled a signature on it, and then jerked a thumb across his shoulder.

"About fifty yards down there is a cargo cage with 'Langley' chalked on the side. Just put your package in there. We'll get to it in the morning." Then he went back in the office and closed the door behind him.

It took me about five minutes to find the cargo bay for Langley, but longer to find their luggage. Two Vuitton steamer trunks were standing on their ends beside one of the cages, like two New York skyscrapers. Both were helpfully labeled "Dr. and Frau Braun" and "Dr. and Frau Hoffmann." The padlocks were cheap ones that anyone with a half-decent penknife could have opened. I had a good penknife and I had both trunks opened in a couple of minutes. Some of the best thieves in the world are ex-cops. But that was the easy part.

Open, the trunks looked more like pieces of furniture than luggage. In one half was a clothes rail with a little silk curtain and matching hangers; and in the other a set of four working drawers. It was the guard at the gatehouse who had given me the idea of what to do. The idea that a bug could be snug in a rug. And not just a rug. But also the drawer in a nice, big cozy steamer trunk.

I opened the packing case and removed the insectary from its nest of straw. Then I removed the mosquito cages that themselves resembled small wooden steamer trunks. Inside, the insects buzzed and whined irritably, as if they were full of complaint at having been cooped up for so long. Even if the adults didn't survive the journey to the States, I had no doubt, from what Henkell himself had told me, that the eggs and their larvae would. But there was no time to use the sucking tubes. I placed a cage inside one of the drawers and then stabbed at the fine net of the cage wall with my knife before quickly withdrawing my hand from the drawer and shutting it and the trunk tight again. I did the same with the second insectary and the second trunk. I wasn't bitten. But they would be. And I wondered if being bitten by several dozen malaria-carrying mosquitoes would prove to be just the right incentive needed for Henkell and Gruen to make their vaccine work after all. For everyone's sake I hoped so.

I returned to the car, and seeing the green Buick again, I thought it a great shame that Jacobs would escape. Out of habit I checked the door, and as before, it wasn't locked. Which looked too tempting to ignore. So I fetched an insectary from the second package on the back seat of the Mercury and laid it on the floor behind the driver's seat. Once again I stabbed through the cage wall, and then quickly slammed the car door shut.

Of course it wasn't the revenge I had imagined. For one thing I wouldn't be around to see it. But it was the kind of justice that Aristotle, Horace, Plutarch, and Quintilian would have recognized. And perhaps even celebrated, in some axiomatic way. Small things have a habit of overpowering the great. And that seemed good enough.

I drove back to the monastery, where Carlos Hausner had a bag of money waiting for him. And, eventually, a new passport and a ticket to South America.

# EPILOGUE

Several months passed at the monastery in Kempten. Another fugitive from Allied justice joined us and, in the late spring of 1950, we four crept across the border to Austria and then into Italy. But somehow the fourth man disappeared and we never saw him again. Perhaps he changed his mind about going to Argentina. Or perhaps another Nakam death squad caught up with him.

We stayed in a safe house in Genoa, where we met yet another Catholic priest, Father Eduardo Dömöter. I think he was a Franciscan. It was Dömöter who gave us our Red Cross passports. Refugee passports he called them. Then we set about applying for immigration to Argentina. The president of Argentina, Juan Perón, who was an admirer of Hitler and a Nazi sympathizer, had set up an organization in Italy known as the DAIE, the Delegation for Argentine Immigration in Europe. The DAIE enjoyed semidiplomatic status and had offices in Rome, where applications were processed, and Genoa, where prospective immigrants to Argentina underwent a medical examination. But all of this was little more than a formality. Not least because the DAIE was run by Monsignor Karlo Petranovic, a Croatian Roman Catholic priest who was himself a wanted war criminal, and who was protected by Bishop Alois Hudal, who was the spiritual director of the German Catholic community in Italy. Two other Roman Catholic priests assisted our escape. One was the Archbishop of Genoa himself, Giuseppe Siri; and the other was Monsignor Karl Bayer. But it was Father Dömöter we saw most of all at the safe house. A Hungarian, he had a church in the parish of Sant'Antonio, not very far from the DAIE offices.

I often asked myself how it was that so many Roman Catholic priests should have been Nazi sympathizers. But more pertinently, I also asked Father Dömöter, who told me that the pope himself was fully aware of the help being given to escaping Nazi war criminals. Indeed, said Father Dömöter, the pope had encouraged it.

"None of us would help in this way if it wasn't for the Holy Father," he explained. "But there's something important you must understand about this. It's not that the pope hates Jews, or loves the Nazis. Indeed, there are many Catholic priests who were persecuted by the Nazis. No, this is political. The Vatican shares America's fear and loathing of communism. Really, it's nothing more sinister than that."

So that was all right then.

All applications for a landing permit from the DAIE had to be approved by the Immigration Office in Buenos Aires. And this meant that we were in Genoa for almost six weeks, during which time I got to know the city quite well, and liked it enormously. Especially the old town and the harbor. Eichmann did not venture out of doors for fear of being recognized. But Pedro Geller became my regular companion, and together we explored Genoa's many churches and museums.

Geller's real name was Herbert Kuhlmann, and he had been an SS Sturmbannführer with the 12th SS Hitler Youth Panzer Division. That explained his youth, although not his need to escape from Germany. And it was only toward the end of our time in Genoa that he felt able to talk about what had happened to him.

"The Regiment was in Caen," he said. "The fighting was pretty heavy there, I can tell you. We had been told not to take prisoners, not least because we had no facilities for doing so. And so we executed thirty-six Canadians, who, it's fair to say, might just as easily have executed us, if our situations had been reversed. Anyway, our Brigadeführer is currently serving a life sentence for what happened in a Canadian jail, although the Allies had originally sentenced him to death. I was advised by a lawyer in Munich that I would also probably receive a prison sentence if I was charged."

"Erich Kaufmann?" I asked.

"Yes. How did you know?"

"Never mind. It doesn't matter."

"He thinks the situation will improve," said Kuhlmann. "In a couple of years. Perhaps as long as five. But I'm not prepared to take the risk. I'm only twenty-five. Mayer, my Brigadeführer, he's been in the cement since December 1945. Five years. There's no way I can do five years, let alone life. So I'm buggering off to the Argentine. Apparently there are plenty of opportunities for business in Buenos Aires. Who knows? Perhaps you and I can go into business together."

"Yes," I said. "Perhaps."

Hearing Erich Kaufmann's name again almost made me glad that I was leaving the new Federal Republic of Germany. Like it or not I was the old Germany, just as much as people like Göring, Heydrich, Himmler, and Eichmann. There was no room for someone who makes a living out of asking awkward questions. Not in Germany, where the answers often prove to be bigger than the questions. The more I read about the new Republic, the more I looked forward to a simpler life in a warmer climate.

Our application forms approved, on June 14, 1950, Eichmann, Kuhlmann, and I went to the Argentine consulate where our Red Cross passports were stamped with a "Permanent" visa, and we were issued the identification certificates we would need to present to the police in Buenos Aires, in order to obtain a valid identity card. Three days later we boarded the *Giovanni*, a steamship bound for Buenos Aires.

By now Kuhlmann knew my whole story. But he did not know Eichmann's. And it was several days into the voyage before Eichmann felt able at last to acknowledge me and to inform Kuhlmann who he really was. Kuhlmann was appalled and never again spoke to Eichmann, referring to him ever after as "that pig."

I myself didn't care to judge Eichmann. It was not my right. For all the fact that he had escaped justice, he cut a rather sad, forlorn figure on the boat. He knew he would never see Germany or Austria again. We didn't speak very much. Mostly he kept himself to himself. I think he felt ashamed. I like to think so.

On the day we sailed out of the Mediterranean into the Atlantic Ocean, he and I stood together on the stern of the boat and watched Europe slowly disappear on the horizon. Neither of us spoke for a long while. Then he heaved a big sigh and said: "Regrets do not do any good. Regretting things is pointless. Regrets are for little children."

I feel much the same way myself.

# AUTHOR'S NOTE

The Nakam, or Vengeance, squads were real. Just after the war, a small group of European Jews, many of them survivors of the death camps, formed the Israeli Brigade. Others acted from within the U.S. and British armies. Their sworn purpose was to avenge the murders of six million Jews. They murdered as many as two thousand Nazi war criminals, and planned or carried out several large-scale acts of reprisal. Among these was a very real plan to poison the reservoirs of the cities of Berlin, Nuremberg, Munich, and Frankfurt, and kill several million Germans—a plan that fortunately was never carried out. However, a plan to poison the bread for 36,000 German SS POWs, at an internment camp near Nuremberg, did go into action, albeit in a limited way. Two thousand loaves were poisoned; four thousand SS men were affected, and as many as a thousand died.

Lemberg-Janowska, the camp where Simon Wiesenthal was interned, was one of the most barbaric in Poland. Two hundred thousand people were murdered there. Friedrich Warzok, the deputy commander, was never caught. Eric Gruen, the Nazi doctor, was never caught.

Adolf Eichmann and Herbert Hagen really did visit Israel. Eichmann was trying to make himself an expert in Hebrew affairs. He planned to learn the language. He also met with Haganah representatives in Berlin.

The Grand Mufti of Jerusalem, Haj Amin al-Husseini, was a ferocious anti-Semite who led several pogroms in Palestine, which resulted in the deaths of many Jews. He had been canvassing a "final solution to the Jewish problem" as early as 1920. He met with Eichmann in 1937, and first met Adolf Hitler on November 28, 1941. This was less than eight weeks before the Wannsee Conference, at which Nazi plans for the "final solution of the Jewish problem in Europe" were outlined by Reinhard Heydrich.

During the war, Haj Amin lived in Berlin, was a friend of Hitler's, and personally raised an SS Moslem Division of 20,000 men in Bosnia, which murdered Jews and partisans. He tried to persuade the Luftwaffe to bomb Tel Aviv. It seems quite probable that his ideas had a profound influence on the course of Eichmann's thinking. Numerous Jewish organizations tried to have Haj Amin prosecuted as a war criminal after the war, but they were unsuccessful, despite the fact that arguably he was as culpable as Heydrich, Himmler, and Eichmann in the extermination of the Jews. Haj Amin was a close relative of Yasser Arafat's. It is believed that Arafat changed his name in order to obscure his relationship with a notorious war criminal. To this day, many Arab political parties, most notably Hezbollah, have identified with Nazis and adopted symbols from Nazi propaganda.

In 1945, the American Office of Scientific Research and Development conducted medical experiments on prisoners in state penitentiaries in an effort to develop a vaccine for malaria. See *Life,* June 4, 1945, pages 43–46.

Philip Kerr's next novel featuring

Bernie Gunther will be available from Putnam

in hardcover in March 2009

Read on for the first chapter of

ISBN 978-0-399-15530-7

## ONE

## *Buenos Aires 1950*

The boat was the SS *Giovanni,* which seemed only appropriate given the fact that at least three of its passengers, including me, had been in the SS. It was a medium-sized boat with two funnels, a view of the sea, a well-stocked bar, and an Italian restaurant. This was fine if you liked Italian food, but after four weeks at sea at eight knots, all the way from Genoa, I didn't like it and I wasn't sad to get off. Either I'm not much of a sailor or there was something else wrong with me other than the company I was keeping these days.

We steamed into the port of Buenos Aires along the gray River Plate and this gave me and my two fellow travelers a chance to reflect upon the proud history of our invincible German Navy. Somewhere at the bottom of the river, near Montevideo, lay the wreck of the *Graf Spee,* a pocket battleship that had been invincibly scuttled by its commander in December 1939, to prevent it from falling into the hands of the British. As far as I knew, this was as near as the war ever came to Argentina.

In the North Basin we docked alongside the customs house. A modern city of tall concrete buildings lay spread out to the west of us, beyond the miles of rail track and the warehouses and the stockyards where Buenos Aires got started—as a place where cattle from all over the Argentine pampas arrived by train and were slaughtered on an industrial scale. So far, so German. But then the carcasses were frozen and shipped all over the world. Exports of Argentine beef had made the country rich and transformed Buenos Aires into the third-largest city in the Americas, after New York and Chicago.

The population of three million called themselves *porteños*—the people of the port—which sounds pleasantly romantic. My two friends and I called ourselves refugees, which sounded better than fugitives. But that's what we were. Rightly or wrongly, there was a kind of justice awaiting all of us back in Europe, and our Red Cross passports concealed our true identities. I was no more Dr. Carlos Hausner than Adolf Eichmann was Ricardo Klement or Herbert Kuhlmann was Pedro Geller. This was fine with the Argentines. They didn't care who we were or what we'd done during the war. Even so, on that cool and damp winter morning in July 1950, it seemed there were still certain official proprieties to be observed.

An immigration clerk and a customs officer came aboard the ship and, as each passenger presented his documents, they asked questions. If these two didn't care who we were or what we'd done, they did a good job giving us the opposite impression. The mahogany-faced immigration clerk regarded Eichmann's flimsy-looking passport and then Eichmann himself as if both had arrived from the center of a cholera epidemic. This wasn't so far from the truth. Europe was only just recovering from an illness called Nazism that had killed more than fifty million people.

"Profession?" the clerk asked Eichmann.

Eichmann's meat cleaver of a face twitched nervously. "Technician," he said, and mopped his brow with a handkerchief. It wasn't hot, but Eichmann seemed to feel a different kind of heat from anyone else I ever met.

Meanwhile, the customs official, who smelled like a cigar factory, turned to me. His nostrils flared as if he could smell the money I was carrying in my bag, and then he lifted his cracked lip off his bamboo teeth in what passed for a smile in that line of work. I had about thirty thousand Austrian schillings in that bag, which was a lot of money in Austria, but not such a lot of money when it was converted into real money. I didn't expect him to know that. In my experience, customs officials can do almost anything they want except be generous or forgiving when they catch sight of large quantities of currency.

"What's in the bag?" he asked.

"Clothes. Toiletries. Some money."

"Would you mind showing me?"

"No," I said, minding very much. "I don't mind at all."

I heaved the bag onto a trestle table and was just about to unbuckle it when a man hurried up the ship's gangway, shouting something in Spanish and then, in German, "It's all right. I'm sorry I'm late. There's no need for all this formality. There's been a misunderstanding. Your papers are quite in order. I know because I prepared them myself."

He said something else in Spanish about the three of us being important visitors from Germany, and immediately the attitude of the two officials changed. Both men came to attention. The immigration clerk facing Eichmann handed him back his passport, clicked his heels, and then gave Europe's most wanted man the Hitler salute with a loud "Heil Hitler" that everyone on deck must have heard.

Eichmann turned several shades of red and, like a giant tortoise, shrank a little into the collar of his coat, as if he wished he might disappear. Kuhlmann and I laughed out loud, enjoying Eichmann's embarrassment and discomfort as, snatching back his passport, he stormed down the gangway and onto the quay. We were still laughing as we joined Eichmann in the back of a big black American car with a sign displayed in the windshield, VIANORD.

"I don't think that was in the least bit funny," said Eichmann.

"Sure you don't," I said. "That's what makes it so funny."

"You should have seen your face, Ricardo," said Kuhlmann. "What on earth possessed him to say that, of all things? And to you, of all people?" Kuhlmann started to laugh again. "Heil Hitler, indeed."

"I thought he made a pretty good job of it," I said. "For an amateur."

Our host, who had jumped into the driver's seat, now turned around to shake our hands. "I'm sorry about that," he told Eichmann. "Some of these officials are just pig-ignorant. In fact, the words we have for pig and public official are the same. *Chanchos*. We call them both *chanchos*. I wouldn't be at all surprised if that idiot believes Hitler is still the German leader."

"God, I wish he was," murmured Eichmann, rolling his eyes into the roof of the car. "How I wish he was."

"My name is Horst Fuldner," said our host. "But my friends in Argentina call me Carlos."

"Small world," I said. "That's what my friends in Argentina call me. Both of them."

Some people came down the gangway and peered inquisitively through the passenger window at Eichmann.

"Can we get away from here?" he asked. "Please."

"Better do as he says, Carlos," I said. "Before someone recognizes Ricardo here and telephones David Ben-Gurion."

"You wouldn't joke about that if you were in my shoes," said Eichmann. "The soaps would stop at nothing to kill me."

Fuldner started the car and Eichmann relaxed visibly as we drove smoothly away.

"Since you mentioned the soaps," said Fuldner. "It's worth discussing what to do if any of you is recognized."

"Nobody's going to recognize me," Kuhlmann said. "Besides, it's the Canadians who want me, not the Jews."

"All the same," said Fuldner. "I'll say it anyway. After the Spanish and the Italians, the soaps are the country's largest ethnic group. Only we call them *los Russos,* on account of the fact that most of the ones who are here came to get away from the Russian czar's pogrom."

"Which one?" Eichmann asked.

"How do you mean?"

"There were three pogroms," said Eichmann. "One in 1821, one between 1881 and 1884, and a third that got started 1903. The Kishinev Pogrom."

"Ricardo knows everything about Jews," I said. "Except how to be nice to them."

"Oh, I should think the most recent pogrom," said Fuldner.

"It figures," said Eichmann, ignoring me. "The Kishinev was the worst."

"That's when most of them came to Argentina, I think. There are as many as a quarter of a million Jews here in Buenos Aires. They live in three main neighborhoods, which I advise you to steer clear of. Villa Crespo along Corrientes, Belgrano, and Once. If you think you are recognized, don't lose your head, don't make a scene. Keep calm. Cops here are heavy-handed and none too bright. Like that *chancho* on the boat. If there's any kind of trouble, they're liable to arrest you and the Jew who thinks he's recognized you."

"So, there's not much chance of a pogrom here, then?" observed Eichmann.

"Lord, no," said Fuldner.

"Thank goodness," said Kuhlmann. "I've had enough of all that nonsense."

"We haven't had anything like that since what's called Tragic Week. And even that was mostly political. Anarchists, you know. Back in 1919."

"Anarchists, Bolsheviks, Jews, they're all the same animal," said Eichmann, who had become unusually talkative.

"Of course, during the last war, the government issued an order forbidding all Jewish immigration to Argentina. But more recently things have changed. The Americans have put pressure on Perón to soften our Jewish policy. To let them come and settle here. I wouldn't be surprised if there were more Jews on that boat than anyone else."

"That's a comforting thought," said Eichmann.

"It's all right," insisted Fuldner. "You're quite safe here. *Porteños* don't give a damn about what happened in Europe. Least of all to the Jews. Besides, nobody believes half of what's been in the English-language papers and on the newsreels."

"Half would be quite bad enough," I murmured. It was enough to push a stick through the spokes of a conversation I was starting to dislike. But mostly it was just Eichmann I disliked. I much preferred the other Eichmann. The one who had spent the last four weeks saying almost nothing, and keeping his loathsome opinions to himself. It was too soon to have much of an opinion about Carlos Fuldner.

From the back of his well-oiled head I judged Fuldner to be around forty. His German was fluent but with a little soft color on the edges of the tones. To speak the language of Goethe and Schiller, you have to stick your vowels in a pencil sharpener. He liked to talk, that much was evident. He wasn't tall and he wasn't good-looking, but then he wasn't short or ugly either, just ordinary, in a good suit, with good manners, and a nice manicure. I got another look at him when he pulled up at a level crossing and turned around to offer us some cigarettes. His mouth was wide and sensuous, his eyes were lazy but intelligent, and his forehead was as high as a church cupola. If you'd been casting a movie, you'd have picked him to play a priest, or a lawyer, or maybe a hotel manager. He snapped his thumb on a Dunhill, lit his cigarette, then began telling us about himself. That was fine by me. Now that we were no longer talking about Jews, Eichmann stared out of the window and looked bored. But I'm the kind who listens politely to stories about my redeemer. After all, that's why my mother sent me to Sunday school.

"I was born here, in Buenos Aires, to German immigrants," said Fuldner. "But, for a while, we went back to live in Germany, in Kassel, where I went to school. After school I worked in Hamburg. Then, in 1932, I joined the SS and was a captain before being seconded to the SD to run an intelligence operation back here, in Argentina. Since the war I and a few others have been running Vianord—a travel agency dedicated to helping our old comrades to escape from Europe. Of course, none of it would be possible without the help of the president and his wife, Eva. It was during Evita's trip to Rome, in 1947, to meet the pope, that she began to see the necessity of giving men such as you a fresh start in life."

"So there's still some anti-Semitism in the country, after all," I remarked.

Kuhlmann laughed and so did Fuldner. But Eichmann remained silent.

"It's good to be with Germans again," said Fuldner. "Humor is not a national characteristic of the Argentines. They're much too concerned with their dignity to laugh at very much, least of all themselves."

"They sound a lot like fascists," I said.

"That's another thing. Fascism here is only skin-deep. The Argentines don't have the will or the inclination to be proper fascists."

"Maybe I'm going to like it here more than I thought," I said.

"Really," exclaimed Eichmann.

"Don't mind me, Herr Fuldner," I said. "I'm not quite as rabid as our friend here wearing the bow tie and glasses, that's all. He's still in denial. To do with all kinds of things. For all I know, he still holds fast to the idea that the Third Reich is going to last for a thousand years."

"You mean it isn't?"

Kuhlmann chuckled.

"Must you make a joke about everything, Hausner?" Eichmann's tone was testy and impatient.

"I only make jokes about the things that strike me as funny," I said. "I wouldn't dream of making a joke about something really important. Not and risk upsetting you, Ricardo."

I felt Eichmann's eyes burning into my cheek and when I turned to face him, his mouth went thin and puritanical. For a moment he continued staring at me with the air of one who wished it was down the sights of a rifle.

"What *are* you doing here, Herr Dr. Hausner?"

"The same thing as you, Ricardo. I'm getting away from it all."

"Yes, but why? Why? You don't seem like much of a Nazi."

"I'm the beefsteak kind. Brown on the outside only. Inside I'm really quite red."

Eichmann stared out the window as if he couldn't bear to look at me for a minute longer.

"I could use a good steak," murmured Kuhlmann.

"Then you've come to the right place," said Fuldner. "In Germany a steak is a steak, but here it's a patriotic duty."

We were still driving through the dockyards. Most of the names on the bonded warehouses and oil tanks were British or American: Oakley & Watling, Glasgow Wire, Wainwright Brothers, Ingham Clark, English Electric, Crompton Parkinson, and Western Telegraph. In front of a big, open warehouse a dozen rolls of newsprint the size of hayricks were turning to pulp in the early-morning rain. Laughing, Fuldner pointed them out.

"There," he said, almost triumphantly. "That's Perónism in action. Perón doesn't close down opposition newspapers or arrest their editors. He doesn't even stop them from having newsprint. He just makes sure that by the time it reaches them the newsprint isn't fit to use. You see, Perón has all the major labor unions in his pocket. That's your Argentine brand of fascism, right there."